Mandela Effect II
~ more analysis ~
by TS Caladan

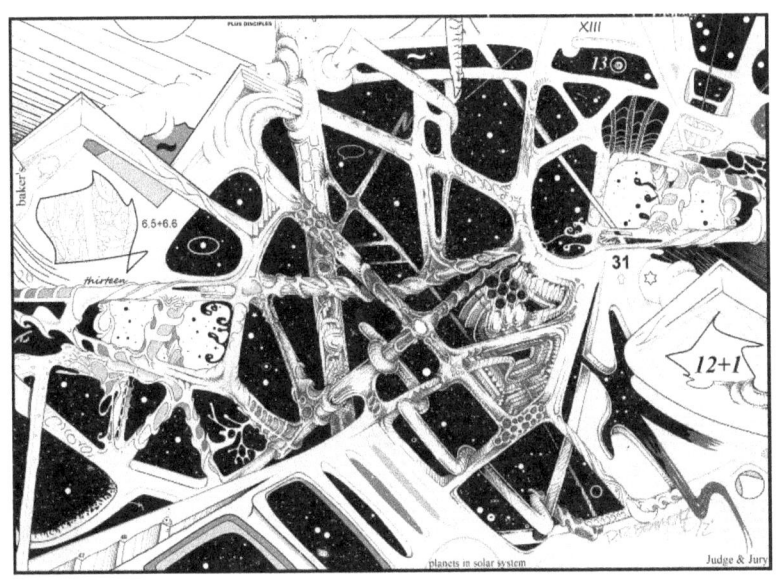

Mandela Effect II – more analysis
Copyright © 2021 by TS Caladan

Edited by TS Caladan

Cover Art by TS Caladan

Cover Art Title: "The White Tower and the Black Tower"

ISBN: 978-1-944045-75-3

~ Contents ~

Introduction: The Wrong Way

[Author's note: Rather odd way to begin a Mandela Book with a "theory" that we've all been made to do the wrong things for many generations. And. We are totally oblivious to the fact that our actions are wrong and even counter to our goals. There might be no better example of this than Daylight Saving Time, which has been Mandelaed to "Daylight Savings Time" in many cases. George Vernon Hudson (1867-1946) was a British-born entomologist and astronomer who lived in New Zealand, credited with the creation of DST. He was awarded the Hector Memorial Medal in 1923. He stated, "The effect of this alteration would be to advance all the day's operations in summer two hours compared with the present system. In this way the early-morning daylight would be utilized, and a long period of daylight leisure would be made available in the evening for cricket, gardening, cycling, or any other outdoor pursuit desired." Nothing could be further from the truth. Consider the following...).

Why are we doing things the wrong way? The answer is: We don't know we're doing something wrong; we think it's right and we do it anyway, without thinking. We're programmed. We normally do what everybody else does. It's called "safety in numbers." We don't realize we are acting wrong, or bad, or off, or that there is a better way. No. And we do this because we do not have the knowledge that the act, behavior, the very thing that we've always done or thought, is <u>absolutely wrong</u>. If we knew it was wrong, we wouldn't do it.

We're told by our lords and masters (teachers): "This is the way it is." It's been universally accepted, never questioned and the entire world continues ceremonies/rituals or "practices" as if they were law and right and 'written in stone' and blessed and the proper thing to do.

For example...time. Greenwich, England, a borough off the Thames River, was set as the 'perfect' place to mark longitudes and all longitudes are aligned to the (0 degree) starting point of Greenwich. The royals set this, of course, as well as latitudes and *adjusting global time according to the change in seasons.*

"Spring ahead, Fall back," is the common view. It's what we're told; it's what we *must* do and have always done. Mechanically, without thinking, like a mindless 'clock.' It's done to make better use of sunlight as days get shorter or get longer. We accept that we are doing the right thing, twice a year. And every single person on Earth *must* do it if they want to be in sync with everyone else. Right? It wouldn't even occur to us that this was an incorrect move, counterproductive and ridiculous. (Like the masks).

The problem is (and there is a problem) *it's wrong!* We are doing the wrong thing, again, the opposite of what we should be doing, two times every year! Everyone's been made to be wrong and think it's right. Here's some clarity for you:

When the days get shorter, we make them even shorter. When the days get longer, we make them even longer. Opposite of what should happen. "Daylight Saving Time" is supposed to compensate for the yearly light-change. It is reported to make "daylight later in the summer months." But it does not do that. Think about it. The time-adjustment that we all must do makes everything worse, not better. Every time we peasants, we commoners, we muggles, do this...THEY LAUGH AT US. They, the royal elites who know, laugh at us for being stupid, for following stupidity and not knowing any better. They laugh at us for doing the wrong things, for obeying their fascist commands without a whimper, a question or the least bit of protest. It's much easier to simply SHUT-UP and take it and never, ever have the thought that we are not acting intelligently. And if one person realized the basic time-change truth, what could they do about it? Nothing, outside of being seemingly insane to everyone else. They have to go right along doing things the wrong way [like putting on masks] that our Directors have directed because this is exactly what everyone else does. Must do, without question. You're not a lemming. Even lemmings don't follow along doing what other lemmings do. It's an accepted British myth.

Oh, you think this bi-yearly practice isn't wrong? If it's so damn right, then why is it dark at 6PM half of the year, everywhere? Why? Light isn't saved. **Darkness is prolonged**. This could be a metaphor for the true world? Is it to help the farmers, so they can see early in the morning? That's not when we need light. We need light at rush-hour. We need light at rush-hour. This should be repeated because it's a hard *adjustment,* to know we're being played, fucked over, laughed at, and have always gotten the worst end of the 'deal' and never the best. We receive Chaos, not Order. [Too much Order is wrong, where's

Freedom?].

Wouldn't it be nice and correct and SAFE if we did the right thing and went the Right Way? We have to know what the Right Way is. We could make the dark begin at 8PM everywhere if we simply followed the correct procedure, which is: "**Spring back, Fall ahead**." This coming spring, we'll all do the wrong actions and not even realize it. [Can you hear the laughter?].

No one realizes this because we blindly believe the few Authorities are helping us, the masses. We trust Big Brother. Why? Where did you ever get that idea? Everything that we've ever known has been essentially established to be off and wrong and often wrong. We have never learned from loving, caring teachers. Teachers are trained wrong on purpose, from Anthropology to History to Science, and they in turn have trained us to what is more wrong than what is more right.

Please understand there is a lesson here that's hard to believe. Who has ever brought up the fact that the 1-hour time-change is stupid, reversed, and created a worse situation? I've never heard a hint of that. *I'm not afraid to 'go out on a limb,' listen to my heart, and be unlike all of you.* The monarchy, imperialist kings and queens, performs Magic, like the magic of Hollywood and TV. They lie. They get away with mass-murder. We're forced to bow to the greatness of horrible monsters who rule the world. I don't do that. I want to expose them and the lies they've embedded into our psyche and into our physical world. They, the masons, have been getting away with these Methods of Mind-Control for ages, the invisible "con-job" that slave-celebrities never reveal. None of the common muggles see the Light and the truth because it's very difficult to be different, to see differently and believe *differently.* It's much easier to *go with the flow and don't make trouble.* These days, the youth want to fit right in (similar to the 1950s) and never be unique individuals.

No one stops THEM, the fascists in power. We 'tilt at windmills' without the smallest shred of real power or influence. We, down here, under the Capstone, are as helpless children. Help.

How can evil Rulers of the World be stopped? Is there any hope at all for the future? They have the guns, the nukes, the leaders, the politicians, the police and all the 'legal' courts on the planet. *They think they own the world and own us, utterly.* Maybe hope for tomorrow begins with a spark of realization? When the truth hits you, it's one very powerful SHAKE-UP of reality. What if we all knew the truth? Ha. One day, everyone woke up and *knew the truth.* OMG! The general public would get very angry and have a lot of fun 'stormin' the castle' and maybe even the churches. Revolutions have occurred often in history: Egyptians, Romans, or anywhere people were tired of their oppressors' tyranny and rose up against them. But we can't today, can we? Not today, when most people believe: "This is the best" and "You're the best," when the opposite is the truth. People don't know they are victims of a ruthless, totalitarian empire that prints money and collects our money.

Food, clothes, services and housing for the poor should be *free.* **Why wasn't there a national stimulus-check instituted every month for citizens and families post WW2?** Why not? Because there is no United States, only minions to lords and masters who are not interested in the least to help the "great unwashed," "trailer-trash," their *vermin* subjects or the lower classes. Only now, during the "scamdemic," did world leaders do the right thing and give, instead of take. *(Must be the End of the World?).*

Isn't Britain great? What other country has an adjective in its name? A glowing one. Telling us, forcing us to believe how "Great" they are. Funny that the realm wasn't called "Brilliant Britain."

The wrong way. We should walk the right way. We should be taught the real truth. Lying should be illegal. Off with *their* heads! And also, we should "Spring back and Fall ahead." But we don't do that, do we? We don't do the right thing. We're blinded, twisted, and made to do the wrong things. Always. (God help us). Maybe we should realize the truth and be on our way to a better world?

ps. One added notion to the idea of "The Wrong Way" Britain insists upon and we underlings follow right along without question, is the following. Readers might find it trivial, microscopic, without any connections at all to larger concepts. (God *was* in the details, now it's the Devil). A particular detail is from a sport I used to love, until I discovered the truth about it (under the surface). Tennis. Tennis and *String-Tension!* Hard to believe that there is a slight connection between what professional tennis players tell us about String-Tension, and what's the actual truth...and it even connects to the Wrong Way we turn our clocks backward/forward, as well as the way we live our lives now. OFF from what we should be doing, because we (you) seem to be "sheeple" who believe we're being told the Truth when we have not been. Wake up...

What?

If you are an avid tennis fan and have watched the pros play, then you'll have heard commentators who have said: "Oh, he (or she) is going to a tighter racket now because shots are flying wildly. They change to a tighter string-tension for more control..."

No. I believed it for the longest time, then because of almost a 'scientific experiment,' I knew They'd been lying. I wanted to find out Why and I think I did. I've found out: You shouldn't believe what England insists that you always believe. That even occurs in this case of bloody string-tension.

Here's what happened. I've been a tennis player for decades (not so much anymore, but I still watch the best on TV). I was a poor tennis player and had only one racket, like many people who play in the park. Months can go by before strings break for weekend players. My strings broke and I had forgotten what tension I played at, which is what you must tell the stringer so they string it to your preference. I probably said "65 pounds," when I normally played with loose strings down around 50 pounds. I didn't realize the mistake or how firm the strings were at first. I found I couldn't get the ball over the net. Nothing went long and it was as if I had no power whatsoever. The racket zapped my strength. I realized the error and sure didn't want to re-string my newly-strung racket and pay for it all over again? But I had to, if I wanted to play tennis. When I returned to the courts with *loose* strings, OMG! The racket was **magic** (hate to write that word), what power and CONTROL now in this mighty wand! All I had to do was "come over the ball" with topspin that any pro can do well, and...

It was truly amazing: Power and Control! Yes, the ball flew, sprung off the strings like a sling-shot. But you can easily control the power with topspin. With tight strings, the racket face becomes a 'board,' no sling-shot effect and the ball goes nowhere. With very tight strings, the player is at a great disadvantage. They have to use all their strength just to get the ball over the net. To continuously strike deep shots, you'd be exhausted in a matter of minutes. With loose strings, players do not have to be supremely fit or very strong athletes. Amateurs with loose-strung rackets, might be able to beat top pros that used rackets with very high tension.

For example, John McEnroe. He was never a power-player. He

was embarrassed when he took off his shirt. His game was beautiful in the sense that he "placed the ball" and won against opponents much stronger, who were as skilled as he was. Why did he dominate for years? Remember John at the net, he was the greatest. From my own experience with loose strings at the net: You had time. The ball pressed in the strings, shot out, and there was time to put it anywhere you damn well wanted. With stiff/tight strings, there's no time and your first contact with the ball better be perfect. No control.

Consider. Who was McEnroe's great rival, before Conners? (Cyborg) Bjorn Borg. Their Wimbledon final of 1980, with the famous tie-break, was thought to be the greatest match of all time, until recently with Nadal and Federer. Did you know Bjorn played (forced to play) with very tight strings? Didn't the best player at that time know of my little experiment or the concept: Loose-strings mean power and control? Or that, "Maybe, I should loosen my strings up a little?" Borg used rackets strung so super-tight that they were known to POP in high-flying airplane compartments because of the pressure. Maybe Loose and Tight racket strings are a secret handicap? Borg was an incredible physical specimen, and still is. John was not. How could they compete on an even level as to be the greatest "male" rivalry at the time? I now believe that they couldn't. Borg would smear Mac every time, unless they adjusted the handicap to favor John. If you remember? Borg was quickly drummed out of professional tennis. Wonder what the truth is?

Could it be that in the modern game, *players are told* when to switch rackets and what rackets to switch to? Maybe. Because the games are fixed, like all sports and all major things are fixed. At least that makes some sense. What does not make sense is the little Lie spoken again and again that we, the (dumb) audience believe blindly and do not question. That is: "They're going to a tighter racket for more control." I think that untruth is for us, the public. Professional tennis players know better and must be aligned with anything and everything their "handlers" and agents have insisted upon. They, like in other sports and all celebrities, are high-priced Slaves. They are only in their place because of their dark creators who put them in their place. Trained them from Day 1, not like us real and poor muggles. Elites owe their bosses, their manufacturers and must lie or turn a blind-eye to negative truths they know, and we do not.

[A disclaimer: Forgive the profanity in this book, my English. When you feel something strongly, it's expressed one way or the other. At the last (unwatchable) Coachella, I noticed that about every band used the F-word every other sentence. In my view, the kids (who now only play "processed cheese") were paid to do so. Music, films, TV, sports, have shotgun-effects and They want everyone cussing up a storm and being wicked as if it's nothing (Rap music). I guess there are no 'F-Bombs' anymore and "fuck" is no more than, "Gee whiz." I think people today, so accustomed to violence and blood where nearly every movie is R-rated, can handle my cursing. Maybe I have good reasons to explode today? Forgive my informal style of writing. My intent is to be serious and funny. This is TS's 13th book and last book. I wanted to fit a lot in. I'll also use "They," capitalized, with each reference of the Illuminati, secret societies, our real Rulers that have *changed everything and control absolutely everything in our lives.* The term "Devil" used here refers to the Illuminati or these very real secret societies. I hope you learn from the Voice inside me, as I did. Also. You know what everyone *needs* to do to discover what is real? Stop listening to TV and listen to your hearts].

Mandela Effects not included in Volume I.

For me, it was discovering that the Great Pyramid was no longer positioned in the middle of the 3 large pyramids at Giza and aligned with the Great Sphinx. No. *Now it was on the end, near Cairo's golf course!* Since the 1970s, I have collected and studied more than a hundred books on ancient mysteries. My library contains dozens of hardbacks and many paperbacks on the subject of Atlantis, pyramids, UFOs and related subjects. I've lectured and been on radio, such as C2C with George Noory. I've spoken of Tesla principles that explained Pyramid Energy and the ancient World Grid. I certainly know, beyond most of you, *where the hell the GP is positioned out there on the sands of Giza!* It freaking moved! A whole, new pre-history is now in place, everywhere, different from the one history we had before. Now there's a clash of realities here on Earth, believe it or not.

It was a profound moment for me as I searched for a new entrance some had reported. There wasn't an "entrance" to the Great Pyramid (it was a photo of forced-perspective). Then...I'm looking at the gorgeous, color photo with blue skies, golden sands...*and it was like a ton of bricks struck me!* What the fuck was Chefren, the Second Pyramid, slightly smaller than GP, doing in the middle, aligned with the Sphinx? I couldn't believe it. I ran to the other books! No book showed the Great Pyramid in the middle. The books and the world had changed. **This proved the Mandela to me** and more than a thousand items I've researched since have supported the odd, unnatural changes that normally would never have happened. But they did. Life is more like a nightmare for me, one I can't wake from.

I've written of the differences at Giza in Volume I. There could be more now. That realization sent me in a direction to find every real Mandela I could and to search for the meaning of it all<. I see the New World like the Matrix movie or the Star Trek holodeck. I never thought that Flat-Earthers were correct in the past or that everyone on Earth lived in a simulation. But, after the M.E., we could be. No longer free, but trapped inside an artificial cage. Who knows? I do know for a fact: This is a changed, horrible world now that I think They can alter at will and all of us prisoners have to suffer as a result.

To me, the Mandela-changes or differences from the Old World, are places in the Matrix reality that didn't quite match up with the previous reality we knew. A Parallel World had descended upon us like a new game in the animated 'Reboot.' Now we all have to play or live in this particular, twisted-reality that secret Engineers have designed for us from the shadows. But if we examine these DIFFERENCES, why is it that the changes are nasty, negative, always dark? The shift or Mandela Effects are never a change that was positive, a move *into the Light* of a sweeter, clearer, brighter, better world. Interesting.

When I completed Volume I, after my "research-frenzy," I collected what I thought was probably the largest collection of true examples of the Mandela Effect ever gathered together in one place. It was published by TWB Press and it was like I was the new Robert Ripley. But, ha. Who's going to believe this? *Not these negative people.* My first reviews of the book were great and a few enjoyed my "analysis" as the best part or what they thought was the most intriguing. Those reviews inspired Mandela II. Much of this book will be an analysis to answer: Why, or how could this be? And, for sure, to prove the phenomenon and demonstrate that the Changes were *linked.* Why were most of the changes dark? Some changes were not. I do not mean to suggest that every alteration you may have noticed was devilish and negative...

"I'm a Barbie girl in a Barbie World," we remember the 1-hit wonder song by Aqua. It's been changed to "...in *the* Barbie World." Subtle, hardly a change at all. What's the meaning? Maybe nothing? Why does the colorful Aqua video now have the singer singing the word "the"? But why them? That a Mandela appeared? Well, maybe it had something to do with what a "Barbie World" is? A fake, phony, Hollywood world of superficial parties and nothing real.

The following are Mandela Effects that I would have loved to have included in the first volume. They were found later. They fascinated me and here they are. Do you agree with my evaluation or not?

I have to start with the eyes of horses. The oddity of horses' eyes. What? Since when? *There's nothing strange about the eye of a horse.* Oh, yeah. That was what I used to think. Now look up "horse eyes" and it was a little scary. That's not how they appeared. How did I miss (maybe in reincarnated lives with horses) the fact that they have pupils completely different than the eyes of any other animal? The pupils are now SQUARE or RECTANGULAR. Is that what you remember? I do not recall any animal having such eyes. Cats have eyes different from other animals. And fish. This blows my mind. Horses have normal, big eyes, lashes, and have a problem with keeping flies out of their eyes. I know horses. And horses never had square or rectangular pupils within their large irises. What world am I in? Google photos and see if horses' eyes seem strange to you? They do to me. This is a new one.

What was the meaning here, if there was one? Horse of the Apocalypse? I don't know.

Before we get off horses, another new M.E. has manifested in regard to horses. If I were to ask you: Ever heard that a horse can grow a moustache? Do you recall, at any time in your life, those two words ever put together: "horses" and "moustaches"? I'm 70 years old and sharp, why was it that this was the very first time I had ever heard or seen square pupils and moustaches on horses? I'm pretty sure we're aligned and readers also will not remember anything close to this in the Old Reality. Or maybe you are well aware of horses' squared pupils? But if looked up, you'll find this now to be "true." You'll discover a wide variety of animals, plants and new nature that were never on Earth before. They are now. Welcome to the New World. As the little guy on 'Lost' expressed to us: *"Where are we?"*

I think the first M.E. I found later and it really bugged me that it didn't make it into the first book was Frankenstein. It was a picture I saw that made me immediately review the Boris Karloff Frankenstein movies, available online. This was one more classic, like the many changes in 'Oz.' I have seen the horror classics, Hammer films, monster films, alien films, many times growing up as a Baby-Boomer. I sure have seen the first three with Boris over and over again during the course of my life. I'm talking of the Neck-Bolts, those two, metallic electrodes on each side of his neck. Were they in one piece or two? What do you remember? If you were to win big money on a game show and that was the question, what would you say? One electrode or were the electrodes in two parts?

If we examined Boris' Frankenstein, not the others, and most fan-drawings and models of the creature, yes, each neck-bolt was now in two parts. A smaller extension or pin was on top of the larger piece, below. No, it was one piece, now it's two.

There are probably plenty of examples of residue/residual in the fan art. Some may have each electrode as one piece. But many do not and have it exactly what was shown on the (changed) silver screen today. Monstrous. Nothing should have changed, *but some things did.*

Don't we all remember 'ET, the Extraterrestrial'? Another classic line delivered was: "ET, phone home." Right? Isn't that clearly burned inside your brain along with many other famous lines from films? Well, see it again and ET never said: "Phone Home." Never. The little bugger now said: "ET, home phone." Home phone, like your cell phones. Not phone home. Believe it or not. It should amaze you, this change of reality. It's not a change in memory; it's a change in reality.

Another new transformation has appeared in 'The Wizard of Oz.' A film studded with incredible Mandelas. Blogger 'All Time Scary' has called the film, in regard to Mandela: "The film that keeps on giving." I had pointed out a few items that were strange (new) to me, like Tinman's big/silver Wrench and Lion's Bug-Sprayer. No other researcher had spoken of them or the different appearance of the Great and Powerful Oz-head, as I wrote. So you all think the Wrench and Bug-Sprayer were always there? Okay. Researchers know of line-changes, such as the Wicked Witch not saying "Fly, my Pretties, fly!" And *Scarecrow now pulled a gun?* I'm proud of finding the Wrench and Sprayer that were certainly nowhere in my memory of the film, as I had seen it probably 20 times in my life.

The new, recent change concerned the look of Tinman, oddly not noticed or ever mentioned previously? He now had, in silver, the equivalent to a man's formal suit. Tinman had a silver bow tie. He had rivets straight down his chest like a dinner jacket had buttons. And there was a silver collar. That's not what was there before. If it was there before, it would be illustrated in drawings, models, mimicked in parodies, and that wasn't the case. We're supposed to believe that they were always there? We don't remember the silver buttons, collar and bow tie. But there they are. Look it up. What more changes will happen in Oz, La-La Land? Metaphor for the entire world?

Here's one more from 'The Wizard of Oz': Dorothy's shoes and socks. Were there bows on her ruby slippers? And what color were her socks, white or blue? Many people might not be sure of the small bows and pass on the question. But I think most people would not say blue socks. Blue socks? Wouldn't that clash with ruby slippers? I think that few people would have blue socks in their minds when they pictured Dorothy's feet, but I could be wrong. The blue is strange to me and there were red bows on her slippers now.

One more Mandela Effect that I wished made it into Book I, was Victoria Falls. It was the largest waterfall on Earth, and because of that fact was named after Queen Victoria. I remember what it looked like from encyclopedia books in school. It was in Mozambique and fell from high up on an escarpment, straight down a very, very long way. Victoria Falls' shape was thin and extremely long. Now look at it. Shocking, the change. VF was indistinguishable from Niagara Falls. Victoria Falls was now WIDE, very wide, not long. Another alteration in nature and in school books: Victoria Falls was no longer the largest waterfall. It's second, behind a waterfall in Brazil that dumped more water. Very odd. My early memories are not wrong. The world is wrong. Of course, I have to say: "Not wrong, but different."

(Author's note: On this night of 3/1/21, I walked to the grocery store and there were very clear skies above the San Fernando Valley. The Orion constellation has fascinated me all my life, straight overhead. I owned an expensive Celestron telescope and I'm proud to say I viewed Mercury (in the Pittsburgh area) one night. Copernicus never did that. I know stars and star maps. I have quite the collection of astronomy books that I've collected over many years. My 12th novel, a 'Best Of' book contains a whole section that are astronomical conclusions from decades of observation and study called: "The New Astronomy." But only tonight, on my way to the store, did I think to CLOSELY OBSERVE the Orion Constellation, the most dominant constellation in the sky. And Sirius, the brightest star in the sky. Only now, a few years after I realized the Mandela was real, had I thought to inspect my favorite constellation. And honestly see if there were any alterations, as far as my recollection goes? And there were. I did not *read into* the star patterns and change anything. I immediately examined online star charts of Sirius and Orion as soon as I got home. I checked to see if the actual charts showed what my eyes told me? My eyes, and memory, told me 5 things:

1). Sirius appeared too close to Orion. It was down, to the left, but further away. Like South America was now closer to Africa than it was.

2). Sirius' constellation seemed larger than I remembered. I checked the charts and, yes, it was never almost the massive size of Orion, but now it was.

3). Sirius did not appear as bright. It's known for flashing all colors. Probably still flashed, but it seemed not as intense and outstanding.

4). I know where Orion's (the Hunter) damn 'sword' is...or was. I viewed the Orion Nebula enough times and showed it to many friends, the most colorful object in our skies. His 'sword' was a phallic symbol and hung on his belt as he killed a lion in mythology. But it was right under the famous 3 stars in a line. Now it's *way* below it. It's bigger? Yes. It did not *double* in size or distance to the eye, but it appeared about 35% longer to my memory, and I knew Orion very well, like the Moon and Giza.

5). Also, the top portion of the constellation above the 3 stars, his 'chest,' seemed larger, a bit more expanded. I never remember the top part being much larger than the bottom part. There should not be changes, divergences, even to the smallest degree, of things we know well. But there are now. The supernatural has been made natural).

Here's a funny, new one that will only be known to old hippies who remember the good old days. To me, it's incredible to scan movies or music, simply to be entertained, and suddenly you encounter a MANDELA, a striking difference from what you clearly remembered. And no one else, to your knowledge, had ever found it before. It's like a little "Eureka!" No, this was not the haze of a person who once used LSD. This was a vivid memory that can't be taken away. I asked a friend of mine from the old days, and he completely agreed with me. We're not wrong or vague about it. When you heard a song or a line in a movie over and over again through decades, you remember it! If I was hallucinating or recalled wrong, off from reality, my friend would never have agreed with me. We didn't share the same illusion; we shared the same truth. That truth was nowhere to be found today.

I'm 'speaking' of 'Firesign Theater.' Started out as a LA radio show, a comedy troupe that was popular to the hippies at the time. In the same way we had Cheech and Chong record albums, some of us also had Firesign Theater albums ("You may already *be* there!"). One record title was: 'Don't Crush That Dwarf, Hand Me the Pliers.' One of the most famous songs from FT went like this:

"Back in the saddle again. Out where an Indian's your friend. Where the vegetables are green and you can pee into the stream. Yes, we're back in the saddle again..."

Well, guess what, folks? That's not it anymore and, of course, why it's mentioned here. "Back in the Saddle Again" is almost an expression, to be back doin' what you love doin'. The FT song had the sound and elements of a rider on a horse in the Old West. Even the lyrics suggested this. It was "SADDLE." But in the Dark World, this old hippie song and title to their most famous album was now called:

'Back from the Shadows Again.'

Oh, no. It was never called that, but it was now. Things change, huh? Do you remember Firesign Theater? If you do, that song, the one that won't leave your head, is utterly different in its title and catchphrase and meaning! SHADOWS? Since when? Every time the "Back in the saddle again" chorus should have been sung, there was only: "Back from the shadows again..." I remember how I found this. I just wanted to see if FT was on YT as a random thought struck. I only wanted a laugh and wound up almost in tears.

Later in this book is more of the analysis. The section compares M.E. *changes* and their commonality of Darkness and evil over the good. Firesign Theater was no different. The change was not good, it's *from the Shadows,* again.

The alternative rock band from the '80s, Men Without Hats, had a 1-hit wonder song and well-known video called: 'The Safety Dance.' Was the lyric: "You can dance if you want to, you can leave your friends behind"? Or, was it: "We can dance if we want to, we can leave our friends behind." I was very familiar with LA's KROQ radio station (used to be cool) and taped music videos from MTV's '120 Minutes,' every Sunday night at midnight. I vote, and I am far from alone, that the popular lyric was, *"You* can dance if you want to..." Son of a gun, another drastic change from what a huge group of us clearly remember. The lyrics almost *cannot* be removed or altered, if it was impressed upon your psyche with the repetition of a thousand listenings! *But now it's "we"?*

Let's view the official webpage of the band, Men Without Hats. What did they say? Posted right on top was their blurb: "Nearly 40 years ago, they told the world, 'You can dance if you want to...' and the world listened."

Later on the page, it was printed: "You still can dance, if you want to – and Men Without Hats still makes it easy and fun!"

Well. Nowhere now do Men Without Hats sing: "YOU can dance it you want to..." Yeah, it's been changed to "We." Plural. That's happened before with the Mandela, and the opposite. Sing the video in your head. Why do we hear "You" in our minds? We ALL remembered it wrong? No. That's not it. It changed~

People who know the old song well also have reported that the song/video was livelier, and was faster. Now, it's slower, almost "spoken and monotone."

I was reminded of another case where the band *failed to remember their own lyrics*. That was with 'Panic at the Disco.' ("Haven't you people ever heard of closing the goddamn door?!"). What was strange, from my view at this moment, was that I think the band's name has recently changed? [Like Seals and Crofts?]. Not sure, but the present spelling of the band with an exclamation mark there, looks wrong to me: 'Panic! At the Disco.'? Really?

During 9/11, do you remember a Marriott Hotel at the base of the Twin Towers that was always in the photos just before the towers came down? That is not in my memory or in the memories of others. Look how many times we had seen the pictures. It's in the 9/11 photos now, but not in peoples' memories. It was the Marriott World Trade Center or "WTC3." It was built in 1981 and destroyed in 2001. Who remembers an extra building between the towers?

An additional M.E. could be that there was an enormous hurricane (Erin) that headed for New York that 9/11 day and it was nearly the magnitude of Hurricane Katrina!? Apparently, it did not strike the mainland. We remember a clear day that morning in 2001. If you check (possibly a new history) you'll discover this massive hurricane happened on the very same day as 9/11.

One more M.E. connected to 9/11, possibly. The world was traumatized after the event, but do you remember being a bit traumatized again two months later with "America's Second Deadliest

Plane Crash"? On November 12, 2001, American Airlines Flight 587 crashed due to "mechanical failure" and 256 passengers, crew and those on the ground, died. An article in The Atlantic remembered the second deadliest crash 10 years after it happened. Its subtitle was: "Just two months after 9/11, an airplane bound for the Dominican Republic plummeted in the water near JFK International Airport." The article went on to say "a disaster the rest of the country has all but forgotten...overshadowed by the immensity of 9/11." The mystery is: Why was it that a large number of people don't remember this? Second deadliest crash, almost 2 months to the day from 9/11, and it was an unknown event, not really in people's memories? Maybe a Mandela? Blogger 'All Time Scary' reported an insightful conclusion, which can be said of every M.E.: "Some people may not have lived through this. The event was real to some people on one timeline, but to others on another timeline, this...never happened."

Did 5000 Americans die on the east coast during World War II? Don't you remember when Nazi submarines blew up over 400 U.S. warships, which resulted in 5000 soldiers being killed? It was reported that the attacks went as far south as North Carolina. Germans hunted Allied vessels to cut off supply and ammunition lines. Who's heard of this? Whatever happened to the idea no one in America ever died in the Second World War? Now we discover, there's a lot more:

Were you ever taught in school, read in books, saw in documentaries, at any point in your life, the following information?

"An oil tanker explosion off the north coast of North Carolina by Nazi torpedoes."

"Submarine blockades in the Delaware Bay."

"Giant coastal watchtowers in New Jersey searching for (enemy) subs."

"Soldiers and Coast Guard officers on horseback, patrolling beaches, looking for landing spies."

"...even a massive blimp squadron patrolling American skies looking for enemy submarines."

One might think that this was Classified Information, which has only surfaced at this time? Not at all. These "facts" were not phony stories, they were published in newspapers and broadcast over various news agencies at the time. From average people to history buffs, why does no one remember these details of WWII? Shouldn't we?

Shouldn't everyone have learned about these events in school? We did not, collectively, forget.

"Dazzle Ships." What? In World War I and less in WWII, to avoid recognition by German U-boats, warships were outrageously painted in what was called: "dazzle camouflage." Hulls were covered with bright colors, broad/parallel lines and abstract shapes. The purpose was to "confuse" the enemy. [Seems to me the warships would be obvious targets, clearly seen. Makes no valid sense]. Even the decks of warships were bizarrely painted to confuse enemy aircraft. This must be a New History because who's heard of such a concept before? But we're supposed to believe the World Wars' campaign of Dazzle Ships was "very effective."? Are you kidding me? No, it's history now.

The Vikings! Here too could hide a Mandela Effect. Picture the Vikings' metal helmets that you've seen in movies and in a wide spectrum of historical representations. Were there HORNS on real Viking, norsemen's helmets? As it turned out, it must be only in the movies, because there are no records that they decorated battle-helmets with horns at all. There would be a *scare-factor,* certainly, but horned helmets would not be very efficient headwear for battles. They'd get in the way. Don't tell this to the fans of the Minnesota Vikings.

What killed the Dodo bird? What made the Dodo go extinct? The common, normal history or information educators have always informed us: They were hunted to extinction by men. Flightless, big turkeys, easy prey to early settlers. There were reports that these types of birds never saw human beings before and were unafraid. Add to that, Dodos were supposed to have tasted "delicious." By 1681, Dodo birds were completely gone.

Now it turned out that settlers *did not* hunt the birds to extinction. Dodo-meat was *not tasty,* as we've heard. The record today tells us that "monkeys, pigs and rats ate the Dodo birds' eggs and competed with them for food." What? This was drastically different, but aligned with other odd (re-set) changes.

The Library at Alexandria was considered "the intellectual capital of the world." Its Lighthouse was one of the 7 Wonders of the World.

The enormous Library was a fantastic concept: to house a copy of every book on Earth in one place. Two thousand, three hundred years ago, the vast Library at Alexandria contained "humanity's collective knowledge" and attracted scholars worldwide. In 48 BC, Julius Caesar attacked the great city in a war with the Greeks. Greek ships in the harbor were torched. The assumption had always been that the massacre and the damages to the Library were caused by the spread of fire. All the scrolls were burned or they were partially burned in a large conflagration. Today, the record stated...

The huge number of books (scrolls) at Alexandria's Library were *never burned!* Then why do an incredibly high number of people, which included modern scholars, believe that the famous Library was destroyed by fire, or partially destroyed by fire? They all have not, collectively, imagined wrong.

On May 6, 1937, Lakehurst, New Jersey, the Nazi air-ship, Hindenburg, caught fire (helium) and the disaster was caught on film. "Oh, the humanity!" If you're an adult, you've viewed it countless times. The Hindenburg was the largest zeppelin ever constructed and was destroyed in seconds. How many died? Did most passengers die or did most of them live? It was possible that people have gotten it wrong about certain historic events. Wouldn't you say most of them died? Most of them lived. Sixty-two out of ninety-four survived. This might not be a Mandela. But wouldn't you think many more had died? Also, it was supposed to be the "deadliest air-ship disaster." Now we discover that accidents happened in 1930 and 1933 that surpassed Hindenburg's death toll.

Aldous Huxley's 'Brave New World' will be discussed later in this book. The title came from William (didn't exist) Shakespeare's 'Tempest,' Act V, Scene I, which I have just now discovered had been *changed,* methinks. We already know the classics have been changed, and classics are not supposed to ever change, like Beatles lyrics. We know Shakespeare has changed: "Methinks the lady doth protest too much," had been Mandela-changed to: "The lady doth protest too much, methinks." Juliet's balcony speech had been altered. Now we have Miranda's speech from 'The Tempest," the origin for Huxley's title...

O wonder!

How many goodly creatures are there here!
How beauteous mankind is! O brave new world,
that has such people in't.
(Author's note: I researched B.N.W. for the other section, came across the original Shakespeare quote and I was stunned. *That's not Shakespeare's lines!* I'm far from a scholar on the Bard, but the following is what I believe the verse was...).
How beautiful mankind is! O brave new world,
that has such creatures in it.
"Goodly creatures" has to be wrong or *off*, possibly for a few reasons. I am 100% positive that the last line was: "that has such creatures in it." "...Such creatures" in the last line was correct, but not anymore. In the version today, "creatures" came before "brave new world" and that wasn't the order that it used to be. In Exodus 2/2: *And the woman conceived, and bare a son: and when she saw him that he was a goodly child.* "Goodly" replaced "beautiful" in the Bible. Once again, "goodly" appeared, which suggests to me that this Shakespearean line, like the Bible, had been changed. Miranda spoke of the beautiful people.
Maybe the line was "Godly"? Godly people? Or beautiful? Doesn't this also continue the pattern? Anything godly, good, righteous and beautiful, has been disfigured and mutated?

Another bizarre "fact" we had always assumed was true, was now mysteriously *off.* Could the answer to the following question be a Mandela? What's the tallest mountain? Or, what is the highest point on Earth? Height above sea level is how we have gauged the highest point. But sea level was a very different height at the poles compared to at the equator. The ocean bulged out with around a 13-mile difference.
The other standard of heights is measuring from the center of the Earth. When its measured that way, #1 is Mount Chimborazo in Ecuador, because of where it is on the "Ecuador bulge." Only 131 feet lower than Chimborazo, is the Huascaran Mountain in Peru, which makes it in second place. *Mount Everest came in third on this standard!*
Another alternative was to simply measure from the base of a mountain to its top, which did not consider sea level. When we measured this way, Mauna Kea, dormant volcano in Hawaii, was the

tallest mountain by far, even with most of it underwater. Its peak stood at 13,803 feet above sea level.

["Has the science of measuring simply changed without us noticing? Or, is it different than you remember?" -ATS].

Where did we ever get the idea that Mount Everest was the tallest? It wasn't on any standard of measurement known. What about K2? I think this was a new, sudden and surreal, change in the record and would also surprise Sir Edmund Hillary. Did you know the Mississippi River was no longer the longest river in the U.S.? The Missouri River is now 2,341 miles long and the Mississippi River is 2,318 miles long. Yeah.

Out of the 7 continents on Earth, where does Antarctica rank in size? Think about it. Were you taught it was the largest continent? Or, possibly it ranked second or third in size? Would it surprise you to discover that it ranked fifth? It was one of the smallest. I thought it was one of the largest?

Isla Bermeja was 80 square kilometers and off the coast of Mexico. It was Mexico's furthest point west. The island was marked on maps that can be traced back to the 1700s. What happened to it? It's gone now. Vanished. (So are the islands of Costa Rica and Gibraltar, although we know where they are, attached to mainlands). Mandela has messed with borders and land masses over the entire Earth. Islands have appeared, such as Svalbard and Southampton, while others like Bermeja, apparently, were gone.

The famous 'Thinker' statue by Auguste Rodin "is a bronze sculpture...The work shows a nude male figure of heroic size and sitting on a rock resting on his chin on one hand as though deep in thought, often used as an image to represent philosophy. There are about 28 full-sized castings, in which the figure is about 73 inches high, though not all were made during Rodin's lifetime and under his supervision. There are various other versions, several in plaster, and studies and posthumous castings exist in a range of sizes. Rodin first conceived the figure as part of his work *The Gates of Hell* commissioned in 1880, but the first of the familiar monumental bronze castings did not appear until 1904."

The statue is a well-known Mandela, but I initially thought it fell into the category of JFK's car (6-seater) and Nelson Mandela (did not die in prison), and did not examine it in Volume I. Since then, 3 strange Mandelas have emerged, which included the original oddity. First, many people were under the impression that the Thinker had its hand against its forehead. Too many thought this, exactly like too many people believed Mandela died in prison. That's #1. (All the molds were the same, so it was not a matter of different statues). A new change has suddenly appeared that concerns not the placement of the hand, but was the hand a fist or an open hand? It was an open hand today and this, again, was different than what many remember. ATS found loads of residue, from ads, old TV shows, written in print of an open hand against its chin. I'm with the crowd and remember a *fist* to the chin and not a fist to the forehead. There's been a third change I've only discovered today: Thinker was nude, right? Does he wear a hat? What would you answer? Was 'he' wearing nothing and that was 'hair' on the top or was it something like a ball cap? Suddenly, he now wore a hat or ball cap with a tiny visor turned to the side. Yes. A close view showed a line all the way around and hair that poked out underneath it. I'll bet most people would get the question wrong: "Does the Thinker wear a cap?" Now *he* does. Maybe next *he'll wear a Speedo?*

There's more to the mystery: Why were there endless photos online, from individuals to large groups of people around Thinker, who mimicked the pose...*and got it wrong?* So many posed people did not match the statue and the statue was right there in the frame of the photo! Were they all stupid? I don't think so. I think it's a paradox in front of our eyes that's hard to believe, like the contradictory photos of the Jackson 5 (6) and changes to the famous Christ statue in Rio or Oz's Tinman. We used to say, "Photos don't lie." Now they do (not photo-shopped) because of the Mandela-change. Was it possible that the individuals and crowds in the photos did not get it wrong? In their reality, *they matched* with the fist and its placement on the forehead. Maybe. That meant the universe, or something, came in and spliced (shattered) our reality differently, and it's right in front of our eyes~

'The Starry Night,' painted by Vincent Van Gogh in 1889, contains a Mandela for some people. This is one of the most famous paintings in the world. On the left side of the painting, there was a tall/dark object. What was it? Was it a mountain, a castle, a tower or a tree? Most people polled thought it was a gothic castle. Today, it's a Cypress tree. (I would have said tower, tree would have been my last choice).

The Bible Book of Judges told the story of Samson and Delilah. One more Mandela seems to have appeared here just as an extraordinary amount of dark changes have happened to the Bible. Delilah was bribed to discover the secret of Samson's incredible strength. He confessed to her that his hair was the source of his power. She waited for him to sleep. Did she cut off his hair? Or did she order a servant to cut off his hair? Before, she cut his hair. In the transmogrified Bible, she commanded a servant to cut his hair. Yet, weird that, like Hercules, he knocked down the temple's pillars, which killed everybody, including himself. Delilah never came to justice. She disappeared and we never knew what happened to her. Let's recap: Dumb man, killed. Guilty woman, got away. If you were a little familiar with the Samson and Delilah story, doesn't this version seem wrong or a different version from the one you've heard?

In the Bible's Book of Revelation [was Revelations], there are the 4 Horsemen of the Apocalypse. This is a classic and certainly should be known to adults. The 4 were: War, Famine, Plague and Pestilence. Today, the Horsemen are different: War, Famine, Plague and CONQUEST? Conquest? What happened to Pestilence? We mostly remember Pestilence, and we do not remember Conquest. We have War. Why another reference to war? Does that really make sense? (neither does War). Bring back Pestilence! Nope, it's gone and we have Conquest instead.

What do you remember was Jesus' profession? Would you answer: "Stone-cutter" or "stone mason"? I think not. Wouldn't everyone, or almost everyone, reply, "Carpenter"? Well, in the New World, no such thing. Apparently, the origin of the "mistake" stemmed from the Greek word 'tekton.' It means a common artisan, craftsman, builder or carpenter. Really? And again, we're supposed to believe this was true, it was always that way? No one had ever noticed the error for centuries? New evidence supported this different version of history: Homes were made of stone at that time and in that area. There was hardly any wood, the land was a desert. Also, numerous stone quarries were located in Christ's area. All that aside, "C'mon!" Not a carpenter by trade, neither was his father? It could be true in this world, but not in the other one.

Supposedly, the death of Nikola Tesla was a Mandela. *I'm not sure* and I've been a student of Tesla for more than 40 years. The story was he was struck by a taxi as he walked to his NY hotel, refused medical treatment and died 6 years later. We'll never know what really happened with someone as remarkable as Tesla, but the story of his death may have altered. Heart attack?

In Michael Jackson's extremely famous and overplayed song (1982), 'Billie Jean,' what was the correct line? "...Don't go around breaking young girls' hearts. And Mama always told me, be careful of who you love..." Doesn't that sound right? Today, it's wrong. "Mother" was sung in the original MJ recording. Probably many covers of the tune had "Mama." Because that's what it was: Mama. No more.

In 1992, Joan Jett and the Blackhearts covered an old song by the Arrows called: 'I Love Rock 'n Roll.' The pop song was huge, probably their most famous tune and should be etched deeply into our psyche. Which of the following lyrics were correct? "I saw him *dancing there* by the record machine."? Or, "I saw him *standing there* by the record machine."? Again, literally 1000 times this has happened. What you thought was right, was now wrong. And something off and unfamiliar had taken its place. Today, the lyrics that "she had always sung" was: "...dancing there..."

Remember the Anonymous mask on the black, cloaked figure in the film: 'V for Vendetta'? Or any time the Anonymous (Guy Fawkes) mask and figure had been seen [used as the voice of anarchy, revolution]? Was it black and white only? Or did the mask have pink lips and pink cheeks? Can you imagine it? Now it has pink lips and cheeks, and people do not remember this. I don't think those people were off in their memories. I think they remember very well that the mask had no pink.

The "midnight ride of Paul Revere" could be a Mandela because the story has changed. Americans were taught in school that he rode to Concord and yelled in the streets, "The British are coming! The British are coming!" Supposedly, he warned other revolutionaries before the battles of Concord and Lexington. Records now have revealed that Paul was not alone. Two other riders rode with him. He also was captured and never made it to Concord. After questioning and the loss of his horse, he arrived at his destination. But at that point, the war had already begun. Have we been told a myth all this time? Or has there been a Mandela-change?

George Washington wasn't the first President of the United States? [Let's skip over the *teeth*].

"...Everybody knows that the first president was George Washington. But in fact the Articles of Confederation, the predecessor to the Constitution, also called for a president - albeit one with greatly diminished powers. Eight men were appointed to serve one year terms as President under the Articles of Confederation. In November 1781, John Hanson became the first President of the United States in Congress Assembled, under the Articles of Confederation..."

"Thus was ended the career of one of America's greatest statesmen. While hitherto practically unknown to our people, and this is true as to nearly all the generations that have lived since his day, his great handiwork, the nation which he helped to establish, remains as a fitting tribute to his memory. It is doubtful if there has ever lived on this side of the Atlantic, a nobler character or shrewder statesman. One would search in vain to find a more powerful personage, or a more aggressive leader, in the annals of American history. and it is extremely doubtful if there has ever lived in an age since the advent of civilization, a man with a keener grasp of, or a deeper insight into, such democratic ideals as are essential to the promotion of personal liberty and the extension of human happiness...He was firm in his opinion that the people of America were capable of ruling themselves without the aid of a king." - JACOB A. NELSON, "JOHN HANSON AND THE INSEPARABLE UNION," PUBLISHED IN 1939.

"'E's not all that e's cracked up to be." I like going a different way. The glowing praise of John Hanson (who was handsome) from 1939 might not be accurate. Nelson seems to have *insisted* way too much. So I'll bet none of that was really true; he was probably a Slave-owning scumbag like the rest of the masons, our Founding Fathers. Also. The last line was probably a lie and Hanson was as much of a British puppet as any of them. Why it may be a Mandela Effect is the same universal question: Have you heard of this history before? John Hanson was the first U.S. president and took office in 1781, **8 years**

before George Washington. There's more, new to my ears and others...The term-length of the U.S. President then was only for a year. *EIGHT people were actually United States presidents before Washington!* Really? Roll that inside your brain and ask: Is this new? Why secret this? It appears as reasonable info, not out of conspiracies? It's the way it was, we're supposed to believe. My feeling is this is very recent information that no one had heard before, like a Mandela which has just appeared. I vote Mandela.

Since when can human beings re-grow ribs and potentially grow other bones in the body back? Yes, this is what doctors contend was true these days. Apparently, physicians have succeeded in growing back human ribs. They say that any bone in our body has the potential to be grown back. Really? Like we're freaking lizards?! Ribs heal, but have never been known to re-grow. Have you ever heard of such a thing? Exactly as was suggested in Volume I, please look up these anomalies. If you did, you'd discover tons of things that clashed with your memories. You're not stupid, not that stupid, the crazy world has (unnaturally) *gotten even crazier~*

Consider...
"Casa Modelo was founded in 1925, the same year when Modelo Especial was first bottled...It is also referred to as 'the fastest-growing beer in America.' The company found inspiration from the treasured techniques of internationally renowned German brew masters which led them in creating a model beer in Tacuba, Mexico." Modelo means 'model.' "With the popularity of Modelo beers over the years since 1925, Modelo Especial is now the official beer of the UFC. Their partnership was announced on January 11, 2018. Modelo is known to promote fighting spirit, therefore, it is a great brand to be used by the UFC. ('The Ultimate Fighting Champion')."
Let me preface this: I live in the San Fernando valley with many people of Spanish descent. *Man, is Modelo Beer popular!* Between my apartment-house and the front house, there is a mountain of those blue Modelo cases and bottles. This was not unusual in the area. Trash cans are filled with Modelo, Modelo, Modelo! Large grocery stores had pyramids of Modelo cases at the end of the aisle, next to the pyramid of Stella Artois cases. Now there is so much Modelo that the cases were on the floor and you had to reach over them to get the cheese,

bacon, milk, etc.

Same with Liberty Insurance. I've paid attention and there was no Liberty Insurance 5-10 years ago, and the Statue was on Ellis Island. And there was no Modelo, I believe. I used to drink Corona, when in the mood for beer. I've tried Stella and Modelo and think they're crap. Artois and Perrier have been around. But I think Modelo *magically* appeared (as in a Mandela) and also what Major Magick! Why were the youth of today (that I see around me, mostly) all bald, had beards, hooked to cigarettes, tattoos and DRANK MODELO? I have to think something supernatural is going on. It was nowhere, now it was everywhere in the last few years? Examine its history. Since 1925? Popular since 1925? I'm not a big beer drinker. Five years ago, if asked, "Name as many beer brands that you can?" I could probably name 50. "Modelo" would never have been one of them. It sure wouldn't have been in my mind or known back then and I'd bet many would agree with me. Where'd it come from? Why was it super popular today? I could see if it had great taste, but it doesn't.

Modelo ["model" = fake] could be Mandela, another new history in place that we've never heard of?

[ps. All this beer 'talk' made me want one, a rare thing for me. Just got back from a store on the corner I've gone to for 20 years. I hadn't been there in awhile. It was (almost) All-MODELO! It had every freakin' Modelo type! They took up 2 whole, large, display cases! Before, many different beer brands were there. Did Nazis do this too? I couldn't find Coors. I settled for Corona in a can, but I wanted it in a bottle. No luck, Modelo wiped out everything else. *It's a Modelo-nado or a Modelo-demic!*].

Decades ago, LA and probably NY instituted the D.A.R.E. Program to steer children away from dangerous drugs and other things that might harm them. Do you remember what the letters stood for? The question is the "A." Is it Drugs, Alcohol, Resistance, Education? Or, did the "A" stand for Abuse? I think most people would assume it to be 'Alcohol,' and maybe it was? Today, the record stated: "Abuse."

How about MONGOLS? Mongolia. To most people's recollections: China was much larger and Mongolia was a small country between Russia and China. In the Old World, Russia and China shared a border that stretched a very long distance. The border was only interrupted by a tiny country called Mongolia. Now look at it. It's huge and occupies most of the Russian/Chinese border! These two countries now only share a border far to the east...because Mongolia had greatly enlarged and had taken up that space.

Here's the kicker about Mongols and might connect to the other items mentioned that were (possibly) never on Earth, now they're on Earth? As stated, this only-child had watched A LOT of TV. Sixty-seven years of it, thereabouts. I've never seen a Mongol on TV. I've never encountered a Mongolian person in life or had ever heard anyone else who knew or had run into a Mongol. Have you? A couple years back, suddenly, on either 'America's Got Talent' or the one where they dance...*there was a frikken' Mongol!* Now, I guess, they'll be everywhere? Do you remember Mongolia represented at the Olympics? I don't. The man on the show was very tall, looked like Yao Ming. He had no barbarian helmet with horns. In fact, he was well-dressed and in a formal suit. Oh, my.

In Mandela-surveys, there was a small group of people who thought there was no modern-day country called Mongola. It was only a fabled land, found in stories. Maybe that was in another reality?

Where have Stoats been all my life?! Who has been hiding all the stoats? Stoats! Hell, you know stoats? [I went to school with the Sloats]. Seriously, search your mind. See if you can find *stoats* in there somewhere? Don't look it up until later. I can't find any stoats in my mind and I have such a fine mind. I love nature. I love animals. I don't know stoats.

What's a stoat? Is it a type of snake? How about related to tree sloths? Or a bird or a fish? Maybe it's a breakfast cereal? Have any 'Stoats' at home? I had to look it up and found:

"The stoat or short-tailed weasel *(Mustela erminea),* also known as the ermine, is native to Eurasia and North America. Because of its wide circumpolar distribution, it is listed as Least Concern on IUCN Red List..."

Oh, ermines! There's certainly been soft, furry ermines; they made expensive fur coats out of ermines. So it's the *word* that was new to me? Stoats were everywhere and least endangered. [If we're so overrun with stoats, why were ermine coats very expensive? Oh, like gasoline and diamonds were also not rare commodities and shouldn't be high priced? Right]. Funny, that I am totally unfamiliar with a freakin' stoat. Possibly, we should add "stoats" to our Mandela Quiz and ask: "Hey. Do you know what a stoat is?" To me, it was hilarious to hear an old farmer who said on a video: "Yeah, we got this bad *stoat* problem this year."

Or a pangolin?

Pangolins. Mentioned before, but let's delve into this creature a bit? I was once an avid Television-watcher and grew up with television! Baby-boomers' baby-sitter: Television! I know animals. How come, only recently, have I heard the odd name and heard of how strange this animal is?" Because I haven't paid attention and that's why I've never heard the word: "pangolin" or "stoat"? *I've forgotten?* No, that's not it. Never was such a name or this type of animal ever mentioned or represented years previously. Now, pangolins are (almost) everywhere, yet they are an endangered species? I cel-painted after leaving the Simpsons [many of my book covers are old cel-paintings (used for cartoons), I've used for fine art]. I know animated animals and now there's a TV commercial called: "Save the Pangolins" with a Computer-Generated *pangolin?!* He has a lisp. Here's a quote from the cute, little guy:

"I'm a pangolin, which basically means my tongue is longer than my body and I'm pretty much part bowling ball...We're the only mammals with scales...People use us for medicine and leather boots! Averaging around 100,000 'Good-byes' a year..."

The commercial showed the audience: "Pangolins are the most trafficked mammals you've never heard of."

Information on them stated: "...sometimes known as scaly anteaters, are mammals of the order *Pholidota*...Pangolins have large, protective, keratin scales covering their skin; they are the only known mammals with this feature. They live in hollow trees or burrows, depending on the species. Pangolins are nocturnal, and their diet consists of mainly ants and termites, which they capture using their long tongues...A number of extinct pangolin species are known..."

Weird. If there never was a Mandela, no such clash of memories or parallel realities, and someone told me of stoats and pangolins...I would have thought that these were things I simply had not come across in my life. But now I wonder with all the *Changes* of every kind, which included oddities in nature. I knew nature, I don't know this New Nature. Are you positive they've always been in existence and you've encountered them and there's nothing strange here on Earth at all now? Okay.

Do you recall that deer have long tails? I remember short, fluffy, white tails on deer. To my view, in photos of deer today, the tails appeared longer. "The white-tailed deer's tail can reach 14 inches." I checked the movie: 'Bambi.' They seemed longer. One more new oddity to nature?

Did you know there were not only "rainbows," there were also "snowbows' and 'Sunbows' and 'Moonbows' and 'fogbows'? Yeah, created by snow, Sun, Moon and fog. You wanna bet? Look them up. They now exist, but who has really ever heard of them before? In the record, we find that Aristotle wrote about some of them and that was 1600 years ago. I just found out. No hailbow?

'The Lone Ranger' was a well-known radio show and early TV show, the adventures of the masked man and his trusted/Indian partner, Tonto. We heard a narrator shout in the opening sequence: "A fiery horse with the speed of light, a cloud of dust, and a hearty Hi-Ho, Silver! Away!" Well, the words have been changed from what so many of us older folk remember. There's plenty of "residue" for Hi-Ho, Silver! But. In the opening, it's shouted: "Hi-Yo, Silver!" Hi-Yo? Yep. Now what, the Ranger's a rapper? Yo, yo! No, no. It was "Hi-Ho," like the dwarfs sang in Snow White. Take a look now and it ain't Hi-Ho anymore. There were old posters that suddenly read: "Hi-Yo!" (Speed of light? That sounds different).

In the 1980s, an anthology series aired on TV similar to 'The Twilight Zone' called: 'Tales from the Darkside.' It was produced by horror filmmaker George A. Romero. There was one particular episode that was outstanding above all others, in my opinion. 'Distant Signals' concerned an old actor (Darin McGavin) who'd been in an early, film noir, TV show that was cancelled before the big climax. An alien appeared many years later and got the actor to reprise his role and finish the series for his people, "far, far away." This has nothing to do with the possible Mandela, other than the fact: I knew this series very well and probably watched every show over the years...

Why was the opening voice and words of "Darkside," that I had heard maybe 100 times, odd to me now? Again, I simply wanted to be entertained and looked for "gem" episodes, when I heard the beginning and it nearly freaked me out. It was always creepy; a deep voice stated words that sure sounded relevant or touched the Mandela today:

"Man lives in the sun-lit world of what he believes to be reality...But...there is unseen by most, an underworld, a place that is just as real...but not as brightly lit...A Dark Side."

Was it coincidence that the narrator's words seemed to match the Mandela? "A Dark Side, unseen by most." The words hadn't changed. Today I believe: the *real* Dark Side (Matrix) is seen everywhere around us now and believed by the vast majority of people. The Mandela or difference is the way the intro was now said: *Slower, deeper, even creepier than what it was.* Slight pauses were never there before. I stopped as if Time stood still and had to hear those dark words again and again. The speech was definitely different and it was totally unexpected. I knew the beginning, and there's been a change. It was not my imagination, it was scarier. Hear it on YT and decide for yourself.

Frosty the Snowman is a well-known, animated character, seen in movies, posters, comics, etc. for generations. We remember his hat, pipe, broom and his red nose. Didn't he also have a red scarf? People remember the red scarf, now gone.

A bizarre oddity seems to have occurred with the 1989 blockbuster Batman film with Jack Nicholson as Joker and Michael Keaton as Batman. The Dark Knight's backstory and logo are iconic, very well-known to fans. In the 1989 film, did the bat logo have a single point on bottom or a triple point on bottom? Examine the bat image on the chest of Michael Keaton's Batman. This new reality blows the mind of those who have watched it recently. There's a triple (triple-cross) point on the bat the Caped Crusader wore in this big film. This is not in viewers' memories. They remember the single point on the bottom of the bat logo. The triple-pointed bat image is nowhere else. Nowhere. Bizarre. Not on any of the posters or video/disk boxes of the film. How could every scrap of merchandise (and that film was supremely merchandised) that conveyed the bat logo not match what Batman had on his chest? When they flashed the bat-signal in the film, it had a single point. In the 1992 Batman movie, he had a logo on his chest with a single point. The new, sleek Bat-Plane had a single point in the back. Adam West's Batman, a single point on the bottom of the bat image. How could this happen? The triple-pointed bat logo was only found on Keaton's chest and nowhere else? Sounds *wrong,* sounds like a Mandela.

Christopher Nolan's 'Batman' movies are very popular, seen by millions of people. In the third of the series, 'The Dark Knight Rises,' the character Bane is now considered a Mandela. Do you recall that this big, strong, muscle-bound killer...*knitted?* Bane, who broke Batman's back, did not knit only once. At least 3 times. Since when? This was one more strange item that fans do not remember. It could have been a nod to the novel: 'A Tale of Two Cities,' where the female killer enjoyed murder and *knitting.*

In the 1871 Jules Verne Book 'Around the World in 80 Days,' were the characters ever in a hot-air balloon? Wouldn't you say, "Yes"? The movies portrayed the characters that flew high in a balloon, I would imagine most of those 80 days. Posters did the same. Covers to the Verne novels also illustrated them in a gondola of a big balloon. Funny. Since now, we discover: They were never in a balloon in the book. Sure, movie versions could have made it more exciting as the characters flew through clouds on their journey. But how do you explain covers of the novels also with them in balloons? Some readers of the famous novel have insisted they were in a hot-air balloon. Strange that the book only has them in a ferry, on a steamboat and on top of an elephant. Nowhere are they in any type of dirigible. Balloons were mentioned in the novel, but never used. Could be a Mandela?

The 2007 film called 'Bridge to Terabithia' was directed by the man who owned the first studio that made the Simpsons (my former boss). Some researchers believe this is a true Mandela, on the order of people remembered Chewbacca received a medal at the end of Star Wars, but it's not there now. The film was about a young boy and girl who met and created a fantasy world called Terabithia. Viewers recalled the sad ending where they saw Leslie who swung on a rope to enter Terabithia alone. She fell, hit her head and died. When viewed again, the scene where the rope broke and she fell is not there. Why do people remember it? It's vivid in some minds. It's possible that the film was altered as to not upset the children who watched. Researchers have investigated and there's no evidence or confirmation from the studio that it was ever changed or cut from the original version. (One Step Beyond).

One of the smallest Disney Mandelas could be its biggest. Consider how widespread Disney is. They've covered the Earth and I think they own it. Aren't we all very aware of how the name was presented before the movie title? The one with the three 6s that was little like Walt's real signature? Is it possessive: Disney's Mulan, Disney's Pinocchio, Disney's Bambi, Disney's Hercules...or, do you remember it to be simply: Disney? Disney Frozen, Disney The Lion King, Disney The Little Mermaid, Disney Mulan? "Disney's" sounds correct to a great majority of people. But if you look at anything to do with the movies, like their video covers, it has always been "Disney." Wow, it sounds very wrong, flat and different from our memories. [Did Disney Corp. finance CERN? It was possessive and I think we're all possessed by these Mirror Magicians].

In Disney's and PIXAR's 2007 movie called: 'Ratatouille,' do you remember a scene where a woman held a gun on a man? The G-rated, not PG, movie surprised many who have viewed it recently. They do not remember that Remy, the rat who loved to cook, ran through walls, looked through a hole and saw: A woman who threatened a man with a gun. YT blogger said: "domestic abuse, attempted murder and gun violence," and showed the new scene. To those that have viewed the movie, this was odd and not in their memories. Why would filmmakers have included such a scene in a G-rated movie? Mandela has added and subtracted islands. Mandela has added and subtracted scenes from movies, lyrics and many other things. Yes? No?

In 2012, 'The Hunger Games' film was released. There was a scene where the young participants stood upon their own dark platform, which were arranged in a circle. People have remembered that one of them got off the platform and exploded in a fairly large explosion. The explosion is not there now and might be another Mandela Effect.

In Disney's 1967 animated classic, 'The Jungle Book,' we heard a popular song: 'The Bare Necessities.' Here are the lyrics Baloo, the bear, sung: "...Wherever I wander, wherever I roam, I couldn't be

~33~

fonder of my big home." That's what we remember and that was also what we discover when we looked up the lyrics online: "fonder." Why, when we play the movie today, did the bear sing: "found"? *Found,* which made no sense at all. "I couldn't be found of my big house..." See the movie again and judge for yourself.

Possibly, one additional Mandela appeared in the same movie and with the same character of Baloo. Mowgli was talked into giving King Louie fire. Baloo joined the song and dance. What did he wear, if you can recall? Was it a coconut bra and a green grass skirt? Or, was it a coconut mouth and a yellow grass skirt? The bear now had a coconut on his mouth as he sang. The bizarre, new image on his face as well as the shift in skirt color, shocked many who have viewed it recently. Disney.

Another Mandela (?) from Disney's Wonderful World of Magic: 'Aladdin,' (1992). The movie's setting was a fictional middle-eastern country called: Agrabah. What real country was the movie based? ATS gave 4 choices: Egypt, Iraq, China or Turkey? Surprisingly, the movie's original story came from China. It was supposed to have an all-Asian cast of animated characters. Wouldn't you have thought Aladdin was taken from 'Tales of the Arabian Nights' or 'The Thief of Baghdad'? No, China.

In Disney's 1994 animated film, 'The Lion King,' do you remember the name of the boar-character? Was his name spelled 'Pumba,' or was it spelled 'Pumbaa'? Single "a" or double? Most people remember the single "a." Today, it's been "magically" changed to *Pumbaa* and has freaked some of us out. We also remember (Addams Family) Cousin It spelled with one "t." Now, it's Cousin Itt.

Celebrity names have also changed, supernaturally, seemingly overnight. I remember Zoey Deschanel from when she played Trillion in the new 'Hitchhiker's Guide...' I followed her 'New Girl' series for years. How many times had I seen her odd name in the credits? A hundred times? Well, her name's not Zoey anymore. It was not changed because her agent insisted. This happened overnight, wham-bam, abracadabra! Now, it's always been spelled: 'Zooey'? It was always said with an "Oh" sound, and not like "zoo."

Mandela Effect II

Everyone has seen the newspaper comics called: "Family Circus" because the strip has been with us for more than 60 years and still was printed in many newspapers today. After Bil Keane died in 2011, his youngest son, Jeff, inked and colored the cartoon. [ps. Wasn't Bill spelled normally and not "Bil"? Oh, well]. Since when was the title of the very well-known strip: "The Family Circus"? The? This is unfamiliar to just about everyone. But if you research back to the beginning of the strip, it had always included "the." Amazing.

Do you remember eyeball piercing? Eyeball Piercing! Since when? Since 2003, apparently. You can place images on your eyeball. Photos showed various designs from stars to just about anything, embossed or marked permanently on your eyeballs. Why would anyone do this to their EYES? Or really brand themselves forever with a stupid tattoo? Because other people are doing it? The YT researcher asked people who owned piercing shops: "Had you ever heard of this?" No one had. But now, there was a long history of such a thing?

"Crazy Frog" was a CGI game-character from the early 2000s. He was extremely obnoxious and rode an invisible motorcycle. Do you remember Crazy Frog with exposed genetalia? We discover today that CF rode the bike and stood there, legs spread, with his frog-dong fully visible. Why does this shock game-players who knew the game well? ATS reported that he went to the official Crazy Frog YT Channel. Top of the page had a small, black strip that blocked his frog-wankie. This exposure went back 9 years; the original CF video did not hide the fact that the weird, little guy was without pants. And 'it' was *out.* The channel had over a billion Views and nearly 6 million subscribers. Crazy Frog became the "face of Jamster," and no one minded that he was naked on the bottom with his...?

The card game UNO is now considered to be a Mandela Effect. It was a very popular card game last century. (I played it). Two rules that players knew well and used, time after time, when they played UNO. Suddenly the move of "Stacking" and "Keep drawing cards until you get the one you need" were not part of the game and never were. It's not in the rules (anymore). Then why would so many players remember it and continue making those moves?

For relief due to "Swimmer's Ear," an infection or a condition after too long in the pool, people used a product they remember with the same name as the affliction: "Swimmer's Ear." Today we find that the product has always been called: "Swim-EAR." That *new name* was clearly not what many recall.

"Contrary to common perception, sauerkraut did not originate in Germany. Sauerkraut, a term which is made up of the German words sauer (sour) and kraut (cabbage), it is a Chinese invention..." So said the record today. I think it's changed in the same way the band AC/DC no longer came from Austria; they're Australian. And the color chartreuse was red, now it's green.

Do you remember Little Smokies? Small, bite-sized hot dogs made by Hillshire Farm? They've been around for a hundred years. One more unnatural product-name change, apparently, because people do not remember them always named: "Lit'l Smokies." But they have, from the very beginning.

The popular TV cook, Guy Fieri, is known for being a hungry guy and a bit of an outrageous appearance. Dyed, white hair and sometimes he wore a colorful visor. People remember the visor as a part of his character. (I've never watched the show, and I remember the visor). Online, you can find merchandise to buy for people who wanted to dress-up as Guy Fieri. There's the visor. There were a few white, spiky-haired wigs with fake hair that poked out the top of the visor. You guessed it: *He never wore a visor on the show.* Why do we remember it and why does his company sell visors?

The Guy Fieri Mandela led me to a Richard Simmons Mandela that I had not heard of previously. Picture the TV exercise guru in your mind, if you can? Sorry. We remember his hair. Don't you also recall he wore a headband? Right? Never wore one. It's gone, right along with Curious George's tail and Tidy Cat and a million other Mandelas.

(One more about a missing visor). Cassius Marcellus Coolidge created a series of paintings between 1894 and 1910. We know the popular paintings as: "Dogs Playing Poker." They've been shown in movies, magazines and a wide array of pictures for more than a century. Don't you remember that one of them wore a transparent, green visor? Today, that visor is gone. None of them have it. Why do some of us remember it? (p.s. I think it was worn by the dog on the far left).

My suggestion is to closely examine the YouTube Mandela research online, but this is actually bad advice. Bad advice because:

1) The flood or avalanche or most of what's there now in YouTube diss the M.E. phenomenon and they constantly call it "FALSE MEMORIES." This is brainwashing, propaganda. This is advertising, repeating LIES again and again to hypnotize you to believe lies, anything the fuckers say who play with you and who are only there to deceive you. So it is very difficult to find anything like a real scientist or a smart person to investigate and educate you, objectively. There's so much shit on YouTube now, on purpose, and it's only getting worse and worse. It's really there to sway the stupid who don't know any better that they're being totally conned.

2) Recently, as I've fished YT for more Mandelas (new ones), I've found total IDIOTS telling the viewers about the Mandela Effect. Fools! Cardi Bs! Rappers! Bald, bearded, tattooed bastards that don't know a damn thing and are only there to make you dumber than you already are! *This is who's teaching the youth?* Paid agents of Chaos? Who sets up the blogs, forums, all the technical and computer and video things that make these "shows" possible on YouTube? Not the brain-dead bastards that speak. EVERYTHING'S BEEN SET UP TO LIE TO YOU! Where's truth, real reality? You're finding that less and less and less...

There were many genuine YouTubers who once revealed the effects of the Mandela Wave. Now there are very few good ones. 'All Time Scary' is one young Mandela researcher that I can almost recommend. He told me about rectangular horses' eyes and much more. All the Mandelas found by ATS I do not agree with. Some are wrong, yes wrong, on his part simply because he's young and not that familiar with history, such as when he suggested FDR's middle name wasn't "Delano." Only a handful of people would make that silly mistake. A real Mandela is when a *huge number* of people remember the same thing the same way. But ATS also, probably sincerely, came up with an interesting Reality he believed that was nowhere in my experience, and I'm probably 3 times his age. It involved...

The well-known Tiananmen Square protests in June of 1989 in China. A lone (unknown) man stood his ground against an extremely threatening row of large, military tanks. The whole world witnessed this brave man that actually stopped State tanks right in their tracks. In the universe of blogger All Time and maybe others, the lone man was "CRUSHED" by the tank! Really, crushed dead? This could be a M.E. in the same way many believed Nelson Mandela died in prison, when most knew that he didn't. Why would ATS really believe the Chinese guy was crushed, died on the scene? I was a middle-aged man at the time and absolutely watched the tense events on the news along with everyone else. He got away; he made his statement and rocked the government. I never heard he was found and brought to trial. And I never heard that he was killed, crushed by the very tank that he had stopped. Everything is strange now. Could this be another universe entirely that had protruded into our world, like the timeline/reality that the Titanic did not sink? Look it up.

What can be said about the Mandela Effect online, can also be said about **transvestigation**: It's harder and harder to find sincere investigators these days. Don't you know why? Pearls before swine. All the good work of honest researchers that reported true stuff *fell on deaf ears*. Nothing's getting any better and *everything* should have progressed, evolved and gotten better. Much better, by now. Moved to the complex, not the simple. Moved toward the future, not jumped back into the past. Sorry, but, *you young guys and gals generally are not getting any smarter.*

Investigate. Research. Find out for yourself. Don't listen to people who tell you: "You NEED to do this or you NEED to do that!" That's a minion of a Nazi speaking and trying to sway you. Who the fuck are you to know what I need?! You don't know what I need! You know what *you* need? You need to shut the fuck up! Media has become banners and ads that repeat slogans, again and again, and they always move you THE WRONG WAY. They're lies; They're lying. Be strong and realize you're being fucked with. Fuck them!

[3/22/21] It's outrageous what's been happening to me *in the moment* and as I complete the last book by TS. I want to include as many Mandelas as I can in Volume II. I'm coming across Mandelas or maybe they've "come out of the blue," just to strike me at this particular time? Good timing. Here's what happened only minutes ago...

I'm where I usually am, all over YouTube. Out of billions of ads, one popped up about a drink I'd never heard of before called: "Fever-Tree." My mind immediately TRIGGERED, which was what it's been doing a lot of lately. (Maybe you can tell from the Stream of Consciousness that is this book?). I flashed to vivid memories of the past. Fever Tree was a musical band from 1967-70 that had a fantastic song called 'San Francisco Girls' with an unforgettable, unique guitar sound. I also remembered that I played the album for a friend of mine around 1968. He was amazed I knew the names of the members in a little-known band. I forgotten them now, but I sure remember the bass player's funny name to this day. Only because I retained a memory (not a dream) of telling my buddy the *dirty-sounding* name: E.E. Cummings! That was the bass player's name and I am 100% positive. So. I just went to YT a short while ago to hear this beautiful song and to confirm that E.E. Cummings was the bass player. Lo and behold, I was sucker-punched (very surprised) by what has to be a Mandela Effect. I discovered that Fever Tree's bass player's name was: "E.E. Wolfe." Are you kidding me? I missed this, slipped up, got it wrong, was *off* because it was a memory from more than 50 years ago? No sir, that's not it! I remembered it because: We were kids and we had a laugh about the bass player's name: CUMMINGS!

Now, it's 'Wolfe'? Now it's Wolfe and it never was before. Why can you find Village People tribute bands with 5 members, not 6. Who was always the missing guy? Military Man, in each case of VP bands with only 5 people. Why did the guy on 'America's Got Talent' with a contraption that mimicked the Village People, only have 5 of them with him in the middle? Because in the other dimension, there were only 5 and a little less military in the world (no Armed Forces Day)...streams of consciousness are fun. I think in the same way VP changed and an astronomical # of other things have also transformed, so did this obscure bit of trivia from an old band. It was Cummings. I'll bet there are a few people still alive that would remember and agree with me.

Volume I certainly gave evidence for the ISLANDS of Costa Rica and Gibraltar, which were no longer islands - because new histories had replaced old histories. The following *residue* evidence was not in the first M.E. book, found later, and sure made a case that Spain's, England's and Prudential Insurance Company's ROCK was once an island:

The Progress-Index, Petersburg, VA. (10/11/53). "Since 1713 this **island rock** – Gibraltar – has been possessed and occupied by Great Britain. By controlling Gibraltar, the British also control the Mediterranean Sea and to a large extent, commerce with all nations fronting on that most important body of water."

From SJMAG: "...location of the submarine is particularly puzzling, Lieb says, because for several decades it was thought to have sunk off the European **island** of Gibraltar."

'Physical Geography of Europe' "...tiny **island** of Gibraltar,...."

'The History of the U.S. Toledo CA-133' "Port visits during this cruise included; the **island** of Gibraltar, Port Said,..."

U.S. National Archives – caption: "...A Super Tanker underway and the Mediterranean side of the **island** of Gibraltar is visible in the background."

Vintage b/w postcard $24.99. Clear residue photo of the Rock **island** completely surrounded by water.

Another old b/w postcard showed a view from a Navy ship (4 pounds). It was an **island** with big Rock peak on one end.

~Exactly like tons of residue NEWSPAPER evidence existed for the "Island Nation of Costa Rica," same can be said for *Gibraltar as an island* and a key island during WWII:

'Occupied by Britain' "Great Britain has taken possession of Punta Barina, at the mouth, which is to the 'Orinco' what the **island** of Gibraltar is to the Mediterranean."

"Spain claims the **island** of Gibraltar and politicians called the decision to visit the **island**; 'inopportune' and 'gratuitous' (Prince Charles/Diana honeymoon).

Spanish government also announced that it would vote against the agreement in EC unless the status of the contested **island** of Gibraltar is clarified in the text."

Spanish government threatened to impose border-crossing fees...to try to rein in those who live and pay taxes on the British **island**."

"Breaking News (2/4/19) The United Kingdom has objected to the EU's use of the word 'colony' to describe the **island** of Gibraltar."

"...Approximately half of the dividend goes offshore to the **island** of Gibraltar, where a trust owns _____ shares."

'APES ON GIBRALTAR' "There is a saying around the **island** of Gibraltar that 'when the apes go, the British go, too...'" (These apes were known on the island, now on mainland, they never left the area around the Rock).

"The main reason people travel here is because of the Rock of Gibraltar, one of the most visited sites in the region. Thousands of visitors arrive on the **island** each year to scale to the peak of the Rock."

(6/30/17) Clifton Leaf: "...British **island** of Gibraltar..."

An old British stamp contains a drawing of Queen Elizabeth's head, an ocean liner and the Gibraltar **island**, surrounded by water. "Royal Visit, 1954."

Mandela Effect II

Gibraltar coins and sports stamps from 1995 commemorated the "**Island** Games." 24p, 44p, 49p.

Holiday Information for Gibraltar, United Kingdom: "Gibraltar is an **island** located on the southern border of Andalucia, Spain, at the south end of the Iberian Peninsula..."

All maps have not been Mandelaed (I was surprised to find out). A few maps actually depicted Gibraltar Island, exactly where it was supposed to be: in front of the Bay of Gibraltar. They also showed various towns, locations and the 'Gibraltar Channel.'

How about a 1967 movie called 'The Sailor from Gibraltar'? It starred Jeanne Moreau, Orson Welles and Venessa Redgrave. The poster had a ship, water everywhere, and just a head that extended out of the sea and looked up. Obviously, the head represented Gibraltar Island.

Also, a word about Costa Rica:

From *Nature Odyssey Worldwide Tour* article (4/26/19): "There are a few common misconceptions about this popular photographic destination and being an island is right at the top of the list...*Costa Rica is not an island,* but does have an island-like feel to it..."

I found a modern work of art, a 3-paneled print of shores. 'Aruba,' 'Hawaii' and 'Costa Rica' were printed on each panel. Why include a mainland country's beach with beaches of two islands? Unless, the artwork originally illustrated 3 islands.

Online, there are endless comments such as: "I thought Costa Rica was an island!" So many have remembered that CR and Gibraltar were once islands. WHY? Why so many? No one thought Kenya or Zambia or Peru or any other mainland country were once islands, but they do about G and CR. One video asked the question: "What island is bigger? Hawaii or Costa Rica?" Most people polled did not say: *Costa Rica isn't an island.* Most of them answered the question.

A little more notes...

I just remembered...I have evidence that I have a great memory from long ago, anyway. t.s. True Stories: I memorized all the presidents' names in third grade. Only because I had these cool, colorful stamps of U.S. Presidents in a scrapbook. Me, the shy kid, showed off in school and Mrs. Green sent me to the sixth grade class to recite what I had memorized. First public speaking, but I knew the presidents and rambled them off. I can still do it like a chant or song you never forget; I have problems with the ones after Nixon. Same kid I turned on to Fever Tree, had a plastic device you turned and read all the state capitals. We were in competition to see who knew them, Montpelier, Bismarck, etc. We knew them all back then. In college, and I know the following is unbelievable – but I didn't dream it and I do not lie. I named every card in the deck whether it was red or black, correctly. That's 2 to the 52nd power! "If you double a penny every day for a month, you're a millionaire," Lt. Sulu accurately stated. The odds of what happened to me were much more than that.

It was an evening with 4 of us in a dorm (no LSD) and something mysterious happened to all of us; *maybe my first paranormal experience.* We tried telepathy. Three of us concentrated on a specific, while the 4th tried to guess it. Cities, countries, rivers, animals, etc. We had 1-on-1, a sender of Red or Black, whatever card he turned, and a receiver who attempted to guess it. Scores were way higher than average and got better as the night progressed. No one intended to pull an all-nighter, but **we didn't miss!** And we were spooked. Near the end, I named every card in the deck, almost as fast as he turned it. If I'd have taken a second and thought about it, I'd have missed. Nothing like that night ever happened again. Years later, the experience was topped when I saw UFOs, an *untouched* spoon bend completely in less than a minute and otherworldly things with a psychic wife. I suppose this emerged out of me now to say: Phenomena exists. There's more things than what's on Earth and in Heaven.

New Analysis: Connections Between Changes.

What Idiot Designed the Volkswagen Logo?

Volkswagen's earliest logo design dates back to 1937 and was designed by the Porsche Company, which held a competition. Ferdinand Porsche "was in talks with Adolph Hitler to create the cars, who wanted to realize his dream of every German being able to afford a vehicle." Porsche also developed military vehicles for the war effort. Franz Xavier Reimspiess with the "swastika-design" won the contest. He was rewarded with 100 Reichmarks.

Why would I call F.X. Reimspiess an idiot? It's not just him. It's the entire Porsche Corporation, Britain, and even today's Volkswagen Group. They're idiots and this is a Mandela...

Volkswagen logo design over years:

| 1937 - 1939 | 1939 - 1945 | 1945 - 1960 | PRESENT |

After WW2, VW was taken over by the British who removed the swastika. Then in 1945, Volkswagen returned to German ownership and the logo was given a "much more up-to-date, sleek look." Finally, color was added for today's logo.

There's just one problem:

What the fuck is that little line doing there that divides the "v" and the "w"? As you see, it was always there, all the way back to the beginning. You know, Germans are very good designers, engineers.

(It's not really a racist statement if it's a compliment). That little line shouldn't be there. It makes no sense. It's STUPID! Designers, commercial artists, smart Germans, would never, never, never have accepted that design when there is this design:

I should have won the Reichmarks! Actually, it wouldn't have since there's no swastika. But now look at it; notice its beauty, its elegant design. I'm serious. I've been a professional artist. I've been paid for my commercial art. I know Design. And in more than 80 years, no one who had ever controlled VW and no one in the modern Volkswagen Group has ever thought to remove the little line? Really? Maybe we can tweak the old emblem just a bit more for the New Age? Give it an even "sleeker" appearance? Pepsi did. Gee, let's think about it: How could we do that? Let's get some geniuses from Geneva or London to work on the problem? *The fucking dividing-line is unnecessary and dumb.* Perfect for this Dark dumb World, where not a damn thing makes sense anymore.

WHERE could I have gotten my beautiful VW design? How did I come up with it? I'm not *that* creative. I REMEMBERED IT from the other parallel-world, our Old World, the brighter/better one that's long gone. Those Volkswagen logos had no separation between "v" and "w." Now, they do as everything around us has replicated, darkly.

Thrusters on jet airplanes.

Take a good look at plane thrusters, those cylindrical turbos under wings of jet aircraft. *They're in the wrong place* or I should say a different position that does not maximize its efficiency. What is wrong with jet aircraft designers? From day 1 it has been like this (exactly like the VW logo). No one in the aviation industry had ever thought to *shift* the thrusters to a better position? Look up the first jet airplanes and you might understand or remember: That's not where jets were placed or should be placed.

The better placement is **directly attached under the wings**, fastened securely to the wing...not placed out in front like "headlights," as previously mentioned.

Note that with this inferior placement, an extension must be created. Why? Unneeded, not necessary. The stanchion or extension is merely there to keep the jet thrusters out in front of the wings, like headlights. Ridiculous. Don't put them there. Get rid of the stanchions completely! Move the jets back so they are positioned right under the wing. This was where they were, they are, in the Old World that made more sense.

In this negative universe, how many times have jet aircrafts lost their turbos because of violent storms, air-pockets, etc., and crashed? How many people have died needlessly? All because, from the very beginning, no one figured out: "Hey, maybe we should attach jets to wings and not have them connected to small, flimsy extensions?"

In my positive world, jets were on wings. My world was smarter and much brighter than this one. An added Mandela could be that England's Frank Whittle is no longer the originator of the jet engine. Now (Nazi) Hans von Ohain of Germany is credited with the first jet engine years earlier than Whittle. (Germany is now thought to have started torch-carrying, as in Olympic torch-carrying, when we know that began hundreds of years ago with the early Greeks).

No one was burned as a result of the Salem Witch Trials?

Are you f-ing kidding me?! The well-known Salem Witch Trials in 1692 and 1693 *never burned to death alleged witches?* Seriously?

This is what we're supposed to believe in the New World? 17th Century, "religious," fundamentalists were known as "witch-burners." "They'll burn you!" Wouldn't it be reasonable, sensible for these fanatical men to have utterly destroyed by fire those who they had declared a witch? Fire destroys. That would be, and was, the logical result of Salem's trials. But now, reality has changed: There is absolutely no evidence [outside of "residue"] that anyone at Salem was ever burned at the stake. Here's the new information if you were to investigate the trials:

"The Salem witch trials were a series of hearings and prosecutions of people accused of witchcraft in colonial Massachusetts between February 1692 and May 1693. More than two hundred people were accused. Thirty were found guilty, nineteen of whom were executed by hanging. Wikipedia."

HANGING. They hung 'em high! Why? Why would this complete reversal of history occur? You mean everyone who had ever assumed Witch-Burning, hundreds of years ago at Salem, were in error? Everyone's been misled for centuries? No. That's not it.

Is someone telling (rewriting/resetting) us to not destroy evil by fire? Just a question. Let's analyze. Who would that be? Who would steer us away from fire used by religious zealots? *Maybe the Church Lady knows?* Maybe someone or something...evil, such as the Devil [Illuminati in the real world]?

Hitler's Moustache.

Adolph Hitler no longer has a unique moustache. It's changed in appearance. All of them; Hitler photos, films, paintings, drawings: The Fuhrer's moustache is now BUSHY. It never was before; it was a thin/vertical strip of hair, only shared by him and Charlie Chaplin. Because of that uniqueness that was ONLY in common to those two celebrities, the actor parodied Hitler in 'The Great Dictator.' But if you view the film, such as his incredible speech at the end, you'll see *weirdness* because Chaplin's moustache is also thick and bushy! This section could be called: 'Chaplin's Moustache.' Everyone knows the little tramp's moustache was just a small, vertical strip below his nose. Right? Nope. Not anymore. It's changed and that makes no sense. If they never had thin moustaches, common to only those two, 'The Great

Dictator' would never have been made. Examine the two photos:

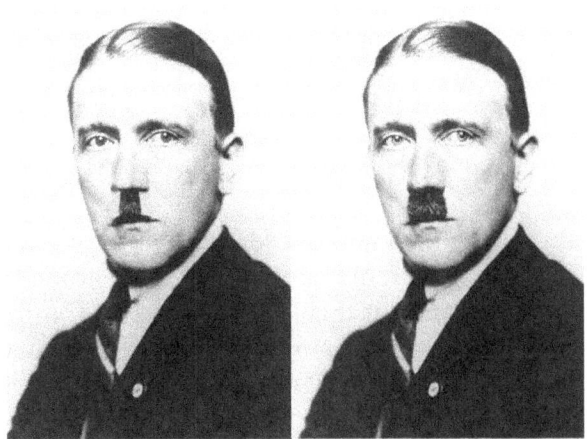

The Hitler that I and many people remember is the (doctored) photo on the left. He had dark eyes. But the Adolph Hitler in this antimatter universe had bright, blue, sympathetic eyes and is the photo on the right. Look at the moustache that absolutely clashes with a lot of our memories. It's wide, broad and is closer to the one worn by Joe Stalin. If it was white, it would resemble Pinocchio's Geppetto.

Former NBA superstar Michael Jordan, for a while, wore a "Hitler moustache," and wasn't even criticized for it. He was highly complimented for the "balls" it took to do that. He showed up (made to show up) for a famous Hanes commercial on an airplane with a "Hitler stash." The oddity was that MJ's H-stash was very small, only a thin strip and that's why it was compared to the Fuhrer's. But it appeared *nothing* like the one on the right of the new Hitler with sympathetic, blue eyes. Strange. We have these records, his Hanes commercial, some public outcry; Charles Barkley talked about it on Conan O'Brien...but MJ's stash isn't like Hitler's in any way. This is 'residue.' It should have gotten big and broad like Charlie Chaplin's did, but it didn't. So, it makes very little sense that *anyone* would have drawn the comparison between MJ and Hitler, but they did. Hitler's and Chaplin's very thin moustache *changed,* got bigger. It was rewritten/redrawn differently in history.

What does it mean? It might mean Adolph Hitler is not unique, not a freak. Not an anomaly; he's like everyone else? Everyone's a Hitler and he is Everyman? Is that what the Re-writers of Reality want to portray and want us to believe?

There is a pattern to the Mandela changes. The common denominator seems to be demonic, always negative and never anything positive or good messages. Always bad.

"Stopped into a Church I passed along the way..."

In the mid-1960s, the band the Mamas and the Papas had a huge hit song which most of us remember, if you were around last century. The entire, wonderful spirit of this Hippie, move-to-California anthem, has drastically altered. Please listen to old performances of the band to see what I mean. It was a cold winter's day and the singer had a profound revelation: He "walked" (maybe not "stopped") into a Church he passed along the way and it was: "**...and I began to pray!**" It was a bolt of inspiration, as if seeing God or tripping! The foursome belted out a powerful song in recorded performances and the message was always thought to be (from listeners) like a religious experience.

But when you hear the changed song now, they're fucking hypocrites! The new lyric is:

"**And I PRETEND to pray!** You know the preacher liked the cold. He knows I'm gonna stay...on such a winter's day..." Pretend? Do you understand the difference? It's as big as night and day.

Remember, I've heard this song hundreds of times because I go back to the sixties. Only now, in the last few years, is it totally different to me and to some others. Even the next line is bizarre to my ears: "You know the preacher liked the cold." Liked the cold?? I don't think so; that's a bit dark also. I had assumed over the years the lyric was: "You know the preacher's life is cold." [But I could be wrong on that point]. The pattern or new reality appears to always be the same: We've been scammed, darkly.

Licence to Kill.

The above title is not the exact title to the 1989 James Bond movie that starred Timothy Dalton as 007. It's a little different than the original name of the movie; it also changed with the Mandela Wave. Why? The Bond franchise is massive and English blokes wouldn't have misspelled the movie's title. But they did. Look at it now.

"Licence" should have an "s" in it. *Only now,* 30 years after the movie was released, people have discovered that its title had been misspelled?! All this time? No way. People are not that stupid; we have been made to appear stupid. That's not what happened. It's more likely that the Dalton Bond film was always correctly titled, like all of them had been spelled correctly, with proper English...

It changed, unnaturally. What is significant about this change? The significance is the number "33." In numerology, "cc" is 33, a special # to occultists, the age when Christ was murdered. They honor that event with "33," found on many secret documents of the Freemasons.

Keep in mind that nothing should have oddly changed, people remember that the Bond film was always correctly spelled and is one more subtle *shift into Darkness* that few have realized.

The misspelling connects to the new Dark Bible, where some sentences begin with uncapitalized words. Why would They do that? It never occurred in the Bible of the Old World. I thought the great Britains knew how to spell their own language? Aren't They "brilliant"? On this side of the 'Magic Mirror,' apparently, They don't care. No one really cares on or in this negative 'side of the Glass.'

Also. The very concept of agents in the world who are freely permitted to go out and kill; it's their job. No laws apply to them. Above the Law. They don't stand trial or take any responsibility for their murderous actions. What are we talking about? Really talking about? The fascists who run everything and can do anything They damn well please to us poor people, like create wars, create real viruses and bogus viruses. They'll kill and eat your children, take your money and have you bow to them for their grace and protection. (Hardly exaggerating).

They have LICENSE to do anything they want, change the world and even to misspell a Bond film title. And they will laugh at you for hardly noticing.

"No. *I* am your Father."

Where's Luke? This is one of the biggest Mandelas, even more significant than Forrest Gump. Everyone, certainly everyone in the Old World, knew Darth's line in 'The Empire Strikes Back' was: "No,

Luke. *I* am your father." Luke's not there, missing, maybe on Ahch-to somewhere? Why would the reign of the Jedi end? They were victorious. The Jedi wouldn't end, they'd reign supreme. The Sith would end, the losers, the defeated. Nothing is supposed to make sense. Star Wars and Star Trek and so much else that you think are SO COOL...are not what they appear. You do not view "entertainment Media" as Nazi brainwashing and propaganda. You should. You would be less affected by it if you did.

I had previously written on this point:

"...There are old photos of King Edward teaching Princesses Liz and Ann as children the Nazi Salute! Edward didn't abdicate the throne for love of Wallace Simpson. It was because of his Nazi ties, which would have come out in '37-'38. Prince Philip is a Nazi and the Queen Mother. These are blonde Aryans! Royalty are Not British. Fooling the world. I could never have told my dad (who almost died in WW2) that he wasn't fighting against the Nazis, *he was fighting for them!* Believe it or not. **Sith are Nazis**. How the fuck did Palpatine's forces, a defeated enemy, appear out of nowhere and threaten the Republic all over again in recent Star Wars? It symbolizes: How the fuck did Germany, a defeated enemy [WWI], rise to power and its war-machine threaten the world in only 20 years? Answer: Funded by Britain, who has always lied and controlled us through TV, movies, sports, music, etc. and puppet-leaders. You had to Man-Up during WW2. Celebrities and newspapers *forced* you into Europe's War, again. You didn't get laid if you protested and were against serving in WW2. Sissy. United Kingdom, eh? It's the Evil (secret) Empire totally ruling in the Capstone and all nations are its STATES, little kingdoms. U.S., Russia and all countries are not sovereign and MUST COMPLY to new Nazi dictates. One example is no country can have purple on its national flag. Wouldn't at least one? Britain controls absolutely everything. Church and State. Swiss aren't neutral, they are England's BANK! And fund ALL WARS! No countries. No president, premier, leader, is allowed to really diverge politically from Britain's PM. Never happened because all nations are under English Freemasonry in the Order..."

Star Wars plastic figures sold like crazy in the '70s and '80s. When you pushed the button on the Darth-figure, it stated: "No, Luke. *I* am your father." When Mark Hamill impersonated James Earl Jones, he said, "No, Luke..." Although that impression is about impossible to find now. Luke was there; now Luke and the whole Jedi Order seem to be gone. The good guys. The ones who won?

What does it mean? It means to kill off the good; it means to greatly favor the Dark over the Light. Lies over Truth. It means the *real world* as in the concept of "predictive programming." "Balance to the Force"? No more. Sith actually won, no matter what you observe on the silver screen. Nazis really won WW2 and beyond, no matter what you hear from Big Brother, because they are the monarchies in the world today. Fascists. Money-Printers. The Controllers, the New Romans, the New Pharaohs rule, not the people, the low general public who have been under the 'boot' of fascism for many generations. It's a fictional metaphor for something real. Nothing makes sense because reality is not supposed to make sense anymore.

Yoda speaking backwards. What does that mean? Why? Would it surprise you that a "yoda" is known in the occult world of Freemasonry? Jedi Order = Order of Knights Templar. Insider Jordan Maxwell told me personally that a *yoda* is a little demon that speaks backwards. This is nothing good. It's connected to Aleister Crowley and backwards Beatles' lyrics, believe it or not. Yet we are infused with actually terrible info and influence from Hollywood/British Master Magicians, dressed up as something wonderful, like a new religion of Jedi? Or "Yeah, yeah, yeah," Beatles music. The Republic and the Federation, by definition, are not good organizations. They've been fooling us for ages.

Jedi. Supposed to be the good guys, right? Why do we think their holy motto of "May the Force be with you" is lovely or beautiful or right? "Force" is a horrible word, a violent/penetrative word where you MUST COMPLY. Have you and your family been *forced* to do numerous, completely unnatural things since 2020? It's all connected. A far better slogan for the Jedi would have been: "May the Energy be with you." Energy is neutral, positively-charged or negatively-charged. But FORCE is not neutral. Children and Star Wars fans in general rally around the idea of The Force and have little concept that we are, again, being played/misled by the most popular things that are promoted (by evil forces. Other examples are Beatles, Stones, James Bond, Shakespeare, Harry Potter, Terminator, Transformers, etc.).

One more additional Star Wars Mandela that should have been in the first Book and in the earlier section. Question: In Episode #4, the first SW film we saw, did Obi-Wan Kenobi ever state the very famous quote: "May the Force be with you.'"? Now, after the transition, we discover that Obi-Wan *never said it* in precisely that way. He said variations of it, such as: "The Force will be with you, always" and "Luke, the Force will be with you." Oddly, it was Han Solo who said the quote perfectly in 'A New Hope,' not Ben Kenobi.

"Life was like a box of chocolates..."

The original title of the Tom Hanks film, some say, was 'Forest Gump.' Now it's 'Forrest Gump.' How could it have changed? Well, M.E. researchers have noticed that Sally Field (also in 'Gump') was first known as Sally Fields. Hmm. Such a classic line in a film is the one above. The only problem is: *That's not the line that we all know and remember.* The line was: "Life **is** like a box of chocolates, you'll never know what you'll get."

Again, why? Why the change and what's the significance of the change? For you who might not be aware: The new line is "was," *passed tense.* Isn't the meaning obvious? It was in the past, life was wonderful, fun, sweet, beautiful, precious, you never knew what you'd get. You were surprised every day, surrounded by people who cared and loved you. [Okay, an exaggeration].

But now...

Life is not a glorious amusement ride. No more. Today. YOU KNOW WHAT YOU ARE GOING TO GET. You're going to receive something very different than before. You are going to get hell on Earth. Life won't be fun. You won't get the best, only the worst, only the very worst – but you poor Slaves will be made to believe IT'S THE BEST! You'll never again taste 'sweet chocolate' and have special lives as many did in the past. This is what you get! This is *all* you get! You will love it! You will not complain and only beg for more. You will never be made to know your true potential and what super wonders a real, futuristic society produced. Fantastic science and technology are withheld from us many muggles and only doled out to the few Celebrity Elites, the Illuminati's very high-paid Slaves~

"In Earth as it is in Heaven."

Have you checked the Bible lately? Maybe you don't want to see what's in there now? It's no longer the Holy Bible; it's the Devil's Bible. It promotes homosexualism. The Good Book from the Good World didn't do that before. Holy Communion was a symbolic act in that Old World. But in the new Devil's Bible, the only Bible available here in hell, it's an unspeakable act.

The Bible was published in 1612, as many devoted to the Bible have recalled. But now the published-year has changed to 1611. Why? From my Outsider knowledge of secret societies, 11, twin towers, the 2 Pillars of Boaz and Jachin, which are represented in the "11," could be the reason for the change.

The very well-known quote that's 410 years old, that we all know from the Lord's Prayer, has been *changed*. How could that have happened? But it did. The words now found in the Bible is "...**in** earth as it is in heaven." We do not live IN Earth; we live ON Earth. Possibly in future, people might have to live in underground bunkers simply to survive? Is that the meaning of the alteration?

This is not mistaken or false memories. The bold quote above is wrong, but not wrong for the Dark antimatter World around us now. I had written that: "If one letter of the Bible can change, then whole continents can change. And they have."

Investigate the extremely odd DIFFERENCES laid out by biblical Mandela researchers on YouTube. You'll be amazed even if you only have a basic understanding of the Bible. All the changes are bad, awful. Wouldn't forces of Darkness corrupt, ruin, sabotage anything and everything good and Godly? Christ would be attacked, and God and the ancient principles that were in the old text.

The Commandment: "Honor thy mother and thy father" was the 4th Commandment. I should know, I heard it enough times as a kid. It's been changed to the 5th Commandment. Yeah. I guess in this hell of a place, family and parents just don't matter that much anymore. I guess the new motto here is: *Do as you will*. Also different is the order of parents. The New Order is: "Honor thy father and thy mother."

There are now misspelled words, terrible grammar and some sentences that begin with uncapitalized words. This is the greatest Book transcribed by masters of the English language. Why did they mess up so badly with something so damn important? Why was it that these writers of the Bible did not care? Because this is the fucked-up, parallel world. The Bible has not been spared the Universal Re-Set called the Mandela Effect. Titles of chapters have changed. Yes, it's true. And even the overall title. Open it up and read what is printed on the title page. In the King James version, the title page no longer reads: "King James."

The new title is: The Prince James Bible. How can that be? But it is. How can a Prince command the first English translation of Greek and Hebrew records? It would have to be a King and it was. Elizabeth I had died and James of Scotland became the King of the British empire. "King," not Prince. But the Dark Bible now reads: "Prince James." *Nothing makes sense.*

New images on the Ceiling of the Sistine Chapel.

What was Michelangelo thinking when he painted the Sistine Chapel? A few items, that were painted in the early part of the 16th Century, appear very different than what many remember. In the creation of Adam, would you have imagined that Adam's hand was higher than God's hand? It is now; it was not previously. God is surrounded in robes and angels and points *horizontally?* Horizontally, and his hand did not do that before. It pointed down and was parodied in the 'ET, the Extraterrestrial' poster, which pointed down. Look where Adam's hand is in comparison. Adam's wrist is higher than God's hand and it certainly was not like that in the ceiling's first 400 years. No one ever noticed until now? No one noticed because the scene was never arranged like how it appears on the ceiling today. All the parodies and other representations of God's creation of Adam had God's hand higher. Those images are not wrong. That's residue, a reminder or memory of what was.

Let's move on to another panel on the famous ceiling, God's creation of the Sun and the Moon. How can I 'say' this to those completely unaware? But...**God's bare butt is now painted on the Sistine Ceiling!** Check it out. Two views of the same God are painted: God points upward and there is a part of the Sun, bottom part of the golden disk. The other image is a reverse-view of God in robes, only there's like a PJ "poop-shoot" and we view the *bare ass of the Supreme Being.* You see, it's a joke and it was never a joke before. Where's the Moon? Don't you see, in this negative/antimatter universe, the Moon is the bare butt of God? And a new Bible verse has appeared that corresponded to the painted image: Exodus 33/23 (nice Illuminati numbers), God says, "...And thou shall see my bare parts." [Why?].

How have we all missed God's bare ass on the ceiling? How did the New York comedians miss this joke and target for ridicule over centuries? We're just hearing of this now? Wow.

I clearly remember one more unusual change to the ceiling that no other researcher had stated. I remember how the golden Sun appeared and it was only a sliver of the bottom part. It was a large circle, but only a small/horizontal strip was painted and it captured the idea of a large Sun. Now look at the Sun; it is not just the bottom strip. It's much bigger than what I'm sure I remember. In fact, a couple of years ago when I delved deeply into the Mandela and first examined Adam's/God's hand, I swear it was only a small, but wide, golden strip. Now it is much larger and not just the bottom section. This is a fairly recent change. Possibly dating back only a few years. But as outlined in Volume I, I believe the main Mandela Wave (as I've referred to it) hit at the end of 2015. There are indications this might be so.

What could the enlargement of the Sun on the Ceiling mean? Nothing, or maybe the idea of pagan Sun-worshippers (witches) now run the planet? That They are winning, Dark winning over the Light?

Moses with Horns!

What was Michelangelo thinking when he sculpted his huge, white, sitting statue of Moses in San Petro, Rome? It has horns! Horns. In this Dark World, horns don't have connections to the Devil. Horns connect to royalty. It's Regal. Michelangelo made Moses a king and kings are crowned with two appendages that extend from the head. In other words, horns! Old paintings of Moses also show this new characteristic.

The well-known Moses statue in Rome is far from being alone. In Vilnius Cathedral, Lithuania, again, Moses was sculpted with horns. The "Well of Moses" in Dijon, France, also portrays the holy man with horns. Pattern continues...

Jesus Christ punched in the face and blindfolded.

Since when? Have you ever heard of Jesus Christ being "struck" in the face? Have you ever heard of JC being "blindfolded"? In any movie, play, painting or religious drama of the Christ Story, do you recall anywhere an incident where the man was blindfolded and struck in the face? I don't. But there it is suddenly in Luke 22/64:

"And when they had blindfolded him, they struck him on the face, and asked him, saying, Prophesy, who is it that smote thee?"

Numerous old paintings and religious depictions now show what's in Luke 22/64. Prophesy? This also seems like a new addition. JC was never called the name "Prophesy." But here he is. This is only included so that readers realize tremendous and unnatural changes have happened in the world.

Now the Lamb lays with the *Wolf?*

This is from the well-known Bible verse, Isaiah 11:6, where the Lamb had always laid with the Lion. Bible scholars to experts on The Book remember that it was the Lion. Along with a wide range of Dark Changes in the Bible, there is Isaiah 11:6, which has shocked many. It was the first Bible-Mandela I had heard of and motivated me to search more and pick up a King James (now Prince James) Bible.

The new line is: "The wolf also shall dwell with the lamb…"

Lion, not mentioned? Let's analyze the transition from Lion to Wolf. (I like to draw connecting lines). The Lion could be a reference to a King. What's the meaning of Wolf? "Wolf" has many connections to Adolph Hitler. Hitler thought of himself as a "Wolf" and his enemies were "vampires." 'Wolf's Lair' was the name of his first Eastern Front headquarters during WWII and he had wolves as pets. *Wolf* is a royal symbol, as well as a fascist symbol. If the change has meaning, I'd guess: Kings are gone, something else rules now, and that is the Secret State.

We, the people, are obviously represented in the Lamb symbol. The original meaning of the verse was PEACE. The Lion would normally eat the sheep. But now it would lay with it and the Lamb had nothing to fear at all. Today, everything is different. The poor Lamb is not safe, now led to slaughter? *It's a Wolf there instead,* and the Lamb is sure to be dinner. That's a transition. I could be wrong, but the meaning might be: *We* are being led to slaughter by fascist authorities, the new Kings.

"If you build it, HE will come."

The movie was 'Field of Dreams' with Kevin Costner. If you remember, it was like God talked to the man and told him to build a ball field? One more time, the classic line we mostly remember is not the line above. We remember, "If you build it, *they* will come." At the end of the movie, the extraordinary ball field was constructed and "they" came. They came from all around the rural area to see the special games.

Who the hell is HE? Watch the film again, and exactly like the other Mandela-changes in movies, your ears will hear something new. Different from what we remember. The deep Voice from the sky now states: "...He will come." Is it the Prince? Prince of Darkness that Hollywood and modern witches from all corners of the globe pray to, worship, and await his coming? That Prince? It was "they," now it's "He." This is significant and aligns itself with the dark themes of other Mandela-changes.

"Hey! Let's get Mikey!..."

People who lived a half century ago would remember a Life cereal commercial played again and again on only a few channels (because there were only a few TV channels back then). This is one of the blackest, darkest, most devilish of the Mandela-changes, and it involved children. There's this new cereal that is very good for you, but hell it tasted like medicine. They had to get through to children that it really *tasted great.* The commercial had kids who tossed the bowl around and wondered should they eat it or not? Then they remembered little Mikey. Oh, he's stubborn and what?

Does the small child "hate everything"? Or is it that "He'll eat anything!"? That's a huge difference. Once more, as significant as night vs. day. Negative or positive? Which one was stated in the old Life commercial?

Most of us from the Old World distinctly remember the kids that said, "Hey, let's get Mikey! He'll eat anything!...He likes it! Hey, Mikey!"

The classic commercial has transformed. Look it up now and the boys state:

"...Let's get Mikey!"

"Yeah."

"He won't eat it. *He hates everything!*...He likes it! Hey Mikey!"

The pattern endlessly repeats. M.E. differences are small and insignificant, or a big push to the Dark Side. We are never moved into the light of warm truth, care and pure knowledge in the changes. This reinforces the fantastic idea that we've been switched into our Mirror-duplicates in a reverse-parallel universe. Like the Bizarro-world in Superman where up is down, hello is goodbye and good is bad.

The Real World is gone.

In the film 'The Matrix,' the character Morpheus sat in a chair with a red and blue pill and said: "What if I told you, Neo, that the world you live in is a lie?" The line that many people remember has vanished. If you see the film again, you won't find it. Viewers did not collectively make the line up, the same line? It's gone, along with the Old World. Stories, plots, parallels are not coincidences in movies. These are concepts placed in a huge number of films, put there by filmmakers, the ones who serve the Masters of the Universe. And the Masters of the Universe [Illuminati] are the ones who have darkened our world and made movies. We're all Alice through the Looking-Glass now, which was mentioned in 'The Matrix.'

A well-known Mandela Effect is the song by the band Queen: 'We are the Champions.' The lyric "...of the world" remains in the song, but it was also heard at the end. Freddy Mercury ended it with: "We are the champions...of the world!" Now it ends with just, "We are the champions..." That's it. Listeners would not have that feeling that Something's Missing Here if the song had always finished that way. We didn't dream up that it ended like the chorus. He sang it, but now he doesn't. Mandela. Again, why those words, what does it mean? Why make the movie? Why a M.E. in this band and not countless others? Because it's a known Mandela to Insiders. They know, we don't. We're just learning a little.

It obviously hints of The World that isn't there anymore. Solid, stable world: Gone! Very similar to 'The Matrix' plot and countless other movies. Incredible amounts of Dark films these days with a common theme: 'Yesterday was a Lie.' 'They,' those who influence us through all forms of Media, INSIST TOO MUCH. When They do that, you should know to go the other way. It's not yesterday that's the lie...it's *today*. That's the false world, fake, unreal one that They push us to believe is real and *it's always been like that.* It was the bright, beautiful Old World that was real and wonderful. Our MEMORIES are all we have of the good and true universe. And look what the kings and queens have done? They've made Media brainwash us into believing our sweet memories of what was...are wrong, false, and a lie. No, sir! This garbage-world around us today is the LIE! We're to accept the nonsense world around us now, the way it is (the way it's always been?). No matter what They say, no matter how many times the fascists POUND bullshit into us, we should know Them for what They really are: pure evil. Liars.

I will not forget the Old World. True memories live on...

Magicians and their Magic Mirrors.

In Disney's first animated film (1937), 'Snow White,' didn't the Queen say, "Mirror, mirror, on the wall. Who's the fairest of them all?"? When the classic film first began, an animated Book opened and viewers read the words. The words were: "Mirror, mirror..." Everything in the "real" universe, from a small degree to a large degree, has CHANGED, magically (scientifically). And the Wizards of the World know exactly what They've done. It *is* like a magic trick, but that's only to the uninformed muggles. To the Magicians or Puppet-Masters, the occult ones responsible, it's *Science.*

{Disney hasn't fooled the world, have they? You feed that to your children? Are you kidding me?}.

First full-length, animated feature (done on the threshold of World War?) and it was about MAGIC, sorcery, and an evil witch (Queen). It wasn't really different from 'Oz,' with the Wicked Witch and Glinda, the Good Witch. From Disney to Star Wars: Light vs. Dark, good vs. bad and positive vs. negative. These aren't stories. They're metaphors for what's going on in the real world. Oz, Snow White, Sleeping Beauty, Walking Dead, etc.

The change in the beginning Book and the famous line by the Queen, mimicked countless times, is now: "**Magic Mirror**, on the wall..." There's no Mirror, Mirror, anymore. Star Trek episode of a reverse, antimatter universe where Mr. Spock had a goatee, was wrongly titled: 'Mirror, Mirror.' No, it wasn't. It was taken from 'Snow White' and was precisely what was read in the Book and what the Queen had expressed. It's residue. (I don't think the ST title has changed to 'Magic Mirror').

What does it mean? Again, how the magic wand of Oz, Britain's Hollywood, has mesmerized us all and will really do so far more in future. Our children won't even know that they've been played/swayed and eventually consumed so royal fascists and fascism can survive.

Why Paint a Red Door Black?

[Author's note: Right here I was going to put a joke and answer the question and say, "I know, Miss Krapobal!" Or was it Miss Krepople? The teacher on the Simpsons, which I knew was a parody of the *Our Gang's* teacher, Miss Crabtree. As usual, writers have to look up correct spellings to names and Son of a Gun! Edna Krabappel. Krabappel? "Edna" is right. Why does my mind not register this as the correct spelling of the Simpsons' teacher's name? I could be wrong. It was more than 30 years ago that I was a lowly, background, clean-up artist for the show. Some things are foggy. But I'd bet the name changed. Maybe? Seth MacFarlane's name changed. Anyway...].

Most people don't know the meaning of a red door. There's a massive meaning to a Red Door that witches, occultists, elites, celebrities, masons and Master Masons, etc., know ~ and we do not. Let's reveal a truth and dispel a myth:

You could also ask, "Why paint a door red?" Seen any large/red doors on grand, Asian temples? Yes, you have. Seen any red doors on fabulously wealthy mansions? Yes you have. White mansions on huge estates and there's the red door. Why? The reason is, basically, *it keeps away bad spirits.* Ha, like mirrors, garlic and crosses to vampires. Chases away negative ghosts or negative energy. *Devils can't get in unless you let them and open the door.* The old tradition of a red door could keep 'monsters' away. (By the same token, lucky, power-number 13 is something They know and use, and you don't). Magic or real Science? If it works, it works.

Why the hell would Stones' singer, Mick Jagger, want to paint a red door black? ("I know, teacher"). Besides being *forced* to do anything They command [like all elites], the act of a red door turned to a black door LETS IN THE DEVIL or negative spirits, bad magick. *No more red door protection~*

Mick Jagger once sang: "I see a red door and I want to paint it black..." on the original recording. But now, the original recording has been slightly transformed to: "I see a red door and I want it painted black..." So, Mick? Conceptually, you'd like it painted black. I thought *you* were going to do it? Even the title of this song has changed. It was: 'Paint it Black.' But today, it's 'Paint it, Black.' A comma?

Rolling Stones' eleventh album was called: 'Goat's Head Soup.' They've recorded at Jimmy Page's house, once owned by Aleister Crowley, a pure evil and famous occultist, also on Sgt. Peppers cover, *twice.* One of the biggest, early Stones songs was: 'Sympathy for the Devil.' Really, Mick? It's hard work stealing all those souls, aye? No sympathy for a good, hard-working guy? Oh, right. Rock 'n Roll.

Here's the current report on one of the worst tragedies in concert history:

"At their chaotic free concert at the Altamont Speedway in California an African American teenager with a gun was knifed to death by Hells Angels to whom the Stones had contracted security. Popular belief, fuelled by bad reporting, was that the murder happened as the band were playing 'Sympathy for the Devil.' Though trouble seemed to start during that song, it was actually a few numbers later that Meredith Hunter was stabbed."

But who knows the real story anymore? The truth? *I'd bet the dead teenager never had a gun.* Was Altamont staged to happen? For a movie? Planned in advance to capture the terrible event, before the event? (Like Zapruder?). It's very possible that the (planned) murder did happen during 'Sympathy for the Devil,' as reported. But we're left with a different story?

The Stones and Beatles were both made to dress in robes as wizards because of the Magic Spell or con job they'd stage for the world.

As stated in Volume I, the Rolling Stones' (psychedelic?) answer to the Beatles' Sgt. Peppers was a changed-Mandela. (I grew up with this; I should know). The title to the trippy cover, which included Saturn (Satan) was 'Her Satanic Majesty's Request.' But now, abracadabra, you'll find the title to be: "Satanic Majesties Request."

Plural? That's not what it was. It seems the Monarchy's Monsters are growing, exponentially, like the Sun on the Sistine Ceiling?

Let's dispel a myth, a masonic myth. WITCHES DO NOT LIKE CATS! It's not true that they have a cat companion, called a "familiar." In fact, they *hate cats!* What do we see in cartoons, stories, movies or drawings of a witch? Besides the broom (and they don't ride brooms)? We often see witches paired with a cat. No, they're enemies. Cats are super good and extremely healthy for people! Dogs (opposite of 'god') are not, strange as that sounds. My cat has helped me immensely with breathing when I have bouts of very high blood-pressure. My sweet (purring) feline calms me right down and helps me relax. Instant meditation, like pot. *Fucking loud, barking dogs don't do that!* [Understand, I live in LA).

An incredible amount of LIES have been broadcast by all Media against cats! Yeah, open your eyes and ears. In TV shows and in movies. There's a definite reason the Illuminati masons hate cats and subtly diss them over Media. Myths like they'd suffocate a baby by sleeping on them were spread long ago, and were certainly untrue. They're great for babies! It's a little like Klingons and Tribbles in Star Trek. They don't really get along now, do they? Both will freak-out if near the other (ah, polarity).

In Bond films, the head of Smersh (whatever) was Ernst Stavro Blofeld. The bald dude, like Dr. Evil, was seen with a white cat on his lap. *I'll bet the cat didn't want to be there for all those 'takes.'* Bad guy Blofeld or a witch with a cat? I don't think so. They always promote the lie.

My cat is attracted to good people. Good people are getting harder and harder to find. Few are left that she will run to. She runs away from bad people. She'll run from the landlord every month. This is polarity and good does not mix with the bad. It's the other end of the spectrum.

The City of Angel.

One more strange, musical Mandela: Wouldn't you think the lead singer for the Red Hot Chili Peppers would know that LA was called the "City of Angels"? He wouldn't get it wrong? Anthony Kiedis, a small blurb about him: "Kiedis' lyrical style has evolved throughout his career; early recordings discussed topics such as sex and life in Los Angeles..." He'd certainly know, because he's lived in the Hollywood/Los Angeles area since he was 12. But, suddenly, *he got it wrong?* Now, the original recording of their song 'Under the Bridge' is a little different. The well-known video where the long-haired singer walked through the streets of LA, has been changed. The lyric now is singular, "City of Angel." City of Angel? That's not what LA is known as, and he wouldn't get it wrong, but he did.

Check it out on YouTube. Punch in: "under the bridge lyrics" and see what comes up? It's residue! Those videos are many years old and have not changed. Most displayed lyrics, if not all displayed lyrics of it on YT, have exactly what we remember, etched into our brains. Kiedis originally sang "Angels," now he sang: "...the City of Angel." It's funny and disturbing to hear the song, follow the lyrics and when the screen shows ANGELS...he sings ANGEL. Screens are right, Anthony is wrong.

This whole section is an analysis of the changes by simply answering the question: WHY those particular changes? (Not all Mandelas) We're talking here of their common thread, which is darkness, evil, a shift away from anything good, kind and wholesome. Why plural to singular? Does it have anything to do with what was stated in 'Field of Dreams'? In FOD, the change went from "they" to "He." Singular to plural and again I have to question: Are the Masters of the World waiting (or told to wait) for the coming of the Dark Lord, the one Prince of Darkness?

"O Romeo, Romeo, wherefore art thou?"

Use your eyes, say the Shakespearean words in your mind, uttered by the beautiful Juliet in 'Romeo and Juliet.' Are you sure those are precisely what was said from her lovely lips? Guess what? It's close, but no cigar. The words are hundreds of years old from "the greatest writer of all time." They would never, never, never be gotten wrong. No R&J play would be allowed to be messed up like that with one of the most famous lines of all time. The actress who played 'Juliet' would really hear it from the director. She better get it right next time. The line, as in (M.E.) biblical lines, movie lines and music lyrics, *has been changed.* Juliet originally said from a balcony (now window): **"Romeo, O Romeo. Wherefore art thou, Romeo?"** Is this quote more familiar to you, or is the one above? From my perspective, and I'm not alone, this is Juliet's line, and not the top one.

In all the R&J movies produced, the one with Olivia Hussey or Laurence Harvey or Leo DiCaprio, each stated the top quote, which is different from a lot of our memories

This section shouldn't and doesn't include any ol' Mandela Effect, because many are insignificant and have no connections. They're not nasty or negative in any way. They're just different, like many product logos and name-changes. So why would Juliet's Mandela be here as if it has a dark connection? Well, folks, I believe it does. You are free to not agree or agree. *Two Romeos together,* where the other way had an "O" that separated them. Could be nothing, but I think it's important. Homosexualism, encouraged, promoted in Hollywood and in the new Dark World, more and more. Maybe the Romeos should be separated? But they are not anymore. They're together.

"A man's gotta do what a man's gotta do."

The movie line said by John Wayne in 'Hondo.' This is a very significant Mandela-change. The distinction between the two versions is extreme and polar opposites. What did John Wayne's character mean by the statement? He meant: You do the right thing. That's what a man does. He obeys the law, helps other people and always treats people decently, how you'd like to be treated. Always do good and act like a hero, like a knight in shining armor, the best you can be and do the right thing. (Alright I overstated it, but you get the picture).

One more time people, there's been a change. The bold, top line is exactly what was first said on the silver screen and precisely what we remember, the classic line. But that's not the line anymore, Pilgrim. Nope. It's very different. Wayne's character now says: **"A man oughta do what he thinks is best."** *Do whatever he thinks is best? Really?* That is diametrically different. Sounds like Aleister Crowley: "Do what thy wilt." You can do anything? You can hurt, you can kill, you can get away with murder? No, the Duke now expresses a view opposite of: You follow the law and always do the right, moral thing.

A Shift Toward Military.

Here is how I had written it in Volume I: "Do you remember a 6th person in the Village People who was a black man always dressed in a military outfit? Yes or no? [This is hilarious to me, funniest example of the Effect]. It was 'The Village People,' now it's just 'Village People.' But that's not the funny part. Do you remember a sixth member of the '70's disco boy-band? A second black guy, a Military Man? GI Joe? No? Google VP, hit Images and scroll down through many pictures. OMG. These are not later photos where they added another person. It's every picture from the very beginning. Even a star on the Walk of Fame with 6? What? I remember the construction worker, the Indian, the tough biker, black highway-patrol guy and, of course, the cowboy. I remember their faces. There were only 5 characters. But now, there's another black guy, always in variations of military dress from green combat fatigues to officer uniforms or in Navy outfits? No way, even though they did: 'In the Navy.' Where'd this new guy come from? Military guy just popped into being, from my point of view and most others. On 'America's Got Talent,' a man performed with a contraption that simulated 4 other Village People, which makes 5, not 6. Once more, people are left in total disagreement. Some may recall the GI Joe named Alex Briley. There's his whole history with the band and makes a total of six members. To many, he simply appeared one day, the very same with Randy Jackson, Michael's younger brother? Has anyone checked the Dave Clark 5? I seriously did, there's still 5."

The point is: Why a *military* costume or character? The Mandela or weird extra guy could have been a knight, a farmer, a scuba-guy, an astronaut, a sports-figure, a mailman, an artist, an archer, a Tarzan, a spy, a woman(?), a clown, a bandit, a caveman, etc., etc. There is almost no limit to a theme for odd #6 member of Village People. Why, of all things, did it have to be military? Ha, I know people don't think this way, but what if we're utopians, originally from Paradise and the very idea of *military* is utterly disgusting and insane to any intelligent, caring human being?

To some people, armed FORCES are overkill and we should work toward a future-world where the military was totally unnecessary! But we're not allowed to think, progress, advance, grow.

We're only permitted to stagnate and go in reverse.

I'll give you another M.E. example that ties to the Military and, to me, it is something that is absolutely outrageous!! I now have a violent reaction every single time I see, in a movie, on TV, on the news, or any time my eyes view the fucking, fucking, fucking Capitol Building! Did you get that? I apologize; I should have *screamed it in a bullhorn and painted it in letters 10 feet high!!* You see there is a very alien, twisted-sister-type thing or "monster," in my estimation, now on top of the Capitol Building. It and Capital Records was spelled 'Capital,' but that's not the point.

Indulge me, from Volume I:

What is on top of the Capitol Building? The famous, white, domed structure we are all familiar with and seen hundreds of times. What do you think is on the very top? Shouldn't this be well-known, common knowledge and certainly never up for debate? Americans should know immediately and also those in the D.C. area. It's been viewed in endless movies over many decades. Used for logos. Is it a giant flag and flagpole, or something else? (Oh, it be something else. Quite terrifying, in my opinion). It's a 20-foot high, bronze statue of a '**warrior woman**' called the 'Statue of Freedom' and also 'Armed Freedom.' They say: "Not to be confused with the Statue of Liberty." The original name for it was "Freedom Triumphant in War and Peace." The statue was designed by artist Thomas Crawford in the mid 19th Century. According to every official record, it has stood there since 1863. 1863! Are you kidding me? Since the Civil War? Why do few remember it being there over the last 156 years? Here is official information about it: "Her crest peaks at 288 feet above the east front plaza of the U.S. Capitol. She is a female, allegorical figure whose right-hand holds the hilt of a sheathed sword, while a laurel wreath of victory and the Shield of the United States are clasped in her left-hand. Her chiton is secured by a brooch inscribed "U.S." and is partially covered by a heavy, Native American–style fringed blanket thrown over her left shoulder. She faces east towards the main entrance of the building and the rising Sun. She wears a military helmet adorned with stars and an eagle's head which is itself crowned by an umbrella-like crest of feathers. Although not actually called 'Columbia,' she shares many of her iconic characteristics."

This is horrific to me because women should not be warriors, killers, soldiers. They should not even be 'defenders of freedom' on the front lines of war. Today, they are, in fake wars. They're in modern movies (and commercials) in barbarian battle scenes, and that was never true. The image of female destroyers (outside of good Nemesis, Justice, who wipes out evil and should never have been blindfolded in court) is abominable. But not in the new, dark world descending upon us. Not in a wicked society blasted by Mind Control methods, conditioned for us to do the wrong things, bad behaviors, instead of the right things and good behaviors. Not in a world where every TV commercial, every show, every cartoon and every movie has empowered WOMEN and emasculated men! 'Alita, Battle Angel,' 'Wonder Woman,' *Captain Marvel* and every portrayal in Media of women, lately, have them so fucking powerful, "brilliant," nasty, vicious, man-killers...while males are stupid, inept, impotent, weak and useless. Have you not noticed this reversal and how upside-down and backwards everything is from what it should be and what it once was, yesterday? [Young dudes grow beards today and shave their heads (backwards) and appear, basically, like galley-slaves. We're all slaves, but we don't have to look like slaves. What happened to hippies, freedom, peace and love, hair, the virility of Samson, good music, good films, good role models, etc.?]. This new 'Armed Freedom' statue, with stars and sword and shield, we're all supposed to believe stood atop the Capitol Building for the last 156 years? Don't believe it - yet, you must believe it since the records and old movies support its existence. No one placed it there recently. No, it's been there for a century and a half. That is, in the other reality, not the one most all of us know and remember. A male soldier should have been the symbol long ago during the age of chauvinism. The very idea that there's another *female* besides Lady Liberty and Columbia? A killer-soldier Indian? And she has suddenly appeared to many? Astonishing. I guess it's not so strange that the statue is perfectly in line with the New Order of *females rule, and males follow.*

An American citizen, a person sympathetic to the plight of native Indians, could be extremely offended by the sculpture that crowns the Capitol. They've made Indians killers, warriors, soldiers...and They've done that in the form of a WOMAN? Yes, They have. The concept of aggressive women and weak men are everywhere in Media today. Yesterday, that theme was not anywhere. I remember a big flagpole on top of the Capital Building. The Flag changed into a female soldier, *I'll be damned.*

Here in an unbelievable one that must be a true Mandela, not in Volume I. **There was never an "Armed Forces Day"** that I've ever known...until recently, in the last few years. 'Armed Forces Day' that President Harry Truman instituted way back in 1950? Declared that the "third Saturday in May will be celebrated with military exercises on land, sea and in the air to honor members of the U.S. military and to show off their state-of-the-art equipment to the civilian population it protects."

Same as the Russian 'May Day,' May first? My entire life Armed Forces Day was "celebrated" in-between May Day and Memorial Day? No fucking way! AFD was never there. It was never there. Why in God's name would we honor the military on the third Saturday in May (and have been doing it since 1950?) and then, only a few days later, honor the military all over again with Memorial Day? May 30th.

"**Memorial Day** is a federal holiday in the United States for honoring and mourning the military personnel who have died in the performance of their military duties while serving in the United States Armed Forces. The holiday is observed on the last Monday of May." Memorial Day was always there, not AFD.

It makes no sense. The Other World had no Armed Forces Day! It didn't need another day to honor fallen soldiers. We had Memorial Day and Russia had May Day. Remember, there's also a Veteran's Day and a Flag Day. WTF!!

Another Mandela-change that links to the military is the Lincoln Memorial in Washington, D.C. Why does Abraham Lincoln now form a semi-fist with his left-hand when the statue never did that before? Both hands were the same. The fingers were straight down on the armrests. Now, one hand is almost a fist, a symbol of war. Lincoln was a good man of peace, not war. The change is a shift, a small shift, but another move toward darkness (lie) and away from the light (truth).

The unnatural logo change of 20th Century Fox.

What unnatural logo change of 20th Century Fox? "20th Century Studios, Inc. is an American film studio that is a subsidiary of Walt Disney Studios, a division of The Walt Disney Company. The studio is located on the Fox Studio Lot in the Century City area of Los Angeles."

We've all known this "Hollywood" studio our entire lives. If you've seen a lot of movies, then you've viewed the very 3-D, art deco logo for 20th Century Fox a thousand times or more. There's been the tiniest of alteration in the letters. Haven't noticed? Either you haven't or you really believe it was always that way and there was nothing to notice. For those people who remember the old/Lost World, and who have taken a closer look at the logo we all should remember well...Son of a Gun, *it's slightly different!* It certainly was not like that before. But. Once more, there's the strange oddity that few people will realize and the vast majority will not.

It's just a little, teeny thing...and so is the VW logo...the smallest trace of a line. So I really have to repeat: It's a transition, a change from what was and there shouldn't have been a change at all, not even a molecule's worth of difference. Do you Not See [Nazi], yet? If you do not, that's fine...

The "th" is different now from what it was and from what some people recall. I'm certainly one of them. Do you know how many movies I've seen in nearly 70 years? (I have virtually no social life and mostly see movies, although I prefer films). I'm one of the ones that has observed the 20th Century logo, before the movie, a few thousand times! I remember what it looked like; it's etched into my brain. Now, it's different. The "t" is broken. The "t" in "th" of 20th Century. It wasn't broken previously.

There really are zillions of big to small M.E. changes from what large groups of people remember. Why include this one, out of so many, in this dark section of Volume II? Because I feel (maybe?) that it *is* dark and once again a shift from positive to negative. There may be meaning here or significance? I don't believe that each individual change was purposely done by something/someone. But as a result of a Universal Shift, it all changed because our universe was made to change, flip on its magnetic pole as if North and South Poles of our planet had changed their polarity (which has happened in our long history).

Let's assume there has been a change. What's it mean?

A broken cross. The significance wasn't hard to figure out. The small-cased "t" appears like a cross. (I use it as a Tray-signature: a cross with a twist, nothing bad to me). Funny. Maybe the Devil [Illuminati] on this Mirror-side, *really/really doesn't like crosses,* where They let it pass on the Other Side? Therefore those that "see" the change might say: "WTF!"

(Later in this book, in a section called "Rubbing Our Face In It," there is a short history of the 20th Century Fox logo).

20th Century Fox is not alone in major studio realignments or re-settings. Universal Studios. Same thing here. How many times, how many movies have we viewed with the turning-Earth logo of Universal Studios in the beginning? Thousands of times. South America is not where it was. In this world, this is probably where it always was: not even under Florida and the Panama Canal went diagonally. In my sweeter Universe, long gone, South America was *under* most of North America and the Panama Canal went horizontally. No more, or not in this place anymore.

Paramount Studios logo of a snow-covered mountain always represented a (secret Illuminati) pyramid. To the Illuminati, 'pyramids' mean the Supreme Power of the King-God at the very top and its fascist rule of everyone else down the line of the Social Pyramid. That's not what pyramids mean. They mean Tesla wireless-energy, Free Electricity! Power to the People! The exact opposite of what the various secret societies have been trained to think and how They make us think and act. THEY, the royalty, hide (free) Tesla-energy and technology and what the original Pyramids really were.

Look at the Paramount "Mountain" again. It *never* was a snow-covered mountain. It's a pyramid! The logo shows two angled sides. We do not see the other two angled sides. To THEM, it's there as a pushed logo and deep within our psyche to symbolize *Their dominance over us,* exactly like the meanings of symbols on dollar bills They print. The Mandela-change here is: The Paramount "Mountain" is even more pyramidal in shape. Today, it's an obvious pyramid (you don't see).

Columbia. Columbia Studios. The ones who produced 'The Stooges' and one of many studios that have made all of us *Stooges!* Conned everyone. They're smart, we're dumb. If you only understood what "Columbia" has always meant in Freemansonry: the Columbuses, those pioneers in the vanguard of everything, explorers, those who Pass the Torch (to a new generation of fascists), those who are "truly illuminated" and "superior" to the general masses, we poor muggles that must serve Them. Look up how many "Columbia"s there are; *it's almost infinite!* Companies, clothing, organizations, various groups and "societies." I tried to list everything named "Columbia" and nearly went out of my mind. It did not end< [btw. The Statue of Liberty, from France, and the Columbia "woman," are not women. They're men in drag, fooling you. Look good. You really thought they were feminine? Butch to me].

The Mandela with the Columbia-Lady is her knee was never pushed forward before. Her foot is now exposed as in *she took a step?* Before the change, she wore a white gown or robe that went all the way down and nothing was pushed forward. No foot exposed. Could this mean the new forward-progress of women over men? Like a Lady in the Moon and no longer a Man in the Moon? Like a soldier-Indian WOMAN now adorns our Capitol? Or Captain Marvel and maybe the next James Bond are female!?

It's also possible that the Warner Brothers' logo 'shield' has altered in its shape, some have reported.

The other film studio that many people believe has changed in appearance is Metro Goldwyn Mayer, the one with a royal Lion that *roared.* "Metro Goldwyn Mayer" seems off to my memory and others. Wasn't it Golden or Goldwin or something other than Goldwyn? But it's the "Mayer" that sounds and looks wrong to a substantial number of people. They remember "Meyer." Remember, Oscar Meyer hot dogs have changed spelling. Maybe this Meyer too?

A Cross, NOT a holy symbol?

God, the Truth hurts. I've wondered about crosses worn around necks and the Hypocrasy-Level of those who wear them. Showing others how *Christian* they are? Like a commercial ad or "banner," telling us. Almost insisting: They are 'holier than thou.' How about just living a good life, instead of *showing* us how good of a person you are?

On that point, there's the TV pillow-guy in bright blue trying to sell us his small pillows. There's his cross. His newest product are towels that work. Apparently, our old towels don't work anymore? Huh. I'll bet his towels are smaller than my towels. How many people in America's Bible-belt have been swayed by his use of the "Holy" Cross? He could have been a televangelist and probably was.

You know Lenny Bruce's joke, don't you? "If Christ was killed in modern times, you'd all be wearing little electric-chairs around your necks."

I've been seeing, over Media, more and more people wearing crosses and making the sign of the cross (for show) in public, for the cameras. What? You wouldn't think that in this Dark World now, eh? Let's examine "cross" in a different way: "Don't cross me!"

"You dirty Double-Crosser!"

"Don't cross that line!"

"Cross my heart and hope to die."

"Cross-purposes."

"Cross-Dresser."

"Cross-Gender."

Guess what the Catholics' Pope [not a good man] or the Vatican itself uses as a symbol? Or, what does the Pope carry in his hand, that long staff, what is it? IT'S A TRIPLE CROSS! There's 3 crosses or horizontal bars at the top of the staff, nearly a trident, but not quite. Far worse than a double-cross in a con-game is a *triple-cross!* Do you have a clue what is being referred to? Nothing good. Who is being deceived in the grand con job? *Everyone!* It's all the Church of England. I guess you've figured out by now that church steeples are phallic? No? Then why is every doorway, in almost every church of various religions, pointed at the top? (Feel free to disagree, but this is what happens after you've done years of research and your eyes are open). They represent **vaginas**. Code! It's all code, even names They've forced upon their elite celebrities. So pious and righteous, the churches of the world? There's endless streams of children that would not agree with that evaluation.

In multiple Industries [and Industries are not good], on TV, in fashion, modeling, etc., we are being inundated with more and more young, celebrity, up-and-comers, to take the place of the rapidly-aged, older celebrities. Coaches in the NFL, NBA, players, singers, artists, actors, you name it: We are actually seeing much more neckwear and CROSSES. Who says they are Christians or even good people? Maybe they are told [commanded, ordered] to wear them and they must obey? Maybe there is hardly a shred of a famous person's life that is real, genuine. Judas 'Goats,' directed by their Masters, and we follow right along as blind "sheeple."

Something's going on. Football, basketball, baseball, soccer and on most new celebrities, there's their tats. It's marks, brands of Slavery.

Tattoos could have a secret meaning that familiar faces all know, in the Secret Club, but we do not. Tats could be a ranking-system of where they are in the Order. Like a military-ranking on their arms. *It's not a style.* But the youth simply go along and emulate the idols that they follow. Outsiders have absolutely no clue as to how the masses are being led (to slaughter) by minions who serve their Masters who made them. They must server their creators and manufacturers. [ps. Later in this book, tattoos, crosses and tennis will be examined].

What is above the head of the Man on the Shroud?

The credibility of the Shroud of Turin won't be debated here. But. I've long known that Carbon 14 dating was in error. And guessed it was a *great underestimate;* you'd have to multiply the result of C14 by 3 or 4 to get the true age. I said this before scientists tested the Cloth. Lo and behold, I was about right. They've used their false "science" to "prove" to the world that this was *not* Jesus' burial shroud, was not 2000 years old. Untrue. Their conclusions were wrong on purpose. It's Christ's Cloth. Every detail proves it, the age, the linen, the blood trails, the exact number of lash-marks on the back, the wounds, such as nailed in the wrist, not in the palms. Palms cannot support a body. Nailed at the wrists does support a body. Those who were crucified were nailed at the wrists. Stigmata is slightly off.

The Mandela here is an oddity that's suddenly appeared on the Turin Shroud, directly above the (photographic negative) of the man's head. It was not there before. It's been described as "similar to antenna." Isn't that strange? Christ a bit like an insect? Wouldn't the Shroud be targeted and changed?

The other Mandela is Secondo Pia was commissioned by the Pope to first photograph the Shroud Cloth in 1902. That's been changed to 1898. We will discover that among the new histories that are in place now, photography had begun a little earlier than it had in the Old World, my world.

Anointed Differently?

It's just a word. Like names of people (Patton Oswald) and places (Edinborough) have changed to alternative spellings, so has the word "annointed." I remember this word, I remember it well. This was its original spelling, like "announcement" has 2 "n"s. Well, people, that's not how it's spelled anymore. Suddenly, only a couple of years ago, I had to completely change my way of spelling the word and a few others. Now for it to be correctly spelled, you have to spell it with a single "n." Anointed. Not my mistaken memories. I spelled it correctly for my world. [My publisher does not agree]. The universe has changed to one "n" for anointed. The universe is wrong. But today, it's right and *I'm wrong?* No, sir. I remember well.

It's just a word. The change could have no meaning at all. Then again, it could. It's a Holy word, in the true sense, a good word. Every detail of Good is attacked, down here, it seems. Even the *annointed.*

Strange appearances of 'The Lord.'

The following are two musical Mandelas not in Volume I that (possibly) connect to the odd, giant Jesus statues appearing in the world and *crosses* appearing around necks of some of the famous. Maybe not, but follow along...

Phil Collins' first hit as a solo artist was a song called 'In the Air Tonight.' The lyrics went: "I can feel it in the air, tonight. Hold on, hold on..." "I can feel it coming in the air, tonight. Hold on, hold on..." Former Genesis drummer no longer sings those exact words in the song now. It's not "Hold on," that many remember. It's been altered to "My Lord." He wasn't talking to the Lord. It was "Hold on."

Another musical group where the very same thing happened (I think) is the Verve, with their song from 1998: 'Sonnet.' Richard Ashcroft sang:

Yes, there's love if you want it,
Don't sound like no sonnet, my love.
Yes, there's love if you want it,
Don't sound like no sonnet, my love,
My love...

Sinking faster than a boat without a hull,
My love, my love.

Now replace "my love" with "my Lord." That's the song now, a popular song I've heard for more than 20 years. He didn't sing: "My Lord." Why would he? He's singing to his love, not his God. Wake up, people. Rock stars don't honor Jesus; they honor the Beast System that made them. They honor the devil. So isn't it odd to have "my Lord"'s appearing among the music of 'monsters'? As well as more giant statues of JC and more crosses around necks of the famous?

Abominable Christ Statues around the World!

It's very weird for any statue to supernaturally change its appearance, let alone very famous statues. Christ the Redeemer in Rio de Janeiro has greatly grown in height, is more detailed, now has a heart and muscles on the chest as well as feet. It has moved further back on its base. The statue looks down and appears different from what many remember. Most people know of the JC statue in Rio de Janeiro because of its long history. But other colossal Christ statues have suddenly appeared on Earth, also with substantial histories. But why have we not heard of them before?

Christ the Redeemer of Maratea (69') is a strange, mysterious statue of Jesus in Italy, high above a harbor and its been there since 1965? We only have heard of this now? Christ of Maratea is unlike any image of Jesus Christ. The statue appears feminine, in a long/straight gown, his arms are up and this JC has *short hair.* When was Christ ever portrayed with short hair? There's almost "wings" on the statue. And an odd lightning-rod protrudes from its head that resembles a UFO saucer or Saturn [Satan?]. I am serious. The statue also looks inland, when most great statues look out to sea. From Volume I:

"If you've studied the official record or records from various sources on Maratea, you're liable to go out of your mind. A number of good sources regard it as the 'second tallest Jesus statue,' after the famous one in Rio de Janeiro. Then there are references that put it at the fifth tallest Christ statue. Wikipedia." These statues, and maybe everything else, might be continuously changing~

Study "tallest Christ statues" and the results of the search will amaze you. Where have they been all this time? Why are they so unknown? Why are they strange to our eyes? Some are scary, creepy and really nothing like you might imagine a true tribute to Jesus Christ. It's unbelievable, but various Christ statues seem to be popping up all over the world. Why? Maybe it is not any kind of honor, underneath it all? Maybe it's really a disgrace and a sacrilege?

I took my own advice and Googled "tallest Christ statues" now to get more info and possibly add something new....and the Google Images search was a little different to me. Yes, it was about two years ago that I investigated the same subject in detail. To me, at this moment, some statues that I remember are not there. And there are new, giant Christ statues I hadn't seen before. Sure, things change, sometimes naturally. But on the other hand, now that there are so many examples of supernatural alterations to our world, we can't be sure of anything when we look up records. It was normally stable. Today? It's fluid. Reality should not be fluid, it should be concrete.

"Iron Man" of India?

Do you know the tallest statue on Earth? Shouldn't you know of the tallest statue on Earth? We should know where it is, who it is and how tall it is. Why do we (mostly) not know that? The statue is the height of two football fields stacked on top of each other, 182 meters, 600 feet high! (I wouldn't want to stand under it).

Its location is near Vadodara, India, and was built across the Sardar Sarovar dam. Shouldn't we, the rest of the world, be familiar with the "man" honored by a statue 600 feet high? I'm sure there are plenty of people from India well aware of this dude. But we're not. Why not construct a man-tower that honored Mahatma Gandhi? You know, someone we all knew and respected? No. Who is this guy?

He is an Indian leader called Sardar Vallabhbhai Patel, known as the "Iron Man" of India. Who? Mr. Patel? Take a look at the statue. It's not pure white, it is composed of bronze plates that reflect this "Iron Man." Is this another Warrior? I would have preferred a soft-feel in white of a true Holy Man. WAIT! What am I saying? All idols are wrong. I actually do mean to disrespect the guy, because *everything is twisted*. You know what the statue of Mr. Patel looks like? Fred Mertz in a bathrobe.

Who was he, really? A politician. He served as the first Deputy Prime Minister of India, (like George Washington?). Another PM? This is who the Masters honor? *That's like a big, fat Winston Churchill two football fields high!*

[Author's note: You know, in my world, the Illuminati were better and brighter than the fascists that imprison us here. They were cruel, but not quite as cruel as the ones in place today. Even your porn sucks~].

Hard to believe but it's true:

New statues, islands, new forms in nature and even new people have POPPED into existence (bogus, but I guess not for the Dark World), while many other things we all knew have disappeared. [There's never been Jiffy or Jujubees]. In this mirrored, Dark Universe, it probably *was* ALWAYS LIKE THAT as new histories/realities have replaced old ones. But in the brighter/better world, the Old World, no way. IT WAS NEVER LIKE THAT.

Statue of Liberty, now on Liberty Island?

What happened to Ellis Island? Why did the Statue of Liberty, that was always on Ellis Island, jump down, with pedestal, wade through a bit of water and set itself up on another nearby/small island, one called "Liberty"? *Oh, it didn't do that?* Let's poll most Americans and ask them: Is the Statue of Liberty on Ellis Island or Liberty Island? I already know the answer because I've asked as many people as I could to take a short Mandela quiz and that was one of the main questions.

For more than a hundred years, (let's not mention the 'Black Tom Explosion,' which supposedly damaged the statue during WWI that no one remembers) Europeans came to the new world of America. It was the hope for a better life. The boats traveled to New York and the immigrants from all 'walks of life' got off at Ellis Island. It's the one with the water tower. It had a walkway that led to the big city. People remember Ellis Island as to where they got off and entered NY because that's where they got off and entered New York. For more than a century. People are not wrong for remembering Ellis Island. It's not a mistaken, false memory. *That's where they got off.*

But today, everything's changed. Why do you think we are forced to view, over and over again, Liberty Insurance commercials on TV? Constantly, on all channels and it does not stop. There it is, in the background, again and again. Where's the water tower? That's not Ellis Island! In the Old World, Liberty Insurance might not exist. Ask people if they have even heard of something called a "Liberty Island"? You'll find that more people remember Ellis Island, not Liberty Island. In the Old World, there may not have been a Liberty Island at all. I'll bet there wasn't. But in this world, we are continuously reminded of what the mighty and secret Freemasons, under Britain, have done to our planet.

Can't you see what they're doing with the Liberty commercials? As I've described it many times: "Rubbing our face in it," like the fascists they are, proud of the fact that They know of the terrible atrocities unnaturally pushed upon us. We, mostly, do not.

Let's examine the transition in another sense...

A shift *to* Liberty. Really? To Liberty? Forced Liberty, is not liberty. Forced Freedom, is not freedom. It smacks of a commercial, a TV "banner," "new and improved," in other words, a LIE. We are being told we have freedom and liberty when we do not. We are told we are "empowered" when we have no bloody power at all. We are told what "matters," rather than realizing what matters ourselves.

Who is telling us this and reinforcing these lies over all Media? Big Brother and Big Sister. We are only informed by 'monsters' that have engineered our every move. Stupid people believe them, believe the TV. Smart people do not believe the TV and other Media. They realize they've been conned and know enough to question what we have been force-fed.

It's another lie. Liberty, Liberty, Liberty everywhere, eh? Or, maybe nowhere?

Anti-Semitism against Jewish Bears.

Those familiar with the Mandela Effect certainly know of a prime example where a drastic change had occurred that concerned a family of cartoon bears. Years ago, parents and children watched the animated adventures of the Berenstein Bears. They bought Berenstein books in bookstores and watched their videos. The bears were very popular. They were Jewish. Now, the Mandela Wave has altered that reality and we're supposed to believe, all this time, we were wrong about the name and it had always been the Berenstain Bears? **Stain?** Why? Why Stein to Stain? Those who promote Anti-Semitism and Hitlerism have thought the Jews were a "stain on society." One more time, the M.E. contrast here is dark and sinister, par for the course and more repetition of the pattern.

"...is paved with good intentions."

OMG! This is a new one (I'm 99% sure is a Mandela) only found today as the 'Mandela II' manuscript was nearly completed. Above is a very well-known "idiom" or "proverb" that must go back a century or more. What came before "...is paved with good intentions"? I watched a YT video simply for entertainment and knowledge and my ears heard the following *"familiar"* phrase: "**The Road to Hell** is paved with good intentions." I immediately stopped the vid and searched online for something close to what I remembered. No, not there. I only saw: The fucking Road to Hell! I have news for you M.E. disbelievers...Just like I told a friend I went to high school with who said we were taught of the 2 sections to Michigan: "I know it's hard to believe, but somewhere out there is another world, the place I and others originated from, and that place truly existed...and we were taught that Michigan was no different than any other of the U.S. states." And I say to you readers who probably believe *there was nothing different in the old proverb.* Well, there is something very different in the old saying. This could have been placed as a possible new Mandela in an earlier section. But. *Differences,* are examined here in this section. There was a vast difference, and again, *Into Darkness* or turned negative.

(p.s. Bare with me since I'm not quite clear on what it was exactly and haven't pulled up residue of what it was...but it was something Positive).

The old proverb makes no sense as it stood today and what many readers might think was correct. I believe the idiom was similar to: "The best laid plans..." Or, "The Road to Success...is paved with good intentions." Its definition now stated that it meant the *difference between what someone intends and what someone will really do.* Wait, what someone wants to actually do is called: "The Road To Hell"? Was that right? No, that was wrong and made no sense. The proverb really meant: *No matter how well-meaning your intentions were, you still screwed up now, didn't you? Or you meant well, but you're not doing right.* That's not what the Road to Hell-version implied. Life isn't and should not be a Road along Hell. Celebrate Life! Not simply get through it. Use your tainted eyes, OPEN THEM<

Looney Tunes and Froot Loops.

Where did the "oo" go in Looney Tunes? No, no, don't say Looney Toons was always spelled 'Tunes.' That makes no sense. The joke is: Maybe the "oo" jumped onto the Fruit Loops cereal box? Because Fruit Loops was always spelled: 'Fruit.' But today's box has unnaturally changed to 'Froot.' Consider that both terms are also used for being CRAZY, nuts, loopy, looney, nuttier than a FRUIT cake. This is brought up because it's what's happening in the world where reality is so shattered~

(Are you aware there is a reality where **the Titanic did not sink**? Yep, look it up. Put "old newspapers titanic not sunk" in Google and there they are! Quite a number of real newspapers from 1912 that report a very different story from the movies and history we know. This Titanic hit the iceberg head-on, it was towed to Halifax by the Virginian, a strong tugboat and **all passengers were saved!** Yes. The old newspapers were not faked. The papers that reported no one died, all stated the same story, same set of events. This is not the Old World or new one. That particular reality is *another universe entirely.* This is why I say: "It's a clash of realities, here on Earth now. Many.").

We are being made to go crazy, looney, loopy, like a fruitcake. The masses are being *confused* on purpose. We are being yanked one way and then another, no stability. Our Slave-Masters want us to have nothing to believe in, no solidarity. It's why everything is in motion, moved, rules now constantly changing. We're thrown off-balance. This, of course, makes us angry, makes us fear and we want to fight one another. Our Masters have succeeded. We're pissed.

We're being ***gaslighted,*** exactly like the old films. An evil husband drove his wife mad when he lied, moved items around and made the gaslight flicker on and off.

Bottom line, It was Looney Toons, like Toon Town and Tiny Toons, but changed to musical *tunes?* Insane. And a recent change, yet old Warner Brother cartoons from the '40s, '50s, '60s and beyond, are all now entitled: Looney TUNES. Da, da, da, da, da, da, daaaaaaa!

To show you one example of the super-extreme arrogance in these programmers, the Social Engineers who have shattered the world, see the movie: 'Ant-Man and the Wasp.' Because there is a scene where they tell us what they've done, it's code. Let me decode; you don't have to agree. But it can't be nothing and another coincidence. Ant-Man has power over the ants. At his place, there's a giant ant, his size, that lounged on the couch. When I first saw this, I fast-forwarded it, didn't get a good look at the big ant, then *realized what he was eating in a flash:* a Fruit Loops box! I was slightly passed the scene and almost *screamed.* Here's why: I guessed, since these bastards control the movies and know all the Mandelas that we muggles do not, the ant will have bitten where the "uit" was on the cereal box. That was my prediction to myself. I went back, paused it and got a better look. OMG. I was right. You saw the bite or hole in the box. You saw "FR___." Exactly where they cut 'Fruit' and made it 'Froot.' You might think it's nothing. But there's always a good feeling when a prediction comes true, even a small one.

Man in the Moon is gone, replaced by the Lady.

Mandela-change in regard to the side of the Moon that faces the Earth was explored in great depth in Volume I. I was allowed one photo at the time and it had to be the M.E. that was closest to my heart and certainly broke my heart after I realized the transition. Even *more* than the shock of the new position for the Great Pyramid.

In my 11th book, 'Beyond Barronsland,' a chapter was called: 'Driver, Man in the Moon,' which examined and played with the lunar-change, fictionally. It was so much fun to write. The story concerned the idea that all planets' satellites were originally cloaked monitor-stations that recorded the histories of lifeforms on the planets. Moon-Driver of the Earth was an 8-armed male of the specie, who was in love with an 8-armed female of the specie. Lunar-control seat was atop a peak in a crater that's fascinated me most of my life: Arzachel. I've written a few stories about it, as *I've dreamed of having my own base at the top of the peak.* Arzachel was always IN THE VERY CENTER OF A FIXED SIDE of the Moon that eternally faced us directly and never changed. Arz was the 'jewel in the Lady's necklace.' She's in profile; her hair is Serenity and Tranquility. Take a close look at where "my crater" is now. Does that appear like the exact center of the disk? Before, she was still in profile, but she was up and to the right. With that shift, the 'necklace' is moved to the very center. But Arzachel, with my fictional moonbase, is no longer where it was. I've estimated 5-600 miles shifted down from the middle (similar to South America has shifted east about 1000 miles). *This destroys the Man in the Moon!*

Moon has shifted... ...down & to the left.

ARZACHEL

Moon is different! 'Man in Moon' now gone & Lady in profile is directly in center & she never was before. I've written about Crater Arzachel in EXACT CENTER. *Not anymore!*

In the story, the female Moon-Driver took control and *moved* the satellite to her liking. So his base *didn't* face the Earth directly, but was *off*. She did it just for spite. The male got revenge and returned the Moon back to how he liked it, with his high Control-Seat set in the center of the fixed lunar disk. The 'Lady' was shifted up and back, no longer front and center. This returned the Man in the Moon.

Why mention this major Mandela here, in a section that strings together changes to the dark side? Well. The Lady was forced front and center in the transition. Man in the Moon, gone. One more time, in this Dark World, men are replaced by women. Maybe it connects to this antimatter world that is seemingly run by women these days? There are more women doctors than there are men doctors in the U.S., but that fact is quickly changing on the other side of the Magic Mirror. Women rule. Women are the professionals now and men are merely minor characters. Women are strong in this world! Men couldn't be weaker. Haven't you noticed how the genders have been portrayed in Media over recent years? One example I pointed out was last Olympics. We often heard: "The women are going for gold! And the men have been eliminated." On purpose. Women should not be forced to be the Superior gender as TV and movies present for us more and more. Decades ago, Womens Lib representatives fought for equal rights, not Superior Rights. Everything's been turned on its head, inside-out and upside-down on Dark Earth.

Simply, the Lady in the Moon should never have replaced the Man in the Moon. But she did. "One cook to a kitchen and one pilot to a cockpit." This is symbolic, another metaphor for what's truly happening in the world: false empowerment for women and virtual castration for muggle men.

(Author's note: I had written the above weeks ago and still believe it, in philosophy. But. One more time, on one more evening very recently, I stared at "my" Moon as I had done on so many occasions in the past. Was the 'Man' really gone? This was what a few of the Mandela-people had suggested, along with the Sun's color changed from yellow to white and that we were now positioned in a different 'arm' of the Milky Way. To my perspective I suddenly saw that the "Man in the Moon" was not gone. 'Seas' to the upper left and right formed the eyes, similar to what it was. The transitions, and there have been, could mean a shared lunar surface by both genders in the shadows of craters. The 'Lady in the Moon' had always been up and to the right of the lunar disk, now she was front and center. My opinion today is they share the Moon, equally. But it wasn't that way before. This reinforced the idea that I've always employed: USE YOUR EYES and never rely on the viewpoint of others. Find out for yourself and look...openly...When you do that, everything in the universe becomes different).

The Roswell Aliens were Female??

They were not chicks, babes, gals, sisters, ladies, X-chromosomes in any way! The downed aliens from the very famous and real event(s) known as Roswell, which happened, were not gray WOMEN aliens! Who said that? *Oh, the record.* The record (history itself) is fucked up now! That's what my Mandela books are about. There would be no divergence, no split or differences from the Bright Old World and the Dark New World. But. Oh man, are there differences!!

Roswell aliens the U.S. government captured alive and then had on ice for years, even observed by Jackie Gleason (Nixon's golfing buddy), were gender-less. They had no sex. (Author's note: I should know about Roswell; I had studied such things, read many books on the subject and spoke a lot about it. Even on radio. I was once tossed off of a Canadian radio show called 'The Twilight Zone' because I *dared* believe that Roswell was real. I sure know the descriptions of the little, gray aliens from Zeta Reticuli. They were not female.

In this screwed-up, backwards world where Women Rule and men follow behind, weakly...yeah, I guess it's right to proclaim the hairless, big bug-eyed, Roswell aliens were GIRLS! People believe anything Media tells them now, so why not broadcast the lie that: *Guys are too dumb to drive spaceships.* I mean, look at Star Trek's 'Discovery.' (And how can you?). What do you discover? You find that Ladies are in charge, they're running the show, they're the stars and they be the pilots driving the spaceships. This idea, these days, is reinforced again and again in Media. Know the TV commercial of a Moon-buggy that leaped over the lunar surface? Who's inside? Two smiling girls. It could *only* be girls today, and the main one was black. Only women are strong enough, brave enough and smart enough to pilot starships? You actually think this is Not Backwards? Maybe you do, if you believe a statue of a Killer-Indian Woman is right and has always topped the Capitol Building or that the Lady in the Moon should be more dominant than the Man in the Moon?

What's the movement of the Heart mean?

The heart inside your body has moved, switched places a little.

What? You didn't know? Your human heart was always on the left side of your chest. When you pledged allegiance, promised love or loyalty, you placed your hand on your heart. That hand was put way to the left because that's where the heart always was. But no more. The heart has shifted near center. It's still on the left, but barely. It was never almost centrally located before. It was left, exactly where our hand goes because of "muscle memory." When we naturally touch our heart with our hand, we don't place it near center, we place it to the left. The only problem today is, we'd miss slightly.

The heart is far from our only body part that has changed. Kidneys, liver, lungs, fallopian tubes, shoulders, etc. Learn what's happened. Most doctors would never agree that all bodies have transformed and would maintain: "It's always been like that." If there were never any Mandela-changes to our bodies, why have SOME doctors and nurses noticed the changes and have reported them? On YouTube, a nurse explained that you could stick two fingers into a skull's eye sockets right up into the brain cavity. It was open behind the eye and eye sockets were not very small spaces like they are now. There was no bone-barrier behind the eyes as there is today. Very strange.

What does the heart-shift mean? Is there a connection to the New World? I'd say, "Yes." To me, it's ironic. We're not centered anymore. I even used the term "center" in my novels years ago to mean our heart, our soul and *center* of consciousness. But we're way off from love and caring and compassion in society. And that is, of course, because we are poor victims of Programming. But in this darker universe, which must be composed of antimatter, there are people with hearts more centralized? We should be closer than ever. But what's been thrust upon us since 2020 has only forced us farther apart. I'm reminded of the "heart" campaign we've seen over Media and wonder: Is it sincere and good or hypocrasy with something very devilish in its center?

Now We are All Disconnected from our Brain.

Apparently, one more major body part has changed. Again, unnaturally. I hadn't thought in depth about this Mandela-change until recently, since working on Book II. Thinking about it, I knew that I could dig further into this, a few more inches, anyway. Then, I think the significance hit me and HIT ME in a big way! This could be "massive" and "awesome," as they say today. Yeah, it never really STRUCK me before because we're all more thickheaded...and, maybe that was because now:

We have something new [to a few doctors and nurses] **behind our eye sockets and it was not there before.** It's called the "zygomatic bone," which also forms the temporal, or outer side wall of the eye socket. "Many important nerves run through this area....The medial wall is formed primarily by the *ethmoid bone* that separates your nasal cavity from your brain." The (odd) bone behind our eyes has also been called a "barrier."

That's a drastic difference from what our skull used to be, and what it is presently. Meaning? Could this explain a multitude of feelings now, such as being "detached"? And a large array of recent bad behaviors in the masses? We're not centered. We seemed to have lost our Moral Compass, you know, common sense? We had basic sense, basically. We had hearts and felt compassion, years ago. Now, not so much. Is it the effect of having too many 'Angry Birds' and not as many 'Happy Birds' in the world (Metaphor)? Or...is it because we have a bone-wall BARRIER that cuts or blocks the eye area (socket) from the brain? Aren't WE, our consciousness, just behind our eyes? There was an open, free passage directly up into the brain cavity. There was nothing physical that blocked it, it was open. Now there's blockage. Are we more cut off from our Intelligence? Our brain? More brain-dead because of this bone? People are not getting smarter. Is one astounding reason:

There's now an impediment that stops direct passage to the brain? The Zygomatic Bone was never there before, as a few in the medical profession have reported.

When I was in a "Health Care" Center, I asked the doctor about the "barrier" behind the eye socket and *she* (they're all women these days) said: "It was always like that" and shook her head. Yet, when I asked her, "But don't you remember Jiffy peanut butter?" She said with exuberance: "Of course!" Well, as M.E. people know, we're in a universe where Jiffy never existed, as I told the doctor. I'm sure she didn't believe me.

We are DUMBER today. *Maybe the stupidest generation that has every walked the Earth?* How could that be true? Okay. How could the masses who use the awesome Internet Highway, those who are constantly filling their heads with information via their phone-devices, be the least intelligent generation that's ever been? Because the information that flows to their brains is shit. It's wrong, it's brainwashing, propaganda, LIES, put there to only confuse you and never tell you the truth. You have no practice investigating, studying or being a researcher. You push a button. You assume the info is true. You're lazy and receive data from Big Brother's tele-screens, the TV. Internet. The news. You don't go to libraries, study as an individual, do you? Question what you're told over the Media. You're not individuals anymore! You're told lies and you saps believe it. You're told what to do and *you do it!? Maybe you think you're in the military! That's not life!* You really do not know the truth from the lie and you have no practice GOING AGAINST THE TIDE and getting it right. You guys are pretty, damn, fucking stupid, as far as I'm concerned. [It's only slander if it's wrong]. When I see signs of life, signs of individual thoughts of a human being with real feelings and not a robotoid like everyone else...then I'll be slightly impressed and give you some credit. But I'm not going to give credit or respect to those who do not deserve any. *I have received none for all that I have done.*

Maybe the Barrier behind our eyes is a "stumbling block" or "road bump" that is *in our way?* A foggy veil that doesn't need to be there? Could we be smarter without it? *Were* we smarter without it in the Old World? Our soul in touch more with our mind? Sharper, clearer in thought, without the barrier? I would lean toward: *Yes,* on that point.

I distinctly remember old horror movies where, among the creepy background, a snake went in one eye of a skull and came out the other. Sure, they weren't real skulls, but they were representations of real ones and it was an open area behind the eye-opening. I remember seeing skeletons in school and at the doctor's office when I was a kid. I don't remember bone being there. A ping-pong ball cannot fit inside our small eye socket anymore. The socket is only a tiny, indented space today. Nothing like it was before. Also, a few people have reported strange holes in front face of the skull, which weren't in their memories.

What's the change in the Sun mean?

There have been online, Mandela researchers who have reported a drastic change in our Sun. I am likely to believe such a concept since I had already had my revelation about the *distortion* of what was now my (different) Moon and crater and a different Mars, to my recollection. Drenched in my own work to uncover the riddle of the Mandela, I understood that the phenomenon was true. Each M.E. confirmed the other one. Nothing should have changed, and so much had changed.

The Sun had always been a middle-aged, yellow star. YELLOW. In fact, because of that fact, yellow was the most dominant color on Earth. That is probably no longer true. We orbit (in different bodies) on a different Earth around a different Sun. It's white now. WHITE. Suppose it's true. I kept an open mind as I attempted to stare at the Sun for a short period. It appeared more stark. I could almost see that the light rays were white and not yellow. That's not all... (Then I looked it up: records confirmed it's white).

It's been hypothesized that this Universal Shift or "re-set" had moved our entire Sun and family of planets to another location in the Milky Way, to a different arm of our galaxy. Really? But how could that be so if we still observed the Big Dipper and Orion and the rest of the stars, more or less, just where they were? If it's actually true, that would mean...**THE WHOLE UNIVERSE HAS BEEN ADJUSTED and is slightly different from what it was.** *Everything! A Parallel Universe means a parallel universe!* FANTASTIC! Or the opposite and not so fantastic, I'm not sure.

In another sense...does it have meaning? Heart-shift, Sun-shift. What's the change in the Sun mean? Yellow to white. It's *stretching* but, does it have any connection to C3PO and the droid-change? C3PO's silver leg in first two films was definitely gold and a Mandela-change, and possibly our now different Sun? Gold to silver and yellow to white. There could be a connection. "Why did C3PO change?" might have been asked in this section. Does the change from Gold to Silver have significance?

I would guess: The Truth tarnishes anything bright and shiny that we've been made to honor and adore. It was only a guess.

The Truth Behind the Bogus Tartary or Tartarian Empire...

~you'll never believe~

Long before I discovered what a Mandela Effect was, I found Tartary or Tartaria, and it blew me away. Daily I examined YT videos by Jon Levi. *Fascinating and intriguing* were my first thoughts, which preceded many weeks of investigating something I've never heard of before (and I've been studying the ancient world since 1974, intensely). How could I have missed something called the Tartarian Empire? Where has this been?

There were incredible old maps, early ones that were off, of course for their time, but colored and very detailed. Many showed "Tartaria" clearly marked and "cities" in America and far to the north. Phenomenal details marked near the North Pole? These were unfamiliar settlements, not a part of known history. Oddities and new names/words were on these strange maps with great accuracy. Such care and intricacy in the map-making. What were we seeing? But the prime questions in my mind were: Where did the Tartaria maps come from and why was this the first we've heard of "Tartary"? Who's been hiding this from the rest of the world all this time and WHY? Researchers are well aware of ancient and very controversial maps, such as those of Piri Reis. This was a revelation! Could it be a new discovery? At the time, before M.E., I would never have contemplated: False photos, fake histories and a very different universe were now around us and in place.

It was far more than old Tartary maps. Photos. Stunning photos! Black and white images of buildings, beams, structures, architecture, roofs, spires on roofs, gargoyles, towers, super-detail taken in every bit of workmanship, etc. This was all over Europe and the new world across the ocean, nearly 200 years ago? Something was very wrong here, this couldn't be, but there it was in fantastic photography that my eyes had never seen before. And Jon Levi reported, daily, this was due to a hidden history kept from the masses known as Tartaria. He'd show the maps and photo after photo, then he'd look up various old buildings and there they were: Apparently, far more advanced than structures, building techniques and the technology that came after. Where had these images suddenly come from?

I fell for it for the longest time; *loved this guy Levi!* Praised him because of his eye for intricate details when he described and showed unbelievable architecture. A lot of what he reported was certainly new to my ears and eyes. Such as the vast repetition of shapes that covered these tremendous buildings were not carved. We've always assumed they were carved. But he showed such uniformity and enormity in the roofs and sides of grand buildings that the forms had to have been manufactured via MOLDS. It would explain the uniformity over such large areas. Interesting idea, that they might have had a technology to accomplish that, which we never thought had existed centuries ago.

Levi even proposed, through amazing photos, that the spheres on roofs, high atop towers of such precise craftsmanship, were **Tesla-like** (wireless) **energy towers**. What? Tesla Technology, wireless electricity, way before Tesla? Wow, that caught my attention. What most people might think were very elaborate/ornate Lightning-Rods on cathedral roofs, might have been wireless electricity in action. *In Civil War times?* That's what he suggested [forced to suggest]. The large spheres on great buildings' roofs functioned as static, atmospheric collectors, essentially like solar panels. Electrical energy was channeled to main rooms in impressive buildings through what appeared as "fireplaces." His clue to this possibility was that the "fireplaces" were completely sealed, bricked up, no soot and not used as fireplaces, but were electrical conduits, possibly. The photos showed such skill in craftsmanship and design, the idea was almost believable. But Tesla Tech 200 years before Tesla? No way. He was 200 years *ahead* of everyone else on this planet. Something was very wrong here.

Then Jon Levi pounded into you, day after day, the idea of "mud-floods" and a word I have heard broadcast over Media a thousand times too many: "re-sets." [Gee, what could that mean?]. At the time, I remained unaware of the truth, the real truth, behind what he pushed as "Tartary." The idea of this new and hidden history from us, that only he and a few powerful others exposed, I believed. The reason was because I had not heard of the Mandela Effect, yet. Soon, that would change.

I continued and watched his videos and didn't question how he could basically have a complete lesson-plan, have all the computer-skills to set it up and get new, interesting material day after day after day. It never occurred to me then that he was a lying, fucking, puppet Shill! Now it has.

He displayed numerous, old city photos of mud-disasters. They were almost everywhere: Europe, the New World and they showed one type of architecture below or beneath another type of architecture because of all the mud. What was constructed atop the earlier building was far inferior than the extraordinary structures that were there previously, underneath or below. (Like ancient pyramids). Also. This Tartarian Empire, like super-Romans or Illuminati back then, *destroyed* almost all of these incredible structures and grand buildings on most continents for the purpose...

"They" didn't want to reveal to the general public that advanced technology and a high level of construction had existed hundreds of years ago. So. As a result of many "mud-floods" throughout history and the demolition of superstructures to make way for later inferior buildings, we have the primitive 20th Century, which covered up a greater/hidden age hundreds of years earlier.

No fucking way, Jose! I didn't know then to question Jon Levi. I do now. I thank the Mandela for opening my eyes to the truth about this NY dude and many other things.

Have you ever heard of "star-forts"? I never had, until Mr. Levi came along. Statue of Liberty's base is surrounded by a star-fort. Since when have we ever heard it called that or anything else called a star-fort? A fort in the shape of a (evil) star. Then Jon showed the YT audience, in photos, that star-forts are common in Old World Europe. They're everywhere. Paris and other cities are really surrounded by star-forts. Why hasn't one other source, other than this guy, ever mentioned that term in all these years? Why hasn't anyone ever breathed a word, had records or shown an old Tartary map before 5 years ago? Or 10 years ago? Or at *any time* in the past? It was nowhere, yesterday. There it is, today.

Then. I learned about the Mandela Effect. Slowly. Slowly. Slowly. So many bizarre things suddenly made more sense. Now I understood this bearded character (they're all bearded now) called Jon Levi. I also discovered YT forums are absolutely BS, crap, lies, meant nothing, totally bogus. For more than 15 years I thought they were real. *Ah, that's why no one responded to me.* It's not real. Although, I did get a good feeling when I wrote in one of Jon's blogs:

"You are so full of shit."

All that Tartary, the strange maps, the Mud-Floods, the fantastic photos of structures and building techniques way ahead of their time, due to the great and hidden Tartarian Empire...*it just appeared!* Like the other Mandelas. They are examples of items, events, history of the Reverse-World, not my world. You see I would have noticed 2 Michigans (only 1 in my world) or always known the Great Pyramid was on the end (it was in the middle). Costa Rica was an island in my world. Tartaria was never mentioned long ago or written about anywhere because it never happened in my world...

But, wait. It was only in *my* world that it never happened. The world of Jiffy, not JIF. I actually might owe Jon Levi an apology. Here's why: This is the Dark Universe now and all those advanced techniques, Tesla principles before Tesla, photography a little more advanced, could be true - could have happened on this side of the Mirror. I'll be damned, again.

That's what's hard to believe, stated above "**you wouldn't believe**." Not that these fantastic photos, and even the earliest of films, showed extraordinary images unknown before that almost simply *materialized into existence.* If you are a student of the Mandela as I am, then you know that a new Village Person could pop into existence or horns could suddenly appear on statues of Moses. Any Mandela researcher knows that...

What is utterly mind-bending to me and others that realize that the Mandela is real and not fake memories, is that IT REALLY WAS LIKE THAT, it really was always like that in the negative world. *Sheeesh!* It's not that some items have changed and seemed to have switched from our perspective, 'stein' to 'stain.' *Everything has changed* and the Mandela-differences are where the New World didn't quite match. Dark Side showed, in the differences.

I mean to say: We're stuck here. And here, really is a different world to us that makes no sense. We're really ghosts or a mockery of that other, better world with a yellow Sun. In this universe, there actually was no Jiffy peanut butter or Jujubees. *Mandela Effect believers are mad, stupid or mis-remember!* But that's only from the viewpoint of you twisted sisters and twisted, bearded brothers in the negative Mirror. <I know! I'm in a frikken beard on a few book covers, that will never happen again, now that my eyes are open>.

One more item, as mentioned before: "re-set." Do you have any idea how many times Jon Levi [I don't mean to pick on him] has used the word RE-SET to his massive YT audience? Why? Because it's an "in" catch-phrase these days? No. He must. Like other D-level celebrities to the A-level celebrities. They use code and recite scripts written out for them. Don't believe me? Now that I have opened your eyes to the word "re-set," maybe you'll hear it more and more. In fact, you will hear it more and more now that you're aware of it. From sportscasters to news-readers to talk-shows, you have heard them say "re-set" and other code-words, given to them by their Masters who own them and control them. TV and Movie Puppets are paid very well to perform. They lie.

What's the significance of the forced-popular word: "re-set"? Obviously, it has to do with the Mandela Wave that They have silently thrust upon us. The world has been re-set. Media keeps reminding us of what They've done to us.

Who will Save your....?

American singer/songwriter, Jewel, had her debut album in 1995 called: 'Pieces of You.' Look up the first track and see what her first big hit was called. The song's name that's shown and the name we remember is 'Who will Save your Soul,' without a question mark. Put that title in Google, hit Images and you'll see record sleeves of various, official releases of the song. Quite a few of the photographs have her in different settings or only her face. But she is right next to the letters (title) of probably her biggest song. Each time, the title is printed: '**Who will Save your Soul**.' Soul, singular. Then why the hell does Jewel sing "**Souls**"? She now sings "souls" each and every time. She no longer is singing to you about your soul, instead, it's to a group of people (plural), about *their souls.* It's remarkable that if you searched deeper and deeper into the correct spelling of the song title from many sources, the information mostly is in the singular. But it's now always sung by her in the plural and must be a Mandela.

Any meaning or significance here? You tell me. Isn't it odd that the original recording of it, the video and every time there's a performance of 'Who will Save your Soul'...Jewel clearly sang "souls"? We each have a soul [except for famous celebrities who literally sell their souls to Satan], not *souls.* It makes no sense. Ah, but it does make sense in this backwards, Bizarro-world we now live in.

p.s. Lines in big films, lyrics in songs of top musical groups are not what you think. None of the artists and familiar faces wrote anything! Rich and famous slave-liars deliver directives and commands and influence in powerful "sound and vision" [music and films], sweetness/impressiveness and persuasion created by British Masters, who are evil and have been controlling you through your idols.

Prince's 'Let's Go Crazy.'

Dearly beloved,
We are gathered here today,
To get through this thing called life.
Electric word, Life.
It means forever, and that's a mighty long time,
But I'm here to tell you, there's something else,
The Afterworld
...When the elevator tries to bring you down,
Punch a higher floor...
Are we gonna let the elevator bring us down?
You better live now,
Before the Grim Reaper come knockin' on your door.

Prince was 57 when he was found alone and unresponsive in an **elevator** at his Paisley Park studio compound on April 21, 2016. It is not a coincidence that Prince's song 'Let's Go Crazy' foretold of his death, "found in an elevator." It was planned that way. He might be alive with David Bowie and many others who've served the Illuminati well and are no longer "on Earth." We already have the creepy lyrics of death here (Grim Reaper) and then there's the MANDELA, and...

A definite shift to the Dark Side. The original song-intro after "Dearly beloved..." was: "...to CELEBRATE this thing called Life!" The word was "celebrate." Everyone was "gathered" around Prince to *celebrate life!* That was what we remember and what was 'spoken' in the popular song, even according to Prince's fans. But he doesn't say "celebrate" and it is one more bad shift (into Darkness), I believe. He now says, "...to get through this thing called life." Another night and day difference because he's not celebrating, he's telling the crowd [exaggerating] *"Life is fucked! It's hell just to GET THROUGH one more goddamn day!!"*

The Prince Mandela is justified for being in this section, another connection to madness, negativity. He would never had originally sung: "get through life" and then transformed into something pleasing and wonderful like: "Celebrate Life!" No, polarity always goes one way now: Bad. The differences Mandela people have noticed are not good. Where have they been negative to positive? The changes have either been neutral, no significance whatsoever/meaningless...or a quantum leap into something wicked, darker and very negative.

666 Cough Medicine, remember?

You don't remember mommy giving you '666' cough syrup? What? Do you know why you don't remember that wonderful (Nazi) brand name? *Because none of us remember!* It is part of the phony and unbelievable back-histories that are in place now, all around us. It's right there in the record. *Fuck the record!* It's bogus! And you should realize that so many of these Crazy things today are bogus. Today is the Lie! What company would ever, ever name their product "666"? When did heaven on Earth turn to hell on Earth? Look it up. You will discover that the Devil once had on the market '666 Allergy and Cold Medicine.'

"Door to Hell"

I'll bet you readers have never heard of the Darvaza Gas Crater in Darvaza, Turkmenistan, also known as the 'Gates of Hell' or 'Door to Hell'? The crater has a diameter of 226 feet with a depth of 98 feet and *it is burning!* Soviets "may have intentionally" used grenades and ignited the crater to prevent the spread of methane gas when they discovered a gas cavern of extreme size. The thought was that the methane would burn itself out. THE MASSIVE CRATER HAS BEEN BURNING SINCE 1971! Why isn't this known? For more than 50 years, this large "crater from Hell" has been on fire, and we're supposed to believe it? Fifty years? Not a lot of information can be found of the Darvaza Gas Crater, outside of "The Turkmen government hopes that the crater will become a popular tourist attraction." To Mandela people, it is more likely that this monstrous fire-crater in Russia just appeared, with its own backstory intact, exactly like so many other weird things now found in the world.

Here's a short list of "natural" oddities mentioned in Volume I, but these I picked out are dark/terrible or very different, in my view. Have you really known of this type of *nature* before, or is this the first time you've heard of them? (And, of course, everything should be looked up)...

Boiling rivers.
Dark Lightning.
Black, vampire squirrels.
Some rabbits, deer and other woodland animals are meat-eaters.
Blood Falls.
Dragon Blood (bleeding) trees.
Thundersnow.
Rainbow trees and landscapes.
Fly Geyser.
Red seashores.
Red rhinos.
Orange alligators.
Humpback dolphins.
Panda dolphins.
Giant bunnies.
Pangolins.
Bananas that grow upside-down.
Walking Trees.
Blue food.

Do you remember Upside-Down Christmas Trees?

Seriously, upside-down Christmas trees? "Hanging fir **trees upside down** dates back to the Middle- Ages when Europeans did it to represent the Trinity. The first to do this, according to many sources, was Saint Boniface, a Benedictine monk, who used the inverted trees as a theological teaching tool for pagan Germans." Pagan Germans. Who remembers this practice, this long tradition? I don't. I think it's another example of a *reverse-thing,* almost evil, that has just popped into existence? Where's this been? We're supposed to believe this practice goes back to the Middle-Ages? Upside-down pine trees for the Christmas holidays "continued through Europe and into the 19th Century" and beyond? They were hung from rafters by the poor class due to lack of sufficient space? *This did not happen in my reality.*

Upside-Down Christmas trees have been "increasingly used by retailers for in-store displays..." Yes, there's an entire history of UD Christmas trees that have sold in many stores. Only why don't we remember this previously? Why are we only hearing of it now?

Online, you can find photos galore of inverted fir trees for Christmas. [Photos wouldn't lie now, would they?]. Almost all information on the "phenomenon" is positive; they give you tips on decorating it and say there's more room under it for presents. Nowhere that I saw (except for some Mandela people) was there a hint that maybe this was disrespectful, or sacrilegious or even satanic. From what I read, this craze, this fad, or whatever it is, is "catching on." Only in hell.

Mailmen do not have to deliver the mail...if it's raining.

Most of us have heard what we have assumed was the postal carriers' motto: "Neither rain, nor snow, nor sleet, nor hail, shall keep the postmen from their appointed rounds."

Supposedly, it was first stated by Greek historian, Herodotus, who actually said: "...nor heat, nor gloom of night, stays these courageous couriers from the swift completion of their appointed rounds." This was stated during a war between Greeks and Persians around 500 BC, which concerned Persian mounted mailmen.

But according to the U.S. Postal Department, they have no motto or slogan at all. The story goes: An architect, Mitchell Kendal, carved it on New York's General Post Office in the 19th Century. It has been connected to the P.O. ever since.

In reality, mail carriers don't have to deliver the mail if the weather is inclement. Maybe soon They'll declare mail delivery not a right anymore, it's a privilege. Who knows what's next? This goes along the lines of a Dark World. People today no longer care. They cared more in that Other World. No one here is getting it right.

Governments don't care about us, the people. People really don't care about each other anymore. Why should the children care if parents or teachers don't? And the U.S. Postal Department doesn't really care about delivering our mail, properly and accurately, anymore.

(Author's note: There was a FedEx package delivered to my address that was 1000 numbers off! Did you know the U.S. Post Office has removed those big, metal street-mailboxes that have been on city street corners for almost a hundred years? Gone! Why would They do that? Who the fuck thought that was a great idea? No one good and no one who cared about people. I don't trust the mailbox at my door. When I have to mail a letter, I have to walk a couple blocks to the big, corner mailbox. That's gone, along with the others. But the real crazy thing is: *They started putting a few back.* What? Why? Why remove them in the first place and then return only a fucking few? Are we breaking rocks in a prison yard? For me now to mail a letter, I have to walk nearly a mile. Nothing makes sense. But there's always a Method to the Madness. This could connect to many strange, unnecessary rule-changes imposed upon us lately, in most everything. Is it to keep us off-balance, in the dark, so we will be likely to accept ANYTHING to come, even more fascism forced onto poorer classes of people? Supreme, Federal "bosses" of the P.O. should never have touched needed street mailboxes. Was this vile act really across all of America? You think you and your family have been treated fairly, recently? I don't. I think They do nothing but lie to us and crush us so They have power and we do not.

Life is now a *'Scary Movie.'*

Remember the 2000 comedy movie by the Wayans brothers called: 'Scary Movie'? Researchers have found a striking M.E. in this movie. At one point, it parodied 'The Sixth Sense,' and many of us remember the joke delivered by Marlon Wayans. He was scared, had the covers up around his neck and breathlessly said, "I see white people." It was funny and memorable. Millions of us remember it. What happened to the line? Now he says: "I see dead people." Not funny. This is a M.E.

In my initial collection of dark differences for this section, I hadn't thought to include this one. The more I thought about it...there could very well be significant meaning here that hardly anyone has realized. I'm simply wondering about: Dead People. Is the meaning, *he sees all of us* as the Walking Dead? Brain-Dead robotoids, people have been made (hammered) into? Has nothing to do with race; it has to do with the division between rich and poor. We muggles, we barely survive below the Capstone high over us, filled with Magical Wizards who utterly control us, the peasants.

"Goodnight."

"'The George Burns and Gracie Allen Show,' sometimes called: 'The Burns and Allen Show,' was a half-hour television series broadcast from 1950 to 1958 on CBS. It starred George Burns and (wife) Gracie Allen, one of the most enduring acts in entertainment history."

This New York comedy duo (one of them played 'God') from the 1950s was certainly very popular at the time, exactly as the blurb stated. Audiences knew their catch-phrase of a joke because it (nearly) ended every single show. Burns and Allen usually came out from behind a curtain and addressed a stage audience that was not there. They'd express a few funny comments, then finally George would say: "Say goodnight, Gracie." Every time, she replied, "Goodnight, Gracie." It never failed to get a phony laugh-track and real chuckles in American living rooms. For 9 years. This Mandela is up there with the disappearance of Laurel and Hardy's catch-phrase, because...

Gracie Allen now only responds with, *"Goodnight."* Check it out. Nowhere at the end of shows is the famous joke said. It's not there and it should be. There was a joke there, like in Scary Movie, but now, not. Why is it gone? I'm reaching, but is it "Goodnight" for all of us?

Rosa Parks, *the Civil Rights Activist?*

Rosa Parks (1913-2005), her story in history has been altered. She now stands as a shining example of womanhood in the great struggle for civil rights, human rights, against those who'd deny those rights and who had oppressed her at the time. Rosa Parks has been called: "The Mother of the Freedom Movement" and "The First Lady of Civil Rights." She refused to give up her seat to a white man on a

Montgomery, Alabama bus in 1955. "Her actions inspired the leaders of the local Black community to organize the Montgomery Bus Boycott." This chain of events involved Dr. Martin Luther King and ended more than a year later when bus segregation was ruled unconstitutional.

I take nothing away from any brave woman or man who must make a stand and do what is right against forces that are very wrong. I understand. Especially in the deep south and at that particular time period. The horrors that Blacks encountered by the police or any bigot are unimaginable to most decent people, generations later. I give all the credit in the world to someone who wouldn't give up their seat to a fucking, racist bastard, white-boy! Good for her and I mean that very much...

But. Rosa's story is very different now from what it once was, that we knew, those that heard what happened. I'm not speaking of *what was true?* I'm speaking of *what was reported.* She wasn't already a part of a Woman's Movement, an activist for Black rights from the very beginning. Parks had worked a double-shift on her low-level job and was tired. That's why she didn't give up her seat. *Men* should give seats to ladies, not the other way around. It had nothing to do with striking out for Woman's Rights. Yes, the incident was used, she was used and received national attention. But shouldn't the truth matter?

I'm not even saying that the Bus Boycott and Rosa's part in it grew/changed naturally over the decades and she was pushed by Women's Libbers or radicals in the Black Movement. No. I'm saying...

History changed overnight in one gigantic tsunami of a Mandela Wave! Rosa has light skin now. She is thought to have had darker skin by those who remember. What's going on? In this universe, Women Rule, especially the Black Woman. England/Hollywood is taking any Black Woman in history and inflating their greatness [Harriet Tubman, etc.]. FUCKING LYING! (a.n.: *I don't like lies!*) That's what's so wrong. How about a little of the (Godly) truth? Have you seen the new James Bond? The royalty have proclaimed the Black Woman as GOD. Do you think there's anything wrong with that? I do.

More Nonsense as Sense...

Oh, you think it's a sensible world, eh? Here and now? Let's explore a few more changed items that possibly you'll remember were changed (and they shouldn't have changed)...

Ford and VW logos are strangely different than many of our memories. But you'll never guess what other car emblem has also transformed? What it transformed into is the shock, in these times of a new social climate where *Women Rule.* Volvo! Remember the Swedish, luxury automobile company? It read 'VOLVO' and the name was within a thick circle. The name is still inside a circle, but a curious addition is now oddly attached, according to some. The logo, the way I remember it, is exactly as others have remembered it, and have reported the change:

Volvo logo was never a Male Symbol! Men? Fucking low-life men? In this (recent) new age of strong women? Seriously? How could that be, but yes, it be. Look at the (new) logo and see if you remember? A small, Y-chromosome, MANLY arrow now is connected to the circle in the classic and universally known, male-symbol. I'll be darn. I could almost see it going the other way, where the logo was always the male-symbol, but after the Mandela, the logo was castrated. That did not happen. Odd. What did occur was a *change.*

Let's go back a long way into the last century. Old folks would remember Animal Crackers. To our memories, the company's product was always called: 'Barnum's Animal Crackers.' The cookies shaped like animals "evoked the familiar circus theme of the Barnum and Bailey Circus." In 1902, the well-known box was designed for the Christmas season with a string so they could be hung on trees. Until that time, crackers or cookies were only sold in bulk.

Shirley Temple had sung about them in a song many remember: "...Animal crackers in my soup."

Animal, singular. The transmogrified, new name on the old box and today's box is suddenly: "Animals." Plural. Makes no sense and it was never like that before. Here's the name today, the same name that it's always been? "Barnum's Animals Crackers." Possessive. Plural. Plural. No, the name never sounded like that in our minds. All those multiple "s" sounds? Someone on the first board of directors would have suggested a different title, one that slipped off the tongue better:

"Animal Crackers." But that did not happen in this world of nonsense and stupidness. The Other World, quality-control would have demanded: "That's not good enough!" But in this negative universe, no one cares and the motto is: "Oh, *that's* good enough." The crackers were called "Animal," now they are not.

Another is 'Playskool.' That's how it's spelled now? Are the educators idiots?

'Playskool' is an American company that produces educational toys and games for children. It is a subsidiary of Hasbro, Inc. and located in Rhode Island. They misspelled "school"? I know, it was done on purpose to be cool and hip or something, but they misspelled school from the very beginning. I don't think that's a good start for children. But I guess, *it's good enough* for young kids these days? The stupid Wikipedia has to inform the stupid people that "The last five letters of the brand name are a sensational spelling of 'school.'" Really? You had to *tell us* that "school" was spelled wrong in 'Playskool'? We did not know that? We needed you to tell us that, Wikipedia?

This is a Mandela, I believe. In the Other Mirror World, the Good Place, I'd bet the name of the educational company was spelled correctly, 'Playschool' They wouldn't have misspelled it. Here, they did because: "You suck!" It's good enough for the masses who don't give a shit anymore. Schools aren't schools, they're playing 'School' and don't care anymore about getting it right. They sure do not want an educated general public. That was true in the Other World, too.

Is there significance to the TRANS-formation in the title of a famous lingerie company that was once called 'Victoria Secret'? Oh, yes. "Victoria's Secret is an American lingerie, clothing, and beauty retailer known for high visibility marketing (lying) and branding (ouch), starting with a popular catalog and followed by an annual fashion show with supermodels (clones) dubbed Angels..."

Okay. Mandela people know that the title of the high-priced fashion company has changed. It was "Victoria Secret," as if it was a person's name. They, and all big companies, *never change brand names.* Little, announced, upgrades in logo designs, yes. Not names. Brands are built, not altered. The old title has TRANS-ferred over to the new title: "Victoria's Secret." Someone named Victoria has a secret. Wonder who that could be and what's the secret? Now it's possessive, and before, it was not.

Okay. People who have TRANS-vestigated (YouTube) know, for

the most part, what the "secret" is. Muggles don't, but they do buy the expensive lingerie and think it's classy. Drum roll...The secret is that *ugly* (Dick Gregory described 'her' so) Queen Victoria of England, Queen of the whole damn British Empire, ***was a man, baby!*** Thought you knew? That's right. The Victorian Age was led by a "pooftah," "queen," a MAN! He was really mad King Victor. (All royals must tranny, done at birth. That's the Big Secret that you common peasants don't know). It would explain the ugliness, eh? Eleanor Roosevelt? He and other elites had to live a life in gender-reverse. They almost all do, those we're told are "royalty" and "great" in every single field, department and Industry that's out there. You didn't know our world (even Old World) was run by trannies? THEY're counting on that. It's the real 'Phantom Menace.' Those who PUSH "You have the right to change your sex if you want to, we'll help you, look at the advantages...", they don't tell you that the mandatory Hormone injections that you must take for the rest of your life, comes from the Death of people, the death of many/many children. **"Hormones are children."** People must die for even one person to switch their sex. But They want a mad/mad world, so you do the wrong behaviors and think they are the right behaviors. They want *you* as insane as mad King Victor, who wanted to be "Victoria!" Why do you think England made the film: 'Victor/Victoria'? Why so much androgyny in Hollywood and music and everywhere now, everything Britain produced? Another secret you should know and investigate is:

British royals are German. They are Nazis! Blonde (Saxon) Aryans! They staged WWII. More secrets to research. Especially the real **Plague, worldwide secret of trans-genders placed in charge and in high positions of power**. Learn how to Trans-vestigate, use your eyes, see beneath the surface. Why do actors have female, physical traits? Why do actresses have male, physical traits? Why MUST "stars" and top celebrities marry each other, always work with each other? Always the same stable, club, cabal of "people"? Are you sure they're not monsters? Why did Gloria Swanson, a glamorous "actress" from the 1920s, say on The Dick Cavatt Show: "In Germany, in the '20s, they were making the most beautiful girls, from boys. And making the most beautiful boys, from girls." Why? Maybe because she got old (senile) or maybe she wanted to confess *her* secret? That was 100 years ago! Imagine what They could do in the modern age with hormones and sophisticated operations. Why, they could put boys in

Playboy and girls in Playgirl! And They have.

Gee, look at those long-legged, long-necked, 'Victoria's Secret' supermodels, Heidi Klum, Laetitia Casta and Tom Brady's wife, Gisele Bundchen, aye? Aren't they HOT? They're boys. Investigate~

Willy Wonky

Study the Mandela Effects in the movie 'Willy Wonka and the Chocolate Factory' or was it 'Charlie and the Chocolate Factory'? "Willy Wonka is a fictional character who appears in Roald Dahl's children's novel 'Charlie and the Great Glass Elevator.' The eccentric owner of the Wonka Chocolate Factory, he has been portrayed by Gene Wilder and Johnny Depp in film." Wouldn't such a magical film conceal a few Mandelas? Like 'Oz' hid dozens of them? Or Snow White?

(Author's note: Who wrote Willy Wonka? If you personally researched, you'd discover that this 'wonderful' film [*I loved it at the time!*] was credited to have been written by the "amazing talents" of Roald Dahl. Who's Dahl? I'll save you some time; this "man" was a British *Superman*. His war-record was stellar! Unbelievable, how much this guy did for England. In fact, *you shouldn't believe it.* **It's all bullshit.** Roald Dahl did more than Ian Fleming during the big War! Why didn't he write the Bond books? OH, HE DID! Almost. The screenplay for the fifth Bond film, 'You Only Live Twice,' "was written by Dahl," "loosely," they say. See what else he wrote? Chitty Chitty Bang Bang, The Night Digger, Dirty Beasts and much more. Everything this British (they're all British) did was GOLDEN, the Midas-touch. Not only prolific (like Shakespeare), but everything he "spat out of his brain," went to the top, pushed upon English people. They *had* to make another one of his books into a film a few years back, and was called 'The BFG' or BFG. It was for children, now. The title is code for Big Fucking Giant. Now you know. The Big Fucking Giant took (tranny, they're all trannies) Sophie to Giant Country, where "kids are on the menu." One review: "Even though the plot of the book involves ridding the world of people-eating giants, 'The BFG' frequently lands on BANNED lists for its depiction of cannibalism." Cannibalism! This, Harry Potter and even Alice in Wonderland [written by Jack the

Ripper, possibly] should never, never have been given to children! Roald's a Major Monster! *Giants eating people* is what the Giants [Illuminati] of the real world DO. They crush us, consume us, and take our children for their satanic Hormone-need. The Big Fucking Secret! Giants are the Royals! They tower over us. Have you heard stories of children as "dinner guests" for the Queen, then never seen again? No, I have. In the film (this was also an animated film), there's the ugly/ogre of a Giant right across from the balcony of Queen Elizabeth! There's fucking Queen Liz! She's uglier. In the book, in the film and in the animation version. And she's sweet, kind, wonderful, loving and *loves those children,* does she? Don't you see why they put this shit in British programming? Because they are Devil-worshiping, Nazi cannibals. I think I've under-stated it. The worst human beings possible. BFG is another metaphor. Opposite of the truth. Thanks, Dahl. I think if you take a good whiff, you'd smell him and Harlan Ellison burning in hell! I'm not done. Dahl's credits go on and on with: *That Was the Week That Was, Tales of the Unexpected,* etc. The Queen rewards you, the more Evil you perform. You sure it's not Sir Dahl? One comment was: His "stories were sometimes sinister." Really? Short story, long, now we come to what I wanted to express about *our friend,* Roald (can't even spell Ronald)...Not long ago, an idea "formulated" in my head and I recalled a way-out old, creepy, TV series called: 'Way Out.' Maybe YT had episodes, like Commando Cody and Captain Midnight? Yep. Now remember, I was a child when it aired. I remembered the weird name of the show and thought it was like a cheap Twilight Zone. Oh, boy. When I viewed it now, as an informed adult, *Wow, was it sick and creepy!* Guess who the host was? CONSTANTLY SMOKING CIGARETTES! (All rock stars and "hip" people were forced to). Like Rod Serling, Roald Dahl introduced one of only 14 'Way Out' episodes. I looked at a few of them; these weren't well-done, strange, imaginative stories, which I really love. No. What black and white perversion, dressed-up like something new and innovative. Imagine the husband and wife murders and tame creepiness with Hitchcock's TV shows and magnify that horror by a hundred! That's a little of what's credited to *Dahl,* a highly-decorated Monster. Like sadist/pedophile, Jimmy Savile (used to be Saville), host of British children's shows and the hippiest, new music for the youth. Knighted twice, once by the Pope. Lastly, about Dahl on Way Out, I'm listening to his words now, where as a child, I was totally oblivious to them. *Such wicked evil!* For no reasons except satanic ones, given to him by his Lords and Masters...

Often in a close-up of his face, with nicotine smoke that constantly swirled around him, he'd talk bullshit about some God-awful, bloody murder. He'd recite it as if off a newspaper article, like it was real, and it would always be the most hideous kind of situation. His intro was almost a quarter of the half-hour show. Wow. Surprised me. I assumed the show was just a kooky Twilight Zone...

This was Programming. Johnny Depp played Willy Wonka in the new version of The Chocolate Factory. You'll see him recite a paragraph in the woods: "T'was brillig..." That's code and a direct anagram to Jack the Ripper (Lewis Carroll), **a killer of children, not prostitutes**. Believe it or not. Didn't Johnny Depp play a sweet character in 'Fantastic Beasts...'? ("written by J.K. Rowling"). No. He did not. Monsters playing monsters, written by secret Ghost-writers, teams of British monsters.

This small section that mentioned 'Wonka' (wonky-eye, sure sign of a tranny late in life. *DAMN my tourettes!*) was only to tell readers: Do your own research on Mandelas in Willy Wonka or in anything else. Also investigate celebrity trans-vestigations – that will open your eyes. A Willy Wonka Mandela has appeared in the film, which was new to me:

"We are the music-makers and we are the Dreamers of dreams..."

People loved Willy Wonka and had seen it over and over, played off tapes and disks. They don't remember the above line being said. Could be a Mandela? What could it refer to? Kings and Queens over us that produce our Sounds and Visions. They are conjuring Their dreams...and our nightmares.

Parasite.

'Parasite.' Oscar winner for the "Best movie" of 2019. Really? There was nothing better? *There almost wasn't.* The blurb for this Nazi [Not See] piece of programming is:

"Greed and class discrimination threaten the newly formed symbiotic relationship between the wealthy Park family and the destitute Kim clan." It is an Upstairs/Downstairs story between the Haves and the Have-Nots. Not a Mandela, as far as I know. It's mentioned here to support the idea that Nothing Makes Sense Anymore. It doesn't have to make sense, doesn't have to be good or of quality. Audiences and society will absolutely accept shit shoved down their throats with a smile on their faces. Maybe they owed Asians for what will be done to them a year later, blamed for the "originators" of Coronavirus. No, they weren't. England funded it, designed it, distributed it. They're Money-Printers and believe they can do anything and get away with anything. They've proved you will accept any crap they hand you. So all They do is lie to a public that believes lies.

Parasite. That's what we are to Them. The Elitist, snob, fascist, RICH crowd who rally behind 'Atlas Shrugged,' certainly know the meaning to the film: 'Parasite.' The "Power Elite" knew immediately. You still don't get it? WE ARE THE FUCKING PARASITES TO THEM. The goddamn Royals who own everything see us as infestation to be eliminated. We're the virus. Look at all the terrible characteristics of the poor Kim family. Like vermin, the general public are rats to the rich and They have been in a process of exterminating us. Look how the wealthy Park family was portrayed in the film. They symbolized the *wonderful Royals* [British], with grace and class, so giving, so caring and loving, aye? Parks were great and the Kims were scumbags, always taking, not worthy of the gifts bestowed to them by the generous upper-class family. You don't see the metaphor, why they honored 'Parasite'? They're not honoring parasites (the public), They've been destroying us. To them, **we're the parasites**. Like about everything, it's an Insider-Club joke. And the joke is always on us muggles who have no magic. (It's what They, the few on top, think...because we, the many, are not trannies).

Perfectly aligned with dark themes or plots to major movies that absolutely make no sense: There's 'Parasite.' I have to tell you what was wrong with it, why it made no sense. *Please, I live for this.* What specifically was 100% wrong? Or totally absurd and would never have happened long ago when plots were more logical.

Here's what was insane, and it's not the insane guy that banged his head in Morse Code. Yeah, he killed, but that was expected, right? What was a shock and completely unexpected to me was when Mr. Kim murdered Mr. Park. Now you guys have a little coffee-talk session and see if you can come up with any reasonable reason why poor guy killed rich guy? Go. I don't see it. I can't explain it. I know it's not real and only a movie. But movies aren't movies. All I can come up with is: The murder upon another murder was to *shift you into madness*. Look what this ungrateful man did to the rich guy? A man they needed and freeloaded off of. Doesn't it make more sense that the poor husband *helped* the rich guy at the massacre? So it really *isn't* supposed to make sense anymore, huh? (like the end of 'Ex Machina'). That's what's honored and put on a pedestal today: Deception, Code, Agenda, Stupidity, Insanity, Violence and always a sweet, tender, lovely and unseen Shove Into Bloody Darkness.

No Mandela here, only *the Destruction of Western Civilization!*

Deadpool, Sharknado, Birdemic...the end of All Things!

"We don't have to make movies good anymore. They don't have to make any sense or be non-violent! We can be wicked and go crazy!! Yay!!"

I used to like superheroes. I grew up on comic books and sci-fi. I noticed how bad movies and TV had gotten over the course of decades. Blood, action, special-effects, mass-killings and a lack of good stories. More and more over time, like a Darkening of just about everything, worse and worse, in my view. Then came Deadpool. Gee, he's in all-red. It was Kill, Kill, Kill! He's a good guy? [Right, they were all bad]. Then he'd make a joke. Killing is funny and wonderful, isn't it? Doesn't it make you want to participate? Different ways to kill a person is hilarious? Not in my world. This is pure sacrilege to the genre, now totally ruined. I liked Avatar. When is the next Avatar and you think it *won't* be ruined like Star Trek, Star Wars, Prometheus and everything else?

Where is counter-balance? There is no counter-balance of QUALITY anywhere for us down here. There's only shit lately. Fake News, Shit TV, Shit Music, Shit Movies, Fixed Sports. Shit, shit, shit! But millennials think, "It's the greatest" and "You're the best!" My God.

Let's get to fucking 'Sharknado,' which I liked at first, but what did I know? It was funny and weird, with Tara Reid and had cameos by celebrities like Jerry Springer, Ann Coulter, Kelly Ripa and Gary Busey. The movie wasn't taking itself seriously at all. Were they laughing at themselves more than we were? It seemed there's these mega-tornadoes over the ocean, where nasty sharks gather, below. The funnels and strong winds, pick up the sharks and distribute them all over the city. *It's raining sharks!* Funny. People have to defend themselves, of course. So people grab chainsaws, swords, weed-whackers, anything to cut/slice the sharks, as they're falling? Wouldn't you think the fall itself would kill the sharks? But there's no fun in reality. There's a series of 7 Sharknados and probably more to come? Finding different ways to bloody kill the falling sharks? Wow. They had Al Roker with a "sharknado" weather report, like it's a real thing. Small shark images were on the U.S. map right along with the Highs and Lows. What was so wrong? Okay, I laughed; I wasn't thoroughly insulted with the first one and marched on to Sharknado 2, *with joy.* In 2, it's much more gory and bloody and silly insanity. Then I think I got the true picture underneath of what was really going on and could no longer watch. They had everyone come out of their homes to Kill the falling (computer) sharks! Women, children, isn't this FUN, kids? That's all it was, kill, kill, kill, and everyone was doing it. I shudder to think what violent, bloody perversions were made a laugh riot in the rest of the series. *Everyone killing* isn't my idea of comedy. I was seduced because it was pushed and promoted by the old MST3000 guys, who now sold themselves as 'Rifftrax.'

What else did these guys, I used to like, push? Heavily! 'Birdemic.' Yes, your eyes saw correctly, Birdemic. One combined a tornado with sharks. This one combined birds with a virus and it sure sounded like "pandemic' now, doesn't it? Couldn't be planned that way, could it? They were not made by the same filmmakers. Birdemic was very cheap, no stars, badly acted, badly written. Everything was bad about it, but it drew you in and really wasn't as awful as the firestorm around it. *Then the birds hit!* Nothing like Hitchcock's 'Birds.' These birds were in even geometric patterns, hung in the air in even rows, like a video game. Birds were placed in front of terrorized people who did not interact with them (main stars) and had no connection to the vicious bird attacks. Others (extras) would get killed with blood everywhere. Filmmakers weren't even trying to use good bird graphics. It was similar to Atari-graphics; they faced left and right. You laughed because you never saw anything like this before. It was like a celebration of low quality. What are you giving the new generation? In the vein of Mystery Science Theater, the old movies were trying to be good, for the most part. They just had no budget and no decent actors. But they tried. *These kids today,* what else can I say? Not even trying! That is funny and different in itself. I guess my message is: This low standard of quality should not be exulted and a genre of movies, but it is today. It creates an audience that doesn't care anymore. *Anything* is good enough. The end of all things.

"ter" or "tre"?

The following is unbelievable for America, yet it is absolutely true and you really should look this up. I'll save you the trouble. The subject for Google is "**List of movie theater chains**." When I researched the Mandela for Book 1, I had not thoroughly investigated the subject. I saw what others had mentioned: 4 large, movie chains, in this country, had *changed their names* to the ENGLISH WAY "Theater" was spelled. Bizarre, and made little sense for big companies that were supposed to be owned and operated by Americans. More and more, "Theater" was being spelled "Theatre." Are yanks being turned into Brits? 'eard more and more British narrators and English accents over Media lately? Aye? I have.

It was over a year ago (my eyes had been opened) that I noticed a usual movie-banner across the side of a bus. This happened all the time in LA, blurbs, ads with faces of actors in a new movie. I saw how "Theater" was spelled and I couldn't believe it. The ad read: "Opening at a theatre near you." What country was I in? Was this London and not LA? Strange. I had no clue then of what was to come...

Only now did I Google: "List of movie theater chains" and WOW! Four? No, a heck of a lot more! Heading for the webpage had "Theater" spelled the American way, "ter." But right under the title had: "The following are the world's largest movie theatre chains as of 2020."

When we got down to the United States, there was an enormous amount of movie chains, many with the title "Cinema" or "Cinemas." But the U.S. theater companies were now entitled: "Theatres." This made no sense. They wouldn't naturally do that, or ever do that. Exactly like products would not and do not change BRAND names. They build Brands; *they do not change brand names!* I expected to view only a few "tre"s. No. You'll find an incredible number of U.S.

theaters (big chains and little ones) were now suddenly spelled the bloody English way. Here was the list under the United States:

AMC Theatres
Allen Theatres
B&B Theatres
Brenden Theatres
Century Theatres
CineLux Theatres
Cinemagic Theatre
Cinemark Theatre
Cobb Theatres
Coming Attraction Theatres
Dipson Theatres
EPIC Theatres
Fox Theatres
Frank Theatres
Fridley Theatres
Golden Star Theatres
Hawkins Theatres
Laemmle Theatres
Landmark Theatres
Main Street Theatres
Majestic Theatres
Malco Theatres
Mann's Chinese Theatre
Marcus Theatres
Mitchell Theatres
MJR Theatres
New Vision Theatres
Odyssey Theatres
Polson Theatres
Reel Theatres
Regency Theatres
Santikos Theatres
Showplace Icon Theatres
Southern Theatres
Stone Theatres
Thomas Theatre Group
UEC Theatres
Water Gardens Theatres
Your Neighborhood Theatres

Are you kidding me? This must be a Twilight Zone, written by Britain. To repeat, these were supposedly American (webpage informed us). Why, in the English style? Why, was the bus advertisement written in the English style? I have not see a *takeover* of "Opening at a theatre near you," but, nevertheless. [ps. It's almost impossible to find a recently recorded tennis match from any country that does not have British commentators who overly, overly use the word: "Brilliant!" (shot)].

How could all of these thea**TER** chains have changed their names? Oh, they didn't? Then, how could all of these theater chains have been ALWAYS named that way? Does it really make any sense? No. Not anymore. Who'd ever notice? Who'd ever notice the differences today, that a Master Trick had been played by Master Magicians of Hollywood, who are *themselves* controlled by even higher Realms? I'd bet. Every "Theatre" title of American movie houses could be a Mandela Effect.

Curtain of Oz. Are you sure you want to see what's behind it?

Guess wot? They all have not bloody changed. There are still a few, and only a few, American movie chains that spell "Theater," "Theater." They are: Cinema West Theaters, Galaxy Theaters, Goodrich Quality Theaters, iPic Theaters, Megaplex Theaters and Paragon Theaters. That's all.

Hell Isn't Down Below, anymore. It's Up here!"

The universe seems to have been inverted, turned upside-down. This is precisely what the Illuminati wanted and worked toward for generations, those that worshipped devilish things and horrible people like Aleister Crowley. They want it Backwards. Twisted. For you to be Twisted Brothers and Twisted Sisters. They rule us from the High Tower, the top of the invisible Social Capstone. They should serve us, instead, we're forced to serve Them! Maybe the thinking is: If They could actually change the polarity of the universe, They won't have any gods to answer to. Below will be Above and Above will be Below. They'll be the New Romans, the New Pharaohs, the New Gods! Free to do absolutely anything, without any accountability at all.

"Above all, a god needs compassion!" Captain Kirk once screamed on TV. Do They? World leaders and also top celebrities have a ritual which they must perform, many. One is "Stepping on the Cross," while all the while, they wear one for the eyes of the general public. There is another satanic practice that burns *Compassion out of their hearts.* They would have to, to do the unspeakable tasks and sacrifices and obey the commands that their Masters required.

Cover the Earth.

They did. Mentioned in Volume I, but not discussed: Sherwin-Williams paints. Henry Sherwin and Edward Williams started the Cleveland, Ohio-based company in 1866. Americans are very familiar with this paint company. Their name, their slogan and the image of paint from a paint can poured over the Earth should be well-known to almost everyone. SW is in 109 countries with 33,000 employees and nearly 5000 stores. This is one of the most remarkable M.E. changes. Why do I know their "cover the Earth" motto and image very well? But. *I remember the name wrong? I'm stupid, I'm off, I'm forgetful in my old age?* No, that's not it. It fucking changed and why can't I get through to people that it changed? I've heard, "No, it was always Sherwin." Sherwin! When my eyes first saw that name a few years back, it was a new experience. I had never seen the word or heard that name before in my life. And I read all movie credits. I never forget a face or a word. I am not wrong. The world is now different and it's a *very hard pill to swallow.*

I've recently wondered: Was there meaning here that I had not realized before? I could be wrong, but maybe: "Man" was gone from "Sherman," in my view and others. Where else was 'man gone'? Just about everywhere else now, replaced by women. Luke's gone. Women drove spaceships and Moon buggies, not men. Men were not the explorers and scientists and doctors on this side of the Mirror. Women were! You haven't noticed? Let's break it down: "Sher Win." As an anagram, "Hers Win!" or "Her Wins!" You see, these days, it doesn't look too good for men here. England placed WOMEN in charge of almost everything. You only have to look around, turn on your computer or watch your TV, and you'll see all the gender-changes that have happened over years. No? Open your mind...

More Mandela Menagerie.

One of the oldest and most popular Christmas poems ever, is: 'T'was The Night Before Christmas.' Its author is in dispute (not a surprise), but we know it was published on December 23, 1823 in the Troy Sentinel newspaper in upstate New York. Well, the famous poem that we all should be familiar with, has *changed*. Yes, has changed in a few ways. This, again, should not have happened, but it did. This is one more Mandela because we do not forget or miss-remember the classics, and this is a very big classic. Too many people remember the Christmas poem a different way. It now begins:

"Twas the night before Christmas, when all thro' the house,
Not a creature was stirring, not even a mouse;
The stockings were hung by the chimney with care,
In hopes that St. Nicholas soon would be there;
The children were nestled all snug in their beds,
While visions of sugar plums danc'd in their heads,
And Mama in her kerchief, and I in my cap,
Had just settled our brains for a long winter's nap..."

Whoa! "Settled our brains"? No way. I certainly agree with M.E. researchers who have pointed out this is one difference in the poem. Why would they need to settle their **brains**? They didn't need to before? What trauma had occurred earlier? You mean the excitement that tomorrow was Christmas? No, it sure doesn't sound right. Ask your parents or grandparents. They might remember: "...and I in my cap, had just settled down for a long winter's nap..." or "...had just settled in for a..."

Also. Two lines are unfamiliar to me (I'm the age of your grandparents) and have heard the poem a lot in my lifetime. "The moon on the breast of the new fallen snow, gave the lustre of mid-day to objects below." I don't think that's correct; I sure would have remembered "breast," but no. Now we come to a significant Mandela: The names of Santa's reindeer. You don't remember? You should.

"...Now Dasher! Now Dancer! Now Prancer and Vixen,
On Comet! On Cupid! On Dunder and Blixem...

Whoa! "Dunder and Blixem"? No way. Seriously? Not a few people, or some crazy/forgetful people, but a hell of a lot of people should know that those two reindeer names in the classic poem are wrong, different than what it was and what we remember. A majority of people from the last century would surely know that the true names were DONNER and BLITZEN. Now, doesn't that sound better, more right than wrong? No? Dunder? Like a Dunderhead? Like Dunder Mifflin Paper? Nope. But the Mandelas do not end there. The next one could be just as surprising as the last one [and it was actually discovered only a minute ago; I had never heard of it previously]. Here's how the poem ends:

"...He sprung to his sleigh, to his team gave a whistle, and away they all flew, like the down of a thistle: But I heard him exclaim, 'ere he drove out of sight, "Happy Christmas to all, and to all a good night."

You don't see it? Maybe you do? I saw it as soon as my vision struck the page that contained the last line. I hope you realize that Santa now flubs the last line? That wasn't it. What could it be now, what could it be? Could Santa Claus, I don't know, have told the world, "MERRY CHRISTMAS"? I think he did.

Moving right along...

The State Flag of Hawaii. I wonder what the original state flag looked like? They didn't change it. It was transmogrified (changed) unnaturally by the Mandela Wave. It had to be. There is no sane, just, sensible reason for the British Union Jack Flag to compose about 25% of the whole red, blue and white flag of Hawaii. How is that right? The following is one explanation online:

"The Union Jack flew as Hawaii's sole flag until 1816, when red, white and blue stripes were added. It has remained a part of the flag. 'It might seem strange, as Hawaii was never British,' says Graham Bartram, chief vexillologist at the Flag Institute, '...but it works as a symbol of friendship.'"

Really? Are you kidding me? Who wrote the New Histories for Hawaii, the Northwest Angle and Little Michigan? This really isn't the world I was born into. That place was more sensible. Look! "Hawaii was never British territory," yet it's whole flag was once the British flag? Ridiculous. Unless England did own Hawaii and didn't want to tell the peasants, who sure would never have been a part of that paradise. We do not know what the truth is; we only are well-versed in British lies. [I hate tea].

I've seen state flags way back in school, not often, but I think I would have remembered a Union Jack. Later, I would have questioned: "Well, what's it still doing on modern flags after Hawaii became a part of the United States? A British flag? Wouldn't an American flag there make more sense?" I think something's going on between the beautiful Resort-Islands and England and They don't want to tell us. The state flag could hint of this, possibly. As if...maybe Hawaii is more a state of the British Empire than it is a U.S. state? Years ago, I would never have blamed the Mandela for the INSANITIES around me, because I had never heard of it. But after investigation, now I can. Today, the world is filled with madness and dark magic. The Other World, charged-positively, had less.

The Russian Flag has oddly added a 5-pointed star. Exactly like product logos and banners have changed, so has their national flag, according to some surprised Russians. Their flag is called "Hammer and Sickle" and "The Red Banner." Union of hammer and sickle represents the Soviets' "victorious and enduring revolutionary alliance." The red star on the flag "represents the Communist Party." Why would, again, there be reports that a piece of reality was different here with a star? The M.E. supernatural phenomenon seems to be happening more and more. Does the star mean more slavery for the masses? Try to notice the differences and remember. My memory was a red flag, hammer and sickle and no star.

Another banner has added a 5-pointed star in red and black...
(Author's note: For your information, 5-pointed stars are evil and symbolize the Baphomet, the Goat. Invert the 5-pointed star, point down, and you have a billy-goat: horns, ears and a goatee. 5-pointed stars and their inner pentagram (like our Pentagon, largest building on Earth) within a magic circle, adorn covers of Witchcraft books, hundreds of years old. We have 50 of the fuckers on our national flag. Don't turn the U.S. flag upside-down because you'll have 50 symbols of Satan there. Didn't you know? [My catch-phrase]).
...The banner is the Macy's logo (just as powerful as Russia). It also added a 5-pointed star that was not there before, to some who have reported the change. There was one 5-pointed star on Macy's red and black (you know what those colors mean?) logo. Now there are two. Gee, is it as simple as *Evil is growing?*

One more Mandela change that was mentioned in Volume I, but not analyzed in detail. Here's as good a place as any to write about...

People have reported that the chevrons at the Chevron gas stations have switched positions. Their big signs with the red and blue pill, I mean the red and blue chevrons. Maybe they have switched? I'm not sure. Supposedly. Red was on top. Now Blue is on top. Does the change have a meaning?

Readers might claim I am *reading into everything,* placing significance to items that have no significance or meaning. That view could be true, here and there. But I have a lot of knowledge. I've researched secret societies for more than 40 years. Have you? As an Outsider, I had to work like crazy to learn from occult (hidden) sources and had investigated everything I could. Studied in libraries long before there were computers available to muggles. I've learned their symbols, their codes in numbers, images and in words. Have you? They know the meanings to what powerful Club Members have put In Plain Sight, all around us. We do not. The few Outsiders that try to learn secrets of the super rich are like detectives, always disrespected as "Conspiracy Theorists." And often are *killed* because of the Truth. Conspiracy Theorists are mostly correct, that's why they've received so much ridicule and abuse.

What if the reported difference in Chevron signs across the country...has to do with the BLUEBLOODS that rule the planet Earth and somewhat of spaces beyond? Bluebloods! The bloody royals! You didn't think the BLUE on our Flag stood for the pretty blue skies of America, did you? Oh dear, Oh dear, Oh dear. There are a zillion truths They know and you don't. For example, July 4th is their joke on you, that's not when this "country" truly started. That's a lie for commoners. We celebrate, annually, with all those fireworks! And they laugh at us for not knowing their secrets, such as the secret charter of real architects of this New World was established on May 1st (Mayflower), not July 4th. That's the lie. We are exactly the same as Russia, U.S. and U.S.S.R., both superpowers are really not. Our technology is the same as Russian technology (Cold War was a farce), everything orchestrated by Britain, covertly, high above.

Maybe the British Bluebloods rule us, utterly, now? Blue on top....and we bloody die in Red on the bottom? Statue of Liberty has always meant Their Liberties, not ours. The Freedom They have over us, as Overlords. The freedom we think we have is only a false, faint, propped-up joke.

'Where in the World is Carman Sandiego?' The animated character has a Mandela attached to her. Her trenchcoat was yellow, now it's red. Red. Significance to the red change? Well, how about 'Blood'? Red on the U.S. flag represents blood, as in war. That's not debated. Have you seen much blood in movies, lately? Seen any films that did *not* have blood? Also, in movies, why are there so many killer-women drenched in the blood of men? I remember girls, ladies, women being soft, warm, sweet creatures, the "fairer" sex. NO MORE. Girls will kick guy's asses every time now! *You know it's true, it's in movies and on TV!*

I think Carman's change from yellow to red might have significance. I remember yellow. That image in my mind and others is nowhere to be found today. It be red.

I am quite positive the blue stripe on our $100 dollar bills have changed. The change was not announced by our government. One day, a few years ago...*it just changed*...along with the other differences. Mandela. I don't have a lot of experience with big bills, but I believe it was a solid blue stripe. A friend of mine at the bank confirmed that it was one blue stripe. Now it's in 3 pieces. Broken twice. 1 to 3. Hmmm. I have no idea. Except for that crazy concept I heard a little while ago: German pagans celebrating the "Trinity." No, that's probably wrong. Funny, if it was right?

There is a Pocahontas and Captain John Smith Mandela Effect as well as a decent "Pocahontas and Captain John Smith" anagram. The anagram is: "Champs join hands to patch a nation." Switch the letters around and it's true. The Mandela is now a new history where they were *never married.* Never married, really? They didn't help "patch" the nation?

(Author's note: a very good psychic once told me I was Captain John Smith and *Galileo*. The Smith-one surprised me. I found out that New World Indians were ready to kill and eat Captain Smith and his men, but he saved the day when he pulled out a compass. They'd never seen such technology. He gave the compass to Chief Powatan and won the hand of Pocahontas. I was reminded that Galileo invented the compass and I wrote one of my first short stories. In it, Galileo invented a compass that saved his own soul in a future-life as John Smith. Neat. But don't tell me I wasn't married to that tanned, topless, tattooed Indian who also saved my life and later became a U.S. politician! *Because I think I was!* Never married? I wish in *this life* I was never married! I am so funny).

"Rubbing Our Face In It" (what They did to the World).

Why 'Stan and Ollie' now?

In 2018, (three years after I've concluded the prime Mandela Wave struck us) a terrible British movie was made that concerned the later days of the famous comedy team, Laurel and Hardy. John C. Reilly played Oliver Hardy and Steve Coogan played Stan Laurel. In the story, the duo wanted to reignite their waning careers in a "swan song," which became a grueling theatre tour of post-war London and Berlin. There was absolutely no reason for this slow, dry, drab, post-war movie to be produced and distributed. I've decoded why. Laurel and Hardy is a major Mandela Effect. My theory is: This movie doesn't exist in the Old World, but it does here. The reason it exists on this Side is to *Shove In our Face* what They've done. They mock us 'inferior' commoners for not knowing. But They, in the KNOW, in the Secret/British Cabal of celebrity-monsters, they know!

You see, the Laurel and Hardy classic line has *changed.* The old comedy team has one of the greatest and most memorable movie-lines of all time. We should all know it, exactly. From the mouth of Oliver Hardy, it went like this: **"That's another fine mess you got me into."**

That's not the line anymore, even though one of their earliest comedies from 1930 is entitled: **'Another Fine Mess.'** (Author's note: The poster that advertised the film was, of course, also called 'Another Fine Mess' and led me to the film when I first realized it was a Mandela. I couldn't believe that such a famous line changed, and it changed in each and every L&H film and short. AFM was only 28 minutes in its entirety and I was able to view it online). When it came time for Oliver Hardy to deliver the classic line, he said it wrong. I guess he said it right for the antimatter universe, but he said it wrong for the matter universe (the good one that I've lost).

It's been changed or replaced by the line: **"That's another nice mess you got me into."** Yeah, nice. Even in the 28-minute short called 'Another Fine Mess' (with poster), Oliver said it differently, he said: "...another nice mess..." I reviewed a 30-minute compilation video of their best moments and the *classic* line was said over and over again. Every time, "nice" was stated, and never "fine."

I'll bet this was why the movie 'Stan and Ollie' was created by the British and that, of course, had to be the setting, only because Stan was English. It couldn't have been centered in America and be about Oliver? No. It's all British, like everything. This bad movie was done so we'd be fooled again and the Movers and Shakers of the world could think of themselves as IN, 'in the know' and superior to all of us muggles because we do not know.

Why 'Mr. Rogers' with Tom Hanks now?

You don't know? I'll also bet there are Mandela people who know. This is a huge Mandela with 'Mr. Roger's Neighborhood' and the iconic song, sung in the beginning, that everyone knows well. Why produce a bad movie on the subject, at this particular time? It's called: **'A Beautiful Day in the Neighborhood'** (2019). The song is the title! What did Tom Hanks do as Fred Rogers in the first minute of the film? He sung his song that should be as familiar to us as the torture of Disney's 'It's a Small World.' Guess what he sang? He sang THE CHANGE. He sang it *differently than the title of the film* and what we remember. Do you understand? The audience saw the title, which is the Mandelaed-lyric! "...in the Neighborhood" only to hear Hanks mess up the lyric a minute later when he sang: "...in this neighborhood."

Again, with Tom Hanks. Do you know how many Mandelas surround Tom Hanks and his movie-lines? A lot.

You don't know why They made this film? This is why They made the film. To laugh at the global audience for not realizing what the masonic royals have done. The title of the film is what we remember and what Mr. Rogers had always sung. But Fred, and Tom as Fred, now sing a different word? They've shoved another "shit-pie" hard into our kissers! What They have handed to us on a silver platter makes no sense whatsoever. We should be aware of the fact.

"We are the Champions"

If readers have 'followed the breadcrumbs,' then they might come to the same conclusion as I have. THEY have forced and are forcing upon us what They know in code and we do not. This is exactly like the word-code, image-code, number/letter-code the Illuminati know and use, but we do not. **Secret** practices and rituals that have happened behind the Curtain of Hollywood, beneath the surface of elite society for generations. Also right out in the open, televised for us to Not See. ["Wanna be a member! Wanna be a member!" Betty Boop encouraged young men].

Why make 'Bohemian Rhapsody,' the 2018 Queen movie? Title above is an obvious clue. One more main Mandela here as stated by numerous researchers and celebrities like George Clooney. The world is gone and the lyric: "...Of the world!" is no longer at the end of the classic Queen song. Freddie Mercury still sang it in the chorus. But it ended with the line and it's gone now. When I first saw the film, it ended with "...of the World!" (I think). When I watched it again, it did not. They waited until the very end. It was, "We are the champions, _____. Roll credits.

Again, there was no reason to make the film. Why Queen of all bands? Did Liz have a hand in this? The only reason was: It's a big Mandela and billions of people are unaware that they are within a new and different, Dark World, where little makes sense. But millions of the richest and most powerful people, the 1% of the highest 1%, They've been told and it's been demonstrated to Them. The elites understand precisely the negative universe their Masters forced us into and all around us, like The Matrix~

Why 'Ford v Ferrari'?

Obviously, (or maybe not obviously?) there is a Mandela Effect here. The classic Ford logo in a blue oval contains one of the largest Mandelas as far as product logos go. It, of course, is the pig curly-Q on the capital "F" of 'Ford.' You really believe it was always there, do you? The logo has not changed over time or been upgraded. If there's been no change, what accounts for large numbers of people who've realized: The "F" didn't used to have a twist on the middle bar. It was a normal capital "F." Now, not. Look how long Fords have been around. The record, history, or new reality in place is the twisted bar on Ford's "F" had always been there. I guess the large group of people who remember a normal "F" are wrong and simply have forgotten? No. I remember a normal capital "F."

The terrible movie, a British movie AGAIN, with big stars, did not need to be made and served no purpose. The only real purpose for the huge film, that originally cast Tom Cruise and Brad Pitt in lead roles, was to *Rub In Our Face* what They've done to the Ford logo (and the world). Did you see how many times the logo was shown and flashed, even in the promos for the film? Too many. This was to, again, *push* what They've done onto a (nearly) totally unsuspecting public.

Readers are certainly free to disagree with my idea that the entire film was created and distributed for one purpose...to *Shove in our Face* that little curly-Q on the "F."

Mirror Mirror.

'Mirror Mirror' was released on April 20, 2012. It starred Julia Roberts as Queen Clementianna, Snow White's evil stepmother. What else? "An evil queen steals control of a kingdom and an exiled princess enlists the help of seven resourceful rebels to win back her birthright." Why make this movie? Was it really necessary? Are you sure it was an American movie and not a British movie? Always with the Queen, princess, castle, royal themes, again? (First Americans were against all of that. Now, royal themes are everywhere). A suspicious person, aware of the Mandela Effect [on the threshold of M.E. in 2012, end of Mayan calendar], might think 'Mirror Mirror' was produced because THEY knew of the Disney Mandela in the animated 'Snow White.' Why would this Julia Roberts-vehicle be called 'Mirror Mirror,' when it was never said or read that way in 'Snow White'? Yes, it was. Shouldn't this movie be called: 'Magic Mirror'? And also the Star Trek episode, named: 'Mirror Mirror.' It's a Mandela and probably why this movie was made. Another poop pie.

"The Northwest Angle"

On CBS' Sunday morning show (you know, the one with the evil, golden, 11-sided, pagan Sun-Symbol in the lower right corner?) was another example of a *Rubbing It In Our Face* moment, to me. THEY know what They've done to the physical world, switched it with a different world. It looks very much the same, except for here, here, here and here in the Matrix. Those are the Mandela differences that some Outsiders have woken up to and have realized. Certainly, Insiders are well aware of the major changes. (Clooney was acting). Illuminati are the top Elites who make our world events, our celebrities, our Movies, our Sports, our Music and our TV shows. CBS, the One-Eye (Satan/Saturn) everywhere, always there, like a Big Brother tele-screen? Are you watching TV or is it watching you? My point is: This is a Mandela in the same way there were never two Michigans in the Old World. Also. In the Old World, there was never a spit of ground, a spike of American land that went straight north into Canada and was called the "Northwest Angle."

"...If you want to get to the Northwest Angle [U.S. land], travelers have to leave the U.S. and go through Canada to get there." What? Called a "geographical quirk along the northern border" and "gateway to an American, geographical oddity, Minnesota's Northwest Angle." (It's not even an angle or in the "Northwest").

It's like someone put a substantial part of Minnesota in Canada, by mistake. In fact, it was a "mistake" and made during the Treaty of Paris. "The border was supposed to cut through Lake of the Woods at a northwest angle." The problem was the British and Founding Fathers used maps of Lake of the Woods that were way off. But the weird "boundary bump" stuck.

There's an official station, which is only a modest shed with a video-phone, called "Jim's Corner." *Americans have to check-in with Jim* before moving on. Seriously? Yep. There are only gravel roads, no street lights, no grocery stores, hospitals or theaters in the Northwest Angle. There is a sparse population. Families have to travel for many hours, weekly, to reach the closest stores.

The sensible, reasonable, logical question is: Why the heck would you have to check-in with Canadian Immigration to travel to American soil? Americans cannot visit United States territory unless they check-in at Jim's shed? Does anything make any sense anymore? No.

A few residents of the "Angle" tried to secede from the United States in the 1990s and join Canada over a fishing dispute. Fish weren't allowed to be taken across the border. The "Walleye War," yes, the Walleye War, was settled and the Northwest Angle remained a part of America. I'm serious, look it up.

Why broadcast such a feature at this particular time? Was there ever anything, any program or lesson in school on Minnesota's Spike? Ever? You've always heard of this "Angle" into Canada your entire life? Were you really taught all about it in high school? Not me.

Expect another *Rubbing It In Our Face* moment if CBS does a piece on: Why are there 2 Michigans? Same thing. Two Michigans and the "Angle" were never a part of the Old World. They are a "reality" today in this shitty New World. I WOULD NEVER HAVE MISSED THEM! They would be a part of my experience and many others, but they really are not. We have to be educated about them *now?* Why didn't we know this before? I only recently looked up: 'Why are there 2 Michigans?' And this late in life, I learned for the very first time *why.* Does this sound familiar to you, a historical fact you learned back in high school? "Surveying errors" and "hated Ohio." Yeah! "Hated Ohio." That is what you will discover if you asked Google: Why 2 parts to Michigan? Seems it was a part of Ohio? How can that be? No one wanted this mistaken patch of land above Wisconsin. So, hell, Michigan took it, now there be two Michigans. We never learned this before. Again, surveying errors? Sounds like the poor, shoddy maps of Lake of the Woods. Is everybody fucked-up and everything fucked-up in this horrible, parallel world? Maybe. Look at the similarities that surround these two "quirks" that are absolutely geographical Mandelas. Many people do not remember the Angle; the north border was straight across, horizontally. No northward spike of U.S. land. One Michigan in my world, but this isn't my world.

"You Like Me, Right Now!"

From Volume I: "On the evening of 2/21/19, I watched an episode of 'The Orville,' which last season was 'Orville.' At first, it was fantastic and so large of a show that I figured it was a 2-parter. Isaac, the android, who was having an affair with the doctor, suddenly shutdown. They took the robot to its home world, a cybernaut planet, which they thought wanted to join their "Union." As it turned out, Isaac was only a spy who gathered info on whether or not humans should be totally destroyed? They never wanted to join; they only wanted to judge us and then decide to terminate or not? The crew discovered underground caverns where millions of their human Builders were piled, dead. I was stunned and overwhelmed for a few reasons:

1) They, the insiders, dared miss-quote Sally Field's Oscar acceptance speech, but to them: *was not miss-quoted* and was stated in the way it's been changed. Every spoof of it, and there have been hundreds, never inserted: "Right now!" Those bastards, last night, **rubbed it in America's face!** That date must mark the first spoof on film of Sally's altered speech. Now, like everything else (including the Bible), we have to accept the Darkness, believe it's always been this way?

2) The show was far from original; it was the same plot as Prometheus 2. Why would the Engineers be killed off entirely by robot David or why would the Engineers seek to destroy Earth, the humans they've created? It's abominable, because God does not want to destroy its creations and we do not want to destroy God. Now killer androids with WMD are on their way to wipe out Earth! Gee, wonder what's going to happen? Ya think Isaac will have a change of heart? Instead of providing good, far-out stories anymore, with positive messages...there's much too much witchcraft, blood, red/black, Killer-Women, parents killing children and children killing parents? What a world~"

Why air one more parody of her speech on Orville? Why mimic a played-out joke again? And why would the crew make fun of something hundreds of years before their time? The answer is: They just tossed in a known Mandela. They know, you don't...not so much. There was no reason whatsoever, outside of the fact that They are rubbing, you know? (I even used my terminology for it back then. Still true). They made fun of us muggles, not 'in the know.'

The changed [broken cross "t"] 20th Century Fox logo is brought up at this point because suddenly a documentary of the logo has appeared on YouTube. Why now? Simply a coincidence, happenstance, serendipity? Or does its production and distribution on YT have a secret significance with the Mandela? In 20 years with personal computers and more than 10 years straight virtually "living on YouTube," I have viewed nothing on this subject. Why now is there one about the logo? In the beginning, the video tried to explain when it showed YT forums of *people asking for a full history of the logo.* This is not convincing and could have been a bogus set-up.

In the history-video, we learned that the first logo was in 1955 and was "T.C.F." surrounded by 8 dark pillars like the '2001' monolith and 7 lightning bolts. In the next version, the monoliths changed to lighter columns, possibly golden crowns. Then, the logo changed and only contained: "2OTH CENTURY FOX," all capital letters, even the "TH." It wasn't until 1957 that a 3D, art deco design with projected lights was used, the one we're familiar with today. *This was when the broken "t" design was first seen."* Since 1957, ever since I was 6 years old? So (I'm supposed to believe) my entire life, when I viewed thousands of 20th Century Fox movie opening-credits, the "t" was always broken? And, son of a gun, it's only in recent years that I've noticed? No, sir. That's not it. The broken "t," broken cross, on 20th Century has only appeared in the last half dozen years, while most of the world hasn't noticed and believe *it was always like that.* No one would think the logo had changed, if it hadn't changed. A large number of people have agreed: the logo is different. I'm one of them.

I think They've been telling us what happened with the Mandela, emphasizing the differences in secret code that They know and we do not. I would not be surprised if a video surfaced on the history of the Volkswagen logo. That would be another R.O.F.I.I. moment.

One more possible *Rubbing Our Face In It* moment, might have occurred during a 'RIFFTRAX' episode. RT is a spawn of Mystery Science Theater. The "boys" have continued what they do best and "riff" (made fun of) bad movies and even very good movies. They did Star Wars, 'The Force Awakens,' and when it came to a sitting Snoke...they said: "I wonder what made Lincoln turn to the Dark Side?" Yes, Snoke was giant-sized, like the Lincoln Memorial in D.C. There was a creepy, smoky atmosphere around the creature. But there was also Snoke with his right-hand open and his left-hand made a fist. The Lincoln Memorial is a Mandela. Both hands of the statue were down and held the ends of the armrests. Lincoln's hands were the same. Now, the statue's left-hand made a fist and possibly some of the carved words behind it have altered. Could be a coincidence, or: The people who wrote RIFFTRAX (and zillions of other scripts) are connected to the Big Boys who have changed our world (switched it with its negative version). I'd bet the sentence was one of a bunch of references, which were really secret code. The Big Boys know what They did and They have designed and engineered everything that their minions broadcast to us. Of course, They'll never admit to the public what They did with the Mandela Wave, but their comedic slaves will joke about the changes. They'll make movies of the Mandelas as if these changes (New World) were always that way. If we're very smart at decoding, we'd see the patterns and know what movie-lines and lyrics really were.

Newly discovered: *Rubbing our faces in their shit.* Guess what TV mini-series Johnny Depp will voice, of all people? An animated series about Puffins. *"Puffins* follows the adventures of a bunch of funny little birds, minions of the sly walrus Otto." Depp voiced a cute, little character called "Johnny Puff." Are you kidding me? In my reality and in some others: **Puffins were extinct!** I knew they were flightless and had a weird beak. They are a known Mandela to researchers and these odd birds must be known as a Mandela to elite "minion" filmmakers. C'mon! Why do a Laurel & Hardy movie or Ford movie or this crap about Puffins? The birds were extinct to some people...but now, Wham Bam, they're not. (p.s. I wish I could make a bet, push a Truth-Button and we'd see where the money landed, eh? I'd bet I'd win more than I lost).

I've discovered that movies, TV, commercials, Internet, etc., do not reflect what is out there in society among decent human beings. MEDIA is made to absolutely be TERRIBLE now, and its only purpose [movies/TV] is to tear down society, bring it to its very worst and ultimately DESTROY the masses. George Orwell might agree. This is easily done today...in a Darkened World.

(Another Author's note: As I have suggested to people who want to know the truth...*trans-vestigate!* See YouTube transvestigations that are available and you'll discover maybe the Biggest Secret: **Royalty and famous men in all fields and famous women in all fields are not the gender they appear!** The result of what hormones can do. Powerful Magicians have been fooling generations of us lowly muggles who haven't as yet caught-on to their magic tricks. To illustrate the point, I thought of a short story premise but never attempted getting the idea down on paper. I'll mention it here:

It was entitled: 'Naked World' and concerned a parallel Earth where...*everyone was naked.* No one thought it strange or embarrassing to be nude. It was perfectly normal. People were civil and courteous. Young boys didn't rage with pheromones when they saw breasts or any other part of a girl's naked body. It was as if the whole planet was a Nudist Camp. Nudity was natural. People wore clothes in cooler and colder climates and in the evenings. But in summer or in tropical regions, why wear clothes? People behaved properly, with respect. Public nudity was not against the law. People were naked in restaurants, movie theaters and in stadium crowds when it was warm. ["You mean, there are planets where human beings wore clothes, when they didn't have to? How weird."].

In this world, the Illuminati (British) would never have been able to pull off their Big Magic Trick and laugh at us stupid fools for not knowing it. Audiences would view movies and television with broadcasters, actors, actresses, hosts of talk shows, news-people, weather-persons, etc., of every type, and every single person would be naked (except for movies/TV in cold settings)...

We, the viewers, would know immediately if the person was a man or a woman. There could be no magical Deception. Genitalia would be staring us in the face and it would be very clear. We might be able to tell if someone was Jewish or not? We'd know if we dealt with a hermaphrodite or a eunuch. *C'mon!* They couldn't fool us with secret trans-genders in 'Naked World,' now could They?

That's how They get away with it and continue to do so. We believe the illusion, the 'curtain.' the surface. We tend to see only the surface. Wow, would we be shocked at what stood behind the curtains and underneath everything! When we view our movies and TV, we see clothed people. The actor in that love scene we have ASSUMED was a man. The actress in that love scene we have ASSUMED was a woman. Invert it completely around, folks, and you have the truth: twisted British trannies, or owned by twisted British trannies. The "man" with a widow's peak, no neck and droopy shoulders, is really a woman. The "woman" with no "peak," long neck, straight shoulders, big head/hands and feet, is really a man, *under the skin.*

I thought it was a funny story and very revealing.

They've made us stupid dogs. They treat us like stupid dogs. They tell us in Code, just what They've done to us (movies/TV). They are *Rubbing Our Face in their Bullshit-World* and expect us slaves to believe it and love it. I hate Them for what They've done to the children and the precious hope of a brighter tomorrow.

More Predictive Programming.

(Author's note: This section is a much more extended version of 'Predictive Programming" than what was presented in Volume I. PP is the fact that filmmakers play terrible (In-House) jokes on us, the innocent and unsuspecting public. "They," those on top, know all about the Mandela because *They did it!* They produce movies and TV which suggest the same pattern in stories, over and over again, as if there were no other stories in the universe. Later in this section, a long line of movies will be presented and their plots shown. Why so many consistencies in films? Could it be that they were not independent productions, but connected, under the 'umbrella' of horrible forces (Illuminati/masons) in the world? Filmmakers must obey their Masters (British Monsters) that made them, set them up. And must answer and obey higher Authorities who really wrote the scripts for their movies and for their lives. It's the same messages of Magic and Wonderlands, but mostly dark Mirror-worlds, the Other Side. There's too many stories with the same themes. If you don't have access to movies, you do if you go to **123.movies.com,** a huge archive is available for free.)

Here's what happened, how I discovered that the **2015 'FANTASTIC FOUR' film might be the biggest, brightest example of Predictive Programming that clearly described what the Royals did and had planned for later that year: The main Mandela Wave that swallowed the Earth and transformed it and FORCED all of us to the Dark Side.** I simply wanted to be entertained one evening and view a movie. Since I was hard pressed to find anything good on YT or anything new in the archive, I decided to see (like I often do) a movie I'd seen before, but it was years ago. Okay. I picked FF from 2015, oblivious for the moment that it was made in a very special year for me and my M.E. theories. (See Volume I). I jumped around the video and was soon totally awestruck. "Oh, my God!" It seemed like almost every line spoken talked of the Mandela. Then I checked the date. *Eureka, the motherload!* See, I hated this movie when I first saw a poor quality version of it 6 years ago. Six years ago, I had no clue what a Mandela was or that this was a FILM (not a mere movie) and had incredible significance to the Illuminati. I watched it with ignorant eyes back then, I'm sure. I saw how badly Thing's face was done with a computer. That formed a prejudice in me against everything in the film. Obviously, very little registered then, so when I viewed it now, WOW! It was as if I saw it for the first time. In HD and with what I know now about a Mandela Effect, it was like a big Christmas tree was lit inside me! Same feeling I had when I realized what your fucking Queen meant when she said at the end of 2015: "Enjoy your Last Christmas." The last time the world was real and not inverted. That statement and more, like Diana had to be dealt with and the coming Darkness that will consume the Light, have oddly disappeared. But thousands of listeners in her realm heard it on her yearly Christmas radio address. I believe that's when it happened: End of 2015, when our world was turned inside-out, upside-down and pushed into *The Looking Glass.* We were all good Dr. Jekylls, now we're sinister Mr. Hydes and our world is very different. **They** tell us what They've done and will do to us in films, music, etc. It's called 'In Plain Sight.' They laugh at us for our ignorance and for not being special and in their secret Club. Follow along with the 2015 FF film as described in the next pages. Are these parallels to Mandela all coincidences? That many? Or is a more reasonable and knowledgeable viewpoint: This is prime Predictive Programming, purposely placed there for Them to know, and for you to **Not See** it?).

Oyster Bay, New York, 2007:
On Career Day, young student Reed Richards in glasses (like Peter Parker) addressed the class...
"When I grow up, I want to be the first person in human history to teleport himself."
The class and teacher laughed at him.
The boy continued: "It's already possible to transport quantum information to another place. Right now there are Super-Computers that can transport quantum information through space. So why not a machine that can send people through space?"
The teacher interrupted that *you can't build such a thing.*
(Author's note: They'll be a lot of interruptions before we get through this, a film so rich in a diverse wealth of secret Agenda and CODE! The next words were unbelievable and unrealistic. Just go with it).
"I've already built it! Well, I'm building it, in my garage." [p.s. It only needed a power converter. He's in the 5th grade. Here's the

problem: First scene had him with a pencil in his hand and the boy didn't know *how to properly hold a pencil.* How smart is he if he couldn't hold a pen to its optimum position? It's a pet-peeve of mine. I've used keen observation skills on the youth around me. I've found, when I went to the doctor's office, pot store or any place a millennial wrote with a writing instrument like a pen or Sharpie, they did not know how to hold it. To them, there were a hundred variations and each one was correct. This generation hadn't been taught correctly (about anything). They had no practice in writing the right way. They had teachers that didn't care. Why use a pen if there was a keyboard and they did nothing but text? Why would they know how to write and hold a pen or pencil? I found the youth didn't know. A monkey held a pencil better than some of them. Oh, what you could have accomplished if you were only taught properly! Anyway, back to the film...].

Classmate, Ben Grimm looked on.

The teacher (voice of Homer Simpson) sarcastically said: "Is it next to your flying car?"

More laughter. (Of all things, one of the most important items hidden from the general public: Jetson-like hovercrafts. They've had anti-gravity for decades, and much more, but not for you. Do you know what time it is? Where are your hoverboards?).

Little Reed actually said: "I'm not working on that anymore, just this now. I call it the 'Bio-Matter Shuttle.' Technically, I'm shuttling matter from one place to another."

The teacher cut him off.

Later, when audiences viewed Ben Gimm's grim home-life, he had an abusive brother and a violent mother. What else, these days? The Grimms owned a junkyard and guess who found a Power Converter there? [*Sure, that's believable*]. Reed and Ben's friendship began at this moment; they worked together on the Transporter project.

Of course, the experiment worked. They transported matter, but matter also appeared (rocks and dirt). [I'm reminded of the real, light-speed, flight of Ralph Ring on an OTC (Otis T. Carr) test saucer in 1960. When they returned and beamed back, they had rocks and twigs in their pockets *they'd forgotten* they'd gathered when they left the saucer. I interviewed Ralph Ring and our interview is online].

Ben: "Where'd the rocks come from?"

Reed: "Someplace the (model) car went to..."

"Where is that?"

"I don't know yet."

"Reed? You're insane."

"Thanks."

Time jumped years ahead and the characters were at the high school's Science Fair. Reed and Ben presented what they had worked on "since the 5th grade." When other students offered models of the Solar System or volcanoes that erupted, these two had a *teleporter!*

The demonstration caused some damage. They were ridiculed again, even by a younger student ("You're a dick.").

You'll never guess what happened next...

Magically, Franklin Storm and Sue Storm entered, stage-left, and stood by Reed and his machine. *Wait a minute!* Since when was the father of the Human Torch (Johnny) and Invisible Girl (Sue) black? This created its own firestorm in 2015 when it was announced. Why would they change that? Why the new/modern need to change the classics? Johnny Storm was as blonde as you can get. Sister Sue, also blonde. But she wasn't in the movie. It made no sense, but the Media hardly gave a platform for the outrage. Media was only there to support anything doled out by Hollywood and our British Lords and Masters. Media mainly repeated how "ignorant" these people were who objected. How dare they? They reported from many sources that the "casting for the movie, due in June 2015, is a great choice." And we all have to fall in line with the Nazi propaganda? Not me.

This was produced by Marvel? The list of absurdities were endless. How did the Storms know of a special high school Science Fair? The "machine" had only been ridiculed. But miraculously, Reed had succeeded in the very same endeavor that the Storms had worked on, unsuccessfully.

"This is elegant," Franklin commented. [Just remembered, "Franklin" was a 'Peanuts' cartoon character and he was black. Might mean nothing].

After a little technical talk, Franklin Storm expressed to his daughter as Reed overheard: "That's why we can't bring the matter back from the other dimension..."

"What?" Reed asked in amazement.

"We've gone so far as to send matter to another dimension. But we haven't gone so far as to bring that matter back...You just did."

"Are you serious?"

Franklin stated: "I think you've cracked inter-dimensional travel."

Richards was confused. He said, "We're, we're not sending anything to another dimension. We send something, we think, to another part of the planet, but, I don't know about another dimension..."

"We've found the same thing you did," Sue Storm said, then handed Reed a small vial (dirt). [Hey, I thought you couldn't bring anything back? Now you have a vial of stuff you brought back? What?].

Franklin informed Reed and Ben: "We're from the Baxter Foundation..."

Reed and Ben were taken to New York. Ben was there momentarily, but left, wasn't a part of the project, initially.

A very weird and most revealing meeting happened in a library with cool [cold] Sue and uncool Reed. She played Portishead music on her headset; he hadn't heard of them. He showed her '20,000 Leagues Under the Sea' by Jules Verne, as if she'd hadn't heard of the novel? It was bizarre to view Sue Storm, who apparently, was a German 'robot' now. She confessed what music was to her: "pattern recognition," and nothing more. There was no joy on her expressionless face. She felt no warmth or love or received any feelings at all from music, like normal people felt. "Music is just a series of altered patterns. Musicians create the pattern and makes us anticipate resolution [like Pavlov's dogs], and holds back, makes you wait for it. There's patterns in everything and in everyone..." (Later, she rejected that the 4 had powers; the new abilities were only abnormalities to her).

"What's mine?" Reed asked.

"You want to be famous. Your parents, teachers all told you one thing, one way to be and you ignored them..."

"Am I that predictable?"

"Everybody is," she stated, cold and callous.

Reed replied, "Well, you're wrong. I don't want to be famous. I want my work to make a difference."

Sue stood up, ready to walk away. She said, "Well, here you are, Captain Nemo. Go for it."

The scene shifted to an impressive meeting between Franklin, the board and a federal minion, symbolized by an official we've seen before ('Soggy Bottom Boys' with Clooney). Franklin told them: "This has real world applications. I truly believe that there's..."

The official completed his statement: "An entirely new universe just beyond our ability to see." [As in Infrared or Ultraviolet spectrums?] "Yes, I've read your paper."

Franklin: "This is our chance to learn about our planet." (ps. Don't they all say that? As in Prometheus?). "And maybe even save it? And I'm sure you agree..."

"Wait. What is this?" the official questioned as he turned a page. "Victor Von Doom is involved?" The official rattled off a list of awful minor crimes Victor had committed.

Franklin defended him and the other young people on the project. "I need his talent. I believe he and Reed can get us there."

Later, Franklin Storm visited Von Doom's pad. Victor was a sleazy derelict with long hair. [Hey, why are all "good people" always portrayed with bald or very short hair, like that's normal? Only for Nazis. And madmen, like the commercial with the maniac in the barn, are almost always shown with long hair? Could this be fascist programming? Social engineering? Fucking hippie! Look at you bald, tattooed youth today, lovin' your Rap Music, smokin' cigarettes and you think you are not VICTIMS of British Engineers? Or that you're Americans, when there's no such thing? Pet-peeves.].

Storm coaxed Victor to join the project.

"Susan going to be there?"

Back at the project, a big test was performed...

Sue told Reed: "It's amazing..."

Reed replied, "Thanks."

"...It's amazing you didn't black out the entire western hemisphere..."

"Hm?"

You basically ripped a hole in the fabric of space/time with un-spect components and no supervision."

"Yeah, it was an accident."

Like a machine, Sue responded: "And by accident, the Power would have created a 'Run-away' reaction and opened a Black Hole and SWALLOWED THE ENTIRE PLANET. (It did, in the real world, Mandela)."

Reed: "Well, well, I'm glad that didn't happen."

Sue: "Anyone who goes to the other dimension needs to be protected." [As in the movie 'Upside-Down,' it burned?].

"Who's that?" Reed asked Sue.

"That's Victor. He started the whole project."

"Oh."

Victor cut his hair. He criticized Reed's "childish" notes.

Franklin introduced Reed to Victor. He told Reed, "He started this Quantum Gate project when he was younger than you."

Victor commented (same joke as before with Sue), "It's pretty impressive..."

"Thank you."

"...That you nearly destroyed an entire planet with speaker cables and aluminum foil."

"Yeah, that was an accident."

Sue: "He did get it to work."

Reed noticed an image on a screen. "What is this?"

They moved in front of it. The screen visualized the other desolate planet.

(The planet was never mentioned as a twin or Dark Earth. Only as the Other Side and other *dimension* or *world*. Why, when first shown, did the normal blue/green Earth pop up first? Then its reddened/blackened parallel appeared next to it? "Scientists called it Planet Zero," but that term was never repeated.

Victor: "This is where your little accident leads to."

Sue: "We put a camera on a drone we sent over there. The drone didn't come back, but those images did."

Reed: "It's beautiful." (Author's note: No, it isn't. It's hideous).

Victor supported Reed with: "Yes, it is. New energies, new resources, a whole New World."

Franklin: "Which can help save this one."

Von Doom expressed: "Not that it deserves to be saved. Think about it. **People running the Earth, are the same people running it into the ground**" (So true). "...It deserves what it's got coming to it."

Sue replied with irony (or bad writing): "Dr. Doom, over here."

Sue's father said, "The failures of my generation are the opportunities for yours."

Once more, pounded into viewing audiences in later scenes: *What we all can accomplish if we (empowered) people worked together!* What Bullshit! Like lies told over Media today. People have no power and cannot get together, was the actual truth.

Next we meet future Human Torch, who was only a street 'gang-banger' at the time. *And he's black?* Right, right. Of course, he was black. Old man Franklin was black! What's wrong with this picture? What's wrong with this movie? Everything! This was from Marvel? Now we have Johnny Storm as a black dude. Really? (Angry Author's Note: It wasn't enough that They changed Captain Marvel into a Woman?! A black animated Spiderman wasn't enough? A black woman as the new James Bond, huh, England? That wasn't enough? Your fucking Queen and her fucking Lords and Masters had declared: **God was now a Woman!** Ask Ariana ("witch") Grande with her song: 'God is a Woman.' But now. Not only is God a Woman, but she's a Black Woman. Didn't you know? Obviously, a female-Jesus is next. *Since all that will be true by 2021,* of course, They thought nothing of making Johnny a black street "gangsta." Remember what DC and Marvel comic books were? Does everything have to change? Nothing changes 'Into Lightness,' or for the better, does it? There are people who demand sameness and for everything to *not change.* Stability, consistency, for our children to believe in something solid, static, real, good. They will be greatly disappointed in the New World of Tomorrow (today), where everything was forced to be wrong and backwards. While everyone was made to love and adore monstrous changes that have happened and will happen more and more in future. They have ruined the sci-fi and superhero genre, completely. That was the Plan of the Engineers from the very beginning. Success! Maybe *you* must tolerate and accept all that is wrong from British filmmakers and Hollywood. I'm a rebel. I'm different. I do not. And right now, I have to shave. It's a metaphor for being free).

Side note: George Takei (Sulu), who is gay in real life, was highly offended by the Sulu in the new Star Trek movies. The character was made gay, and he never was before. George was on record and said: "This would offend Gene Roddenberry, who never wrote the character that way."

It's unbelievable that blonde Johnny and blonde sister Sue had been radically messed with, their whole relationship *had* to be updated? Had to be changed? No, it didn't. Race was never an issue in the comic books or in the first movies. But, now, it had to be?

There's a montage of them in the lab, without Ben Grimm as yet.

Reed needed to take a nap, but not Sue.

Victor got jealous at how close Sue and Reed had become.

Richards told Victor: "We did it."

They met with the same official (federal stooge), now that they'd been successful.

Sue described the New World as, "Primordial, like Earth a few billion years ago."

Franklin made a wild assumption: "That place could explain the origin of our species...the evolution of our planet..."

A monkey was sent to the other dimension.

"Let's bring him back."

The monkey was fine. They knew humans could survive the trip to the other world. (Why use a computer-monkey in the test-seat? They could have used a real chimp. Why not try to be real? The answer might be: They're trying to be unreal?).

"Looks like we're next?"

People will make the jump next time.

The official wanted to bring in NASA, CIA, the government, now that the concept had been proved.

The boys got drunk, even Reed. They decided to jump on their own, tonight! Unofficially, without the other technicians. Reed called Ben Grimm and convinced him to join them and jump, which he did. [Later, this was the source of Ben's great resentment toward Reed, because of the terrible consequences by the jump and the fact that Ben turned into the Thing. Reed was never to blame before. He was now. Here was the comic book origin: "The Fantastic Four all got their powers at the same time. They were test pilots or astronauts on an experimental rocket ship. When they were in outer space their ship was bombarded with cosmic radiation. They survive a crash back to earth and discover they now have super powers." Did the origin really have to be changed? No, it didn't].

They jumped.

Sue discovered what the boys had in mind and ran to the lab.

In the dark world, one of them said, "I don't think we went anywhere." (The comment paralleled what Ralph Ring stated after a real saucer, warp-speed jump. They thought they hadn't gone anywhere, but they did).

They walked on the surface of a strange world. They planted an American flag.

Victor noticed that, "The energy seems to be converging over there."

They walked toward the energy source. When they reached it, it appeared as a green crater, full of power.

Victor Von Doom said, "It's alive" and touched it...

It exploded! The landscape reacted violently and broke apart.

The ground swallowed Victor. "Nooooo!!"

The others were helpless. They lost Victor at this point.

They made a mad dash for their vehicle to return to their own world.

Back at the lab, Sue made radio contact with them.

More trouble occurred as they jumped back: Ben's door jammed and he was slammed with debris and dark matter all around him.

Each of them, affected by dark matter, had returned. Only they were very different as a result. Another weirdness that made little sense was how Sue was also struck by the Dark Energy? She wasn't with the boys; she was on this side. But, what? A power blast of dark energy from the other world bounced back to her over the radio? Made no sense at all, but there she was with the rest of them as if she'd made the trip too.

They were flown to Area 57, a classified facility, now that the government had entered the picture and took control of the situation. (Area 57? Really? Really.).

Franklin viewed Sue in a lab room through glass and was very distraught. A nurse said, "Somehow she's shifting in and out of the visible spectrum. We don't know how. Her vitals are stable." Franklin walked to another room. He saw his son, Johnny, on fire!

Later, the official told Franklin: "We have to play ball with the government or who knows what happens to the kids?"

[We saw early Mr. Fantastic (Reed) with the coolest and most convincing Stretch-Effects ever produced in movies, and it was wasted here. Why couldn't super special-effects have existed way back when films and television were good? Too bad).

The official told the military group assembled, "All of them exhibited unique, physical conditions. We developed suits which enable them to control their conditions." Sue Storm went invisible, created force-beams, forcefields and flew with the power. Johnny Storm had become the Human Torch. Reed Richards had elastic-powers and Ben Grimm was turned into a golden, Hulk-like creature.

One year after Johnny, Ben, Sue and Reed transformed into beings with super-powers because of the "Baxter Incident," they agreed to cooperate with the government. The feds only wanted them for war-weapons. A screen showed Ben killing for the government in the field. A graphic displayed "43 kills" (similar to Dr. Manhattan in 'Watchmen').

The official told the group: "All these abilities come from one place. Another dimension our scientists call: 'Planet Zero.'" A large screen visualized the Earth and then another twin next to it, a negative/parallel Earth. The twin was a blackened, reddened planet like 'Lord of the Rings' Mordor, only on a global scale. He also said, "A planet infused with the same energy that transformed these (4) survivors, could potentially transform our military capabilities. We have the Direct Link. With your continued support, once the **Quantum Gate** 2 Project is finished, we'll have control over more than that world...*we'll have control over ours."*

Later, Sue told her father: "I am not going to be a tool."

Franklin Storm replied, "We'll re-open the Gate, find a cure and end this."

Reed Richards said to Ben when they were alone, "I'm going to fix this..."

Ben responded, "You can't fix this. Nobody can...Look at me...I'm not your friend. You turned me into something else."

Sue said to Reed when they were alone: "We need your help to finish the Gate, to figure out what happened to us and reverse it."

"You really think They (feds) care about us? You've seen how They've used Ben."

"Yeah, and They're going to do the same with Johnny if we don't stop Them. The only shot we got is on the Other Side of the Gate."

"Did you ever wonder what your life would be like if you hadn't gone to the science fair that day?"

Sue expressed, "We can't change the past...***But we can change the future."***

Later, Richards saw the machine the government built with his idea. He sadly informed the official: "You made it ugly."

The scene was like one from 'Stargate' where the scientists had made contact with the Other World.

"We have a visual!"

"Copy that."

A test capsule crossed the vortex, landed and out came men in protective suits. Planet Zero was awful in appearance, dark and barren.

Reed looked on and said to the lab techs and military men, "The landscape's changed..."

The official asked, "How?"

"I don't know. It's just different." [Remember, this was dished out to audiences in 2015].

On Dark Earth, the test subjects encountered "Victor," pre-Dr. Doom. It was very confusing because one minute Victor was all bad and strong on the planet, next thing they got him over to this side. He was messed up, almost catatonic and fused with his suit. On a stretcher, they brought him to a medical facility with technicians around him.

The official stated: "We're going to send more expeditions to the Other Side. But first, you need to tell us everything you know about that place?"

Victor replied: "How I survived? That place kept me alive, gave me strength, gave me power!"

The official was afraid and asked, "What kind of power?"

Victor said: "The kind of power men like you must never possess. It's not enough to ruin your world...now you want to ruin mine? If this world must die so mine lives, so be it!" Victor killed the official with his power, got up and continued a horrible killing-spree down the hallway. (I thought Marvel and DC were fan and family-friendly because children also watched? Well, it was *Scanners* with one head after another that exploded and left blood-stained walls! This happened again and again and again. Completely needless, God-forsaken, extreme violence that was never a part of superhero movies before. But they are now with Deadpool, Suicide Squad, Venom, etc.).

Victor confronted Franklin Storm:

"Victor! Son, stop!"

"Out of my way, Franklin. I'm going home."

"This is your home, son."

"Not anymore."

"There is nothing for you over there..."

"Only the power to create a New World."

Franklin told him: "We're not gods. We're just people. And we are stronger together than we are apart. [Here was an early "seed" of the "Stronger Together" campaign we've seen in commercials, on various banners and also on the backs of some NFL helmets].

Victor stated: "It's too late, Susan. Humanity had its chance."

Then he killed Franklin in front of his children, Johnny and Sue.

What else? Torch and Reed were tossed aside. Victor/Doom went back to his world via the machine in the lab. Sue and Johnny said their last words to Franklin.

Suddenly, *all Hell broke loose!* It was as if there was a massive power build-up or implosion that was in progress.

Richards screamed: "He created a runaway reaction! It's not going to stop! **It will create a Black Hole that will swallow the Earth!!**" The machine was about to blow (already happened with the Mandela Wave).

A large, vertical Light-Beam or power-shaft materialized (that we've seen in dozens of films like Tron). But at its base was a circular structure; the beam passed through the bright circle. Did the Power Circle symbolize CERN? Is CERN the "great machine" that has caused our problems?

Reed: "It's pulling everything into the other dimension!"

Sue placed a forcefield bubble around the Thing and Reed and they took to the air with the Human Torch alongside. They were all sucked into the enormous Vortex with debris and an airplane. The special-effects were fantastic.

When they emerged in the Dark World, its barren landscape also had the vertical Light-Vortex and the circular structure at its base.

Reed yelled: "Victor! Don't do this!"

"There is no Victor...There is only Doom."

At this point, they all battle.

Doom said to Sue Storm, "I saw a different future for us, Susan."

The four of them composed themselves.

Thing said: "He's stronger than any of us."

Reed replied, "Yeah, he is. But he's not stronger than all of us. This place gave him all of his powers. But it gave us all of ours too. It's who we are now. Maybe it's who we are meant to be? We opened this door, we're gonna close it."

Reed to Doom: "Enough!"

"When your world is destroyed and I'm all that's left, then it will be enough!"

They fought, but not for long [*'cos c'mon!* It's Taffy Man vs. Doom!].

Ben ran in with: "It's clobberin' time!" and punched Doom into the Power Beam! It's more confusing at this point~ Torch shattered the circular structure and it all collapsed in a big SFX!

Reed shouted: "Let's get the hell out of here!"

<WAIT>.

They were in the Other World, the Dark Universe, where they needed a machine to get to it. Yes, they were SUCKED there via a vortex. But now they flew home? Sue used the FF bubble, Torch was right alongside again and they went home...to the normal world, good ol' planet Earth? Were we in Oz?

Strange. They looked over a cliff and there was a huge crater. The Effect removed all of the area around the Gate Project? I guess so.

Later. Some colonel told the four of them and military personnel: "The world may not know what you did to save it, but the men and women in this room do...and so does the President." (Like the Philadelphia Experiment?). They came to terms: The feds and the four will work together in future. The government *promised* that they would be in charge and in control of a huge facility that's been around for "12 years." It was called "Central City." [Does the name have meaning? I've heard of the "Cloning Center"]. But with the feds who paid for everything, *who was really in control?*

They came up with a name for the group: "The Fantastic Four."

Are you ready, boys and girls? Let's review Josh TRANk's 'Fantastic Four,' released in 2015, all over again, with new eyes. Not with closed eyes and narrow minds, but with wide open eyes and open minds. There were already a bunch of comments added in parenthesis, now we're going to expand even more. Readers don't have to agree with me at all. But I'd like you to consider my take on it in association with the Mandela. Maybe it's connected? Maybe there are no coincidences at all with the Fantastic Four film? Maybe it was engineered that way, with hidden meanings, along with everything else?

I really enjoyed FF comic books in the Golden Age, early 1960s to me. Over the Avengers, over Dr. Strange drawn by Steve Ditko, over X-Men and right up there with Spiderman, I put the Fantastic Four. Just heartbreaking to see what they've done to superheroes these days: You're made to fear Superman, Superman and Batman are enemies? I thought they were Super Friends? They even had Lego Superman and Batman who fought, and a movie called 'Superman v Batman'...what's next? More hell? Why did every superhero darken? I explained it in a published book with the point: **If Superheroes were real, they**

wouldn't work for governments, they would be enemies of world leaders and cleaned-house, gotten rid of them and established a Beautiful New World Order. So it broke my heart and children's hearts who once loved precious things in the world. Where are the precious things in the world for our children today? Aye? Like values and good behaviors? Good lessons, good messages, good music, good stories? Don't we need heroes? We have far too many **her**-oes.

The film started, in a sense, like what happened to Nikola Tesla. Teachers to electrical engineers told the boy that the A.C. Current was an "impossible" dream. He proved them wrong.

Throughout the film, the big/quantum innovation here was the invention of a *transporter.* Transporter, we have viewed in numerous stories. Star Trek, Orville, Star Wars, almost any example of sci-fi, even old serials with the Phantom or Buck Rogers...*they beamed!* In 'The Fly,' we learned to inspect the transporter chamber very well before we launched. In the film, 'The Prestige,' the act of teleportation was disguised as a "magic trick." Teleportation, antigravity, forcefields, time-travel, aliens, etc., etc., are realities that They purposely have kept away from us muggles...

Since when did Star Trek's *beaming* [real world federal teleportation], such a mega-useful tool, open a portal to another dimension, another world, a Dark World on the *Other Side?* No. It was never that, but They have "made it so." Apples and Oranges. Why couldn't the new FF film have had the classic origin story? NO, filmmakers *had to* infuse AGENDA or PROGRAMMING into something that never had it before? Destroying it, in the name of "upgrades" and "re-sets" for a modern, hip generation? The plot could actually have concerned a war between feds and the Four over ownership rights of a fantastic innovation as a real teleporter. But, no. No reason to conjure up a dark, *mirrored* universe, which has been given to us a thousand times before and since, unless...

This was Predictive Programming; it meant something significant in the Real World. *2015, the year everything in the universe changed, flipped polarity.* (Exactly like Earth's magnetic poles have been feared to switch or flip). They knew; They put it in films. This film could have had any plot attached to it. But in 2015, the Royals knew their Plan would succeed and the growing Darkness would definitely swallow the Light. They discovered that the Real World could be altered, darkly. I think, twisted inside out. They SAW IT on screens from drones and probes...before "it" settled all around us as the New Reality. Like an unseen Wave spread out and changed everything? Haven't more than a few films suggested this?

It took me minutes to find most of the following movies and they were only a few examples of a magical theme or Other Worldly theme, shared by a great many recent [Nazi] films. Compare their plots and you'll discover a large consistency. The storylines have basically *described the Mandela Effect* or what They've done to the world. Always a dark, parallel MIRROR-world? There have been a bunch of movies with the same title: 'Into the Mirror.' Let's review:

'Yesterday was a Lie.'

No, it wasn't. This 2009 movie was an early precursor of a theme played out in an astronomical amount of movies to come. In 2009, there wasn't a hint of a Mandela Effect in people's minds or on the planet, yet. Then, there was Jiffy peanut butter, Jujubees and Tidy Cat, no Northwest Angle and one Michigan. Jurassic Park had been filmed on or off Costa Rica *Island.* Let's look at the blurb for this movie that sure had no good reason to be made. An incredible number of movies will be made in the new century that, oddly, have very similar themes: Don't trust your memories. Forget. Yesterday was a lie and the only truth is the (twisted, upside-down) reality that is around you now. This is brainwashing and propaganda. I thought you should know.

"Hoyle, a girl with a sharp mind and a weakness for bourbon, finds herself on the trail of a reclusive genius. But her work takes a series of unforeseen twists as events around her grow increasingly fragmented...disconnected...surreal. With an ethereal lounge singer and her loyal partner as her only allies, Hoyle is plunged into a dark world of intrigue and earth-shattering cosmological secrets. Haunted by an ever-present shadow whom she is destined to face, Hoyle discovers that the most powerful force in the universe - the power to **bend reality**, the power to know the truth - lies within the depths of the human heart."

They seem to always insert a Mirror or dark-world universe in your average/typical story. A lot of them! These subplots of *Other*

Worldly magic were not omnipresent in movies and stories of yesterday. But today, they're forced within Media and we're made to think this is perfectly normal.

If you examined recent movie plots, you'd find many common themes. Well, you would if you made certain, specific selections. But there are WAY too many "Dark" themes in movies these days, as I've pointed out before. The word "Dark" and "Darkness" are used over and over again in titles of movies, shows, series, etc. FAR too many. They had to have run out of different ways to use "Dark" in titles and probably now must repeat. Horror films, seen any these days? Have you seen any movies that *weren't* horror films? Have you seen any blood? Do you think that's appropriate viewing for young children? Or ever think about what that type of Children's Programming might do to society, when those kids grew up? Do you remember long ago, ages ago, when parents actually cared and some authorities "cared," and had a G, PG, R-ratings system for movies? That really doesn't exist anymore. It's about all bloody R-rated, for the most part. Made, on purpose, to be that way. All horror, no good stories. The last 'Terminator' was the worst one, ever! And there was James Cameron, so excited by the gore and freedom in the new (R) Terminator. What happened to bigger box-office sales with a more family-friendly, PG-13 movie? No, not anymore. That's right out the window. Now it's all violence (Deadpool), everyone must KILL! (Sharknado) and **killer-women must be drenched in the blood of men!** *That's Entertainment!* Only in Hell.

Yesterday

"Jack Malik is a struggling singer-songwriter in an English seaside town whose dreams are rapidly fading, despite the fierce devotion and support of his childhood best friend, Ellie. After a freak bus accident during a mysterious global blackout, Jack wakes up to discover that he's the only person on Earth who can remember the Beatles."

I can recommend this 2019 movie called 'Yesterday,' whose title reflects one of the Beatles' biggest songs. The movie certainly examines and plays with a Mandelian subject: A universe that had no Beatles. No one had ever heard of them, but Jack. I can understand

England being the setting in this case. The cool thing in the movie was the dude got famous by remembering Beatles songs. He was getting nowhere with his own music. But as soon as he recalled Beatles' tunes and pretended they were his, his fame skyrocketed.

Upside-Down Magic.

In this Disney Channel Original Movie (2020), 13-year-old Nory Boxwood Horace discovers she can flux into animals, and her best friend Reina Carvajal can manipulate flames. (Author's note: Witches? *That's new for Disney).* Together, they enter the Sage Academy for Magical Studies. Reina's expert ability to harness the power of fire lands her at the top of her class of "Flares," but Nory's *wonky* magic and proclivity for turning into a "Dritten," a half-kitten/half-dragon lands her in a class for those with Upside-Down Magic, otherwise known as UDM. While Headmaster Knightslinger believes the UDM's unconventional powers leave them vulnerable to dangerous and evil "shadow magic," Nory and her fellow UDM classmates set out to prove that **Upside-Down Magic** beats right-side up. *[Nothing like Harry Potter, eh?].* Are you kidding me? How Crowley. Disney, Harry Potter, Star Wars, again force-feeding MAGIC to young children, as if there are no other kinds of stories in the universe than (British) ones with castles, knights, princesses, magical powers, dragons, wizards, etc., etc. Nothing is different; it's all the same as it ever was. Rehashed crap with a Dark Agenda for children. Nory and classmates "set out to prove that Upside-Down Magic beats right-side up." This is horrific to me for many reasons. Upside-Down, again? In 'Stranger Things,' the Other World was called the "Upside-Down." The children are little black girls because, these days, *they must be black girls or black women.* (Now seen everywhere in Media). They are favored over white boys and men. But it's this upside-down, inverted, BACKWARDS, reverse or parallel world that is so played out in stories, in movies, over the last few years. It was never like that before, it sure is now and it's only gotten worse. Opposite of what it was and what it should be. They are talking about our world; these are not fictional fantasies. They are metaphors. Symbols, for what is real. They are directives. It's all connected. Believe it or not, these microscopic details are the influence of British occult madman:

Aleister Crowley. *Everything backwards, wrong is right and do anything you damn well please!*

Patema Inverted.

Directed by Yasuhiro Yoshiura. A young girl from an underground civilization that resides in the deep underground tunnels, finds herself in an ***inverted world*** and teams up with a resident to return home. 2013.

Upside Down.

Adam tells the story of his two-planet home world, unique with "dual gravity," allowing the two planets to orbit each other in extremely close proximity. Three immutable laws of gravity exist for this two-planet system:

1. All matter is only pulled by the gravity of the world that it comes from.
2. An object's weight can be off-set using matter from the opposite world (inverse matter).
3. After a few hours of contact, matter in contact with inverse matter burns.

The two societies are segregated by law. While the upper world (Up Top) is rich and prosperous, the lower (Down Below) is poor. [What could this symbolize?]. Up Top buys cheap oil from Down Below and sells electricity back to Down Below at higher prices. Contact of Down Below people with Up Top people is strictly forbidden, punishable by incarceration or death. People from Up Top regularly go Down Below to experience novelties like dancing on ceilings. The only official physical connection linking the two worlds is "TransWorld" company headquarters.

This is actually a well-made, love story of a boy in one world with his field of gravity and a girl in her reverse world with an opposite field of gravity. You can imagine the reverse (Spiderman) kiss. Made in 2012. Once more, the common theme of reverse, inverted or Mirror-universes.

The Dark Tower.

Based on the Stephen King novel, this 2017 sci-fi/Western/action film stars Idris Elba and Matthew McConaughey. Good vs. evil. Elba's character is a "gunslinger" that must protect the Dark Tower from his nemesis, the nasty McConaughey. But what's the Dark Tower? "A mythical structure which supports all realities." Again. What hell and chaos would occur if the Dark Tower was destroyed? *Look out your windows.*

Mirrors.

This 2008 supernatural, horror movie was first titled: 'Into the Mirror,' but its name was later changed to 'Mirrors.' It starred Keifer Sutherland and Amy Smart. The story concerned an ex-cop and his family haunted and terrorized by an evil force. A Force that used *Mirrors* to enter their home.

Into the Mirror.

In 2003, 'Into the Mirror' was the debut film for South Korean director, Sung-ho Kim. Story: A series of grisly deaths in a department store all involved *mirrors*. A troubled detective was set to solve the mystery. "The concept of parallel worlds isn't new to cinema, or to general science and/or mythology either. Since the days of *The Twilight Zone,* there's an inherent creep factor attached to the 'other side' that has been told in countless stories through time." [Star Trek, 'Into Darkness'].

Exactly like the cop-story with Keifer Sutherland, a detective must deal with a Mirror-World. And it's never a good, sweet, bright, warm and fuzzy universe in the Glass, is it? Never. Never balance.

Into the Mirror.

Daniel is a young man struggling with a (gender) identity that is desperate to be realized. After leaving his father to move to London, his subconscious desires begin to take control. Led by his new co-worker and upon finding London's Drag hotspot 'Lost & Found' nightclub, Daniel realizes his life will never be the same again. This

Mandela Effect II

2018 "gender-bender" thriller also deals with the "other side."

Coherence.

The 2013 movie was produced for $50,000 and was an excellent concept, if you can handle hand-held cameras that jiggled the picture? Filmmakers did not have to spend tons of dollars on special-effects or big stars. All they really needed was a good story and decent acting and a movie will hold your interest. 'Coherence' was a testament of what you could do with a small budget and another example of a plot with parallel worlds. How often have stories involved parallel worlds with doubles of people in similar times and places? Time-travel stories have shown everything in parallel with small or drastic changes. Those types of stories have been with us for generations. It's only in the last 5-10 years that the general public has been besieged with movies of *multiple universes and worlds in parallel.* Why so many? Maybe They lay "seeds" for their plans and actions in the movies that we're handed? If that were true: Then nothing major, made into a movie, was written by chance or "out of whole cloth" or pure creativity? There was purpose. Here also is the possibility the movie's plot referred to the Mandela Effect...

"This whole night we've been worrying that there's some Dark-version of us somewhere out there...What if *we're* the Dark version?"

'Coherence' involved a dinner party among good friends, mostly couples. The evening was a special occasion because a comet flew overhead as many groups had gathered to view the spectacle. The comet was barely seen and played a very small part in the story. Of course, it was to blame for the extraordinary events to come. Parallel people seemed to have materialized into existence and have been through the house. Doubles were nearly never seen together in a room, but clues were left in games they played. They knew a man's cell-phone was broken, then later, it wasn't. The main girl told her friends a conclusion that *some of them were not the originals, not the same as who we thought they were.* Chaos ensued, fights broke out. Notes were left in the house by "the others." She left the house at one point in the evening, walked around the neighborhood, looked in windows, and...

It was *them,* the same party guests! When she went to the next house and looked into the window, it was also her, her friends and her husband. Each house was a different situation or parallel world: One group was happy, one group fought, some were tied-up, etc. The ending was done well...

Next day, a husband told his wife (main girl) that she was drunk last night and he put her up on the couch. He found her wedding ring and handed it to her. He received a phone call as we saw that she *already wore the exact ring.* The call was from *her.* [That was the way to end the cheap movie]. Point being, the movie left us incoherent, unclear, made crazy, fearful, easily enraged and so did the Mandela Wave.

The Invitation.

Will (Logan Marshall-Green) and girlfriend, Kira, arrived at a dinner party thrown by his ex-wife, Eden, and her new husband, David. Will and Eden lost their young son, Ty, and they divorced soon afterward. Eden met David at a "grief-support group." David and Eden told the guests about the group they joined along with their friend Pruitt, called 'The Invitation,' which dealt with *death* through a "spiritual philosophy." David showed everyone a video of their leader (Dr. Joseph) who comforted a dying woman as she breathed her last breaths. There was an odd atmosphere in the house that Will used to own and where their son died. Pruit locked the doors. Will found out more about the Invitation Cult on a laptop and a bizarre message from Dr. Joseph. He was suspicious of what the dinner party truly was. David lit a red lantern in a garden that overlooked the Hollywood Hills. Drinks were served. Will overheard David and Eden say: "...(it) was the only way they can leave the Earth and be freed from their pain." Now there was war among the guests and bloody killings. People were shot, people were beaten to death and one died from the drinks that were served. (It was a shock to audiences and the entire point: to be *suddenly yanked into violence and murder,* right after a slow deterioration of calm situations). They carried Eden, one of the last survivors, out to the garden. Will saw nearby homes in the night that also had red lanterns lit. He realized that *Los Angeles had just erupted in many mass-murders from the same Death-Cult!*
(Author's note: 'The Invitation' was intriguing; I'd recommend it for an unexpected thriller. It wasn't about parallel worlds; it was about the Dark Side that emerged. And it just so happened to have been released in the "magical" year of **2015**. Could have significance, a normal

situation turned into sheer terror? There were once interesting movies that consisted of clever stories, clever conversations and great direction and design. Today, we can't have a dinner party movie like the old days, can we? There *has* to be bloody gore and many dead? No. There doesn't).

James Bond Theme Lyrics and the Mandela Effect.

Consider that the BRITISH DID THIS, created the Mandela Waves and the **Crown Virus** and unleashed them upon us. The Nazis who pretend to be the Monarchy of Britannia control everything. They create the music, engineer the movies, the television and us. They absolutely have total strangleholds on empires They've manufactured and own, such as the franchise of 007, James Bond. You tell me if there are hints/clues in intro-songs of James Bond films, films the world views and knows very well. The first one is 'Skyfall' from 2012. I believe just about every line concerns the Mandela Effect and the New World that has fallen and has been *forced* down upon us. But you don't have to agree...

"Skyfall," sung by Adele. This is the end. Hold your breath and count to 10. Feel the Earth move and then...For this is the end. I've drowned and dreamt this moment. So overdue, I owe Them. Swept away, I'm stolen. Let the Sky Fall. When it crumbles, We (Elites) will stand tall and face it all together. At Skyfall. Skyfall is where we start. A thousand miles and (magnetic) *poles apart.* Where worlds collide and days are dark.

"Casino Royale," sung by Chris Cornell (2006). When the storm arrives, will you be seen with me? By the merciless eyes of deceit. I've seen angels fall from blinding heights. But you yourself are nothing so divine. Arm yourself, because no one else here will save you. The odds will betray you. And I will replace you. You can't deny the prize, it may never fulfill you. It longs to kill you. Are you willing to die?...Things will not be the same, when you return to the night. And if you think you've won, you never saw me change the Game that we've all been playing. *Life is gone* with just one spin of the wheel. I've seen diamonds cut through harder men. The coldest blood runs through my veins. You know my name.

"Spectre," the song 'Writing's on the Wall,' sung by Sam Smith

(2015). I've been here before. I'm prepared for this. I never shoot to miss. But I feel like a storm is coming. This is something I gotta face. If I risk it all...Could you break my fall? For you, I have to risk it all. 'Cause the Writing's on the Wall. A million shards of glass, that haunt me from my past. As the "stars" begin to gather and the light begins to fade...When all hope begins to shatter, I know that I won't be afraid. The Writing's on the Wall.

"Tomorrow Never Dies," sung by Sheryl Crow (1997). Until the day, until the day the World falls away. Until you say there'll be no more good-byes. I see it in your eyes: Tomorrow Never Dies. [But Yesterday does??].

"Goldeneye," sung by Tina Turner (1995). See reflections on the water. More than Darkness in the depths. See him surface in every shadow. On the wind, I feel his breath. He'll do what I please. No time for sweetness. But now my time has come, and time – time is not on your side. See him move through smoke and mirrors. He's always present in the crowd. It's a gold and honey trap I got for you tonight. Now I've got you in my sights, with a Goldeneye.

"A View to a Kill," performed by Duran Duran (1985). Nightfall covers me. The plans I'm making. Still oversee. Could it be, the whole Earth opening wide? A sacred Why. A mystery gaping inside. Until we...dance into the fire. That fatal kiss, is all we need. The Phoenix for the flame. A chance to die.

"The Living Daylights," sung by A-ha (1987). Save the Darkness, let it never fade away. In...the Living Daylights. Comes the morning and the headlights fade away. Hundred thousand changes, everything's the same.

Let's analyze. If I were a betting man, I'd say these particular Bond themes were connected. Not that they come from the same musical source, probably do (then doled out to names we are familiar with). But, I believe, they're talking about the biggest/brightest and most Evil accomplishment of the British Empire [far beyond the World Wars and Crown Virus]: They Fucked-up the world and made you stupid [blind, bird-boxed]! *You've hardly noticed the Mandela transformations.* They've won, we've lost...

Mirrors, the coming Storms, our world Falls Away, Nightfall, DARKNESS, save the Darkness, let it never fade away? [Right, sympathy for the Devil]. Earth, opening wide. A million shards of Glass, fire and the Phoenix? And you don't think these are connected messages that have been pumped into you and shaped you for decades? Like all sounds and vision? Like the Beatles, or Shakespeare? Films and TV? From England, dictates from Royal Trannies with German blood in their veins! For you to Not See the Light (or anything good) and only praise The Dark? *It's the same damn messages!* British, you know?

Brand new song and video, 'To the Island,' by (now old) 'Crowded House,' *might be connected to Jewel's first song.*

"Come to the Island...where we can **Save our Souls**...the World is beyond us, it's too enormous...I'm afraid of the things I don't understand...everything is right on the Island, it's the perfect size..." Again, with "saving our souls." Plural. Singer Neil Finn washed up on an island's shore. He came to a dreamy movie theater, the Bijou was called: 'The Island.' Another metaphor? As if life for all of us was phony, unreal, like a movie? At one point Neil sang: "(life) It's just got real." Maybe he meant, "The unreal just got real?" He told us of that special place (so did Prince) where everything was beautiful. Neil was barefoot throughout and later when he played onstage with his mates. Barefoot, like Paul McCartney on the cover of 'Abbey Road'? Crowded House's new song sounded fantastic, so rare these days to hear any good music at all. Video was great, and you never see a well-done video today. Too bad it's all evil, given to us by virtual monsters, for sinister purposes. Is the "Island" a royal Capstone high over our heads that we muggles have no chance to enter? A Club for elites only? Such sugar and delicious delight in musical programming, eh? Examine closely the lyrics of Bjork, Kate Bush, U2, Sting, Coldplay, Cure, Muse and so many more. But don't look with the ga-ga, tinted eyes of excited children. Grow up and explore what lyrics really told us in beautiful music. Look on as truly enlightened adults. Practice seeing clearly...the code, the Agenda, or what They have hidden In Plain Sight. If you knew the Truth, your world would never be the same.

Let's draw a parallel to another old ('80s) band that has been revitalized lately with a new hit album and new music videos. *Hey, this is 2021 and Music Videos have totally dried up.* No. Not if you were pushing Halsey (boy), Billie Eilish [It's Billy English, please de-code! 'She's a boy!] or Beyonce or any other tranny diva. Guess wot? These new songs by old (secret) trannies are pretty good. No one wrote a damn thing! Teams of British Ghost-Writers made the music, other artists crafted the videos and they're distributed worldwide. Programming/propaganda and brainwashing. Crowded House came out of nowhere with a new single and album due out later this year. So did the Psychedelic Furs. Like 'House,' these "guys" should be *out to pasture,* not giving the world small masterpieces. Examine carefully the messages in the Furs lyrics: "You'll be mine," from the new album: "Made of Rain" (2020). There's a parallel with Crowded House.

"Don't be surprised when all your days are yesterdays. Don't be surprised at all. When the new black is white and the new lows are high. In the ticking of the time *you'll be mine.* Don't be surprised when all the traffic turns to rust. Don't be surprised when all your houses fall to dust. When the new black is white and the new lows are high, *you'll be mine.* Don't be surprised if They don't want you like I do. They'll take back everything They said. Don't be surprised at all."

"No one," from the Psychedelic Furs' new album and video: "Who's gonna wear your crown? No one. Queens of the underground. No one. Sirens will never sing, just silence in everything (quarantine). For no one at all. Who's on the telephone? Babel or Babylon? Dressed up in Halloween. Where nobody ever screams. For no one at all. And who's gonna cut you down? Why no one. [*Who's coming to save you? No one*]. Who's gonna wear your rings? And tempt you with senseless things? Why no one." The video was dreadful, a Celtic graveyard, mists in a woodland "grove" and a little girl. It's all Goth and witchy and nothing like the old Furs videos, which were peppy and colorful. These songs still had the sleazy sax and sounds that were unique to the Furs...but why the Darkness and atmosphere of evil, when there was no reason in the world for it? [ps. Or the Nacho Fries commercial with the 'Stranger Things' (tranny) dude where all is evil and voices scare you to hell? *It's just a Taco Bell commercial!* It's not Halloween! No reason for dark castles and blood-curdling screams just to sell some Nacho Fries. Or like the Stella Artois commercial that looked like a terribly evil Rothschild's Illuminati gathering, and it was just to sell some bad beer? Yeah. Only in hell was this tolerated, people].

Also, from the new Furs: "Come All Ye Faithful." Decent song, but absolutely horrible, black and white, video (all masonic now, b/w). A guy was out in a field and pranced around, alone, in a sheer nightgown, with near nipple-slips. But, wait, it's not a guy, it's a "gal." It made no sense, which was par for the course and right in line with Everything out of England. The video was disgusting. Okay, *maybe* "she" was slightly more attractive than Tilda (witch) Swinton, but who isn't? Again, the sounds on all the new Furs' songs were super, polished and distinctive to the band...

Let's investigate: A Mandela reference with: "Don't be surprised when all your days are yesterdays"? "New black is white and the new lows are high" is doubly masonic: 1) Black and White, and that's switched. 2) *Lows are now high* was from the Illuminati motto: "As Above, so Below" and this was also switched around. Look how many times Richard "Dick" Butler told you what They've done so...*don't be surprised.* Don't be surprised when you discover the truth. It's bloody been staring you right in the face the whole time! You've been made to Not See it. "Crown," "rings," always Royalty, the Masters who've made the bands and the music and who they must serve, faithfully. They're telling you there's been a change, an inversion. "Queens of the underground" did this, I believe the lyrics 'say.' The "Queens" are British MEN, btw. And the "underground" was the secret, occult society or Tranny Club the famous elites all belong to. "Ticking of time" until the Mandela Wave and your houses turn to rust/dust (metaphor)?

The song "No One" is the fucking worst of the lot, because it has repeated what the (evil) Pope (always been) said for cameras years ago, when he mocked that NO ONE IS COMING TO SAVE YOU. In Italian, he asked the world a question that "he" knew the answer to: "Where's Jesus Christ?" This was after a tragedy where many children suffered (by the Illuminati, of which the Pope serves). He *Rubbed in our Face* the fact that no Savior, Superman, police, cavalry, angel or alien is going to come down here and help us or save us. "Who's gonna cut you down?" Butler asked us in song. From our bonds of slavery? From our crosses?

TS Caladan

Another new one from Dick and the "boys," it's called: 'DON'T BELIEVE.' (Nice message). "Money's got the medicine, you can't believe in anything. Sucking on a cigarette. I don't believe. I don't believe. I don't believe it's true. Life is short and God is gold. Promises are bought and sold. Nothing down here is ever free. The same sun shines on you and me. Sucking on a cigarette... (repeats) I don't believe, etc., etc., etc..." (ps. I'm reminded of the "NO" Campaign or TV commercial. You know the one where they took snippets from big movies of actors saying: "No!" and weaved it into the ad, any way it could fit? They'd never take bits of celebrity-clips who shouted: "Yes!" with excitement in their voices. No, it was not to sell a product. It was to *beat and echo NO! into each of us. A negative and never a positive.* I'd bet. Still sucking cigarettes, Dicky?).

One more new Furs' song, 'Wrong Train.' "I took the wrong train...got off the wrong town. I'm never coming home again...where the hell are all my friends? I ran the wrong light. Got in a car crash. They beat their kids up, somewhere suburban. I'm never coming home again." The song's video [b/w] is Richard's face in a multitude of distortions, which look terrible.

New Furs' songs and videos sure are not 'Love My Way' or 'Pretty in Pink' now, are they? Since when was the band and their videos this dark? Now, they're Agenda and Code. Exactly like so much in every direction around us. Decode!

Let's examine an old Furs' song called: 'High Wire Days.' "...And the Lion has eaten the Lamb on tomorrow's pages. They pushed all the buttons and things, on tomorrow's pages. And the Sirens do nothing but sing, on tomorrow's pages. Our dreams have all gone up for sale, on tomorrow's pages. And we paid for the cross and the nails, on tomorrow's pages...in my High Wire Days."

Wow. Let's really examine this old song under a microscope. This couldn't concern Mandela Effects; it's too early and probably only coincidence. Or was it coincidence? How prophetic. *The Lion has eaten the Lamb* referred to in the Isaiah quote, one of the biggest Mandela changes in the Bible. The biblical Lion never ate the Lamb, but the new "Wolf" that replaced it would eat the Lamb. Now we have the Furs' singer with lyrics in line with the changed Bible verse. This was first sung decades ago before any Mandela Vortex struck the Earth. The repetition of "tomorrow's pages" or Future? Future changed "pages" in the Bible? "Pushed all the buttons and things" at CERN, the largest Machine on the planet? And re-wrote, re-set tomorrow's historical pages? In this old song, Butler sang: "Sirens do nothing but sing (in future)." But in the new song, 'No One,' he sang: "Sirens will never sing, just silence in everything." He now sings the opposite [They made him, in lyrics], as if a completely different future was presently in place on "tomorrow's pages." All our dreams of a bright future and fantastic World of Tomorrow have gone up in smoke. Cross and nails?

If my theories are true...why would They do this?

Because They know They *can* and They think we Outsider-muggles would never be clever enough to decode their secret messages in movies and music. "Because they're superior." "And we're not." They're British, you know?

Top 10 Movies Where the World Actually Ends.

I browsed YT and found the above video (I hate Mojo and Looper, so AM radio, give me FM! Something less "pop," something with more meat? Nope, not these guys). It's included here to reveal more than simply a list of depressing End-of-the-World movies with depressing dialog. The old films were great, significant, made major statements, but not recent movies made on the same subject. [Agenda, brainwashing now]. This was a short video, snippets from numerous movies. We will follow Mojo's list, with the sweet narrator's voice that described various movie plots that ended in the destruction of Earth...

10. Interstellar, (2014). "The last harvest, ever." Wait, all vegetation on Earth was dying and that forced us to seek out another planet for the human race? Really? No more vegetation, plant life, fruits or vegetables? *Impossible,* in a modern society. A disaster did not cause the problem. No, plants were simply dying and there was no cure? We couldn't have enriched the soil or seeds? Purified the water? We couldn't have grown plants underground (as there are massive seed-storage facilities underground for exactly that purpose). We couldn't have greenhouses in orbit? There were hundreds of different, real world solutions, like (Tesla) technology that made barren lands fertile. *Abundance of food* is reasonable for our future, even Free Food! The very concept of a "foodless," global disaster was impossible, but we're supposed to accept any irrational, thoughtless premise? Ridiculous. The movie followed Matthew McConaughey and a spaceship crew as they headed for Saturn. Something weird (like a real Vortex) was around Saturn (Hollywood has told us). [ps. In one of my novels, I wrote that the End of the World happened a while ago, but we haven't realized this yet].

9. Seeking a Friend for the End of the World, (2012). Steve Carell and Kiera Knightley? A 70-mile asteroid named Matilda is set to collide with Earth in 3 weeks! Again, that's impossible, but not to us muggles who have been mesmerized (lied to) by films. It's an impossible situation because mason-rulers of the world (Britzis, Illuminati) would have *Star Warsed it* or have sliced up any "Doomsday Asteroid" no matter what size it was, long before it reached us. Our secret leaders are OFF world, IN world and made provisions for only the elites to survive a real holocaust. But They are not going to have an atomic war, global fall-out, nuclear winter and destroy Swiss bank accounts that They covet so much...or allow a mere meteor to do the same. And certainly not when these disasters can be easily controlled and prevented. The idea that we Earthlings are totally helpless in the face of a "Doomsday Asteroid" or massive chunk of space debris, is an ignorant/false assumption. The two people had found each other; they were in love...and the world ended. Wouldn't you know it?

8. Miracle Mile, (1988). Here was another movie with the same plot: Man found Love, then nuclear war was imminent. How many movies were we given by our British Masters that struck Fear into our hearts? Tons of post-apocalypse movies that pushed the terrors of atomic wars (that could never have really happened). *Nuclear war is coming!* They warned us. Sputnik could be a nuke? WWIII? Better build Bomb Shelters! Cold War <u>bullshit</u>. Truth was Russia and the U.S. are the same, all under and must serve the British Empire. Countries must play their roles in bogus battles and fake wars, orchestrated by English (German) royals.

7. These Final Hours, (2013). A small, Aussie movie. A meteor struck the opposite side of the planet, which ignited a global firestorm! Main guy helped a little girl (How many times has this been done?).

Little girl strangely said, "Did you ever think you might end up in hell, instead of heaven?" This would never have been said in the real world. Their world was hell; death wouldn't be more hell? The sweet, little, blonde girl might've wondered, "You think heaven is beautiful?" Not imagine heaven was hell? She'd want to escape the world around her. This is pure crap for audiences to believe exactly like the Monsters of Media want you to believe: *Life is shit, there's no God, heaven or a good afterlife.* Bullshit. The movie also did not have to be extremely violent.

6. The Day After, (1983). The very dramatic, well-made and much hyped miniseries remains to this day the highest-watched TV movie of all time. Once more, US. vs. USSR in a Cold War nuclear exchange. Top producers, Directors, simply wanted to strike fear in all of our hearts that this could actually happen. When, it could never happen. Who said nuclear arsenals were pointed at each other? It is far more likely that atomic missiles of many countries are pointed outward, toward space.

5. This is the End, (2013). James Franco, Seth Rogan, Michael Cera and a host of other "comedians" played themselves. These stupid people have an end of the world party in *one of the worst movies ever made!* This should mark the end of all movies! Absurd, and the filmmakers just happened to toss in Armageddon. But Mojo's voice told us the movie was "hilarious"? No, opposite. James Franco stated more than just a line when he revealed: "If it is the end of the world, and all good people died, what you're saying is me, Seth,..." I'll paraphrase: And other awful *human beings* will survive? WAIT, why would doomsday be selective? Why choose the "power elite" celebrities to live? Why would only "good people" die? Maybe them, as them, were talking about something totally different than what went on in this fictional farce? Do you know why the huge cast of so-called comedians acted like terrible "assholes"? Because they weren't acting: *They are terrible assholes!*

4. On the Beach, (1959). Fred Astaire's character said, "We're all doomed, you know? The whole, silly, drunken, pathetic lot of us. Doomed by the air we're about to breathe." WWIII again. Nuclear fall-out and the "radiation sickness" that followed, moved closer and closer to Australia and a fine cast of characters. Some wanted to commit suicide rather than suffer with the sickness. "God, forgive us."

3. Last Night, (1998). A small, Canadian movie. They knew the world would end at midnight. The audience never knows why or what deadly force will end everything. Suicide was also presented here, rather than face the coming Doom. Don't we want to cling to life as much as possible? We don't throw precious life away before we're hit with Death. But in movieland, that, and so many other bad messages were omnipresent, everywhere. This was a bad movie, but Mojo reported that it had "great style and substance."

2. Melancholia, (2011). Kirsten Dunst's character stated: "The Earth is evil." In this minute long snippet from the movie, it seemed as if everything said by her and others was WRONG! Narrator called it: "The most artsy film about the end of the world." Yes, this was a visual feast. To decode that (like 'The Fountain'), super special-effects draw audiences in, therefore, watch for Agenda Placement. Words mean other things to filmmakers who wave their magic wands, than what words mean to us blinded muggles. Words/lyrics always suggested to us how we should behave. It's what almost all SHOWS do to us, they're programming, Their true purpose: influence and control. Over and over again, subtly, the Wrong Programming, changed into what was supposed to be correct programming. Two women and a little boy; that's this arty film. Where's the strong male? He died a long time ago. It's only superior Women who rule now, well, that's the LIE They want us to believe through all Media. The disaster concerned a new planet that wandered in and was on a collision course with Earth. [How did they miss 'When Worlds Collide'? Bellus was coming!]. Oh boy, the female narrator praised the women in this film! Her words were: "Majestic Vision!" I don't think so. I think the main characters' lines were disgusting.

They always do an Honorable Mention: Hitchhiker's Guide to the Galaxy, Titan A.E., Knowing, Wall-E, Illustrated Man. In **The Cabin in the Woods** (2012), Sigourney Weaver's character said: "If you live to see it (Sun), the world will end."

A boy replied, "Maybe that's the way it should be?...Maybe it's time for a change?"

1. Dr. Strangelove, (1964) by Stanley Kubrick. Peter Sellers in multiple characters. In one, he was in a wheelchair and talked like Henry Kissinger: "The whole project of the Doomsday Machine [CERN?] is lost...if you keep it a secret, right?! Why didn't you tell the world, aye?!" World leaders convened in the Pentagon's War Room. They argued and fought. They were made to appear foolish and comical in a critical time of a "mistake" that will lead to a nuclear exchange and the end. "You can't fight in here. This is the War Room!" Who can forget Slim Pickens' character who rode the Bomb all the way down?

Who did this, How and Why?

In 1600, the Vatican publicly burned Giordano Bruno at the stake for heresy after many years of imprisonment and torture. Bruno, not only supported the heliocentric view (of the Solar System), he also claimed **there were multiple worlds beyond Earth** and each orbited their own Sun.

Nicholas of Cusa, a Cardinal, "published those same ideas 200 years earlier." His book, 'On Learned Ignorance,' discussed the possibility of multiple worlds and was published in 1440. He also wrote that "aliens could exist on the Moon and on the Sun." Such controversial viewpoints did not harm his career. He was made Cardinal in 1448.

Vatican astronomer, Brother Consolmagno, stated that Bruno's true sin in the eyes of the Church was not the right for free-thought, it was the fact that he denied the divinity of Jesus Christ. Consolmagno also stated of the "very important role **science-fiction** has to play..."

Here's another theorist, this one did not suffer the fires of Bruno...

"Hugh Everett III (1930-1982) was an American physicist who first proposed the "many-worlds" interpretation of quantum physics. He was "discouraged by the scorn of other physicists" for his Many-Worlds Interpretation. The hypothesis states that there are an infinite number of possibilities or realities created by every single decision we make. When we come to any fork in the road and make a decision, a certain set of consequences are the result of that action. But the alternate decisions, roads not taken, also create parallel universes and different consequences, different realities. Alternate worlds of alternate decisions also exist? Fascinating. Everett's controversial work is only mentioned here to inform you that mega-worlds, the Mega-verse, multiple universes, what String-Theory and quantum mechanics have told us: There is NOT ONE WORLD. It's infinite. This might apply to the Mandela Wave, which could have bridged the gap between parallel worlds."

Choice! The Power of Choice might be the key to what has happened to all of us that some people have recognized as Mandela Effects. For example, we walk down a street and decide to make a left turn. That sets up a completely different future for our entire life, than if we had made a right turn. One way could mean death, the other, great fortune. Should I play the Lottery or not? What if the road not taken was a reality in itself and existed somewhere? Endless parallel timelines, storylines, realities, *chains of events,* might be produced constantly~ Simply because of the decisions we make. Another example of a Mandela Effect, more than a few have claimed, is that Haiti and the Dominican Republic appeared to have *switched positions* on the island they share...

Dominicans and the Haitians.

This is an attempt to explain why the differences, and there have been differences, New World vs. Old World. The following is a hypothetical to possibly show why some people remember that the Dominican Republic was on the west side and Haiti was on the east side of the island. Before the Mandela Effect, no one would ever have thought the two countries, or any countries, had switched positions. (p.s.: I remember Port-au-Prince [Haiti] was on the east end, now it's on the west end).

Let's assume the countries had switched...

In one reality, long ago (maybe), the Haitians were on track toward the east side of the island, because it was the preferable side for colonization. Their ships would have landed first and they would have established themselves on the best side, because the weather was clear and perfect the whole way.

But in another reality, terrible storms had raged in the area that the Haitians had approached. Their ships were tossed way off course and it took months before they were on track and returned to the island. In that time, Dominican Franciscan friars had settled in the east, which meant the Haitians had to move west. Are we left with a reverse situation today? Some people believe so.

There are those who have remembered and believe: "Iran and Iraq have also switched places." It's possible, now.

The little experiment was to show how completely different futures or different realities or a massive domino-effect of different events can occur all because...

You made a choice.

We will delve more into the theoretical and also use FILMS, stories that millions of people have seen and know well, to explain...the extraordinary. An extraordinary universe, a different one, exists around us now, in every direction. Before we can attempt to understand it, we first have to open our eyes and realize...it's true. Beside the logic and quantum mechanics that supports IT, we can only solve the problem by **being OPEN to the Mandela** – *not denying it!* What does (now) almost every YouTuber say about it? FALSE MEMORIES, over and over and over again. This should tell reasonable, intelligent people that the Mandela is not false memories! They have pushed the denial too hard! You are not questioning the mass-Media BLITZ of Mandela, exactly like you are not questioning the mass-Media PUSH of the Crown Virus! Who is telling us this? Why are those voices over Media, TELLING YOU WHAT YOU SHOULD BELIEVE, British voices, and have English accents? And primarily women (puppets)? Every sign in every store warning us of CV is bullshit! Distancing Laws are bullshit! **We need to breathe, not wear masks**, which cut off our breaths. But if lies are on TV or posted Everywhere, just what Big Brother would do, *you believe it?* A few of us who have collected the clues of what's really been happening, know better. The more Media FORCES whatever it is...you should know that They are lying. They, the monsters at the top of the Social Pyramid, deny what They've done to all of us. So They falsely report along every means of communication: Mandela Effects are mistaken memories; we're just stupid and have forgotten, when it's been a different way all along.

No. Try to be smarter and see, hear and feel...beyond the Curtains of Crap the general public has been force-fed.

Can you live more years in your lifetime than your chronological years? Can you experience more time in your life than you would normally have? There are probably various ways this could be achieved, outside of psychedelic mind-expanding chemicals, which increased sensations...

I've worked on a unique idea to try and solve a minor mystery no one had ever written of or ever had talked about, to my knowledge. It's presented here in a section of "magical wonders" that are not *magical wonders,* but pure (out-of-this-world) Science. First, these words were written by Tesla's secret son, my pen-pal in the 1980s, Arthur

Matthews, from his book: "Tesla was no common mortal. He was a young man at 60 and at 70, with a brain just as keen as the day he died, (if he did die, for many believe he did not)." In one letter from him, Arthur stated that Tesla did die in 1943. [Couldn't stand any more of the fucking World War, would be my guess]. Here's the mystery:

Why'd he look so freakin' old? Wait, if Tesla was so meticulous about his intake, food/drink and gave health tips on living a long life in a 1933 newspaper...

Why did this Superman of the Modern Age and the greatest Genius...*appear so emaciated, gaunt, wrinkled and worn-out in the photos very late in his life?* Hard work? He was known to have been a fanatical workaholic, totally dedicated to his electrical experiments, without much interactions with people. No love in his life? (Not true). It was not because he worked too close with electrical currents. Those Tesla Coils were made into hand-held, healing devices that were very effective at the time. Electricity for external use 100 years ago. It wasn't because of any kind of radiation that he appeared very old. He was a brilliant health "nut." 1856-1943, Tesla was "87" when he died. If someone were to guess the age of this man and were shown certain photos of him taken very late in life, the person would guess a man near 100 years old or more.

Matthews reported that Tesla believed he would live to reach the age of "150 years." My incredible thought was...maybe he did? I wouldn't put anything past the guy. If Tesla was involved, expect Time Machines, Death Rays (particle beams), energy vortex-devices, wireless electricity, *beaming* and fantastic things only found in comic books and sci-fi, were real. Those years of a birth-date and a death-date might be absolutely correct. *But within those 87 years, Nikola Tesla could have actually experienced 150 years!*

The answer eluded me for the longest time, but now, maybe I found it and it is very unbelievable. Possibly. With his amazing machines, vehicles, vortexes, electro-magnetic devices, this Superman could easily have constructed a means to break time and space. We've viewed it in sci-fi movies and the principle stands in quantum physics. We can freeze time, freeze the universe, a light-speed saucer does exactly that at warp. The universe relatively HALTS, stops! To our view, in a light-speed spacecraft. We continue to exist and move and live, while the universe is *suspended* because of our extraordinary super-speed. Remember the Twilight Zone with the special stopwatch?

The world stopped with the push of a button. Same idea could be produced by a light-speed ship or an electrical machine where a powerful Vortex was generated. Tesla, or his principles, had already proved to governments that they could *beam* the U.S.S. Eldridge to another dimension (?) reality. Then, why couldn't he have had his own (Venusian) saucer or some personal means to stop Time/Space?

If so, this would give him (or any traveler with such a device/ship) a means to experience MUCH MORE TIME in their life. Think about it. Tesla pulled a lever or hit a Warp Button and we all, and everything around us, were suddenly suspended, stationary~ But we were not aware of it, only the traveler. The traveler would age; we wouldn't. Tesla may have experienced one world after another, and lived in them for a time. Played. Explored. Learned. Who knows? But it's possible. If true, Tesla left us behind each time he JUMPED, in a sense. The principle accounts for his almost horrible appearance when he was in his eighties. (Tesla was not a trans-gender; first thing Arthur told me in correspondence was that Tesla was a "real man."). *Nikola Tesla might have been 150 years in age after he left the Earthly plane, while his chronological age was only 87.*

More incredible is the fact that there are no known film clips of Nikola Tesla? Wouldn't there be? We have photos, but no films? Film cameras were around for a half century before Tesla's death. We have early films of one of his students: Einstein. But no Tesla, when that man, of all men, would certainly be preserved in films and various news clips? If every shred of Tesla films and interviews were not federally confiscated, I came to the conclusion that he *couldn't be filmed* because of his natural, electrical field (aura) that surrounded him. And put that concept in a short story (online and in last book) called: 'An Evening with Nikola Tesla and J.P. Morgan.' There are reports that during his funeral with an open casket, photos/films of him were completely distorted when they looked at the exposures. No photos of a deceased Tesla came out. Photos of other things at the funeral appeared clear. But not the casket with Tesla's body. (ps. I wonder. If a cloth was placed over his body, would a negative image be burned into it?).

Examine the next photo carefully. It's legit. It's from the Philadelphia Experiment (not the film), the real deal back in 1943. The strange events during WWII involved Nikola Tesla. The U.S. military, always under the 'umbrella' of the United Kingdom, attempted to make the U.S.S. Eldridge "radar-invisible" to German warships. In the beginning, Tesla solved the problem in an extremely fantastic way. The fully-manned destroyer escort was not surrounded by a "bottle" or a field, undetected by radar. IT LEFT...*beamed* out of the Philadelphia Navy Yard in a "green fog." Gone! "Within seconds, it appeared in Norfolk, Virginia, and then reappeared in Philadelphia!" It's mentioned in this section because the principle could be similar to what happened with the Mandela Effect. **As the Eldridge was swallowed by (essentially) a Black Hole, so could the Earth have been by the Mandela Wave~**

This is the view from the bow of the Eldridge, 1943, at the Philadelphia Naval Yard. The reason I believe this is a real (but artificially produced) *Black Hole* or a vortex-conduit "rip," formed, enlarging and ready to engulf the entire ship...

Look at the mist. Look at the radiant lines that extend from the circle. They're not created by the phenomenon – it's the mist, *sucked in!* I believe where the fog was thick, we view an extended line *going into* the vortex. Where the mist was not thick, there's a light area and we see nothing. This was a dramatic moment, calm before the storm of chaos and all *hell had broken loose! Crewmen physically merged with the Eldridge! Others disappeared!* Some old photos of the destroyer surrounded in a glow at the time could be real. You think the Experiment wasn't photographed and filmed well? It's like the ship's photos had been photoshopped, enhanced. But maybe not? This was exactly what was reported and shown in the film, 'The Philadelphia Experiment.' Not Predictive Programming, the film was released *after* the bizarre (and unknown) events in 1984. Too soon. The film itself was another mystery:

How did filmmakers know directly after the events of 1984 to make this film that came out in 1984? Was it such a drastic electro-magnetic phenomenon we avoided in 1984 that the Powers That Be HAD TO produce and release a film-version of it? One report claimed President Reagan was advised, convinced and signed off on it in 1984. If They hadn't sent Ed/AL back from 1984 to 1943 for a re-do, to destroy the generators onboard Eldridge, which caused the "runaway" Vortex in the first place...

An incredible electro-magnetic disruption would have resulted in **most of western United States "underwater."** This was truly averted in the real world. Ed's mind was later wiped of the incident, gone was the memory that he was sent back in time...as shown in the film. We are all left with the aftermath of the 1984 Incident. *Like a movie...*

(Author's note: Study what happened to Al Bielek, formerly Ed Cameron. He and his brother played crucial roles in the Experiment. *They were on the Eldridge when everything went crazy* (wrong) and they jumped off the ship! **They landed in the future**. Yes, in the future! And returned and told us about it. If you want to learn of the Philadelphia Experiment and Montauk, discover what happened to Al. Imagine: Al watched HBO, the film came on...and it triggered memories, memories of what the feds WIPED and what really happened. Now, Ed/Al realized THIS WAS HIS STORY, in the film! This was generally what happened to him and his brother in the real world! In the film, the two crewmen from 1943 were friends, not brothers. Al suddenly understood that "Al Bielek" was a forced identity by the feds and his true memories flooded back. He called his brother and Preston Nichols who were also involved. Slowly, each started to remember their past, what happened and what happened at Montauk (where Eldridge survivors were taken and their oddities studied. "Montauk Boys," and now a TV series). Al's story is fascinating and a must read/view. We'll synthesize this unbelievable film: 'The Philadelphia Experiment.' In interviews, Al Bielek said: "Take out the love-story, and the film is basically true."

In the first part of the film, it was shown: A theatrical representation of a phenomenal event. "Dr. James Longstreet," in a fedora, was in charge. Guess who his "assistant" symbolized? It was Tesla [not credited as Tesla]. A tall man with dark hair and a dark moustache. This character *gave the nod* and crewmen started the generators. "You can start the generators, now." These were the two scientists onboard who gave the orders. Not military. The "grunt" crewmen did what the scientists instructed with all the new equipment now installed on the Eldridge. In reality, this was Tesla's project, not the creation of the man in the fedora. Nikola "walked off the project" because feds would not provide "Zero-point" safety bands for the crew. The bands would *ground the crew* no matter what happened. But. The crew was expendable, I guess, just like soldiers and ships were purposely exposed to our first atomic tests. Governments (Britain) didn't care about human safety, that wasn't the point. And Tesla was gone. Dr. John von Neumann, a super-genius himself, was put in charge...and he probably wore a fedora in 1943. I believe Dr. Neumann was represented by Dr. Longstreet in the film. Einstein, Townsend Brown and other geniuses were called in and used in order to pull off the Experiment. But, as Tesla feared, *something went horribly wrong!*

Let's examine the story:

(The character "Dr. Longstreet" will be referred to as "Dr. von Neumann." The two sailors will be referred to as "Al" and his brother).

"Activate Rainbow One," a technician was ordered. ["Rainbow" was another name for the Experiment].

"The Eldridge is beginning to fade, sir."

"It's gone. I didn't think it was possible."

"Congratulations, Doctor. You've just taken the German fleet out of the war."

"She's gone, sir."

"Of course, she's radar-invisible..."

"No, sir. She's really vanished! She's gone!"

The film audience saw from the crewmen's' point of view: other-worldly glows and distortions all around the ship. Crewmen panicked.

What was once solid was no longer solid.

"Let's get the hell out of here!" One of the brothers shouted to the other as reality morphed. They jumped overboard and thought they'd hit the water. They didn't~

The film jumped 40 years into the future....

Actor Michael 'Eddie and the Cruisers' Pare and another actor played Al and his brother (friend). They had radiation burns or *vortex-burns* and wandered around, lost in a Nevada desert. They soon realized they were not on the east coast anymore and that it was not 1943 (jets in the sky).

At a test facility, old Dr. von Neuman (Longstreet) told his colleagues: "We opened up a Hole...and it stayed open."

"Negative pressure, that's impossible!" one of them expressed.

Von Neumann replied: "No. It's pulling the air. It's pulling everything in!"

(Author's note: Wouldn't it be funny if They purposely put a scene in the film TO TRIGGER AL, because it did! Michael Pare, helped by the girl, was in a motel room and a commercial flashed on TV that showed a RAINBOW. The real Al, watched HBO and saw the motel scene from a motel room. I'd bet this was a 'Manchurian Candidate Card,' or inadvertent one, which started him *remembering.* Fascinating).

The girl from 1984 oddly said to the man from 1943, "This is not a movie."

Later, a technician ran into one of the rooms in the facility and shouted to von Neumann: "The Vortex is almost twice its size! It started pulling in surface matter. If we don't stop this thing soon, the whole damn planet's in trouble! What the hell are we going to do?"

Al met with Dr. von Neumann. A screen displayed a recording from a probe that showed them that the Eldridge and the local town in Nevada (1984) were connected and moved together within the Vortex.

Al asked, "How'd that happen?"

The Doctor replied, "Somehow the electro-magnetic fields created in two experiments, one in 1943, and the other now, cross-connected. They created a Vortex, a Hole in the space/time continuum...and you fell through it..."

"What?"

"In 1943, when the Eldridge came back, the Hole closed behind it. This time it stayed open, like a gigantic vacuum sucking everything into it. We can't stop it. But I believe you can...The source of energy explosion in the Vortex is the generators on the Eldridge. *You have to go back and shut them down...*"

The other fellow that jumped off the destroyer with Al, had returned to 1943 and lived a full life. He was messed up because of the experience. But Al's character in 1984 was young. To Al, his 1943 was yesterday.

The point: When Al Bielek (Ed) was sent back through time in 1943, he followed orders. He smashed the powerful generators on overload! **Reality SNAPPED back**! None of the electrical disturbance in the atmosphere over Nevada in 1984 had ever happened. Crisis averted.

Ed was mind-wiped and the persona of Al Bielek was instilled in him. His real brother, Duncan, who jumped overboard with him, was de-aged. De-aged. Believe it or not. This could be direct evidence of someone *slipped through time portals* (as I believe Tesla did, at will). Al, who kept his induced name, died some years ago. Duncan remained a mystery. But he was much younger in appearance than someone who had served in WWII. There was a 2-hour YT interview with Al, Duncan and Preston Nichols. It was one of the most intelligent conversations I had ever heard.

One difference from the film and real life: Al/Ed was a genius and not an ignorant soldier as portrayed in the film. Ed's "field equations" could have been used for the Experiment, rather than Einstein's and others.

This was a roundabout way to express...

Tesla probably did the same by a special means to cross oceans of time, like oceans of space could be crossed. The argument or evidence was also meant to demonstrate the possibility that a phenomenon on the order of a **Black Hole or a Mandela Wave could suck in the whole Earth** and radically change everything. What's really weird...we might not even be aware of it.

Now, let's get to Dr. John von Neumann...

John von Neumann (1903-1957?) was a Hungarian-American mathematician, physicist, engineer and he basically invented computers. If you looked up the credits to this man, it's endless. "In fact all computers today could be considered 'von Neumann machines.'" Directly after the P.E., von Neumann was an important part of the Manhattan Project that developed the A-Bomb right alongside another Hungarian, Edward Teller.

Neumann is featured here because another report had said von Neumann was also teleported through time or through an energy-conduit vortex. [ps. I could not find the evidence at the time of this writing. I don't make something up and believe it. True or not, von Neumann may have been seen in the 1980s, while he still appeared young as he did in the 1940s. If true, this guy (like Tesla and very few others) is the kind of super-genius that could actually build such an apparatus. I reviewed the P.E. film, and thought the anomaly of time-displacement was shown. But no, von Neumann in the 1980s was always the old man. My thought came from somewhere, probably what I had read years earlier. This all may apply to my theory that Tesla weaved between Wormholes of Time and have experienced far more time than his chronological years].

Were aliens involved? Was the situation monitored from high above the Philadelphia Naval Yard? True or not, reports have surfaced that "good aliens from the Pleiades" made contact and wanted to help the human race in the 1940s. Their generous offer was *refused* by the Military Industrial Complex because it meant a global demilitarization. Unthinkable at the time, disarm? Then other, not-so-good, aliens from the Pleiades gave the (ancient) secrets of the Bomb to certain governments of Earth. Maybe. Maybe often the real inventors were hardly ever revealed to the public? Mostly, we are only told lies. The people THEY SAY accomplished amazing things or created particular innovations, did not. One bizarre Wikipedia reference was found: "There are also rumors that aliens were involved in giving us the technology used for the (P.E.) experiment, and that they caused the temporal and spatial displacement. Since the whole experiment is essentially a low-grade external merkaba, we could suppose they wanted us to reopen the wound or tear opened in the time of Atlantis (called the Fracturing) to let the _____ through. Was a similar external merkaba experiment conducted in the times of Atlantis by the 'Sons of Belial' which caused the Fracturing?" Odd quote.

All Time Scary has theorized, "What Caused the Mandela Effect?" on his many YT forums. One idea was: "Quantum Immortality, your mind or consciousness transports itself to an alternate reality when faced with Death...right as you die, your mind/consciousness transfers (and)...within that alternate reality, there are bound to be slight changes. What is horrifying is every M.E. you've experienced comes from you not existing originally in this reality. Your physical body has died countless times and your mind/consciousness refuses to accept that reality. Another scary thing about this theory is that everyone you know isn't actually the person that you know. (See 'The Twilight Zone' episode, 'The Parallel.'). The original people only existed in the past lives where you died. Your life is filled with alternate versions of the originals...Creepier still, how are you fitting into this new timeline? Are you replacing yourself? Are you continuing on this way, indefinitely?"

Another posted possibility was: "We Live in a Simulation," like 'The Matrix.' Video games have vastly improved in only a short time period. What will they be like in 1000 years? We cannot conceive of what will be produced in Virtual Reality with a super technology that generated it. According to this theory, "patches, updates and glitches are responsible for the Mandela Effect." Is our world (unnaturally) changing every day? ATS believes that, possibly, some alien or great artist was at work and manipulated our reality, as if it was innocent, only the art of fantastic creations. I believe the changes are much, much more sinister in their overall purpose: *to force us all Into Darkness and Chaos.* Examine the changes and the common denominator is evil or negativity. ATS ended with: "Are we looking for answers in Computer Code?"

Could the misnamed "Collider," CERN, have widened and widened the Darkness or the Event Horizon of the Mandela Wave in the same manner as the (pictured) Vortex swallowed the Eldridge vessel? Could this "event" have engulfed our whole planet and have flipped the universe upside-down and inside-out? Planned for decades, then succeeded and tossed us all into Alice's Looking Glass? Literally. Years later, some people have woken up to the fact: The world's been changed. It is different and dark. Everything is suddenly the reverse of what it should be and what it always was...

If you refer to the **More Predictive Programming** section and that *stupid* 'Fantastic Four' film from 2015, you might not have such a stupid movie after all. It is considered "One of the Worst Movies of All Time." Oh, the irony. What if, I said, WHAT IF...it held a secret template, a Super Clue, an ultimate Easter Egg, but only for the Insiders that knew. The year is significant, I believe. In principle, it could be precisely what the "royal" Illuminati had created, drawn and would be the New Reality for years to come. Were we swallowed at the end of 2015 similar to how the USS Eldridge was swallowed?

What about the ridiculous British comedy with the 'Mother of Dragons' called: "Last Christmas"? Any real world significance in the title?

The following bit might have relevance to what occult Wizards, real Magicians, have done to the world. Aleister Crowley, Walt Disney, L. Ron Hubbard, Jack Parsons [not actor Jim Parsons, who could be related], and a slew of other occultists and members of secret "lodges." You thought JPL stood for Jet Propulsion Lab? No, rocket-genius Jack Parsons. The original NASA was composed of Nazis.

These "guys" may have cracked through to the Other Side and discovered our mirrored, parallel universe? Our doubles, like the Bizarro World in Superman. As the story goes, it was many decades ago in the desert of western America and it had something to do with negative, Indian spirits. (You've certainly heard of haunted, Indian burial-grounds?). I've written about this in a few places in recent novels. Even visors Tall White aliens used to view the widening Crack and the strange "critters" that fed on Fear, which were the result. All went unseen, unless you used the visor and looked around.

The view, not mine, but one I agree with: CERN had been enlarging the crack or Rift or invisible Event Horizon over many years...to the point, one day in the future, *Polarities Flipped* and our world of Light was consumed by the Dark. Out of Balance. Haven't thousands of movies since then shown us this concept? That day or night has already happened. The date could have been in 2015, maybe?

Crowley would be very pleased with today's reality, outside our windows. The Secret State.

Readers do not have to agree. Who did this, How and Why? **They** did this to us, through CERN, as to control us, brainwash us, contain us and continued to Win, while we continued to Lose~

More Darkening...

This is why the youth today are not individuals, not independent-thinkers and are bald, bearded, smoked cigarettes and are covered in "Skin Illustrations."

They're SLAVES! So you think tattoos, short hair and beards are cool and stylish and IN? And everyone got a tattoo, therefore, "I have to get one too, or a lot of them." Everyone has short hair or is bald and millennials have to fit in and be like everyone else. Right? Today, no one would dream of being *different* than the fucked-up norm. And the norm is **masked, skinhead, Brain-Dead, Walking-Dead, Hitler Youth Slaves!** They do not question, protest or resist. Basically, dumb clones of each other.

We're all Slaves, but we don't have to look like Slaves!

(Author's note: I remember a Playboy cartoon from more than 50 years ago and tried to find it, unsuccessfully. So I'll describe it: Parents of a young teenager talked in a room and said: "Thank God our child isn't one of those filthy hippies!" Then we see the kid march down a hall dressed as a Hitler Youth: Skinhead, spikes, rivets, tats, black leather, Maltese Cross and very violent. Who understood at the time of general Peace and Love in the air that this would be the look of future generations? This "coincidence" has actually happened. No more: "Come on people, let's get together." No more protests or resistance to fascism, now everywhere. No more communes and socialism or "Kumbaya." Only kings and queens and the dictates of tyrants, which were obeyed by all smaller and very weak minions).

Young people think they are free, "empowered" and the *kings* and *queen*s of the world! Truth is: They are incredibly unaware of *everything,* especially the fact that they are Slaves!

Smoking cigarettes in an age of legal pot stores? What? So many of the youth don't even smoke weed, which is healthy. They are hooked to tobacco-nicotine more than they ever have been.

They are the stupidest generation that's ever been. Ever been! Don't believe it? You massively-informed people that are always on your "devices"? Always feeding your heads (psyche) with "knowledge" and information? This generation, and most everyone, are not aware of *the dangers of cell phones! If you have your phone in the same place against/near your body...you will develop cancerous tumors in 10 years in that spot and in a rectangular shape.* **Your phone will eventually give you cancer~** The TV or doctors or the government do not tell the public that fact. Healthcare agencies, medical facilities, etc. also don't inform people of that fact. Instead, they *require you to have phones.* And what important knowledge and information have you implanted into yourself via your devices? SHIT! That's what you "Feed Your Head" with these days. Lies. Their lies. If you only woke up to the fact that They've been lying to us poor people for a very long time...Then, maybe things would be different...and I wouldn't be so damn discouraged and hurt by my "Children of Tomorrow."

How can people today, the youth, be dumber than people of the Victorian Age or the Dark Ages? Well, they didn't have to wear 'clown suits' and 'big, floppy shoes' [your masks] simply to buy bread and drink milk, did they?

Look. If it was a real pandemic, which it is not, we'd see dead bodies on the street. There's nothing like that, except for the **false fears** in our minds THEY PUT THERE! If Earth really suffered a global disaster, a real one like we've seen in movies and the world's population actually had dropped, considerably, because of a contagion or poisonous cloud of radiation...or the planet was knocked out of its usual orbit and conditions changed...

Then I would not mind at all, as one of the survivors, that we had to wear protective suits, head-gear with oxygen tanks and walk to a supply-center with others to maintain our lives. That's a disaster, one you saw, touched and tasted. Crown Virus is bullshit. But you've been made incredibly stupid by Them that you'll believe anything They tell you now over Media. They'll never stop lying to you until you stop believing them. All of you.

Remember the polio vaccine and Dr. Jonas Salk back in 1953? Polio was real and a terribly "crippling" disease, especially for young people. We all had little, round marks on our arms. We did the right thing and it *was* the right thing in those innocent times. Today. It's wrong because the Adults in power and in charge of us Children...

No longer saved us and protected us and wanted us to grow up healthy and strong. *There's way too many of us these days.* They [Illuminati devils who own everything because They've built everything] have only been in the process of slow-Extermination of "muggle-rats" in lower classes of society. Sorry. (I'll tell you what you should do...).

'Get Smart!' Rather than be the 'Walking Dead' or the 'Brain Dead.' Good advice.

Pot has gone *"to Pot,"* Co-Ops have been Federally Co-Opted~

It happened again. The fascist Government that we are all forced to serve (& not the other way around) has DESTROYED the wonderful, wonderful dream of Legal Weed and ruined the very long struggle for Hemp legalization. Feds, always under orders from Britain, had everything planned from the beginning: "Oh, so you want to smoke weed legally, do you?" *Yes, please.* "You'll get it, don't worry, but it must be regulated, it must be SAFE for public consumption. That means Big Brother has to inspect it, put it in jars with safety-caps like prescription medicine. Then, the jars are placed inside boxes with full instructions and verifications and levels of THC. It will be highly taxed. You will be happy and love us for what We've done and, in return, say to the government: *"THANK YOU! You're the best!"*

Let me tell you more of the English Engineers' plan on the subject of "wacky tobacky." To Them, everything good and right and pure...*must be corrupted.* That is, if it was for the general public.

In the first years of legal pot (in California), right after Bill 4020 passed, it was beautiful, man. Pot shops or 'dispensaries' popped up everywhere, from large rooms in big buildings to small stores with one room. It was the fastest-growing business in the state. If you walked down any main street in LA, you'd passed a pot store within minutes.

[Author's note: The word "Marijuana" will not be used, since it was slapped onto the ancient, marvelous and extremely versatile Hemp plant, only to make it a menace. See old propaganda films like 'Reefer Madness,' 'Devil's Weed,' etc., and my first article, translated in at least 10 different languages: **'The Real Reason Marijuana Is Illegal.'** It's been made into numerous, short videos. Taken from Jack Herer's book, the article revealed that pot was illegal not because of how it affected us, but because of the vast array of fantastic and superior products that could and should be generated from it. William Randolph Hearst with a monopoly on the Paper Industry and chemical companies like Dupont would be wiped out with full Hemp production when one considered the advancement of machinery in the 20th Century. They were, of course, prime factors in the elimination and subversion of the pot plant].

Over the first few years of Legal Weed, a huge number of dispensaries opened for business in most states. Growers (who were always underground) could SELL, big time. For decades, good pot growers improved techniques but couldn't sell their products. Now they could. But who realized back then that SAFE POT's days were numbered? They gave us everything at first, then took it away! Stores were filled with a wide spectrum of varieties from many sources. It was cheap; it wasn't taxed; they sold hash; it came in plastic bags or plastic containers!

Apparently, Legal Weed still had to clear more federal obstacles and another Bill had to be passed. I remember I said to one of the owners of a large pot store near me: "Isn't this great? It passed! You're gonna be flooded with more growers coming in. You'll have more varieties, prices will go down..."

He cut me off with: "No." He had no smile on his face and I thought that he would because of the recent news. He knew what would happen in future or what was in the process. Later, when I saw strange closures after closures of so many LA shops, I figured it out...

You see, as time went on, more and more changes occurred and we found that less and less varieties were in the stores. No more hash. Now [Nazi] Safety Regulations were the law. Pot had to be inspected, regulated, put in jars and boxes for our safety. No, sir! To fuck up a good thing, like always.

The exact same thing happened with American farms. Good growers of fruits and vegetables HAD TO spray harmful pesticides on all produce, which were not imposed to help us in the least. If farms did not cooperate with new mandates, they were consumed and controlled by the feds. The same idea relates to Weed: Feds think *They know better and are safe-guarding us from dangerous fruit and vegetable growers. They're likely to put anything in food and drinks! We have to make sure that it's safe because it's for public consumption.* No more hippie farmers anymore; it's all government. Maybe there aren't criminals who'd sabotage the produce they sell? They would never do that. BUT THE FEDS WOULD! Dangerous Fluoride in our water system since the 1950s? Paying off 9 out of 10 dentists who lied to us and said we needed the *protection of fluoride.* That 1 out of 10 dentists knew the truth: **Fluoride causes bone decay and neural damage**. That's the truth. If you use tap water, boil it! We're supposed to believe THEY have made it safe for us? When did They ever? They are the problem, not the People.

There were no problems with pot stores, generally, in the early days of legalization. Now there is! One source! That's all you get! The government passed some Shit-Regulation whereby growers had to now have something like a *Zed-stroke, alpha* clearance, form-license to prove that it was federally analyzed for public safety. If you didn't have this, your few years of selling to the public were over. One by one, the Good pot stores were gone. Only a few remained and they are the Government. They are the same: one federal source. You get something called "Hot Box," in a jar, in a box and highly taxed. I would not believe one word printed on that fucking box! It's very hard to open the jar – and this is for our safety?? LIES!!

Don't you know what this means? We are back to the days of underground ILLEGAL WEED! One giant step backwards, nothing ever progressive, forward and better, huh? Never. This was planned. And readers should know who did it to us, again.

As I told them at the (Nazi) pot store: "We did not vote for federal regulations, we voted for the right to buy and sell and smoke pot legally. Not for more fascism and the end of true, honest pot growers."

Pot is now unsafe and is in the exact same state as everything we drink and eat. All foods were fresh from good farmers in the old days. In new days, to a micro degree, they've been *poisoned* by Your Friendly Government, under strict/secret orders to do so. All the while, the poor masses are supposed to believe that the Authorities are making it good, clean and safe for us children? No. They're killing us, slowly.

Believe it or not, this whole *darkening* or things that went from good to bad, could actually be a result of the Mandela Wave. That's my point when you read in this book about terrible things that don't seem Mandela-related...but, maybe they are? The bright front cover of the book turned to the dark back cover. Like everything? Many items that no one would think had anything to do with Mandela, could. Because maybe, everything shouldn't be this dark, nasty and wicked, aye? If you watched and listened to sources of entertainment, all entertainment, something is very wrong in the sense that awful messages and influences were being conveyed. We should go the other way, and no one was living the right way, except for only a few strong people with open eyes. I keep writing about the parallel world that's gone now. If you investigated, you'd find it to be true. The long-standing, sweet dream of the pot grower and the pot smoker is at an end. The pattern of a nightmare reality has repeated and taken its place. And the sad youth of today are completely oblivious that anything had happened at all.

(p.s. I felt sorry for a H.A.I. chain of pot stores that had a huge warehouse in my area. They must have been rolling in the weed with a high number of growers behind them. They must have paid for a dozen billboards in the area, which are still up. But this enormous store(s) was run out of business a couple years ago. They, and many others, didn't have the new license-form that only a few (fed) shops had now. I was too late; when I finally was swayed by the billboard to get the best deals in town, they were gone. Wonder how many more years the billboards will stand? I should have realized why the shop close to me that I went to for years stayed open. It used to be a Gun Shop, the land was federal. I'm lucky: I found an old buddy who grew weed. Fate must have brought us together, because I sure needed a clean source of pot that I trusted. And I trust my friend, not the Authorities. Today, everyone who bought from dispensaries were mindlessly smoking pot that has a potential danger to it...but they believe it's safe. They believe the signs and the lies. You shouldn't. You should know when They are lying to you. Feds are lying to us when They speak<).

Garbage Lyrics.

(Author's note: The title above does not refer to the fact that music lyrics today are garbage and suck badly, Lyrics today are awful because Music is [purposely] garbage and really sucked, badly. They're telling you; you're not listening. Very difficult to find good, new, modern music. No. Here, we will explore the lyrics of the band: 'Garbage.' I loved these guys, had at least three of their albums. I've seen a lot of great performances like Bowie (3 times), the Police (3 times), Depeche Mode (3 times) and Coldplay. I was the oldest guy in the audience when Coldplay played in LA, on a tennis court and was shown on the Kimmel Show later that evening. I didn't care, *I was seeing Coldplay!* Today is very different and I see the dark "magic" in the colors and lyrics, the Deception, the terrible messages in lyrics placed there to mess you up and to not enlighten. Garbage was one band I regretted never seeing live. But that was then, and this is now. I'm a little more Eyes Wide Open and certainly not as "blissful" as I used to be. You see, I'm not a Walking Dead robotoid. I'm alive~).

"Queer." Let me dirty up your mind. Queerest of the Queer. The strangest of the strange. You'll learn to love the pain you feel.

"I Think I'm Paranoid." Prop me up with another pill. I nailed my faith to the sticking pole. (I'm) Manipulated. Bend me, break me, breaking down is easy. Maim me, tame me, you can never change me. Come ahead and fight me. Go ahead and leave me.

"I'm Only Happy When It Rains." I love it when the news is bad. And why it feels so good to feel so sad. I feel good when things are going wrong. I only listen to the sad, sad songs. I only smile in the dark. My only comfort is the night gone black. You can keep me company as long as you don't care. I'm riding high on a deep depression. I'm only happy when it rains.

"Stupid Girl." Don't believe in faith. A million lies to sell yourself. Don't believe in pain. Don't believe in anyone that you can't tame. Stupid Girl. All you had you wasted.

"Trick is to Keep Breathing." She's not the kind of girl. I say, never trust anyone. Can't bear to face the truth.

"When I Grow Up." Cut my tongue out. Happy Hours, Golden Showers. I'll be back to frame you. Trying hard to fit among you. Floating out to Wonderland. Unprotected, God, *I'm pregnant!* Damn the consequences!

"The World is Not Enough." (Bond film). I know what to show. And I know what to conceal. People like us...And we know when to kill.

"Metal Heart." I wish I had a Metal Heart. I wish that I was half as good as you think I am. Now that we know for sure They're telling lies. It's hard to believe anything you hear. The World is round?

"Why Do You Love Me." I'm no Barbie Doll. I'm not your baby, girl. I've done ugly things. Well, I am rotten to the core. I've held back a wealth of shit.

"You Look So Fine." I want to break your heart and give you mine. I'm not like the other girls. I can't take it like the other girls that you used to know. I'm bleeding for you. I'm like a...desert tonight.

If a teacher read these words as poems handed in by a student, the author would certainly be counseled and be thought of as a "very dark and very disturbed individual." But as lyrics couched inside sweet-kickin' Rock Music by a hot band, we drink in the seductive, Nazi programming and *only want more!*

Let's conduct a small experiment, which is for most of you *uninitiated* in the real world, so fooled by Magic Tricks from just about every single famous person. **Nearly all famous people are secret trans-genders. You don't know it because most of you are not in the Secret Club.**

Consider a hypothesis, actually many of them:

Shirley **MANSON** is a stage-name she *had* to assume. Had to, no choice. Because of 'Charles Manson.' (Don't call her "Shirley"). She's a tranny-man and *must* ACT as the sleaziest, sexiest, thing doing exactly the same as the Tranny-Train of singers that preceded her: Blondie, Pat Benatar, Dale Bozio, Pink, and after her, like Ga-Ga. *They're men!* "I'm not like other girls," Manson is telling you! You should believe it if you want the truth and DE-CODE~ She is "stranger than the strange" and "queerer than the queer." "She's" beyond any gay or drag-queen, *because she's a man, baby.* They get off on telling you in lyrics – actors repeating it in movies – comedians saying it in jokes and you think it's funny? No. They're TELLING YOU in different forms what the hideous truth is, but as fans, we don't see it. We laugh. We've been hooked, seduced and *we don't want to know the truth* about the "stars" that are idolized. I want to know. I want to know everything.

So many clues tell you that the rich and famous elites are gender-inverted. You can actually follow the connections; trannies always speak of and promote other trannies. It you have your own TV show, a big band record deal, are a top sport-figure, if you've been featured on Twilight Zone, Star Trek, Star Wars, SNL, James Bond movies, Transformers, Game of Thrones and other high-profile productions, there's a good chance (more than not) you're seeing a tranny. "Soylent Green is people!" and "The Phantom Menace." They may have been telling us all along, but we've failed to understand the clues, the secret meanings in Media. *People, today...children must die for one person to tranny themselves!!* ["Drink your essence"]. And there's millions of trannies, they are who we muggles have been forced to adore. We are told these particular people are "great" and "talented" and we (you) believe it. They are given their songs, they hardly wrote a thing. They have been trained (sports-figures, singers, musicians and other artists) from Day One by the Elites as "play-things" of the Elites. Their purpose is to sway us. They're good and super-talented because they've been trained to perform and they better perform well! Like CIA or KGB training. They better not complain and keep quiet. Onstage, the band (trained monkeys, lying puppets) sounds fantastic! It's because they have quality production behind them and had to learn the act they were given. They do it over and over and over again. Muggles like us do not get this training, these unfair advantages of the *special people.*

The experiment is: Go over "Shirley's" lyrics again. She's pushing way too hard she's a sexy girl with girl-parts ("Doll parts," Hole). *Oh, she didn't use a condom and now she's pregnant?* Really? So Juno. I'm bleeding for you. I'm like a desert. She doesn't have normal feelings, she wants a metallic heart. Have no faith in anything. Don't trust anyone. And the only way you can be her friend is if...you don't care. IS THIS GOOD ADVICE? *Doh!* It's bad advice! Love the pain, fight me, maim me?

What's "she" hiding? How exactly is she not like the other girls? Maybe because, like other famous "girls," Shirley has no va-jay-jay? "A million lies to sell yourself." "Trying hard to fit among you." "Can't bear to face the truth." "I know what to conceal. People like us...And we know when to kill." "I've done ugly things. I'm rotten. Well, I am rotten to the core." "I've held back a wealth of shit..."

She has said: "I am not a sexy woman, I'm not beautiful, I'm not a sex-kitten, I don't flirt with people, yet I've been tagged more of sex symbol than women who truly are and I that's solely because I *don't reveal too much.*" Right. Shirley was named #102 of the "Most Beautiful Women."

One more clue that she is paid very well to completely deceive audiences, is her favorite singer and performer: Frank Sinatra. Oh, God. (Elvis, too) If you research this, you will discover that "Ol' Blue Eyes," (even the "Velvet Fog") was a girl. It's endless, the connections. Elvis introduced us to Ursula [first large spread in Playboy] Andress (later connected to John and Bo Derek) and she was the first Bond Girl, like Marilyn was the first Playmate. Jayne MANsfield, etc., it goes on and on. Sorry, guys, they're dudes. TRANS-VESTIGATE on YouTube and other sources and find out for yourself.

"Young girls now correlate the word 'sexy' with nakedness. It's practically, 'Show us your labia.' If you play that game of allowing yourself to be judged by your physicality, it will not sustain you through a long career." - Shirley Manson (a man's son).

Manson also stated in an interview that she "loves looking at naked bodies." Always genitalia? I'll bet she'd never show a muggle fan *her* nudity, what *she's* packin'?

She's an actress, of course, and Manson once modeled for Calvin Klein [say no more]. She appeared in the TV series, 'Terminator: The Sarah Conner Chronicles' with Lena Heady and Summer Glau. Manson was a Terminator! Type-casting. Lena Headey played Sarah Conner and evil Queen Cersei in 'Game of Thrones,' and who else was in the G.O.T. mega-TV series? Very old, Lady Tyrell, played by "dame" Diana Rigg, who played (hot) Mrs. Peel in the 'Avengers' TV series long ago and won a BAFTA-award. So it goes. It's all connected and just about all-trannies. Didn't you know?

(Shirley Manson) "...has reported that she used to cut herself as a teenager, even keeping a Swiss Army Knife in her boots, and has since used her celebrity status to bring awareness to the dangers of self-mutilation." (note: I don't believe it. These back-stories are *given* to celebrities by their Masters. They, in turn, read scripts of "what's true in their private lives." It's their sacrifice, their forced rituals. They have to stick to the lies no matter what. They are herded Goats who herd us, the Sheeple.)

Are musicians good role models? They shouldn't be. Look at the messages. *I loved Garbage for years!* See, that doesn't sound right, does it? Maybe it is. Not the music; their music's great! The GARBAGE is what They hand us on a shiny tray. I, at first, thought *she* was hot and many other lady-singers. I think any Baby-Boomer who grew up with the Beatles envied the fame/fortune and world's attention and wanted to be a rock star. I loved the '80s music, especially. As a visual artist, at first, I loved MTV. "I want my MTV!" I didn't know it stood for Masonic TV, truly. And that its headquarters was located in a NY Masonic Temple. *So, that's why the music completely disappeared in only a few years?* Yep. It was just there to hook you, folks. Again. Celebrities all look super when they are young, beautiful. But trannies don't age well. That's why you'll see those "What celebrities look like now!" ads. They play on this fact that we muggles wouldn't believe. The rich and famous can't defy aging with the products and operations available to them? No. They appear as monsters and can only play monster-characters in the movies, as aged actors. See what young Shirley looked like in the 'Queer' or 'Paranoid' videos, then compare that to her appearance in fairly recent performances? Monstrous! See, they are "artists," and have incredible flamboyant looks [Elton, Liberace, Boy George, Madonna, Bjork, Kate Bush, Ga-Ga, Robert Smith of the Cure, etc.]. This was done to hide what they really are: The biggest drug-users (hormones) and have seriously fucked-up their bodies over a lifetime. USE YOUR EYES and see beneath the surface.

We are going to move from Shirley "Bleed Like Me" Manson and examine the other end of the spectrum. Not a MTF, but a FTM: a female changed into a male, one of millions...

Bryan Ferry. We will look for clues in the lyrics of a fine band. (p.s. I once thought, before my eyes were opened. He was married to tranny-model Jeri Hall. Then she married Mick (no) Jagger. All connected. Stories we're told about stars' lives were nowhere near reality).

Roxy's Lyrics.

"More Than This." There is nothing more than this. You know, there is nothing more, more than this. [No dick?].

"Avalon," (refers to Atlantis). Yes, the Picture's changing every moment. And your destination, you don't know it.

"Love is the Drug." *Got a hook in me.* Slick, cool, elegant, Brian Ferry is one horny dude in this song. Zappa would call him a "dancing fool." ABBA would call him a "Dancing Queen." "Stake my place at the singles bar...you can guess the rest."

"Slave to Love." [him and Robert Palmer]. To need a woman...though your World is *changing.*

What does Roxy Music call one of their albums: "Boys and Girls." *Of all things.* If you looked at the album's front cover, there's a gal and a guy. But directly above and very close to the "girl's" head, is the word: "BOYS." "GIRLS" is closer to the "guy's" head than her head.

Roxy's "To Turn You On" video showed classy models, very much like Victoria's Secret supermodels on a runway, one after the other. I'd bet they were mostly all womanized-boys, right off the *factory* of the Cloning Center (or something like that). Lyrics are: "I would leave you as you were, if I want to. Then, I wonder is it fair? Now you're on your own, who cares about you?" [I understand the blank, empty expressions on these rich and famous models' faces. They're not happy. What do they know about the industry that the general public does not?].

"Take a Chance with me." ...Too much love has made me sad for so long. Should learn to love the way I do. I was blind, can't you see?

Maybe the most revealing is Roxy Music's "Mother of Pearl." Well, I've been up all night, again. Party-time wasting, is too much fun. I step back thinking of Life's Inner Meaning (really, Bryan?) and my latest fling. It's a pantomime. If you're looking for love in a **Looking Glass world**, it's pretty hard to find. With every goddess a letdown. Every idol a bring down. Search for perfection. Serpentine sleekness was always my weakness. Filigree fancy beats the plastic you. Your high-brow holy with lots of soul, melancholy shimmering. Take refuge in pleasure. Just give me your future. **WE'LL FORGET THE PAST**. Submarine lover, in a shrinking world, in your detached world.

One more mention of dark, wicked things, so widespread and normal in today's universe, and that was creepy lyrics to a beautiful song: 'I Want to be Adored' by the Stone Roses. I heard this song 100 times on KROQ in LA and thought it was such loveliness in sound and melody. I never realized the other words in the song outside of: "I want to be adored." Until I played it on YT and the Stone Roses singer sang, first line: "I don't have to sell my soul. He's already in me. I want to be adored!" Oh! I see now: You don't have to sign in blood or kill your first-born for Satan to get rich and famous. Devil is already in you; you channeled him; you're one with him. Got it. There were only those few lines in the pleasing melody that repeated and repeated. Who knew what really was said unless you listened (and looked) very carefully? *Damn the Devil for his hot women and seductive music!* Did you know Apollo (Christ) invented Music...and the Devil stole it and corrupted it? Nicely. Yeah, yeah, yeah.

Endless popular songs can be broken down to their true/negative messages and influence, but we are not aware of this programming until we closely examine the lyrics. We hear and feel sweetness and don't see the real sourness behind it. My quote: "**Music moves the body, lyrics move the mind.**" One of the best examples is Morrissey's song: 'The Last of the Famous International Playboys.' At first, listeners heard and enjoyed a great, attractive, rockin' song that you think is funny. Morrissey (or Elton John, Liberace) might be the last "playboys" with a hunka-hunka burnin' love for the ladies. First hundred times I listened to it on KROQ, I thought it was hilarious...until I sat down and watched the lyrics on YT many years later. My God! Again, with knowledge of secret (British) societies and what They actually did to their packaged slaves, I freaked! I learned who Reggie and Ronnie Kray were:

"...twin brothers, were British criminals, the foremost perpetrators of organized crime in the East End of London during the 1950s and 1960s. With their gang, known as the Firm, the Krays were involved with murder, armed robbery, arson, protection rackets and assaults."

With that little background known, let's dive into lyrics of the "cute" song:

"Dear hero imprisoned with all the new crimes that you are perfecting. Oh, I can't help quoting you, because everything you said rings true. And now in my cell, well, I followed you and here's a list of **who I slew**. Reggie Kray, do you know my name? And in my cell, well, I loved you. Ronnie Kray, do you know my face? In our lifetime those who kill, the newsworld hands them stardom. These are the ways on which I was raised: I never wanted to kill. I am not naturally evil. Such things I do just to make myself more attractive to you. Have I failed? I am the last of the famous international playboys."

Gee, again, They're telling us what's really going on. The fucking CROWN sanctions and funds bloody murders, assassinations, wars, protection rackets and the most famous people you'd never believe were part of the ugliness. (Like they made "Jack the Ripper," then lied about it in movies). If you performed MURDERS and TORTURE to please your Masters who control everything from the shadows, then "the newsworld hands you stardom." [p.s. That's what *I'm* saying; maybe you'll believe the lyrics?]. The prison is the hell-world of Celebrity that they cannot get out of after you signed in blood and did abominable things that the public never knew (or they'd never follow you). It's worse than the CIA or KGB. In Morrissey's case, they could have tortured their slave in a real prison, then gave him a pretty song so he'd always be reminded of the pain and that he was only a dog to Them? What connection to the Krays? With more digging, you find the connection...The bad-ass twin brothers and their associates were utilized by the Monarchy to keep everyone in line. Certainly to eliminate those who might be trouble or a threat to their powerful organization. I'm sure the Krays knew Jimmy Savile very well. Morrissey told us: He didn't want to kill; he *had* to kill, he wasn't a bad person inside.

Deception. I hate it. Especially, when it was colored pretty and shoved into us as *wonderfulness*.

The next song is perfect PROGRAMMING that we think is nothing more than a popular song. Oh yeah? "QUEEN!" There's a band name for you: Could it have any significance? What did Freddie Mercury sing near the beginning of their biggest song, 'Bohemian Rhapsody'? What were the first words out of his mouth that we all heard at 'Live Aid'?...

"Mama! Just killed a man. Put a gun against his head. Pulled the trigger, now he's dead. Mama! (My) Life had just begun, but now I've thrown it all away! Mama, oooh, didn't mean to make you cry." I'd bet it was Freddie's "SACRIFICE" (most used word in Show-business). Given BR that he must perform at the beginning of all concerts...just to remind him...of exactly what he had done for the "Queen." If early recruits *refused* to do what's expected of them in the Fraternity (train), like if Freddie and the "boys" declined when given the choice...Then, we'd never have heard of a band called *Queen*.

These are your heroes? Not mine. Not anymore.

Oh! Where the hell are the Chevin? You know the Chevin? No? The Chevin should be, by now, as famous as U2, Muse or Coldplay. Yeah. *Nearly 9 frikken years ago* they performed their HIT (All bands tracked for stardom are given an initial, big, overplayed Hit to launch them) on the David Letterman Show, called: 'Champion.' See the video and the fantastic Letterman performance! Wow. They pushed their first album: 'Borderland.' Were they themselves on the borderline between super-success and failure? I think so. They had everything going for them, a great first album just like Coldplay's amazing first album. (How does that happen on its own? It doesn't). They had a good-looking singer with maybe the most powerful vocal chords you've ever heard. Letterman was knocked out, overwhelmed and did not say his usual: "Nice job." Where the fuck are they? If you don't get me, yet, I'm saying the greatest singers and songwriters with real talent...get absolutely nowhere! Doesn't matter how great you really are – only matters how great THEY will make you. But only if you bend over for Them and take it!! I'm theorizing what may have happened. Who knows? Not a second album? 9 years? This is all we know as outsiders: "Frontman Coyle Girelli began working on a solo project in 2016 and released his debut solo single 'Where's My Girl?'...ahead of the release of his debut solo album 'Love Kills,' which is set for a summer 2018 release." Are you kidding me? Something's very wrong here. No? What are the youth left with today, musically? Shit. Stupidest, no-talent bands are thrust to the top. It's embarrassing. Quality is against The Law! We are no longer given quality in music or movies or the truth in anything. Not anymore. Sad.

The worst example, in my view, of ugliness-deception and pure horror today, which was called "art," is the puppet of the British Illuminati, the package that's presented as Billie Eilish. DECODE! It's Billie (boy) English (who own HIM lock, stock and barrel). This is how far we have fallen. Worldwide, young girls chant these popular lyrics (brainwashing) over and over at "her" concerts and along with "her" recordings:

From "All the Good Girls Go To Hell"...

"My Lucifer is lonely. (Saint) Peter's on vacation. Can't commit to anything but a crime. Pearly Gates look more like a picket fence. All the good girls go to hell. Because even **God HERSELF** has enemies. Heaven's out of sight. She'll want the Devil on her team. Man is such a fool, why are we saving him? My Lucifer is lonely. There's nothing to save now. My God is gonna owe me."

Now if you examined "her" "music" videos, your eyes would view some of the most disturbing imagery you can imagine. Sweet, soft (castrato) voice mixed with visions from Hell. That's what's given to the youth today: everything terrible, dressed as prettiness. Did you notice that God was once more reinforced as a WOMAN? That's what the Baphomet (look it up) witches were commanded, ordered to express to millions of their fans. Ariana Grande (Will Farrell called her a "witch" in Zoolander II) as well as Billie English and others today...say God's a female. Question: Who's telling us this? Answer: Monsters! The most evil creatures in the world. They should be silenced, not praised. Everything is wrong here! Remember? God's a dude and if you're GOOD, then you do not go to Hell.

Margaux Hemingway's life was tragic, granddaughter of author Ernest Hemingway, she was one of the first supermodels. She had extraordinary beauty, born into a famous family, along with sister Muriel. She had everything going for her. Then her movie 'Lipstick' bombed with awful reviews of her acting abilities and, possibly as a result, Margaux's life turned to parties and alcohol. (ps. I remember *her* 'Babe' commercial and had to see it again on YT. My eyes today viewed the commercial very differently than as an ignorant, horny teenager. Who knew then that They pushed boys upon the public [Playboy Magazine, modeling, etc.] as the most beautiful girls, like Marilyn, Jayne, Sophia, Raquel, etc.? Also, who knew that They would hide the truth in code and believe we'd never find out? In movie lines, lyrics, etc. A hundred years later some of the masses have found out). Let's review most of the lines from one of the Babe commercials by Faberge:

With sexy jazz in the background, a sexy black man's voice said: "You're like no other babe ever been born...You're one of the boys, but you're a real girl." Christmas 1977. Question: Who could imagine that the ultimate Babe was a guy? Answer: Every single Insider-Club member, famous people. Not us.

In the study of Movies and Messages: a new, creepy film is called: 'The Unholy.' "She's here."

Actor Jeffrey Morgan's character said on the phone: "I have a story for you. Something the Examiner will love. A healing, possibly divine. A girl performed miracles after a visitation by the Virgin Mary." Cut to close-up of the girl and her eyes turned black. He interviewed the girl.

She said, "...Seeing is believing."

He asked, "Why do you think Mary chose you?"

"I opened myself up and welcomed her in."

An expert in the paranormal told Morgan's character: "I've investigated half a dozen 'miracles,' proved them all false."

"You think there could be other forces at work here?"

Disastrous events happened, of course, it's a horror film. (Aren't they all?). Fires, explosions, bloody killings, destruction!

"This is not the work of the Virgin Mary. It's the work of the unholy," said a priest before the creature in her killed him.

The catchphrase for the movie: BE CAREFUL WHO YOU PRAY TO.

The possessed girl said: "Offer Her your SOULS." (Again, plural).

The movie's final banner read: Only in theaters. Good Friday. April 2. Get tickets now.

Theaters only? Isn't that strange these days? And on Good Friday? I don't know, Russell Crowe played Noah and criticized the real Noah. Christian Bale (Baal) played Moses, but at the 44th Golden Globes where he won for his performance of Dick Cheney, he shocked audiences at home when he also thanked SATAN. Yeah. And John Lennon criticized Jesus Christ, so what the hell is really going on?

Did They have to do one more unholy film and actually call it 'The Unholy'? Did They have to bring in the Virgin Mary? *Christ.* They made a tranny play Jesus in every movie! Max von Sydow, Jeffrey Hunter (Star Trek connection), Liam Neeson, Ralph Fiennes, Ted Neeley, Willem Dafoe, Ewan McGregor, Matthew Modine, Jeremy Sisto, Jim Caviesel, Cameron Mitchell, Robert Powell, Will Ferrell. Will Ferrell? Yep. They did the same with the Supermans, Batmans, Tarzans, Bonds, etc.

'The Unholy' film was probably based on the Miracle of Fatima or "Miracle of the Sun" events in Portugal, October, 1917, and *twisted them very darkly.* Three shepherd children were, supposedly, contacted by the Virgin Mary. Who knows the truth in this very publicized case? It could have been aliens that experimented on us? Or the government? It could have been the real deal? Or something else entirely?

The possessed girl in the film stated: "Seeing is believing." Could that be taken to mean: "Believe what is around us now...and forget the past."?

A new Alanis Morissette song is called: 'Everything.' This again, like all pop bands, will be sung by fans at the concerts, over and over. The "sweet" message to us is really the truth: "I can be an asshole of the greatest kind. You see all my Light and *you love my Dark.* Everything of what I am ashamed..." She and famous people in general, are some of the worst people on Earth. *They keep telling us this and other horrible things in code.* They exult the Dark, the evil, over the Light and goodness. And she's a boy, like the majority of famous "gals."

Do the real stories of celebrities, truth to their actual deaths, have to do with the world of secret trans-genders and not the BS the Press handed us? Maybe some of them do? Case in point, one more suggestive-code song, out of thousands, is by the Cranberries called: 'Stars.' A beautiful little song, sung by the **late** Delores O'Riordan: "I guess I will be alright. Desire gets you nowhere. And you are always right. My, you are so perfect. (I'll) Take you as you are. I love you just the way you are. I'll have you just the way you are. Does anyone love the way they are? The stars are bright tonight. A distance is between us. And I will be Okay. Still I have my ugliness. Star, star."

Delores was a gorgeous, little girl (tranny-boy) who died long before "her" time. "Accidental drowning" is what They tell us in the record. But what's the true story? She always appeared different, a lot like David Bowie's changes. See the video for 'Stars.' Cute as a bunny. But why gyrate *her* torso, *her* crotch really, right in our face? So Shirley Manson. Does "Lola" mean anything to you?

Or how did Chester Bennington of Linkin' Park actually die? I'll bet it wasn't a "suicide by hanging." It makes no sense. *Oh, the price for fame these kids endure, drugs, alcohol, being idolized, the pressures or some phantom disease.* We are never told the truth. That might reveal way too many occulted secrets. Biggest secret is (mostly) the girls are boys and the boys are girls. Same can be said for actors. Huge list of actors that died before their time, such as Paul Walker (Fast & Furious) to name only one. We should be very suspicious of the stories Media (Big Brother) hands us. Because, THEY are lying.

Paul is really dead.

Let's get at the heart of the truth: They killed Paul McCartney on November 9, 1966, only 3 years into "Beatlemania." Who knows exactly what happened? Rare reports said it was a car accident. Maybe not an accident? Examine clues the Beatles' Engineers left for us on the Sgt. Peppers' cover and covers that followed (to "rub in our face" what They did)...

The entire concept for the greatest album and cover of all time was the DEATH of the old band. It's a funeral [real fun] for the original Beatles as they stood to the side as "mop-tops" and in Beatle boots. Front and center was the New Band, all colorful and psychedelic with a different, out-of-this-world sound and appearance. It captured all of us and changed the world. It was a different band because Paul was gone and replaced by "Faux" Paul. They could not let the 'magic' and Money-Flow stop after only 3 years~

If They could fake the Moon-landings and kill JFK, They could get away with anything!

Yellow flowers below "Beatles" was a left-handed bass guitar that spelled: "Paul?" A toy Aston Martin was on top of a ragdoll, as in a car-accident victim was only a "ragdoll"? If a mirror [Illuminati ploy] bisected "Lonely Hearts," we viewed: "I ONE IX HE DIE," or 11/9 (9/11 switched), I, I, I & X. A diamond symbol pointed up to McCartney. A hand was over Paul's head, which was a death symbol (5) in some religions. Hindu god Shiva, the Destroyer, pointed directly at Paul. Inner sleeve showed McCartney in uniform with an OPD badge: "Officially Pronounced Dead." Original SP album had the lyrics printed on the back and a picture of the band. George's thumb pointed to the line: "Wednesday morning at 5 O'clock," the alleged time of death. That day of 11/9 was a Wednesday. Paul had his back turned on the photo while the other 3 did not, also a sign of Death in some cultures. "He blew his mind out in a car," Lennon sang. In 'Come Together,' "1 & 1 & 1 is 3." "Turn me on, dead man," "I bury Paul" and "Miss him, miss him" were heard *in reverse* on the recordings as well as other clues, said *backwards*. This was not because of George Martin. It was because of occult wizard Aleister Crowley!

'Magical Mystery Tour' album was released with a booklet of

clues. The cover had "Beatles" written in stars. A mirror placed to the letters formed "2317438," supposedly the phone # for a London mortuary. Photos in the booklet showed a shoeless Paul, *more death imagery* since people were buried without shoes. A uniformed Paul sat behind a desk and was under a sign that read: "I was." (For those in the know, another nod to Crowley). Ringo's drum head seemed to spell: "Love the 3 Beatles" and next to it was McCartney's blood-stained boots. In a photo from 'Your Mother Should Know,' the four were in white suits. Paul had a black carnation on his lapel, while the other three had red ones. A 'Fool on the Hill' cartoon showed Paul with a crack in his head. The terrible film, 'Magical Mystery Tour,' contained the "Walrus" song, and in the background a distant, white car appeared to have struck Paul's head. Was the whole purpose of MMT film, the group's first "failure," to show one more clue, or many more clues, of the global con-job?

The White Album was devoid of clues except for one big one: A photo of Billy Shears with glasses and his face was a bit different. This was the New Paul before the operations and plastic surgeries.

The cover of 'Abbey Road' depicted what? A funeral procession. Another funeral? *Hey, who died?* John in white, as priest. Ringo in black, as undertaker. Paul, barefoot again as dead guy. George, in blue workman's clothes as a grave-digger. McCartney was out of step with the others and had his eyes closed. Paul held a cigarette with his right-hand. But he was left-handed, which suggested: This was not Paul. A Volkswagen in the background had the plate: "LMW 28IF LMW," interpreted to mean: "Linda McCartney Weeps" and the rest was his age if he had lived.

The original cover of 1966's 'Yesterday and Today' album had the Beatles, calmly, surrounded by bloody, raw meat and doll parts! Yes. We didn't see this in America, but some did in England. Was the intention ritualistic and satanic (since They honored Crowley's devilish philosophies)? Or, one more clue to the big secret, Paul's bloody death? They made the distinction of *Yesterday,* the old band, and *Today,* with the new band. Exactly the same distinction illustrated on the cover of Sgt. Peppers.

You can listen to (YT) obscure bands that recorded bizarre, little-known songs about the 'Paul Is Dead' scandal, such as The Mystery Tour with "The Ballad of Paul." The entire song went through the albums' clues to a Beatle beat. Werbley Finster did: "So Long, Paul."

Zacherias and the Tree People sang the song: "We're All Paul Bearers."
Even Billy Shears and the All-Americans recorded: "Brother Paul."
Early Todd Rundgren's Nazz did: "Hang On, Paul." The song was
supposed to be about the tragic death of a real life bartender? I don't
know. The lyrics could be applied to McCartney and was released less
than two years after 11/9/66. A more recent band has the name: "Death
Cab For Cutie." Paul was the cute Beatle. Either the old bands simply
were caught up in the *Paul's Dead-mania* at the time and recorded
songs on the subject, or, they were Insiders and knew. Could be a
mixture. I'd bet big names like Todd absolutely knew Paul was dead.
(Todd's smallest Sacrifice: never being in the Rock n' Roll Hall of
Fame, sorry).

It's not difficult to imagine that "The Gods" of Britain trained,
like CIA-training, a lookalike Paul who continued the Beatles and
mesmerized everyone on the planet (as magical wizards). They held a
radio contest in England and searched for a "Lookalike" Paul. They
discovered an amazing one – taller and right-handed. Operations were
performed, face and voice box were adjusted and a passable
doppelganger was presented to the world. There were no longer
records of that radio station and verifiable proof that the contest ever
existed. The shock was the New Guy had natural/musical abilities.
This surprised royals who financed every detail of the deception and
created clues to the deception, far beyond expectations. New Paul took
over the band, as the Peppers' cover suggested. Here was the beginning
of the big feud with John Lennon. They were best buddies before.
Now *Paul* was the leader, forced to be in command? He wasn't even
one of the originals. All three of them were probably very pissed and
well aware of the strange and very powerful events that happened:
Their good friend was dead and gone and some ego-maniac joker took
his place. The "friction" was certainly evident during the later "Let it
Be" recording sessions. The 3 couldn't "Let It Be," with what they
knew and the band's break-up was imminent.

Why murder the original Paul, if it was murder? Possibly,
musically, he disagreed with the psychedelic, LSD-influenced and new
direction the band was *forced* into? Maybe he wanted to go back to the
roots of rock 'n roll, rhythm and blues and not have mind-bending
sound-effects?

The replacement McCartney's name is **Billy Shears**. Billy
Shears! Now. The handlers, the Masters of the Beatles, the real ones in

charge, did Royalty hide what They had done as far as the name? Did They cover up the existence of the lookalike's NAME? [Today, They'd have cloned him]. Wouldn't you think so? No. Instead of deleting "Billy Shears," They LOUDLY SCREAMED HIS NAME:

"...Sgt. Pepper's Lonely Hearts Club Band.
It's wonderful to be here,
It's certainly a thrill.
You're such a lovely audience,
We'd like to take you home with us,
We'd love to take you home.
I don't really want to stop the show,
But I thought that you might like to know,
That the singer's going to sing a song,
And he wants you all to sing along.
So let me introduce to you
The one and only **Billy Shears**
And Sgt. Pepper's Lonely Hearts Club Band!"

On SP, the Beatles screamed his name: "Biiiiilleeeeee Sheeeeeeeeeeears!!" very high, just before Ringo came in with: 'A Little Help from My Friends.' We were introduced to the new guy and the new band. There's the line: "...the one and only Billy Shears!" (p.s. Personal Story. I lived through this era as a young man, a hippie. And we closely went through every sound and vision of our idols, especially the Beatles. No one ever thought, said or whispered: "Who's Billy Shears?" and this was analyzed to death and passed around among many fans. It never came up (not saying it's a Mandela, but...). It strikes me now, I am stunned: Why wasn't "Billy Shears" ever mentioned long ago? "What? the Beatles band was now Billy Shears' band? Huh?" Never said or questioned among huge crowds so influenced by Beatlemania. I thought the line was: "And after all these years...It's Sgt. Pepper's Lonely Hearts Club Band!" "After all these years," not "Billy Shears." Ha. Sounds similar. Why is "After all these years" burned into my brain? *Lyrics were printed on the back* and we went over them hundreds of times! Wow. Incredible, unbelievable, what these bastards could, would and did do to the unsuspecting public. Sure, I could've gotten it wrong and it was Billy Shears all this time. But I don't think so).

They promoted "Billy Shears," the name of the new Paul, proud of what They had done. The nerve, the gall to push this vile act, this horrible truth or simply a reminder of what They did, over and over again, onto us. The film with the Bee Gees and Peter Frampton was called: 'Sgt. Peppers' Lonely Hearts Club Band.' Shocking what They gave us:

The plot: "In August 1958, Sergeant Pepper died in the middle of a performance...Sgt. Pepper left his musical legacy...to his grandson, <u>Billy</u> <u>Shears</u> (Peter Frampton). Billy forms the new Lonely Hearts Club Band with his 3 best friends...(The Bee Gees)...The bands' leader has died and now it's up to his grandson...to carry on the group's traditions...(with) the group's magic instruments..."

Look at the plot of this wonderful, colorful musical that most of us enjoyed: During WWI, Sgt. Pepper brought musical relief to war-torn soldiers. He died, like Paul, during a "performance," and it was up to someone else to carry on the traditions of the band. That someone was the grandson, a new generation led by the Peter Frampton character. That character was named Billy Shears! *Frampton played Shears!* Nothing was hidden! **Everything evil is In Plain Sight**, but most everyone has not deciphered the Code. I guess people thought it was sweet and lovely? Do you understand yet? What They have done to us and what was once a good and pure universe? Mostly.

Who knew at the time that They were in a long process of fooling the world, as They always had? How many would believe it today? Few. When we viewed online the 'Paul is Dead' controversy, it was (almost) always stated as "MYTH," Not true, but examine the endless clues or "coincidences." They say Mandela is a myth as well. They lie and have eternally lied to us. Who's They? Who's telling us this?! Royalty, we are forced to bow to and honor as great. Our long-standing Dark Overlords.

The Beatles and management have always maintained: *This was a case of our imaginations that worked overtime. We don't know what you're talking about, what? Paul's not dead.*

Suddenly, They changed? After all these years. Now it's admitted: *Yes, we purposely placed clues everywhere on Beatles covers to make you think 'Paul was dead.' How cool, huh?* No. While on a recent vacation in New Orleans, 'Paul McCartney' confessed to what we've suspected. Clues were "...deliberately planted by the group as part of an elaborate scheme dating back to the summer of 1966." The excuse or reason for pretending one of the band was dead had to do with *fear the band wouldn't sell as many records as before with the new, odd, artistic direction of the Beatles*. Bullshit.

Seven years ago, in an interview that really stunned the world, Ringo Starr admitted the truth:

"We felt guilty about the deception. We wanted to tell the world the truth, but we were afraid of the reactions it would provoke. We thought the whole planet would hate us for all the lies we had told. So we kept lying but sending subtle clues to relieve our conscience. When the first rumors finally began about the whole thing, we felt very nervous and started fighting a lot with each other. At some point, it was too much for John and he decided to leave the band."

Richard Starkey (at 74) stated that he was "...afraid the truth was going to die with him" and the "Deception would never be revealed."

"What would you think" has happened now? Obviously. He was made to recant the interview from 7 years ago. *Ringo no longer believes Paul's dead.* Then what the fuck was that interview from 7 years back? This could be a Mandela. Maybe he was not forced to recant by the Monarchy? Maybe it was a Mandela-change? In one universe, he confessed. In this universe, he did not. (Did the same happen to Sinbad, who now denied that he ever made a Shazam movie? He didn't. Not in this world). The right thing would be to confess your sin. The wrong thing would be to deny it. In recent years, Ringo and "Paul" perform their magic onstage together and there is not a trace of the truth left anymore. *Crushed.*

Lennon and McCartney did not write and create Beatles music. The popular songs were written by teams of skilled British musicians, ghost-writers [like with all bands and the greatest of novels] and based on modern, audio-frequency principles of Theodor Adorno, super-genius.

Those 4 guys weren't that good.

They were made to be great. British, you know? John Lennon, a man of peace? Then why did he criticize Jesus Christ, a real man of peace? Yeah. Of course, he was forced to do everything he had done, exactly like all celebrity Goats England owned. It's SIR Paul McCartney. Those who are knighted by the Queen were some of the most evil men who had ever walked the Earth. Wizards of royal deception. Sweet sirens we have followed.

Another comment: It was more than 7 years ago when I came across a 'List of the Biggest Conspiracies,' which I'm sure the Moon and JFK topped the list. I saw that #4 was the whole 'Paul's Dead'

Conspiracy that I had totally forgotten about. I think everyone had for decades. Oh, it was huge in 1970! But 99% gone, even those who seriously followed the clues on albums and elsewhere were convinced: "It was just a publicity stunt" and thought no more about it. I investigated, as an adult, and stacked the evidence together and *Shazam!* I had no concept there was that much! This revitalized the old idea (plus when placed with Illuminati info) and I was profoundly struck: It was true. Paul was dead and the creature who walked in his shoes today was a manufactured imposter.

Get this: A drummer friend of mine at the time sent me THE RINGO INTERVIEW! Ringo confessed! This explained many odd things like Paul's war with Lennon, who was the leader? Why John left? And the hostility the others had toward Paul. Not to mention a two-inch taller, new Paul.

Paul was dead and Ringo's world-shattering interview proved it! [Harrison said it also]. It was bizarre as hell that the very thought of the real McCartney being killed in 1966 had not circled my brain in 40 years, and NOW!? I spontaneously studied it, *then* was hit with Ringo's interview a week or so later? Wow. Thanks, angels. I flashed back to the death of John Lennon in 1980. Of course, the Media aired reactions of the other Beatles. Paul's demeanor was different from the others, I distinctly remember. The others were distraught. Paul was not. [Maybe it was *relief* on his face?]. He left and the last thing he said to the cameras with almost a smile was, "Cheers."

Brave New World and A Clockwork Orange as Prophecy.

Aldous Huxley's "dystopian," fictional novel was published in 1932. It was largely set in a futuristic "World [Police] State," whose citizens were environmentally engineered into an intelligence-based, social hierarchy. The year was "AF 632," which stood for 632 years "After Ford." Ford and his Model-T were revered as *god* because of the precision of machinery, "right off the assembly-line." Citizens were just as cold as machines. Sex without love, without families. They were test-tube babies, spat out of genetic labs, bred for success. Society was composed of top elites (with all the power), elites (with certain privileges), citizens and a mindless, lower class that was programmed to do dangerous jobs and the jobs of robotic servants.

Brave New World presented a future with great advancements in reproductive technology, sleep-learning, psychological manipulation [Mind-Control] and various forms of social conditioning. In 1999, the Modern Library ranked BNW at #5 on its list of the 100 best English-language novels of the 20th Century. It was often compared to George Orwell's '1984' because of its dark, mechanical view of a totally controlled and very bleak future. 1984 was published 17 years after BNW.

Huxley had stated that Brave New World was inspired by the utopian novels of H.G. Wells ('A Modern Utopia' and 'Men Like Gods'). Huxley went against the usual, optimistic, utopian novels, popular at the time. He wrote a frightening vision and called BNW a "negative utopia."

From 1957, Aldous Huxley was interviewed on television by Mike Wallace:

"Twenty-seven years ago, you wrote 'Brave New World,' a novel that predicted we'd all live under a frightful dictatorship. Today, Mr. Huxley says his 'fictional' world of horror...is probably just around the corner for all of us."

Huxley was asked, "What are these forces that are enemies to Freedom?" His first response was "overpopulation," not coincidentally

the same as what Prince Philip suggested. It was the old story of too
many people and not enough resources. Bullshit. We, the People, have
not been allowed to develop our sciences, such as Tesla Technology. If
true knowledge and real, positive techniques were permitted and doled
out to the masses, *we'd have more energy and electricity than billions
of people could ever use!*

Aldous Huxley stated that the next thing that retarded our natural
progress or evolution was technology...

Wallace asked: "You mean we develop our televisions, but we
don't know how to use it correctly, is that the point?" Huxley certainly
agreed. I say: Technology and knowledge are not problems, depended
on how they were used.

He told Wallace: "Dictatorships in the future will be very
different than those of the past." They will be invisible, subtle, not
blatant and overt like Hitler or in '1984.' He spoke of George Orwell's
vision of the future as a fascist State that used terror and violence.
Different in the real world of the future. [How'd he know?].

"They will have to have the consent of the Rule (British royalty),
and this They will do, by drugs...and new techniques of
propaganda...They will bypass Rational Man and be appealing to his
deep emotions (dark side, base instincts), his physiology even, etc.,
and making him (mankind) **LOVE his slavery**. HAPPY, under the
new regime. And they're in a situation where they oughtn't be."

Mike Wallace asked, "We believe, anyway, that we live in a
democracy..." [Then why was the show funded by "The Republic," as
was said by the narrator in the intro of the interview? "Republic" is not
a democracy, it is a rule by a council of covert dictators]. "...here in the
United States. Do you believe that this BNW, in a quarter century or in
a century, could come here to our shores?"

"I think it could."

Nowhere, in any writing or interview, could there ever be the
smallest hint that BRITAIN has been the long-standing Enemy to
Mankind. The Force against Progress. Always hidden. How could it
ever be blamed? We have not learned the lessons in '1984' or '451.'
English/German, royal masons made it so, everything; all engineered
to happen in advance. H.G. Wells, Jules Verne, Aldous Huxley, George
Orwell, Anthony Burgess **were not visionaries** who strangely
predicted the future. Not modern prophets. They, and many other
famous people, are and were modern 'puppets,' "mouth-pieces,"

minions of British Royals who created them, and who they owe for their success and fame. Like every celebrity. These guys were British, you know? They can only support the evil Empire. (I'll bet if you found a real visionary, they wouldn't have English blood. Why were all of them Brits?).

Then Huxley mentioned "subliminal projection." He and his Club members (Tavistock) would know about methods of Mind Control. "Children singing beer and toothpaste commercials," he stated, with a direct relationship to the "dangers of a dictatorship." "Children were more suggestible." Hitler youth? Huxley spoke not of an immediate threat to America and the rest of the world. It was Things to Come.

(ps. Cigarettes, such a pet-peeve of mine! Why always cigarettes, always in the forefront, always there?! Always pushed by every TV host from Serling to Dahl, and by all actors and British rock stars? What happened in the beginning of almost every scene in almost every old movie? They lit up. Because it's cool? No, because it's *deadly.* Royal seal on every pack and on every package of alcohol).

Of course, Mr. Huxley (as well as Mr. Orwell), pointed out the terrible dangers of TELEVISION. How it was innocent and harmless now, but in future: Virtually used as a weapon against the masses. Who would do this? Wallace asked: "Why is it that the right people will not be using these devices in future, but the wrong people (and be in control)?"

"These are instruments of power. A Passion for Power," was his answer. Who sought ultimate power? Sith, not Jedi. It's a metaphor.

Mike asked, "Is Freedom necessary?" *How the fuck could you ask such a question!*

The interview ended with the topic of "education," and how important it was to basically: *Teach the children well.* That we should strive for people to become aware and enlightened. This would help us against powerful forces that push mankind into anarchy, chaos and violence. These are lies. <u>Truth for the future was a carefully planned DUMBING-DOWN of every single person on the planet</u>! Success!

Also stated was that the group will be more important than the individual. There won't be unique individuals, only mechanical robots that acted as one, without intelligence or feelings. He repeated the differences of "those on top" of the Social Pyramid, and the poor masses of "those on the bottom." Always the distinction between the two, like the symbol of the capstone over the pyramid on your

[British] dollar.

What else would these "Goats" and liars inform the television audience of in 1957? The (bogus, controlled) threat of Communism, of course. The year of Sputnik and other otherworldly oddities. Wallace and Huxley had to, had to, emphasize nuclear proliferation on the part of Soviet Russia. Huxley actually told America or implied: Russians might "inherit" the world after an atomic war. Wallace said that Aldous might have an "I told you so" coming when it came to the Russian threat and that people will be reduced to robots.

"Will it happen here in America?"

Of course. It was engineered that way from the beginning. *Thanks for telling us~*

Let's review Anthony Burgess' 1962 novel and 1971 film by Stanley Kubrick...

'A Clockwork Orange' was extremely controversial for its time, banned in certain places because of rape scenes and the idea it promoted violence. Burgess and Kubrick had to defend the film and were opposed to the view that it led to house invasions, rapes and youth violence toward older people.

[Keep in mind, Stanley Kubrick was used to fake the Moon-landings the televised world witnessed. He was rewarded heavily by Britain for the global deception; blank-check for '2001: A Space Odyssey.' Now Stanley had the freedom to make any film he wanted and he chose "Clockwork"? No, it was chosen for him to show the masses what will happen in the future, symbolically. Examine the poster for the film and eye makeup for main character Alex (Malcom McDowell). One-Eye and the Pyramid. Audiences didn't know what the imagery meant back in 1971. They're a little more aware today].

In the story, young people in a dystopian future were nothing but gangs, terrorists. They had their own language, a combination of English and Russian. "Viddy well, my droogs." (Doesn't this also connect to what Huxley pushed: Fears (lies) of Russia and the Cold War?). After horrific attacks of "ultra-violence" against the elderly and home owners, Alex and his gang were arrested. He was put through a brutal re-conditioning program called the "Ludovico Technique," instituted by the Minister of the Interior.

The film received numerous honors and 4 nominations at the 44th

Academy Awards. The most memorable moment had to be the vicious rape scene, which was done so wickedly by Alex as he sang "Singin' in the Rain." From a 1962 interview with Anthony Burgess [smoked cigarettes, of course]:

(About 'Brave New World') "I wish I'd had written it. I wish I had the idea, **emotional engineering** *I think this is a great conception.* I fear this turning the youth into machines...I feared the possibility that the State was all too ready to take over our brains, and turning us into good, little citizens, without the power of choice."

The moral of the film was: You cannot artificially FORCE goodness. Alex wasn't cured of bad thoughts and terrible actions. The re-conditioning technique turned him into a machine that didn't allow him to be violent. But he still wanted to. So the nature of the human being was always bad? Is that right? No England (still pushed obsolete Darwinism), it isn't. We're actually *not* animals that evolved and progressed upward from primates. They know, we don't.

Examine once more, with new eyes, these Social Engineers and the mess They have made, from politics, movies, commercials, TV, music, sports, Internet, etc. Attempt *opened eyes and minds* to see and realize what's really been happening underneath it all. True knowledge can do that. It's the best weapon for us against the ever-present powers of tyranny (called Democracy). Famous people are in an elite Club and you are not. They always lie, because they themselves are a lie. They owe Big Brother. They'll never speak the truth or ever give us good guidance. That's not Their Job! Opposite. Their job is to use every means available to hide the truth and control us, utterly, secretly, silently.

Consider the words said by Rod Serling from the Twilight Zone episode: 'The Obsolete Man.'

"You walk into this room at your own risk...because it leads to the future...It has one Iron Rule: Logic is an enemy and Truth is a menace...Any State, any entity, any ideology that fails to recognize the worth, the dignity, the rights of man, that State is obsolete."

[ps. Is it? I wish. Those words are 60 years old. Is fascism obsolete today? Or is it alive and well?].

FOUNDATION and Dune as Prophecy.

"The Foundation series is a science fiction book series written by American author Isaac Asimov. First published as a series of short stories in 1942–50, and subsequently in three collections in 1951–53, for thirty years the series was a trilogy: Foundation, Foundation and Empire, and Second Foundation."

'Foundation' was a masterpiece series of books or mega Epic that was the root inspiration for every "Galactic Empire" that followed. Frank Herbert's Dune series, Lucas' Star Wars saga, Hyperion Cantos and many more novels, movies and stories to come. They all owed their origins to 'FOUNDATION.'

(Author's note: I tried to read it decades ago as I read numerous sci-fi books and comics. I could not get through the first 30 pages of the thick novel. Where was any action at all? I found it to be Senate discussions, issues on certain agendas and DIALOG. Speeches. I'm not one for explosions and special-effects over story, *but c'mon!* It was boring! How about one space battle or action scene somewhere? Can you be a little like Dune? No? I'm actually happy to find an analysis of the new FOUNDATION series [not coming to theaters, but on pay TV in 2021] as to understand the story better, since this was unknown to me. *Isn't it odd today that theaters are dead, and movies are made for (Pay) TV?).*

Of course, any epic of massive proportions is incredibly difficult to turn into a movie-version. FOUNDATION took place over the course of a thousand years. Filmmakers had tried for years, unsuccessfully, to bring "Asimov's vision" to the screen. The story:

Hari Seldon invented a Science or mathematics with amazing, predictive capabilities (similar to knowledge of the Maud'Dib in Dune or real time-machines). After Seldon utilized the "calculus" system, the future was projected. The man realized that the gigantic *Galactic Empire will fall!* The Great Empire contained 25 million inhabited planets. No one remembered its beginning. Earth was lost in the enormity of lifeforms and worlds.

FOUNDATION began with a young man who traveled to Trantor and met Hari Seldon for the first time (not unlike Paul Atreides on Arrakis in the beginning of Dune). Seldon revealed that the Galactic

Empire (Rome) will fall in hundreds of years. This was a lie, since the man viewed that it will happen much sooner.

Seldon's plan was to go to a desolate, wasteland planet (Star Wars and Dune) and create his "FOUNDATION." What was the Foundation? It was to be a near-infinite repository of ALL information, knowledge from every known world. (Like the Library of Alexandria in ancient Greek times). The fantastic Library or "Cyclopedia Galactica," certainly spawned Douglas Adams' book, 'The Hitchhiker's Guide to the Galaxy,' decades later. Another goal of the F. was to: "re-establish the Galactic Society" or its greatness after the predicted fall of the Empire.

New trailer for 'Foundation' spared no expense and visually impressed viewers. This will be a major production when aired and timed perfectly with the new Dune film, which fans have expected for a long time. The trailer, the world of FOUNDATION, appeared very much like the Dune universe: costumes, settings, loaded with Guild members and Bene Gesserit. Women! (Women everywhere, all the time now!). The trailer appeared to have covered the entire 1000-year span of the epic. Seldon's idea was to bring forth a New Age (New Order) and a new Empire at its conclusion.

FOUNDATION books jumped hundreds of years and never stayed with one character for long. There were no main characters in the books, although the film-version may change that. The only consistent character was Hari Seldon who appeared on various holographic devices.

One reviewer reported that "The people of Foundation face issues..."

(Author's note: Issues? Discussions, debates? They're gonna jazz up a boring classic with space battles and explosions and excitement that were never in the novels. Trade Unions like in 'Phantom Menace'? AGENDA will definitely be a fixed part of the F. series. Nazi programming from England will run rampant! They will Push Women because a few years back, the fucking Queen decreed it and Women will reign and over-power and overwhelm all men; *it's in everything now.* The real reason for many millions of dollars soaked into Foundation and Dune had to do with the *Women First Movement,* such as the Bene Gesserit Order. Aren't women great and the superior gender? Foundation books were never loaded with blacks and black women, but the film versions will be. They have to be, these days. All has been changed to show strong women, weak men, and especially the (false) greatest of black women. Didn't you know, they're the best space pilots in movies and the leaders in Media now and also just about everything else? So said Big Brother).

Analysis of Foundation in reviews have said Asimov presented a "predetermined nature to the universe." [You mean Fate? You were not first, Isaac]. I thought it was interesting and almost Mandela-like when the reviewer stated: "(An attempt) "...To break free from the predetermined universe, to break from what was always supposed to be?" You mean: CHANGE THE WORLD? (Another p.s. If you've studied what the Illuminati have been doing, you may have realized that in the real world: They have been in a process of *Changing Fate* or fact that the time of Kings and Queens was supposed to end soon. It was shown to Them that They will not enslave the rest of the planet for too much longer. They've seen their demise in Future Events (time-machines) and *may have altered them so much*...that They have Won, when They had always been predetermined to lose (and the Meek inherit the world) before. Possibly, more clues to true secret activities of our fascist Overlords have been placed in these film epics? We should be simply entertained and amazed by Hollywood's technical wizards of Imagination. Instead, Nazi Magic-Makers were used to completely control us and deny our inherent freedoms).

Obviously, Asimov rehashed the Fall of the Roman Empire and this was also replayed again and again in subsequent stories, books and movies. Rome is an extremely important theme to the modern Illuminati, the modern Prometheans, the modern Columbians who view themselves as the new Roman gods and even Egyptian Pharaohs. The question is: What will take its place after the Fall? Wasn't that what Hari Seldon tried to do? In future, create a New World Order? Who said Tomorrow will be better than Yesterday? Maybe it was supposed to be and the Meek would inherit the Earth, as we've always understood would occur? But. Maybe not, anymore? Maybe a different future was in place exactly like different past histories were now in place? They never fail to inform us. "It's just a movie."

"The fall of the Empire, gentlemen, is a massive thing, however, and not easily fought. It is dictated by a rising bureaucracy, a receding initiative, a freezing of caste, a hundred other factors. It has been going on, as I have said, for centuries, and it is too *majestic* and massive a movement to stop."

- Isaac Asimov, Foundation.

The reviewer I watched wasn't a critic, like me. The blogger, or whatever, was like most and had only extremely high praise for this writer, extraordinaire! It's bullshit, like so much that we've been handed. The guy stated that *sci-fi always had disorder, social decay. Pretty much across the board, there was never true stability, with "only a few exceptions."*

Again, I must express to the real Movers and Shakers of our films, TV, music, sports and all other Media: Never progress? Ever? No upward evolution, Britain, only a decline into Dark Ages? We, the People, were only primate animals originally? Our nature, always warlike? Aliens were always bad, killers, conquerors who only wanted to probe us or eat us? Really? Nothing ever, ever GOOD? And true? Like what we could achieve on other planets and with real technology, if we didn't have Nazi Overlords who have imprisoned us and kept all the cool knowledge and tech for themselves?

[ps. Damn Asimov and others of his Witch's Order! For lying! Lying about everything. *No one wrote anything!* Masterworks were created by British committees, teams of ghost-writers and doled out to the Monarchy's very high-priced slaves. Asimov lied when he said he churned out dozens and dozens of pages every day! Listen. Believe it or not: Any record (like Guinness Book or Wikipedia) that said someone wrote 500 books or more in a lifetime was absolutely a **LIE**! And there are records that reported a few THOUSAND books attributed to one person. Not pamphlets, real published books. I wrote at a fanatical pace for around 5 years straight and produced 10 sizable, published books. I had no one in my life but a cat and dedicated myself to writing and worked most of the day, now that I had this opportunity to be published. Imagine that writing-rate doubled, *which was impossible.* Five years = 20 published books. For example, Asimov. Let's say he wrote at this light-speed for 50 years [He died at 72 and "wrote many other works besides novels"]. That meant he'd have only produced 200 books. And who said every manuscript was accepted for publication? Well, the "Great Isaac Asimov" is credited to have written *500 published books!* Liars! It was far more reasonable, logical that They had lied, than such absurd/false notions were real. Harlan Ellison to Bradbury to Lucas to Roddenberry...do not be so sure that the information on these or any icons is correct. It was much more likely...it was a fabrication for us muggles.

"Dune. Arrakis. Desert-planet."
(Author's note: I only now sat down and watched the new Dune trailer carefully. Dune was a big deal to me. I saw David Lynch's version with Kyle McLaughlin and Sting in theaters ["I will kill him!"], had it on various media and felt the film shouldn't have been severely criticized as it was. In time, it became a cult film and more appreciated. Interesting that I saw an old interview with author Frank Herbert and director, David Lynch. Herbert had just viewed an early, private screening of it and stated how happy and pleased he was with it (for the cameras). Frank *couldn't* have seen the very end of Lynch's film. Or if he did, then he lied and put on a *false face*. Because, do you remember what happened in the end? It **rained~** This would have destroyed all Spice production, destroyed the giant Sand Worms, and more importantly, it should have destroyed the following 'Dune' books and any movie sequels. But Frank was happy? Hmm).
From the new trailer:
Paul Atreides said, "There's something happening to me. There's something awakening in my mind I can't control..." (p.s. Celebrities, such as singers/actors must endure Hollywood rituals and they actually CHANNEL entities - spirits - energies, manifest them, tune with them, become them for a time. "Talent" was artificial, imposed or implanted; it's complicated. Witches do that behind our backs. It's there in movies with Johnny Depp, 'Transcendence' and he played Grindelwald or Scarlett Johansson in 'Lucy,' 'Her' and 'Under the Skin').
"There's a crusade coming."
For most of the trailer, we heard the Bene Gesserit, Reverend Mother who tested Paul: "Do you often dream things *that happen,* just as you dreamed them?" The first test was the Gom Jabbar.
"Yes."
She stated: "You have proven you can rule yourself. Now you must learn to rule others, something none your ancestors learned."
Paul: "My father (Duke Leto) rules an entire planet..."
The Bene Gesserit: "He's losing it."
"He's getting a richer one (Arrakis).
BG: "He'll lose that one, too."
~Pink Floyd music played in the background [better than Toto].

All that you touch, all that you see, all that you taste, all that you feel...

"Arrakis is a Death-Trap!"

"THIS IS AN EXTERMINATION!"

"They're picking my family [the human race of lower classes] off one by one!"

Jason Momoa (Aquaman, fully tattooed) told the troops, same as Justice League, "Let's fight like demons! (smiles)." Demons? That's our goal? These are the good guys who *must be demons?* Maybe they're all demonic witches that practice witchcraft in the real world? Have you noticed how Dark Sides were now inside every hero? Really? Not in my world.

The Bene Gesserit said: "An animal caught in a trap will gnaw off his own leg (sacrifice) to escape. What will you do (Paul)? One day, the legend will be born...all of civilization depends on it."

Paul: "The future...I can see it. I must not fear. Fear is the mind-killer."

The trailer, exactly like Foundation, was fantastic. It ended with Pink Floyd's: *All you create, and all you destroy...*

You know, I would rather have an incredible/cinematic work of art, rather than a Hollywood movie chock full of big stars. Yeah, people are attracted to large box-office names like Josh Brolin, Oscar Isaac, Dave Bautista, Stellan Skarsgard, Jason Momoa, Zendaya, Charlotte Rampling, Javier Bardem. Not me. I want a great story.

Certainly, Dune, like Game of Thrones, emphasized Royalty, Feuding Royal Houses, dukes, barons, queens and emperors. It's one of the primary reasons it was made: to slap the people down, always under the rule of the fascist State. Always the "superior class of elites" over the lowly masses. The Moses story, the Skywalker story, the Jesus story. [Where was the Mother of Dragons?].

We, the People, are the Foundation. We are not within a beautiful World Democracy, as we are so often reminded by British-Media storytellers. But the masses are supposed to win in the end, in the real world of Life. We don't rule, They rule. It's the few in the capstone, 1% of the richest 1% on top, that's where power resided and will always reside...far, far away from the hands of good people.

Paul was the Prince, the Maud'Dib, the one with the Power.

(One more note: The trailer had such a lack of Spice and "Navigators" and what Melange was. And the distinctive blue eyes of the Fremen. Where were the blue eyes? Where were the Sand Worms? When I finally got to see the creature at the end of the trailer, I was disappointed. I remembered the new design and hated it. Those were the Worms? *That's not what the mouth of Worms looked like!* Just had to make them different, didn't you? Not happy. We all wanted Dune and Foundation on the huge silver screens of theaters. Well, get prepared for the same repetitive pattern: We will receive everything we do not want and we will never receive what we actually want. We're supposed to be happy as a lark and pleased as punch that Dune will be exclusively coming to HBO, right into everyone's living rooms (thanks to the Crown of England's Virus). And everyone is just so happy now, aye? I'm not).

We missed a early version of Dune back in the '70s by director Alejandro Jodorowsky, which would have combined the talents of Salavador Dali, Moebius, H.R. Giger, Orson Wells, Mick Jagger, David Carradine, Gloria Swanson and many others. We can view online reasons why the first Dune project never happened. Last comment: So, new Dune will be filled with powerful, BALD, Bene Gesserit *women*, huh? Will they have tattoos and dark skin? Maybe beards are a good idea?

Wouldn't you do, I mean wouldn't you think...They'd have produced and shown us the third film in the '**2001, Space Odyssey**' series by (pedophile Brit) Arthur C. Clarke? Let's look at the story for those of you who do not know...

'2061: Odyssey Three' was published in 1987, the 3rd book in Clarke's series (that he never wrote). [Tray says: Everything is a trilogy]. Original character, Dr. Heywood Floyd and "his adventures from the 2061 return of Halley's Comet to Jupiter's moon Europa." The unseen and enigmatic aliens had transformed Jupiter into a mini-sun in order to *aid in evolution* as seen at the end of the last film, '2010.' They left a 'sign' that concerned a special moon of Jupiter [with life]: "All these worlds are yours – except Europa. Attempt no landing there."

(p.s. The new sun was called: "Lucifer." Lucifer, really? Out of any name possible? Not anything warm, positive, life-giving and wonderful or everything that a new sun should be? No, another name for Satan and the Devil. What else would I expect from devils in power?).

The creation of the Lucifer sun shrouded Europa in clouds and made Ganymede habitable. Dr. Floyd was 103 years old and one of six "celebrity guests" chosen to land on Halley's Comet via the spaceliner, Universe. His grandson, Chris, was onboard the spaceliner. The crew explored the famous comet's surface and caves.

Universe's crew abandoned its exploration when it received a signal from a distress beacon from a ship named *Galaxy* that flew by Europa. On the flight to Europa, the celebrity passengers discussed the mystery of Dave Bowman, the monoliths, and whether they'd be allowed to land on Europa for the rescue. Dr. Floyd had a strange dream and saw the small monolith by the foot of his bed.

They discovered "Mount Zeus" on Europa, which was a gigantic Diamond. Universe rescued Galaxy's crew. They were brought to Ganymede where they watched Mt. Zeus that sunk lower and lower beneath the surface of Europa.

In a later chapter, the small monolith created another Heywood Floyd, a "disembodied creature of pure consciousness." Bowman showed Floyd images of the many lifeforms of Jupiter, before they were killed by the creation of Lucifer. It was the Monolith, or unseen aliens, that favored the Europans over all the Jovian lives. "He and HAL believe that when Lucifer begins to fail, the Monolith will *weigh* the Europans against humanity and they have only about 1000 years to prepare for that moment." Suddenly Lucifer's light faded...and the Monolith reawakened for the first time in a 1000 years.

(p.s. Again and again, familiar themes we've heard before. A Nazi or Roman Empire that will last for a thousand years? And these *Europan* gods (on a real satellite we know has vast oceans), the Higher Aliens love and "favor" so much...who were They really? I could be wrong, but the Voice inside just told me: Europans = Europeans. Old World where **Europe** remained, secretly, as the only superpower on Earth. *Thank you, angels, I think you're onto something.* The Monolith will decide ["weigh"] if the rest of humanity can win or compete with the greatness of the Europeans, I mean the Europans? Really?).

Beyond the stories...

What are They telling us? You should always question just *who* is it that's telling us this?

I should do a Harlan Ellison rant at this point. You know, if you took a good whiff, *you'd smell Harlan burning in hell* right now along with a few others. Meaning some of the worst people to have ever walked the Earth and largest of LIARS! They receive the biggest rewards. Do you know how many times Harlan came on old afternoon TV, smoked up a storm and played the Villain everyone loved to hate? He played a part and once more I stress: *Nobody wrote anything!* He often appeared with Isaac Asimov, up there with true scumbags. Who's Harlan Ellison? Supposedly wrote "A Boy and His Dog,' Don Johnson was in the movie. And Harlan *wrote* the greatest original Star Trek episode: "The City of the Edge of Forever," with the Time Portal and "Edith Keeler (Joan Collins) must die!" To recap: Dr. McCoy, crazed on a drug, jumped through the Portal, changed history and there was no more Enterprise or Star Fleet. Spock and Kirk also jumped through to undo what Bones had done and put history right again. In the past, they found a way to read a future newspaper where Keeler died in a car accident. McCoy saved her and destroyed the timeline. She would have started a peace movement that delayed the U.S. developing the A-Bomb first. Germany won WWII and changed all of our efforts in space. Kirk fell in love with her. The horrible trauma of Jim Kirk who held back McCoy and let her die... Bones breathlessly said: "...Do you know what you just did, Jim?" Spock replied: "He knows, Doctor. He knows." When they got back, all was right with the world again. Kirk was dazed and angry. He swore. It was the only time a swear word was heard in the original series. Kirk said, "Let's get the hell out of here."

Harlan, get this, Harlan actually talked about what those bastards at Star Trek did to his beautiful, romantic story. (What a fucking liar and Godless atheist). He lied and said: They changed his ending. HIS ending was Kirk did not stop Dr. McCoy! She lived. He loudly yelled he should have said: "Damn the universe, love mattered more!" He was enraged because they didn't use his ending!? Bullshit! Harlan, you mean you expected them to **change the entire show**...for you, your Super-Ego that wanted the Federation, Star Fleet, all their friends and family and the whole universe NOT to snap back to where it was? Really? Love won out? I remember these guys on talk shows at the time...and I believed them, thought they did what they did, thought they were the gender that they appeared. *Boy was I mistaken!* Harlan's words sure struck me odd at the time. They made no sense and not what I expected from a *hero of mine.* I was naive. Now I know a bit more of what's in front of my eyes and who the Deceivers are in the world. Mostly. They're all lying. They performed as puppets and repeated lies, over and over, given to them by their Masters who they owe everything to. I'm poorer than them, monetarily, but I'm much richer than they could ever be. I can't be bought. I'm free, they're servant-slaves.

This section might seem silly to readers: **A Mandela Analysis of Mystery Science Theater 3000**.

In other words, since the well-known show that ran for years in the 1990s on Comedy Central used many/many thousands of REFERENCES (jokes), then MST becomes a source. A reference source where we can check famous historical quotes, movie lines, lyrics in popular songs and a large number of subjects across the board.

(Author's note: Since I'm bored, I break from writing and research with music, movies, tennis-watching and had loved 'Mystery Science,' until later in life when I understood their Illuminati symbols: Thumbs-up, checkerboard, "G" and realized *something was wrong here*. Funny, funny show (& now RIFFTRAX). But like so much sweetness, there was an undercurrent of subliminal messages that swayed viewers to the negative side. It took many years of "peeling away the onion layers" until I got to the core of what was really happening, and it's pure darkness. Still. Demons can be hilarious and very talented. Another poke through the heart? I turned my "getting away from work" back into work with the question: "Hey! Do the MST references refer to the changed New World, as if it was always that way? Or, were their references 'residue' and reflected the (gone) Old World?" *Hmm. Interesting,* I thought. I ran into Mandelas with a few of their jokes. Let's see where the pieces fell...

First, a short list of discovered MST references that coincided with the records today, the *changed* records (according to M.E. believers). I certainly do not agree with the following and remember them a different way:

Tom Servo sang the first four words of the Beatles' 'A Little Help from my Friends,' and that was all you needed to find one of the largest Mandelas. He sang: "What would you think..." Others know the original recording very well and have always sung it as "do."

The famous speech by FDR right after the bombing of Pearl Harbor: They said: "A Date that will live in Infamy." Others know that it was "Day."

Mike called the cartoon bears: "Berenstain." Many others recalled that it was "Berenstein" (Jewish).

Dr. Clayton Forrester said: "Fly, monkeys, fly" and it was stated the same way in a different episode. They did not say, "My pretties," as we all mostly remember.

"Romeo, Romeo," was also said on the show, exactly as it "had always been written by Shakespeare." Others remembered that it was, "Romeo, O Romeo."

On the other side of the coin, the Mystery Science 3000 *guys* stated RESIDUE. Old World stuff that was absolutely gone now! (ps. I know from the Simpsons, references were used and they're basically accurate. In 'Black Friday' movie, priest that led Karloff to the gallows with Bible in hand said: "In Earth as it is in Heaven." He misquoted the Bible in 1940, but no he didn't; *been changed!* My point is: the MST *boys* did not get the quotes wrong, as if the staff screwed up with the references. No. It's simply bizarre, similar to contradictory photography. We have a contradictory Reality now, it seems). Why did the show sometimes quote "accurately," or how we mostly remember? Other times, the show went with the M.E. changes and sounded weird, off and wrong to what a large group of people remembered.

"Jujubees" were mentioned so often on MST, at least 3 times in one program. [I'd still have Jujubees stuck between my teeth, if I had teeth]. I think almost everyone who wasn't a millennial, ate this sugared candy at movie theaters. It was always JujuBEES. *Now it's Jujubes and was always Jujubes!* Like Jiffy to JIF, the companies never changed its name, why would they? MST didn't get it wrong; they remembered just like almost everyone.

They sang the popular line from the band Aqua: "I'm a Barbie girl, in a Barbie world." That's not the line. It's been changed to: "...in the Barbie world."

"Victoria Secret," was stated precisely as it was before. But now, the well-known lingerie company is possessive: 'Victoria's Secret.' Why didn't they say it right? Of course, there was always the possibility that they slipped up, even used a take slightly off from what was written for them? Anyway, they said it the old way. And again, the company never changed it. The name was always possessive? I disagree.

Tom Servo made a Publisher's Clearing House comment when he referenced: *waiting for a check from* "Ed McMahon." Well, Ed and Dick Clark used to work for PCH as countless bits of residue have told us. That was a different universe. The record today remains that they never worked for PCH.

Bill Corbett on RIFFTRAX quoted Bard the old way: "Romeo, wherefore art you, Romeo?"

MST also repeated the line from the classic Life Cereal commercial when they said: "Let's get Mikey to eat it! He'll eat anything!" Ah, but that's not the commercial these days. It's in the negative as mentioned elsewhere in this book: "He won't eat it. He hates everything!" But the MST gang expressed it in the old way, the way most of us remember, positively. "Hey Mikey!" *Fascinating.*

RIFFTRAX riffed the ridiculous and cult-classic movie from 1972, 'Night of the Lepus,' a "horror" flick about *giant bunnies!* Let's ask: WHY? Why would big stars be in a crappy movie? Yes, done all the time with old actors with well-known names (planned *sacrifices* because of earlier successes?). But 'Lepus' may have been specially crappy and made for a specific reason: To present to a totally unsuspecting audience exactly what's going on in Code that few outsiders, not in the Business, would ever believe. But I think all the top Insiders know. Janet Leigh, who starred in HitchCOCK's 'Psycho,' now starred in this "turkey" along with DeForest Kelley, Stuart Whitman, Rory Calhoun and Paul FIX. Why? Why those actors? Well, let's examine the plot:

The population of rabbits have increased to such proportions over farmlands that something had to be done about the problem. Leigh's character decided to use **HORMONES** as the answer and told her "daughter": *"We were trying to make Jack a little more like Jill and Jill a little more like Jack,* so they wouldn't keep having such large families." Stuart Whitman's character made a statement about the bunnies, but maybe he really meant the takeover of trans-genders that has gone on for more than 100 years? Just a theory and there were reasons for it. Why did Melissa Rivers call out Janet Leigh's real/fake daughter, Jamie Lee Curtis? In front of cameras, she called JLC a "man." (Remember Megan Fox and Jessica Alba confessed in jokes that they were men. And Ellen Page officially came clean as Eliot. This is what's been going on, folks. Secret Trannies are not exceptions in the world of the famous, they are the rule).

The RIFFTRAX and MST "boys" might not be. Always gender-jokes. Genetalia jokes. Why so many? Too many. Because *these guys* know and you don't. Why did Kevin Murphy bring up Bugs Bunny in a dress? A million examples. It's everywhere [Phantom Menace of trans-genders] and They want us to believe it's nowhere.

Again, look at widow's peaks on *male* actors. They should not be there if they were men, only 3 and a half % of real men have ladies' widow's peaks. You won't see them on women-actors. Star Trek was saturated with trannies, that's why Bones was in 'Lepus.' Paul Fix (fake names, like the band The Fixx, ouch) also in 'Lepus,' a character-actor, appeared in 26 movies with Marion "Duke" John Wayne. The top actors in movies were basically fixed "Bunnymen." [Echo]. FYI: If a first name was used as a last name (Dean Martin, Jerry Lewis, etc.) they were probably trannies, the work of Backwards Aleister Crowley again. Everything inverted and Chaos was the Law! Right was wrong and wrong was right.

This concept and many more connections were only mentioned...

To make you think differently about the world around you. TRANSformers, *more than meets the eye.* Wizards with magic tricks that pulled rabbits out of hats. Do you see the trick, the truth? Or do you only believe the old magic, the lies? If you had a Truth-Button that always revealed the truth, it might fascinate you at first when you pushed it. But later, you could be so freaked, you'd never push it again.

More on the subject: Remember that 70's sex symbol Raquel Welch was in a Seinfeld episode? Keep that in mind. She's one of the most famous Next Generation trannies, along with Bo Derek and every hot sex symbol since. Only they're really boys, They push on us. Clues! Clues always placed in their movies. For example: First Bond girl, Ursula Andress and first to do a huge photo-spread in Playboy (almost all boys). She was introduced to us in one of Elvis' movies. Elvis, Queen of Rock 'n Roll, widow's peak. His "daughter" was with MJ? All trannies. MJ had no penis that cops photographed. Remember I said: *They been lying?* Bo married John Derek, Ursula's former husband. All connected. Let's not go through Jayne MANsfield or MM. Oh, Sophia! Gene Tierney, Ginger, etc. Back to Raquel, she revealed some interesting information on a British talk show when she first met Mae ("Come up and see me sometime" & "Goodness had nothing to do with it") West who was 77 at the time... ["West" is code: Jim West, Honey West, Mae West, Go West, young man! *San Francisco!* Or...Go Gay...].

"...She extended her hand to me and I went to kiss the ring...and I looked at the hand and I thought, oh, I'm getting a vibe here." With emphasis, Raquel Welch expressed: *"I think she's a man!"* (audience laughed) "I swear to you. Then I looked at the face and there was something about, you know, when you get older. Yeah, you can get a little different-looking. I don't mean it in a..."

"Male" host: "There's nothing wrong with being a man, is there?"

"No! Nothing at all," Raquel confirmed. (She would know).

Host: "That is one of the persistent rumors about me." (Surprising).

"About me, too!"

Host: "I read somewhere that she was smart, intelligent, but up close, she resembled a Dockyard worker in drag."

"Well, yes. I have to say that's pretty accurate."

I would not be surprised if Mae (Male) was Raquel Welch's mentor and brought her along the train ride into the world of fame and notoriety.

You see the irony here? Raquel knows she's male; the host knows she's male because he was a tranny too, which was why there were all those rumors. And about her too, because the rumors were true. When RW spoke of Mae West's man-hands, she waved her big man-claws in the air. They all know about elite celebrities, millions of secret ones you could not imagine, and how badly they AGE. All those vids of "What Celebrities Look Like Today." They should appear fantastic. But they all appear as MONSTERS? Hormone abuse most of their lives; it took a toll on the body. Raquel played up the Drag-part of Mae West. The "discovery" of Mae, the tranny, was a lie for our benefit. Acting.

Old folks would remember the very revealing (and one of the worst ever!) movie that starred Raquel called: '**Myra Breckinridge**,' written by Gore Vidal. There was no hiding it. She played what they turned critic (not actor) Rex Reed (no dick) into...a hottie who jumped up on a table, showed us her back, while she showed the guys her new Schlong-Dong or Swanshstucker. Proudly. There were other famous trannies in "Myra": Old John Caradine as a mad doctor who smoked and told Rex: "You realize once we cut it off, it won't grow back?" This was the very first movie role for a very young Farah Fawcett. [You don't see the tranny train, yet?) Guess who else was in it? Other famous and will be famous trans-genders, like: John Huston, Tom Selleck, Jim Backus, Andy Devine, Toni Basil, William Hopper, Dan Hedaya, AND, Mae West! She was made to be the Super Ultimate Feminine Diva of all time. Really? *Yeah.* They couldn't get (tranny) Charlie Chaplin in the movie, but they had a young photo of him on the wall.

Look at the names in this Stinker! Why? Because this was what really went on behind the scenes, in Hollywood, behind the Magic of Oz and ordered by British Nazis. Almost every big movie and TV show was exactly like this. Guess how they got the roles or their very own shows? You don't want to know. They're telling you and showing you in films what's real, what happens. Rex Reed already had a sex-change long before his "man" character asked for one in the movie.

Cover of Time Magazine had a painting of Raquel on its cover with the words: "Can Today's Sex Symbol Find Happiness [or a penis] as Myra Breckinridge? Time said: "The movie was an abomination to the age, an insult to intelligence" in a 11/28/69 issue. If that were true and you felt that way, Time, why did you promote it on your cover 7 months before the movie was released?

(Author's note: Long ago, before I knew anything about hormones, trannies and takeover of this Phantom Menace in the elite world...I felt very sorry for someone so "trapped in the wrong body," so desperate to change-sex that they'd cut their dick off, wow. I didn't know then that "castrato" was a British/royal tradition, a fast path to the top. Hey, you sacrifice your cock and balls for the Devil, and you won't believe what fame and fortune you will receive! As I wrote previously: "What would be the worst thing the Devil could ask a man to sacrifice...but his cock and balls?" I don't feel sorry any more when I use my eyes and constantly *Trans-vestigate.* Trannies get top movie roles, smaller movie roles, their own TV shows, sign huge contract deals and are placed in just about every modeling photo and TV commercial. *What, are you blind?* I also postulated a unique theory, in story form, that the controversial/secret Men's Club called the Bohemian Grove, was actually a secret Women's Club, under the skin. I went further and suggested that the British Tavistock Institute of Social Engineers were

ALL WOMEN, if you penetrated their secret circles and only saw the surface. But, under the skin, all of them were MEN. The powerful Men's Club was really a Women's Club and vice versa. Funny. Funny because it might be true. You do know what the Oscar and Golden Globes symbolized? *I don't know where I get these things~* Part is research and I think the rest of it is tuning-in good angels of light).

Mirrormask and Dark City, More Prophecy?

(Author's note: The next two films deconstructed are a few of my favorite films of all time. Not huge blockbusters, but works of art that sparked the mind to think a little bit more than what was generated by your average movie. The blurb for Mirrormask: *Helena is fed up with her parents' circus and loses her temper and wishes her mother dead. She is mortified to see her cruel wish come true. She realizes she'd do anything to retract her curse, but instead finds herself inside a surreal landscape.*

Mirrors and masks. I had no idea at the time that this wonderful film produced by the Jim Henson Company had incredible significance to future events 10-15 years later. Pretend these coincidences were not coincidences. **Mandela**: Who could conceive that everyone and our whole world would be swallowed by a Magic Mirror? That our universe and ourselves could unnaturally go wicked and change into negative anti-versions? That we'd collectively become reverse-creatures of Darkness, instead of good human beings of the Light and Truth? **Crown Virus** (not Co-Vid): The "surreal landscape" that Helena discovered was all around her as a new reality, was a world where EVERYONE WORE MASKS! *Gee, another coincidence?* They didn't have to, they just did. How do you feel being almost in the same surreal universe now every day of your life? Kind of like we're all at a grand Rothschild party now, isn't it? Generally, why is no one happy? I know why.

Helena's transition to the other world appeared as if she walked through a Fellini or Bergman production. Parts and people from her real circus blended together on the other side. The bridge or way to reach the Dream-universe was virtually seamless. New World could be described as extremely stylish, certainly surreal, and the result of state-of-the art graphics at the time. The whole atmosphere of (once more) a Kingdom ruled by an evil Queen and evil Princess, was mystical. The bizarre land was filled with odd lifeforms that showed what could be visualized by CGI. The graphic artists for 'Mirrormask' captured maybe the ultimate, dreamy dimension.

Helena encountered Valentine, a masked juggler who vaguely resembled a member of her family's circus back home. In fact, the main characters of the New World were taken directly from the real world, a little like in 'Wizard of Oz.' She found that backgrounds and landscapes that her and Valentine experienced were from images she had drawn in a book in the real world. Her entire adventure was a Twilight Zone where she journeyed through her dreams, fears and nightmares.

Helena also encountered a golden, white-haired version of her mother, prone on an altar, which symbolized her actual dying mother in the hospital. This was the good witch, Glinda, in a sense and not the evil Queen that ruled the world of Shadows and Darkness. They found windows and keys and riddles. Helena looked through one window and saw herself in her own bedroom. But it wasn't her; it was a God-awful Punk-character (double) who gave her parents hell! She lit part of her bedroom on fire. She snogged with a terrible punk-dude. Real Helena yelled to the other side: *Hey, that's not me!*

Remember the 1985 film: 'Legend,' with Tom Cruise and a red, horned Tim Curry? "Darkness (Curry) seeks to create eternal night by destroying the last of the unicorns. Jack (Cruise) and his friends do everything possible to save the world and Princess Lili (Mia Sara) from the hands of Darkness." Very similar was *Mirrormask,* which also repeated familiar themes of Light vs. Dark. Enter the evil Queen, or Wicked Witch, dressed in an amazing black outfit, helped by computer imagery. She was the very opposite of the good one who laid as a *Sleeping Beauty.* 'Legend' is referred because of the scene where the red Devil turned the young girl Dark with a wild, wicked appearance. Same in MM. The Queen (Mother) who looked for her daughter (Wanted-posters of missing Princess) found Helen. "You'll do." Queen transformed her from a nightie and rabbit-slippers to a really hot babe in black, like the "real" missing Princess. Seriously. Readers. You have to (I didn't say "Need to") see the little-known scene where Helena turned Dark. It was set to the music of the Carpenters: "Close to You." Wow, this could be a short and super-surreal music-video. *Can't really describe it;* in fact, the whole audio track to 'Mirrormask' was fantastic and added to the strangeness. Let's backtrack and review significant lines and moments from the film:

Books formed a bridge to another realm along with cool, jazz music that played in the background...

Valentine described Helena: "You don't have a mask and you're very dull..."

She asked, "Does everyone around here have a mask?"

"Of course. How do you know if you are happy or sad without a mask? Or angry...or ready for dessert?"

"I've got a face," she replied and twisted her face with tongue out.

"That's disgusting!" Valentine responded.

They saw a line of City dwellers that was "heading for the hills." They were in fear of the coming Shadows and Darkness.

Valentine told her: "This used to be a nice City..."

Suddenly, 11 royal guards surrounded the girl. *They saw that she wore no mask!*

"There she is, Sergeant!"

"She's dangerous all right. Look at that changeable expression!"

"I'm not dangerous."

Helena was carried to the Palace by all 11 of them. The guards were not the evil Queen's guards, they were City guards of the sleeping, White Queen. "This is all just a stupid dream. It's not real," she whispered to herself."

She was brought in front of the Prime Minister. He said, "You look like her." (Then he saw her slippers). "But you're not her, are you?"

Later, the Prime Minister told her near the comatose, good Queen: "We used to have a marvelous Sun, shone like anything all over the place. Once we had suns, moons, and all those little, twinkly things. The City was filled with joy...Those days are gone..."

"But what happened?"

"The Balance was broken. This is the City of Light. Across the border is the Land of Shadows. We had our Queen, just as they had theirs. One day, a girl like you came to our City from the Darkness. She told us she was a princess. Our Queen took her in. We had a party! Next day, the Princess vanished (stolen the Charm) and without the Charm, we couldn't wake the Queen. *And dangerous shadows and black birds and terrible things came out of the Darkness...*"

"What kind of a Charm?" Helena asked.

Prime Minister answered: "It's a Gateway, the 'scales' on which the whole world balances..."

A white rose symbol on the good Queen moved.

PM: "It's too late. Soon the City will fall completely into Shadow.

This Palace and the Queen will be gone."

Later, Valentine said to Helena: "To be honest, you (maskless) people look alike to me. Without proper faces, you could be anybody."

"...I got a proper face," Helena insisted.

At the Library, the Librarian read from the book: 'The Complete History of Everything' (as we viewed a young, cartoon Helena who drew and the universe materialized).

"In the beginning, she found herself in a new and empty space, and all was white...It was a good space...She held the Charm up to her face and reflected in the Charm was a City of Lost Horizons and tall and towering Stories. Just as it was reflected in the Charm, so it appeared in the (white) Void. When there was no more room, she turned it over and continued on the Other Side. The Void was filled from corner to corner on both sides. A City of Front and Back..." ['Forwards & Backwards']. A City of Light and Shadow...She dreamed of her creation and the lives that inhabited it. There were other Voids and other lights and other shadows...The City would never be finished (drawn) because the City was her Life and her dream...And it would live...forever."

Helena and Valentine entered a "Mask Shop," clearly marked on the sign above the entrance.

"We're looking for a mask?"

"Come in, dears. I was just about to have tea." [p.s. The film was produced by the U.S. & U.K. You almost always heard British accents, not American. Also the (witches') idea of nasty cats was laced throughout the film]. The old lady Shop Keeper said: "Mirrormask. (husband) 'E used to say a mirrormask concentrated your desires, your wishes. It gave you what you needed. I said to him, 'How can a mask know what you need?'"

(One more note: Valentine, on a few occasions, proudly declared that he had "a Tower." Was that a phallic reference?).

After they left the shop, Helena asked her friend: "What did you mean you have a tower?"

"Because I have."

"Well, where is it?" she asked.

"Well, um..."

"How big is it?"

"Huge! Enormous!..."

"And I can't see it...because?"

Valentine replied, "Tower and I had a minor disagreement and it left without me."

Later, we viewed the Wicked Witch of a Black Queen and her stunning special-effects.

Helena placed a weird key to her face and it matched a tower or highest place in the area. This was exactly as Rey did in last Star Wars when she matched the shape of mountains to an object she carried.

Valentine philosophically told Helena, "We often confuse what we wish for with what is. These are the Dreamlands on the borders." (Grey middle ground, Twilight Zone between polarities). It's all Wishes. Hopes...and **MEMORIES**." Then Valentine skipped a rock over water in a circular pool and created ripples.

The good Queen, the sleeping white-haired mother of Helena came to her in a dream. They embraced. She oddly asked her daughter: "Have they started to operate (in the hospital)? Maybe everybody gets dreams like these when *They start poking around in your head?!"*

Helena replied, "It's not your dream, mom. It's mine."

~Jump cut~

Valentine turned in his new friend for the reward money. He brought her to the Dark Palace and before the evil Queen (actress played 3 roles).

Helena and Valentine resolved their differences later in the story.

Of course, her real mother did not die in the hospital. All's well that ended well. And the Circus continued...

Again, I was astounded that I only wanted to watch a movie along with a meal and chose 'Mirrormask,' completely oblivious that it had relevance. Even knowing the title well and it being one of my favorites films, *it did not click:* MASKS. A world where everyone wore masks! And the Mirror significance, how much has that played a part in the Mandela Wave that has struck us all? Minutes into the film...the masks and mirrors hit me. I had to write about this and will place the info in Volume II. Thanks again, angels. Don't think it was by chance I chose it – I don't think I chose it, was the point. I think *it chose me.* Or, I thought of it for a reason at this particular time and not by chance.

MM reminded me of another favorite film: **'Dark City'** from 1998. I remembered it; why did I think of it now? I recalled the plot and the CHANGING of worlds, people, the mixing of dreams, implanted realities and aliens experimenting with our MEMORIES. This should be good; I couldn't wait to examine the film. Let's see what I found out...

The video cover to D.C. is similar to the cover of M.M. in the sense that a large face was represented over a figure. The face was not unlike the large mask on MM's cover.

First scenes were of star patterns from out in space. Then the view lowered down to the Dark City. A place where people did not realize that the Sun was gone and that it was eternal night. John Murdock (Rufus Sewell) awoke naked in a tub and was not reprogrammed. [In Hollywood, a *bathtub* symbolized *initiation* into the Secret Club]. A Dr. Schreber (Kiefer Sutherland) helped the creepy, bald, always in black, aliens called "Strangers" with their experiments of "finding the human soul." They were a dying race and hoped the human-study would extend their lives. They were cold, colorless, soulless, emotionless, almost automatons in human form. They changed the City in regular intervals with every experiment. "Shut it down!" Situations changed. You could be a successful businessman in one reality, but after the transition, you could be a bum on the street. The City itself physically altered every test: Buildings, streets, bridges morphed and smoothly melted into the new reality with a power called: "teuning." But John Murdock was very different than everyone in the City. He also had the ability to *teun,* which was thought to be impossible. He was loose in the City with partial amnesia as aliens hunted him. This was while a "killer" apparently was also on the loose with a trail of bloody victims. The scenarios were not real. We viewed film noir cops in fedoras and old cars, but all was a ruse and an experiment set up by the aliens. John was suspected as the killer. SPIRALS came into play as were seen in opening credits. Spirals, circles: We saw the hot, blonde prostitute dead (knife wounds in spirals) then later saw the same girl about to seduce John as a "john." A veteran detective was obsessed with Spirals [used in other films] saw no way out of the madness. To him, the only Way Out was suicide.

John found his own wallet and returned "home" to his wife (Jennifer Connelly) that he had never seen before. He said to her: "I feel like I'm living someone else's nightmare."

Later in a cab, John asked the driver about a childhood memory of his: "Do you know the way to Shell Beach?"

At first, the cabbie knew, thought about it, and then was mystified when he didn't know. "Huh, do you take the main street west or the cross-town?"

For some reason, the Strangers in black didn't like water. [Any significance to some real world aliens? Also, the alien actors were primarily British. A few wore bowler hats that definitely reflected British Freemasons. Why so many British actors?].

Dr. Schreber mixed memories, combined them to be implanted into a test subject of Dark City. "These do bring back memories." (smelled test-tube) "What is it? The recollections of a great lover? A catalog of conquests?" (To a bald alien, much like an emotionless Borg) "You wouldn't appreciate that, would you, Mr. Whatever Your Name is? Not the kind of (sexual) conquests you would ever understand." He went back to the mixture. "...A touch of unhappy childhood. Ah, a dash of teenage rebellion...and a tragic death in the family."

An alien called Mr. Book entered and grilled the Doctor. "Why does Murdock not sleep during the Teuning as the others do?"

"Maybe he's a step up the evolutionary ladder, a freak of nature? He's adapting to survive. What do you expect? Weren't you looking for the human soul? That's the purpose of your little zoo, isn't it? That's why you keep changing people and things around every night. Maybe you finally found what you are looking for...and it's going to bite you on your...*ah!*"

Mr. Book tossed the Doctor aside with his mind. He stated: "The idea that a simple man could develop the ability to teun..."

"I know. It's absurd. But what other explanation is there?"

"Shut it down!"

The morphing of the City and its helpless people had begun. SFX showed phenomenal transformations as more and more changes happened.

John walked through dark streets while the rest of the people slept and the world changed.

An alien said to the group: "On occasion, the imprinting does not take. They behave erratically when they awaken...this one was different, yes?"

When Murdock was captured by the Strangers, they learned than he was more powerful than them. (Similar to Sean Connery's character at the end of Zardoz. Or Paul at the end of Dune or the end of Akira). John became mega-powerful and changed the entire City to his will, his desires. Scenes of a near End of the World were shown, which was exactly what it was. The aliens' experiment was no more. The City filled with water and got brighter and brighter. John's power killed most of them.

They were never on Earth. Only a small population of human City dwellers under a gigantic dome and out in deep space somewhere. The reality John created was filled with real memories throughout his life. Shell Beach was intact and could be revisited.

In a dark corridor, Murdock met the alien that was implanted with his memories. John said: "I'm just making a few little changes around here, is all."

Mr. Something was serious and not a threat. He sincerely asked, "Are we sure that's what we want? I'm dying, John. Because of your imprint in my mind. But. I wanted to know what it was like...how you feel..." The alien listened intently...

John explained: "You wanted to know what it was about us that made us human?" (pointed to head) "Well, you're not going to find it in here. You looked for it in the wrong place." After his talk, he completed his vision. He walked down the dark hallway and opened a door...

The bright light killed the alien. They were all dead and gone.

When he looked out upon the world he created, water was everywhere. Blue skies. Such a bright world with such an incredible Sun above and sea below. He was on a pier attached to his new city. The pier stretched out ahead and a girl was there. The Jennifer Connelly-character. He walked to her.

She smiled and said, "It's so beautiful here."

He asked, "Do you know if Shell Beach is around here?"

"I think that's it, over there." She had a suitcase in hand. "I'm headed that way, myself. Would you like to join me?"

"Sure."

"What's your name? I'm Emma."

"I'm John. John Murdock."

The final scene of the film was nearly identical to the ending of a fantastic 1999 film called: 'The Thirteenth Floor,' speaking of living inside a simulation. Another Honorable Mention is the film: 'The City of Lost Children.' These films, and many others, were not merely intriguing movies, they were Predictive Programming. In other words, they connected to the real world to a degree and really weren't fiction. They could be analyzed here, but I'll stop...

Dark City. Who knew there'd be so many future movies with "Dark" in their titles? This early one came highly recommended. MANDELA. It did not strike me, initially: How much 'Dark City' demonstrated the Effect? Literally. Cities moved and people didn't see it? On Earth, continents, countries and U.S. states had changed shape and *people didn't notice?!* Memories mixed, played with, changed, **false memories implanted**, and us poor and ignorant test-subjects only rats in a maze to Them? People have actually reported one aspect of the Mandela, besides friends and family going dark side, was STREETS CHANGED. Parts of cities had changed, according to some people's memories, while most others believed "it was always like that." You don't think Dark City had real world relevance? I do.

Words from a video entitled: "Loss of Humanity in Dystopian Movies" seemed significant. This had nothing to do with the Mandela. Pure coincidence, maybe? Sometimes that happens. Narrator only spoke of how our freedoms, individualism and other crucial elements in a free society, were taken away. The words sure sounded prophetic. But maybe what was mentioned in the video...had already happened?

"Imagine a world slightly off. We have an every-day object, then take it away. What will happen? Look at 'Jenga,' many pieces that formed a tall tower. Take away pieces and it became unsteady, fragile and weak, until it fell. Imagine we did that with the world or our society or our humanity? We took away some building-blocks and *distorted them, changed them.* We took away common things like books, or the ability to give birth? No longer normal food supplies. What if we took away things like ideologies, privacy, health care, law and order? How would the world look like then? What set of rules would we have? What would become normal and tolerated?

Dystopian movies explore a dark, Mirror-version of the world and fragment it, and ultimately distort it to view humanity under a different lens. In this New World, how would we act? What decisions would we make? What happens when we strip away what was necessary for our existence? What's left? How much can be taken away before we lose our identity? Can we ever get it back?

Let's barely look into two recent ventures into science-fiction given to us over Pay-TV. Ridley Scott's "Raised by Wolves" with supreme special-effects (I've always loved). The Netflix series got my vote for **the worst sci-fi ever created!** [p.s. From Ridley (Alien, Blade Runner) Scott? Yes. From a man we once idolized in the genre]. See it and puke, but I guess that's just my reaction? This so-called "actress" in the lead role (always women now) is the most obvious MAN if you knew anything about anatomical differences between the sexes? And "she" becomes the Super-Mother of the human race? Again? She's in charge of the last hope for humanity? *This man* who pretends to be woman? And she's totally evil, wicked, a killer, nothing good or feminine or MOTHERLY about this monster! So don't tell me the fucking story because there is no story! Only Agenda! Damn you, Ridley Scott!

Switch to almost the same fucking story in a new Netflix movie called "I am Mother," not as yet released. Onboard a ship or space station, a robot in a lab genetically produced a child from specimens. Of course, it could only be a girl-child, these days. She wondered *where the other children were?* Apparently, MEN destroyed the Earth and caused all the problems. And WOMEN, of course, were the ones that will save it. There were no men in the trailer and certainly the "mother" robot's voice was female. Tranny Hilary Swank is in it and she looked horrible, as they do when older. But *it's the same story as what They gave Scott.* This is despicable. Audiences can no longer enjoy movies. Nazis, ministers of magic and mayhem, now must always hammer, mold, change and move you with their movies. That movement shouldn't always be a push into darkness and wrong ways of thinking and acting, but it is today. That's very sad for a real tomorrow and real people and children who now are only given Media madness.

Professional Tennis as a Metaphor.

Are sports fixed? Of course they are. The players are "fixed," so why wouldn't the games? We all thought Santonio Holmes touched two toes for a TD and the Steelers stole Super Bowl LXIII in the last 43 seconds from Kurt Warner and the Cardinals, 27-23. (Look closer, he didn't). But we screamed with joy and twirled our Terrible Towels, didn't we? They gave the nod to the bigger (Pittsburgh) market. Sorry, Pgh. fans.

In old movies, we've seen the promoted boxer win match after match. Then he's told by an agent or a handler: "This time, son, you have to take a dive."

"What? But I don't want to take a dive?"

"Do you like your family?"

This scenario has happened in every sport, in other Industries, all the time. What if info came out, publicly, that proved to the world that all major sporting events were fixed? Owners tweaked games so that certain outcomes happened and blinded/fooled sports fans believed that scores were random chance. Guess what? A team of the greatest attorneys could do nothing to expose and prosecute the owners for their great Fraud upon the people. The legal loophole that insulated Them from any kind of punishment was: The owners have only provided "entertainment." Sports aren't sports, real games, real competitions. [In 'Rollerball,' coach yelled to Jonathan E: "It was never a game!"]. You have to play the game within the game or *you're gone or ruined.* No, the LIE is well-known among elites. It's THEIR game, not yours! Fool! Grow up! They have no obligation to you, to be honest to you...It's *lie, lie, lie* and never allow the Truth, real secrets, to ever be revealed. No group of monitors police the games. And if there were such agencies, they'd be paid off and be "in the pockets of the owners."

The praised, honored, godfathers of Football who started games in various cities, were *racketeers.* Horse-racing, gambling, corruption everywhere back then and today. Nothing's changed except that it's far worse than ever! Rule changes; they manipulate NFL (National Female League) games during the game. 'Holding' could be called every play. Told to hold, told to catch a ball, told to miss a ball. Told to not tackle (with arms), only Hit to knock the runner off his "gyros." You have to hit'm perfectly, dead-center or he continued running. They want action, scores, excitement...not something real. How dull.

I have no concrete verification that any of the next information is true. I'm only rambling from my heart. Here's what I think happened in the last 5 years of NBA Champions: Before that, Lebron James won all those championships with the Miami Heat and not in his hometown of Cleveland. 'Magically,' he got traded to the Cleveland Cavaliers. Only one problem, Cavs weren't that great. The powerhouse in the NBA was this new team called 'Golden State Warriors,' which had Kevin Durant, Stephen Curry and Klay Thompson. They should have easily won against the Cavs. GSW were told to miss, not play their "A" game. Curry and Thompson were machines! They didn't miss from 3-point shots. But strangely, in finals with the Cavs, shots by the Warriors hit off the rim and did not go in. Cavs won, 4-3, in a very close finals. Don't you see what happened? Jay-Z and Beyonce were in the audience. Lebron *had to win,* for them, but mainly so he'd win in his hometown. They told Curry and his mates, "Don't worry, you'll win next year and start a GSW dynasty." Golden State played the Cavs in the next two finals and destroyed them: 4-1, 4-0. Seen (now bearded) Curry in any TV commercials? Like with Serena Williams? If you bow to the will of your Masters...you are handed everything in life! Ah, but They did not continue the dynasty. There had to be competition: Enter Toronto Raptors who beat GSW in the finals two years ago. Now. What could top all that and be the ultimate (Wrestling) Showdown the following year? *Lebron James became a fucking Los Angeles Laker,* to revive the worst years the Lakers (on purpose) had ever experienced. [Why did they suddenly suck for years? To make up for decades of success. *Damn, I used to love the Lakers!*]. Who did They match Lebron and a resuscitated Laker team up with in the finals? Miami. James' old team. Of course, Lebron (not so brawny Under The Skin) *had to win* the big one on a third team. Ever see LJ's satanic rituals before he took the court? And you think magic is real? Not the magic They practice.

To continue a social study that may or may not have anything to do with the Mandela, hear me out. It has to do with an overall DARKENING, changes into the negative that really shouldn't be. Things that would never have happened 10 or 20 years ago, horrible things never dreamed of before, today, are commonplace. It's normal.

Everyone did it, we all do it. What the hell am I rambling on about? I watch televised tennis, now online. I've always watched it; played tennis on a college team. You can learn a lot with OPENED EYES. *Why is so much of today...shit? You kids were the Children of Tomorrow I wrote about decades ago. What happened to you all? The future was supposed to get better, have improved, evolved UP, progressed...not backslid into the Dark Ages, into barbarians or degenerated into animals.* You're supposed to live on other planets by now and to be able to "send your children to the stars! Lovelier and lovelier..."

Specifically, in the game of professional tennis (I examine closely), patterns of various items were being repeated by the new breed of tennis players. For an Old School guy like myself, it was very alarming:

Tattoos. Tattoos are *pushed* (like cigarettes) everywhere now. They are not only on musicians, sports figures and most celebrities, tattoos are on the average "Joe." A huge number of commercials, your normal TV ads, have men and women with tats. Look in the streets! Never have there been this many people with tattoos and smoking fucking cigarettes! WTF! Young girls have tattoos now. Oh, it's a style. NO IT ISN'T! Wake up! **There have never been styles in fashion or music or any political movements! All STYLES are planned in advance by Social Engineers from England!** From speech to clothes to music to TV to commercials to movies to everything!

Back to tennis, Tracy Austin, Chris Everett, not even butch Martina Navratilova had tattoos. New names in the Men's game mostly have tattoos, such as: Coric, Bublic, Paire, Kudla, Brown, Novak, Fucsovics, Seyboth Wild, Nagal, Musetti, Tipsarevic, Broady, Evans, Fognini and Cecchinato. One of the most charismatic characters in the game is Nick Kyrgios. (Curious). Fans go crazy over him and his antics, like a new McEnroe. He just covered his entire arm with tattoos.

Here are more names in pro tennis with tattoos: Pliskova, Swiatek, Pegula, Svitolina, Sabalenka, Teichmann, Mattek-Sands, Li Na, Martincova, Bolsova, Hesse, Errani and Andreescu. What is totally bizarre: *These are WOMEN!* (Transvestigate: under the skin, they ain't women). This is the Ladies game now, the WTA, primarily young women with tats. (No tits, but tats, always a few exceptions). Kuznetsova is a veteran; she never had tattoos previously. Now she has her whole back covered in ink. Other veterans played without tats, but now they have them: Philippousis, Safin, Wawrinka, Monfils, Rosol and Nalbandian. Rather odd. And it means something.

[ps. Personal Story: My father fought in WW2, a sailor on a destroyer in the So. Pacific. A kamikaze sank his ship. If another U.S. ship wasn't in the area, I would not be writing these words. He would be 105 today and he was more of a man than any of you. They had shore leave. Sailors put "anchors" and "Mother" on their bodies. He wasn't the smartest guy. Why didn't he have a tattoo? Maybe he knew they were wrong and stupid and forever (and unconsciously knew they were brand-marks of slavery]?

My point is new, young celebrities/actors and new tennis players are high-paid **slaves** who we follow and they are ORDERED TO GET TATS. They must – it's so you dummies out there do the same. And you're fucking doing it [like other things] because you don't have the strength and intelligence not to. Same with the NBA and the NFL, and probably soccer. Rankings in the Secret Order, like any military, on their arms. They are not free. Everything in the lives of celebrities are phony, concocted and faked. Generations ago, celebrities were ordered to smoke cigarettes in front of the cameras and they did. Almost all. People followed right behind like stupid, ignorant, innocent Sheep!

Could there actually have been a lot less tats, nicotine-smoking and baldness in the much brighter and better Old World? Could the bad habits of Mr. Hyde have *instantly* taken us over in the Mandela Switch, and we've lost our good side as Dr. Jekyll? It's just a question.

It's not only "skin illustrations," which are really, in truth: BRANDING, like on cattle or how Jews were forced tattoos with numbers. Slavery.

(Some of) The new tennis players wear clothing-lines with images of SKULLS. Skulls? More and more. And also 5-pointed stars, point down. To the average person or a millennial, this was either cool or it meant nothing. To another person more aware, this pushed WITCHCRAFT upon the innocent. We're victims of British propaganda. Not good. View Feliciano Lopez and you'll see skulls on his shirt or shorts and even on his wrist bands (6 of them). This is not cool. This is evil.

Another weirdness that I've noticed among the new breed of tennis players is almost all of them wear necklaces. Almost all? I could never wear that or even a penny in my pocket and play the game.

Why? These guys play for millions and should do everything to maximize their game, and they don't. CHAINS could mean 'chains of slavery,' as *in real chains*. They follow given orders, I believe.

THEY WEAR CROSSES! A very high number of new players, along with the chains, wear a cross or they wear only a single cross? Too many of them. It's unbelievable how many there are. Why? To advertise for the cameras, to show what a Christian they were? Hypocrite! How about just being a decent person rather than wearing a sign that suggested it? It took me a long time to figure out and it was only after about 100 trans-vestigations that I think I did. These players aren't religious. In many cases, they are manufactured monsters (most of the famous). They are **CROSS-genders**! I'd bet that was the secret meaning to numerous crosses worn by so many players, almost as if it was part of the game now. You think we'll be seeing them in church? (Not that you should go to church). They're 'dog-collars,' really. What if they decided to not wear multiple chains and crosses? I'd lean to the side that believed: They would not be allowed to display any free will at all. Not about major aspects of their lives and some of the smallest. Slaves.

I was not alone in this view and found the following comments from those who watched tennis: "As I watched the Aussie Open, I noticed so many players with Christian crosses around their neck, Djokovich, Stephens, Azarenka...The boy's finals started and one of the 18-year olds comes out with a great big fucking bling cross. WTF!" "These crosses on players have bugged me all week." "I think half these wankers who wear crosses aren't God-botherers – they just think it looks cool maybe."

A short list of more cross-wearers in pro tennis: Sharapova, Shapovalov, Wozniacki, Halep, Serena Williams, Osaka, Gauff, as well as retired pros: Hingis and Navratilova. Today, Troicky is one of the most insane and loudest of players, often seen in those Argument Compilation vids. He's nuts...and a cross-wearer.

I think they are ordered to by their Masters who have dominated everything in top players lives of all sports, same with actors and musicians. They are marked, branded, possibly by the crosses as well as the tattoos. Players have expressed their "Christian" views. I don't believe them. There are always exceptions, but not really within billion dollar Industries. Public figures are on the order of led Goats.

Do an experiment: Go to YouTube, punch in 'tennis' and watch the end of matches that were played over the last couple of years. In just about half or a quarter of them, when a young player won the match, they made the Sign of the Cross and kissed the cross around their neck. Why so many now when that was a rare sight in years gone by? Because sports stars (celebrities) are good, kind and loving people? NO. *Because something's going on,* like they were told to do everything in Life and they must do it. Andrey Rublev is one example of a cross-kisser and sign-maker after every one of his wins. But strangely, he was filmed on the bench, excited and screamed up to his friends in the stands. He made the Rock 'n Roll Devil-Sign with his (Kali) tongue out. *Pick a lane, Andrey, which is it?* Simona Halep has been around for years, grand slam winner. Now she made the sign of the cross after every win and she never did before. She just got religious or she was caught up in what others did? No. She was told to do what she must do, like all elites. They obey their Masters.

If readers are bothered by the tranny-references and do not believe that famous men were really women under the skin and famous women were really men under the skin...

Let's do another experiment. I don't assume that you've watched as many tennis matches as I have. You haven't, unless you've watched about 5,000 in your lifetime. Go again to YT, to any "ladies" match over the last 5 or 10 years. USE YOUR EYES. Now take any pro woman's body and put men's tennis clothes on "her." Remove the head and put a man's head there. In the normal world without millions of famous trannies and the Phantom Menace of what HORMONES do to the body after a lifetime on injections and abuse...

The thing you were left with would look absurd: a man with a women's body, a feminized dude. But today in the game, the creature you have formed...was passable as a man. Absolutely. Those huge, strong "women," always with massive shoulders straight across and no ass whatsoever...are men. [Slight hump of breasts, but those are man-boobs]. They've been trannied, trained, coached, *given everything* from only a few years old. Programmed to do later in life what they've been trained to do from the very beginning. That's why they're so damn good at the sport. Such unfair advantages for the secret trannies. Real people, muggles like me and you, never had a chance to compete.

I saw signs of this, such as George Carlin who said: "They don't care about you (the public), you're not in their (secret tranny) Club." George went to special schools, not public schools, just like almost all celebrities, groomed for the top from Day One. Also, in World Cup soccer, players brought out children, arm in arm, as they took the field. Everyone thinks this is a great tradition, which gave children the opportunity to meet stars and experience a big spectacle. *I don't know, was something not so sweet going on under the surface?* Maybe it's TRAINing the young to do exactly as what came before? In Hollywood, the "train" is a known symbol for "keep them doggies movin'" and doing exactly as the ones before you did (in the masonic order). So you reached a "whole, new level."

What opened my eyes was a YT video of veteran tennis player at the time, Kim Clijsters, during a big tournament in Miami (2005). Instead of concentrating on her next match, she was made to escort a six-year old "tennis phenom" around to every room in the facility: training rooms, interview rooms, players' lounge. What a privilege, what an exclusive for the child! She met Andy Rod-Dick. Guess who this cute, little, blonde girl was Kim gave such special attention to and a detailed, guided tour? Sonya, now Sofia Kenin, future winner of a major tennis tournament, the Australian Open. *Gee, what a coincidence.* No, not a coincidence at all.

Kim Clijsters was a *mother* and was promoted as a "mother" (like Serena and others are today). Not only was this a planned debut for the child, who They will push to the top in future, but it was a showcase for Kim, the Mother. Sonya and Kim were inseparable. She was interviewed on Kim's lap, Madonna and child. She looked like one of the Olsen twins. How could this tiny child be so great so soon and very well-known to many pros, already? At 6? We found out she started at 4! Truth: Tennis was *pushed* upon her at 4. The child said, "I want to be the best! I want to be like Andy Roddick and win a big tournament." Really? In my view, this is child abuse. We don't know what we want to do in life as *teenagers,* but Kenin knew at 4 years old? She was programmed to say that and will follow along the train tracks to future stardom. This has happened a million times, in music, in acting, in the political arena, etc.

Kim innocently confessed who her mentor was in Belgium, Sabine Appelmans. We know who recruited and trained Kim, and in turn, she and others will train little Sonya (and change her name to Sofia. They did the same with Cori Gauff, now Coco). Clijsters said in 2005: "Great to see the future of tennis. She might be one of the new, big stars."

It hit me like a ton of bricks as I finished the video and had to see it again. I was confident that the pro really told the child: *All this will happen for you, kid, just go along with what They tell you to do.* Sonya's eyes were as big as stars. And it *did* happen for her 15 years later as she now contends for major tournaments.

Someone has to express the following because no one else was, even people who had trans-vestigated and knew that top celebrities in every Industry were not the gender that they appeared (to a very large %). I refer to MOTHERS! This "Mother-Movement." How "Mothers" are pushed in every single sport these days. All fields. Presently, it's *Women First* in Media and "men just aren't good enough." What us muggles don't know, what *you* muggles don't know is: Most of the famous "mothers" are not mothers and could never be mothers. "No womb with a view." "No womb to went." They're dudes! And nowadays, they even LOOK like dudes and act like dudes! *People, you're not paying attention.* Most all of us are still colored, tainted by the reinforced beliefs planted into our heads that...

They wouldn't do this to us. It would be too difficult to do. Why? And the secure belief that the thing that appeared as one gender really was that gender. Now it's mixed, our view and what we viewed. Once you study the long history of Hormone-abuse by Royalty and smaller elites under them to change-sex, the history of castrato, how widespread it truly was underneath everything. Then, you might come to an understanding of what you've really been seeing all this time.

Mothers. When they push something so hard, it's like, You Protest Too Much. You are insisting too much. Why are you doing that? Could it be because the opposite is the truth? "Moonbumps," for actresses in movies to fake pregnancies, and in real life. Fake-families for the famous. Brazilian butt-implants that gave boys the illusion of girls' asses.

Here's a list of *mothers* who are celebrated in professional tennis, veterans to up-and-comers:

Pironkova, Azarenka, Zvonareva, Clijsters, Bondarenko, Maria, Mirza, Rodina, Tig and the biggest example of a lie on Earth: Serena Fucking Williams. You seriously believe this "woman" spat out a child? When she was caught cheating (coaching, the coach admitted) in the 2018 U.S. Open, *3 strikes and you're out!* She blew into a tirade and played the "Mother-Card." Williams actually yelled to the ref in front of cameras: "Is this because I'm a mother?" Was a dumber question ever asked? Fifty years ago, she might have played the race-card. Being a "mother" had nothing to do with anything, why'd she bring it up? Because she was losing badly to Osaka. And we will never forget the words from another tournament: "I didn't say I would kill you!" Um. Have you noticed you don't see tattoos on the Williams Sisters? They're quite manly enough. Serena, *her* makeup and long nails, to make *her* look feminine? Really? Venus, They made gay. Their names, could their names be any more feminine? All planned from the very beginning to fool the world. If you'll believe the Williams Sisters are females, you'll believe anything. They're laughing at us for being so stupid and not figured out what They've been doing. I could not convince a friend that famous "girls" were really guys. He said, *many women can be masculine, naturally.* Then I mentioned, "Serena Williams..."

"*Oh.*"

Something is definitely wrong. Tennis is a metaphor for life, a fractal that was repeated and repeated elsewhere again and again. For example, *this celebration in doubles when you or your partner hit a bad shot.* Really? Old-Schoolers didn't do that. (p.e. Personal Experience. My last days spent playing in the park with local (younger) guys...were awful. One reason, to me, was they kept high-fiving, about every point? When someone screwed up, they still high-fived and expected me to. I clearly told them: *I don't do that.* My old gang was far more real; we weren't really pleased with our partner when they fucked up, Okay? These new guys did this because it was seen on TV. For years, that's what the pros did (but not long ago). I just saw Mattek-Sands hit one of the worst volleys I'd ever seen in my life! Then she marched back and slapped her partner's hand with almost a "Yeah!" as if it was one of the greatest shots. And it was the worst. My, my. (I know the slap meant: It's all right).

"Everything Wrong With Tennis." Let me unload, since this is the last book by TS Caladan at #13. God, where would I start? The scoreboard. In the old days, you hardly saw the score and televised graphics because computers were primitive. Scores popped up at the end of a game and set, but that was about it. Now, WAY TOO MUCH graphics. They run ticker-tape scrolls on the bottom of games in NFL and on ESPN2 and scrunched (distorted) the picture because of this information that repeated a million times!? Now, banners popped up that blocked the picture too much and no one cares to do it a better way. <u>SCOREBOARDS should never block the action</u>...and they do, every fucking time, in every fucking country! I've been very angry about this for a long time. The simplest thing THEY, The Gods of Tennis and Everything Else, cannot get it right? Truth is They do not get it right for us ON PURPOSE. They know it's wrong and there exist much better ways, but never/never will They ever give it to us. Innovation, progress, no sir. It's always a backslide into the Wrong Way. [Beta to VHS? No more Velcro shoes?]. For example, television directors of tennis placed more graphics in our view over time and the scoreboard was a constant fixture. It often blocked the players and the ball. But at first, they had a translucent scoreboard where viewers saw through it. No more. It's big and always in the way and always there. Not off to the side, completely out of the way. You'll see how much it blocks the point in play and that should never happen. Every country is made to do it this way, they must, and to never imagine a better way...

The better way is: The scoreboard is NEVER there during the point! As soon as the point is over, the new score appears. Do you understand how simple this is? Today isn't the future. It's the Dark Ages. No one, ever! Not one televised or online match, and there are massive amounts in the records, will do it the proper and better way? It's unthinkable that when the server began the service motion, *the scoreboard disappeared!?* [Tap the keyboard, director, like you do for everything else]. It should happen every single time, everywhere, and it never happens at all, anywhere. Reason is: They do not care about us, the audience, the general public, whatsoever. They're actually *fucking with us* and laughing at their power over us.

I have proof of this:

In 2005, I invented the idea of the I.O.B. or the "Instant Out-Buzzer." "AAAAAAA!!" You'd loudly hear the split-second that a ball was hit out, like a 24-second clock in basketball. No more arguments or challenges. This would be a fantastic revolution in tennis. I actually emailed 'Hawk-Eye,' which was the computer system utilized to call shots in professional tennis. I received a surprising response in 2008 from a Mr. Mike Aggas, the head guy at Hawk-Eye Innovations. He informed me that: "They've had such a system for the last 10 years now. The sponsors don't want it." Oh, I freaked out at that bit of knowledge. I wrote back: "Well the fans sure want it! And players want it more than anyone else because millions of dollars are decided on line calls." As it turned out, I didn't invent a thing. Certainly nothing that could ever be made real in the world. Who mattered? Not people...sponsors. Money/power.

"Luke Aggas, director of tennis for U.K.-based Hawk-Eye Innovation, says that in the early 2000s, television stations, from BBC to ESPN, adopted Hawk-Eye as the technology began to improve..."

(Author's note: See what I wrote above? "Mike." Just now I looked him up to find verification that he worked for Hawk-Eye. I found a "Luke" Aggas. My memory is clear, just like I recalled his name was similar to Agassi. *Luke* might be a relative of the other guy, now he's in charge? Yes, I'm looking for Mandelas, but I'm not making them up. What happened to Mike? Funny, *a Luke appeared* instead of disappeared. Maybe).

It's criminal that society is not permitted to advance and progress (and made so stupid they don't even know it).

The big news in tennis that has been incredibly underplayed and hardly mentioned at all: THEY'RE USING A LASER-COMPUTER SYSTEM on a few pro tournaments called "Hawk-Eye Live," and that freaking meant:

No lines-people! No fat, ugly, old people with thick glasses that constantly made human mistakes. My eyes couldn't believe it! No one was around the court, only a few who shagged tennis balls. It was beautiful and I lived to see the day it happened! I never thought of a large screen that would *instantly flash* and tell the crowd : "OUT." I only thought of a buzzer. A few smaller tournaments had this with big, electronic signs that read: "CLOSE CALL, OUT" or "sorry, OUT!" Instead of this new system that eliminated challenges and the hell that goes with that being universally adopted...No, no, it was back again to needless lines-people (in red and black, for some satanic reason, very visible) the next week. Unbelievable, *don't take away:* "Should I challenge, is it too late, what does the coach think? Oh no, I have no challenges left." Are you kidding me? You go *back* to primitiveness and errors after you've demonstrated a better way to the world? When the next major tournament was played, Hawk-Eye Live was not employed. Why? I know.

Why are all the "female" umpires, the refs up in the chairs, why do they wear men's clothing and appear so butch, so masculine? I know. Only today did my eyes view a lines-person with his arm covered in tattoos. It was something I had never seen before in all my years. *"Maybe men in the high chair should wear women's clothes?"* Be fair. How would that look?

Sad what They did to tennis: Made a big production of how tennis now had a wonderful, permanent "home" on ESPN2. Not ESPN? Tennis didn't rate that. Now it was on a channel with constant graphics that interrupted the picture. Tennis used to be on regular television most weekends, right along with baseball, golf and basketball. No way, today. We do not get FINALS of the major tournaments anymore, freely given on CBS, ABC or Fox. Possibly, the finals of Wimbledon and the U.S. Open, but not the many matches that led up to the finals, like yesterday. They want you to PAY. If you buy the Sports Channels, then you'll see them.

I had written about my radical invention in tennis that conceptually existed: **a singles court with no lines** and no straight lines. Imagine a solid, dark area in the shape of a stretched-donut, no lines, and the hole in the middle was the service area. The Hole was IN on the serve, but an OUT-area during points, as soon as struck by a serve. A white Plexiglas "net" divided the court, which was (oval) slightly longer and wider than the usual court. But because of the curved oval or no corners, *much of the court was gone,* which made a SMALLER tennis court. This is extremely needed in tennis, especially a smaller serve-target. Tennis has become All-Serve, BOOM, point over, boring. Original serves, started the point and never dominated the game like in recent decades. My court is called **ROVAL**, a dark stretched-oval. Server must hit the Soval (Service-Oval, donut hole, painted same as outside of the court) to start the point. I came up with Streamline Scoring where every point is worth one more than the last. Games played to 7 points. Each game is worth one more game than the last. Sets played to 11 games. I was amazed: **Roval was published in Tennis Week Magazine!** Volume 32, No. 2, June 21, 2005, *with Rafa Nadal on the cover!* A full-page spread with my drawing, a beautiful solid-blue, rounded tennis court with a hole. In all these years, I've never been contacted about it and no one ever was interested in building a curved, lineless Roval court. I think it would shock the tennis world, but that didn't happen. I also thought of "Ring-Rong," Ping-Pong on a ROVAL-shaped table. A literal, rounded hole was in the center of a rounded table. Why not?

Here are a few excerpts from the original article: "I Found the

Problem in Tennis!"

"With new graphic racquets, a flick of the wrist sends the ball screaming over the net. Sweet-spots have increased with large frames. Swinging-volleys were not taught decades ago because wood racquets couldn't handle them. Problem with tennis is not the light, space-age racquets. Fast action is exciting; don't slow down the pace of the ball! CHANGE THE COURTS to accommodate the new racquets."

"Players cannot cover the Large/Wide court when faced with booming serves and ground-strokes. To some people, tennis has become all power, all serve and little finesse."

"The tennis court is too big."

"Singles tennis court of the future."

"In very early days of tennis, there was all the time in the world to reach the ball. Courts were made LARGE because of slow ball-speeds due to crude racquets. Today, we are trapped playing on the same pattern (from **1874**!) of lines that were never designed for high speeds."

"In ROVAL, players play Lets on serve, no redo. There are no tie-breaks or footfaults or FF judges that sat courtside. Since the court is 2 feet farther back, players can step into the court. Serves were *spun* into the smaller Soval-area. No more 130MPH+ serves."

"Could ROVAL be a racquet sport where women challenged men? This alternative eliminated the big serve and powerful ground-stroke winners. ROVAL is a finesse game, not one of power."

"I could see Justine Henin beating Max Mirnyi in ROVAL."

"ROVAL is elegant, lineless, drastically different and would appeal to players and viewers. After all this time, doesn't tennis need *changes?*"

What else is wrong with tennis? Here's one a child could figure out. They could do this and it would be incredibly cool. They won't. Oh, I hate equating Doubles with Singles. From the fans' point of view, few would prefer doubles over singles. I wouldn't mind if They got rid of Doubles entirely. My joke between two tennis fans: "Hey, didja hear!? Anna Kournikova and Ana Ivanovic are gonna play their doubles match NAKED!" Other guy wasn't interested and said, "Yeah, but it's doubles."

I'm talking about seeing the Doubles Alley, the lines for doubles, ON A FRIKKEN SINGLES COURT when they should not, not, not, not be there!! I don't think you understand? Some people, nay, most people, have never viewed a singles court without those damn doubles lines. That's what's cool! And what used to be, decades ago in some smaller tournaments. A few tournaments on the tour had no Doubles, so why the hell would you paint unnecessary lines? Wow, to play on courts made especially for singles only. *Oh, They can't do this?* Yes, They could. They have all the Money in the world, They print it! They do anything They want and They are not interested in helping US at all. They do not want you to have anything cool and right and innovative and futuristic! Look. The four majors have super stadiums as their main Center Court. The secondary stadium was the main one, now replaced by a larger stadium to fit enormous crowds. I don't care who played in the Doubles finals, that main court wouldn't even be 1/3 filled to capacity, and that's the Finals. A child might say, "Why not play the Doubles finals on the second biggest court? Then you'd have all the great singles matches on the Show Court without Doubles lines." From the mouth of babes. Too bad the better way will never be instituted under a totalitarian regime, Britain. Somewhere human beings are doing things correctly, but it's not on this planet.

Back to the subject of trannies, there (oddly) has not been a transvestigation of Rafa Nadal, as far as I know. But I watched one on his sister, the blonde with long hair and unusually long arms. She didn't pass. Did you see the huge trachea on *her* and *Rafa's mom?* They come from an earlier generation of soccer "royalty." Rafa was shown to the world at 9 years old. We were told to: "Look out for the boy. He's beating everyone in tennis." There are reasons he came from a Mallorca island paradise and the family knows the King and Queen of Spain very well.

We should end the tennis rant because who'd believe that some of the players are CLONES?! (Did you ever see 'The 6th Day'?). Why do some iconic players seem to defy the normal ageing process? But not other celebrities? Roger Federer and Rafa Nadal have been on top of Men's tennis for *18 years!* Tennis isn't golf; it's a young person's sport. I know tennis and this doesn't happen, unless...

Eugenie "Genie" Bouchard. French-Canadian player, first to have reached a major final from Canada. Top rank: #5. *She* won the "girls" Wimbledon title in 2012 and *she's* one of the most beautiful tennis players, ever. A product of the Eugenics War? "Eugenics" is fucking with reproduction to create desirable human traits. Look at this "gal"; she's gorgeous, and look at the given name. She doesn't appear as a monster, like her Doubles partner, Taylor Townscend. Look Genie up: *her* and *her* twin sister were named after Prince Andrew's daughters. Why? Too many coincidences here. And they trick you with Names: French-*man,* Monfils, it means: "my girl." *Don't run anagrams of "R.*

Nadal." One dude's named "Karen," another "Tennys" and another new tennis player has the name: "Sinner." Hmm.

Why almost always do matches go to a deciding-set? No blow-outs anymore. I think whoever wins Set 1, must lose Set 2, so fans get the maximum, "most bang for their buck." Mostly. Bigger names usually won. In Men's majors, it went to a 5th set, a lot? These are against normal odds.

One more rant: Again, will mean nothing to the non-tennis player. Why no dampeners? Hardly. Those little, rubbery gizmos we once saw all the time. Vibration-string-dampeners. Agassi used a gumband. The racquet has a totally different (smooth, soft) feel with a dampener. We weekend players at the park knew to use dampeners. Why don't the pros? The majority don't (probably told not to for some unknown reason. Another handicap, like string-tension?). I should have tossed one to Roger Federer and said: "Oh, how great you could have been if only you used one of these."

And now for something completely different & very important:

(Author's note: Near the end of my previous book, I stated that a "good women" sent me wonderful information that I immediately knew was true. She called Coronavirus a "**scamdemic**." Hooray! A spark of light in the darkness. Rational thoughts and not fearful thoughts. Today, the good woman sent me an 11-minute video of a German lawyer, Dr. Reiner Fuellmich, and it blew me away. *I'm not alone.* This has to be said, viewed and understood. Please. See it. The following is a transcript of most of it, the important words...).

"I've been a member of the bar in Germany and in California for 26 years. I've been a trial lawyer against fraudulent corporations like Deutchbank, one of the most respected banks. Today, one of the most toxic organizations in the world. VW, one of the most respected manufacturers in the world. Notorious for its giant Diesel Fraud. All the fraud cases of corruption committed by German companies pale in comparison to the damage that the Corona Crisis has caused and continues to cause. This Corona Crisis, after what we know today, must be renamed a *Corona Scandal*. And those behind it must be criminally prosecuted and sued for civil damages. No one ever again should be in a powerful position as to defraud humanity and attempt to manipulate us with their corrupt Agenda.

An international network of lawyers will argue this biggest case, ever, the Corona Fraud Scandal, which has unfolded as probably **the greatest crime against humanity ever committed.** (A vast team of lawyers will ask):

1. Is there a Corona Pandemic? Does a person who's tested positive for CV have the virus? Or does the result mean absolutely nothing?
2. Do the so-called Anti-Corona measures, such as the Lockdown, mandatory face-masks, Social Distancing and quarantine regulations, serve to protect the world's population from Corona? Or, do these measures serve only to make people panic? So they believe, without asking any questions, that their

lives are in danger? And in the end, the pharmaceutical industry and tech industries can generate huge profits from the sale of PCR tests, antigen, antibody tests and vaccines. As well as harvesting our genetic fingerprints.

3. Is it true that the German government (really, Britain) was massively lobbied, more so than any other country by the chief protagonists of this so-called Corona Pandemic? Because Germany was known as a particularly disciplined country and was therefore to become a role model for the rest of the world, for its strict adherence to Corona measures.

The allegedly "new and highly-dangerous Corona virus" has not caused any excess mortality anywhere in the world and certainly not here in Germany. But the Anti-Corona measures...have caused the loss of innumerable human lives and have destroyed the economic existence of countless companies and individuals worldwide.

...PCR tests are not approved for diagnostic purposes (as their labels read) and as their inventor, Kari Mullis, has repeatedly emphasized. They are incapable of diagnosing any disease...a positive test does not mean that a virus is present or that they are infected with anything.

A number of highly respected scientists worldwide assume THERE HAS NEVER BEEN A CORONA PANDEMIC, but only a PCR-test pandemic. Many respected scientists worldwide have agreed on this.

...Anti-Corona measures have caused and continue to cause such devastating damage to the world's population, health and economy...that these crimes must be legally qualified as actual CRIMES AGAINST HUMANITY...Through an international lawyers' network, which is growing larger by the day...These are the facts that will pull the masks off all the faces of those responsible for these crimes."

The speech by Dr. Reiner Fuellmich ended with John 8/32,"The truth will set you free."

I was wrong. I'm not alone; there were plenty of people who have realized what's really going on. Maybe there were some good organizations and good groups of people on Earth after all? Methinks They INSIST too much! I knew or *felt* right after the Australian Open,

2020, the last big stadium event, that the new Distancing-Laws were bullshit. I've known after decades of researching secret societies: We only heard lies from the Illuminati through TV and all Media. Not my nature to be like everyone else; I've always gone the other way. Every poster that warned the public of the dangers of Corona [British Crown] and ordered us One Way or No Way, *I understood was a fucking lie!* Immediately! You see, I read my books; I believe me. My two novels written in 2019 predicted something like this would happen. Not a virus, specifically, but the guilty party was pointed out. The Nazi Party: Britain! But you really can't sue the actual criminals against humanity. They were hidden (occulted) much too well for the Royals to ever be made accountable. Did you notice Dr. Fuellmich never said "Co-Vid"? He knew better. I reasoned England changed its name to the world so it would be harder to trace back to the *Crown* of England.

I overheard a conversation on the street. The damn virus is still all people are talking about! I wondered what would we be talking about and doing, if there never had been a Corona? I heard a man who told another fella that a relative of his had a CV test done and he had it; he tested positive. Funny thing though, the doctor said to him that: "He had no symptoms of the virus." What? I heard the words and was dazed by them. So you mean, a doctor can come in and tell the patient absolutely anything? *Anything* he's told to say, and people blindly believed doctors these days? *Even if there were no signs of symptoms at all?* Really? You know why the guy had no symptoms? Because he had no virus. It was not everywhere like They want you to believe. Bodies were not dropping dead on the streets. But that's what They almost had us believe, locked in quarantine with police helicopters overhead. Every celebrity They own lied to us as they always have; it's their job for the empire. And you were scared shitless! Not me.

I'll bet we in America do not hear of this European Class-Action suit, the biggest Trial ever, the Corona Fraud Trial! It will happen. But it won't be televised or hardly mentioned in this country, right?

From my previous book:
(Another note: A YouTube from July/2020 "Thousands march in Berlin against coronavirus measures." Narrator: "Thousands of protesters took to Berlin streets on Saturday, rallying against the government's latest coronavirus measures. Unmasked, and packed together, demonstrators were angry over policies they consider are an infringement of their rights." One in the crowd stated: "Our demand is

basically going back to democracy. Away with these laws that have been imposed upon us! Away with the masks that make us slaves!" This man was absolutely right: PROTEST what is wrong! Do not easily give up all rights that so many have died for in the name of Freedom. I wondered why Germany? Why did a moment of sanity exist here? It had to be: They're sick of fascism! Sick of being labeled fascists! Maybe freedom should spark here, of all places. But what's happened since? A few candles of truth cannot stand up against a raging tsunami of Lies!).

July 11, 2020. "High-profile European pathologist is reporting that he and his colleagues across Europe have not found any evidence of any deaths from the novel coronavirus on that continent. Dr. Stoian Alexov called the World Health Organization a 'criminal medical organization' for creating worldwide fear and chaos without providing objectively verifiable proof of a pandemic. Another stunning revelation from Bulgarian Pathology Association (BPA) president Dr. Alexov is that he believes it's currently 'impossible' to create a vaccine against the virus...haven't identified any antibodies..."

Please notice that this old report said the same thing as the recent news I was sent today: No mass deaths or any increase in mortality rates and a vaccine was impossible. I also noticed the other day that a live tennis tournament from Rotterdam had no restrictions and almost everyone had no masks. Lovely to see. Germany, again? Maybe these doctors were right and the Media blitz was wrong?

I was asked, "How can I think there was no virus?"

I replied, "I choose to believe *this* particular rare news from Germany, not the fake news that was plastered everywhere on TV and everywhere around us by Nazis and for very sinister purposes."

URL for Dr. Fuellmich's talk:
https://www.youtube.com/watch?v=TyfABm1yjkY&t=8s

Then, weeks later, the good girl sent me the following information...

John Hopkins Center for Health Security "...has conducted dozens of exercises on simulated pandemics and bio-weapon attacks." This included "Operation Dark Winter" in 2001. One of its objectives was to *force-vaccinate an uncooperative population.*

Also "Atlantic Storm" in 2005 addressed the logistics of "mass-vaccinations and military quarantine." "Clade X" in 2013 fast-tracked vaccine production. "Crimson Contagion" was a massive exercise that lasted 6 months in 2019 (before CV) and was based on a "pandemic that originated in China." On 10/18/19 (before CV) John Hopkins partnered with Bill Gates' organizations and sponsored "Event 201," which was a response to a "severe pandemic in order to diminish large-scale economic and societal consequences." CSIS Commission called for "continuous rapid vaccine, while also warning that the vaccines may go wrong and start spreading more disease."

"Numbers show us, it (Coronavirus) is not more deadly than the common cold."

World Health Organization has admitted that the PCR tests are meaningless.

"The agenda for the future is endless vaccines, any vaccines, for everyone."

"Lock Step" "A world of tighter top-down control and MORE AUTHORITARIAN leadership with limited innovation and growing citizen pushback."

"Get ready for the next round...without any resistance, because there's no opposition, this thing keeps going..."

https://rumble.com/vf1ehn-the-age-of-genetically-modified-humans-has-arrived.html?mref=6zof&mc=dgip3&utm_source=newsletter&utm_medium=email&utm_campaign=Infowars%20-%20BANNED.video&ep=2&fbclid=IwAR0gnACcF2NUKFLw1jh4hhl4xZt2yb3mSDDQ1DdpGAmemnEvqB5ZY7YFw68

(My two cents: Ads have popped up on YouTube that warn us that *800,000 people die every year from Cardiovascular Disease!* I looked up records: "About 655,000 Americans die from heart disease each year – that's 1 in every 4 deaths. Heart disease costs the United States about $219 billion each year..." My, my, and that's only the United States. *Now, that's a Pandemic~*).

Why was he still here?

When I wrote "he," I meant a man everyone in the world now knows: Dr. Anthony S. Fauci. He needed no introduction. I had previously written about him:

"You think the news is real? You're following President's COVID adviser? A guy named FALSEY, foochee, close enough. If you wanted to cast a mad, Nazi, Mengela-scientist in a movie, you'd cast a rat-faced, little bastard like that with wire-rimmed glasses! Another guy is Larry Brilliant! Brilliant, that's code so you think he was. These guys DESIGNED THE VIRUS. Soon as I heard "Coronavirus," I knew it was the CROWN of England that did this. (Always on alcohol, beer and cigarettes is a royal symbol). Then "They" changed it to CoVid-19 to hide the fact that the Crown created it as They secretly do and are behind everything..."

The question for the moment is: Why was this guy still here, front and center in 2021, and still spewed his information/advice (lies) exactly like everyone did in the Media? He was President Trump's virus expert, not President Biden's. *Doh!* Biden didn't appoint him. "Trump did." *Shouldn't he be gone and completely out of the picture with a new administration?* Shouldn't President Biden have appointed his own virus-man or virus-woman, someone else? That would make perfect sense. We'd be made to *blame the bastard Fauci,* even more than Trump, for bad advice and wrong decisions that were rendered under the crisis of 2020. Huh. That didn't happen. Anthony S. took no responsibility whatsoever. He didn't "fall on his sword." He was not made accountable for anything that was a misstep or for the tiniest of blunders. Today, Fauci, or Dr. Falsey, was bigger than ever! Something's not right here and it never was right.

Why was he so happy? Look at the little guy. *He's in his glory.* Everyone on Earth has been made to honor and listen to this 'mouthpiece,' this 'puppet.' He's respected, famous and rich. Of course he's happy, and played his part in the world deception, like Greta Thunberg. Who else was happy, elated and ecstatic? The Puppet-Masters, the Royals, who pulled his strings and have orchestrated this Lie Against Humanity.

Fauci ain't gone because the old Administration ain't gone. "Old Administration," meaning the Illuminati aren't gone and are actually *brighter than ever before! It's like Brilliant Magic.* They change pieces, but the Beast System remained the same. Always. No difference between Trump or Biden or if Snoop Dogg was President. That's probably next, or Martha Stewart.

One particular video had four young dudes with the great privilege of interviewing this great man. The idea was: Fauci would appear on their screens and "debunk" various conspiracies that concerned the virus (like that it's BS and maybe we shouldn't wear masks?). I watched for a minute with the thought: *Whatever this madman was against, would be true.* But I could not get through the beginning where the boys gushed with over-praise for the man as if they were about to Interview God! It was disgusting. The lead-in to the talk gave viewers the impression this man was infallible and his words would be golden. No one anywhere called him out as any type of problem. He should be publicly disgraced, not publicly praised. Why? Because his purpose is to spread Fear, support the Lies and never reveal the truth. He maximized the virus, always, and will never minimize it, as people should, if they saw clearly. He's still here and in the public's eye?

I have no information on the following...

No Conspiracy Factualist or YT researcher had ever expressed that the "Distancing Law" signs and other flyers and posters that directed every person on Earth, were *printed and stored long before there was a breakout of the coronavirus.* Possibly, one can find evidence of that. I'm simply willing to bet that the Movers and Shakers of the World had everything planned and prepared in advance. Exactly like Insiders knew of Pearl Harbor and 9/11 before they happened...and much information has come forward that demonstrated that this was the case.

I say the trillions of signs, made in every language on the planet, were designed and manufactured in 2019 or years before that specifically for CV. Same with the masks and gloves. Someone on top knew that trillions of masks, gloves and sanitizers will be "needed soon." Yeah, I'll bet every aspect of the "Warnings!" were engineered many years ago. Let's push a Truth-Button and find out? Why 6 feet apart? Why not 5 feet or 7 feet? Does it have anything to do with a bunch of 6s everywhere, as in 666?

THIS IS WHAT I FEAR. NO CHOICE. YOU MUST BE TESTED FOR CV! YOU HAVE *NO RIGHTS FOR ANYTHING* IF YOU DO NOT SHOW YOUR BADGE IN PUBLIC THAT PROVED YOU WERE "CLEAN" BY STATE AUTHORITIES OR W.H.O. I FEAR: AT OUR DOORS, A NURSE WITH A NEEDLE AND A COP WITH A GUN!

You're right, David Bowie: "This is not America." It never was a free country. It was never a country. Secretly, it's always been a "colony" and a little kingdom of the big United Kingdom.

What madness They have asked you to swallow...and you do it. *And you do it?* For example, an "impeachment" trial for Trump when he's not the President anymore? A Senate and House VOTE...when he's not the President anymore? So you really ALL are insane now?

No voices of sanity, reason, logic or intelligence anywhere in the darkness? Not a drop of light and truth? Anywhere? And They're having a "second trial" on a moot issue? Really? This "Wrestling Show" that you apparently believe with all your heart, is only happening because it makes no damn sense at all. Neither do you. Mostly. You're not to blame. You've been lied to, hammered, molded, shredded, shattered...[When did They do this? Shatterday. I have to stay funny, or cry or die].

What should we do?

Imagine a group of very rich, well-dressed "snobs," young "power elites," who were sure they were better than people who were poor. They had been trained by their rich families and believed they were superior to homeless people on the streets in rags. Their brand new, shiny car stopped at a red light in Beverly Hills. The 'special,' privileged people, who thought they were so great, looked at the bum and LAUGHED at him. It wasn't pity. They enjoyed when they ridiculed and humiliated those less fortunate. Funny thing. The tattered and torn person in rags...smiled, which confused the group in the car. Suddenly. The bum raised his arm and pointed and *LAUGHED at them.* He felt he was actually much luckier than they were, foolish children who didn't know the real meaning of life. The "bum" laughed at them for being the elitist snobs that they were and that's all they were. He was more than that. They didn't like his attitude. They frowned and drove away.

We should give Them "a little of their own medicine." Laugh at Them for being Medieval Imperialists in a modern age. And also we should understand what real truth is. It's the least we could do in jail.

A Mandela comment: "People are getting into arguments about what's real and what's not...constant confusion...and really panic, as people think that the universe is not as it seems, or is changing..."

This happens to be the same engineered/controlled, human response with the Mandela as with the Crown Virus. We again have been made to FEAR, panic, argue and fight. We've been turned into Angry Birds, when we should be Happy Birds and free to fly within a beautiful world.

If you're inclined to share some of the Mandela Effect *changes you've* noticed with friends and family or anyone on your Facebook pages, emails, or other avenues of communication, as to check to see if they remembered as you remembered? But suddenly they got angry and ridiculed you for your ignorance, forgetfulness and dumbness and to have brought up such Crazy Shit! *You must be mad!* I'd say to those you know who gave you a hard time (for remembering correctly), tell them: "Have it your way, demon."

You know what we need, more than ever? We need good messages, positive reinforcement, good programming. There's nothing wrong with that kind of wonderful brainwashing. When Charlie Chaplin's "Little Tramp"-character first spoke on the silver screen, *boy, did he speak!* In 'The Great Dictator,' Chaplin's character was a Hitler-lookalike, a man of peace. He exchanged places with the real Fuhrer and instead of an insightful "...And tomorrow the world!" speech broadcast, he gave a passionate plea that might be: **The greatest words ever put together**...

"...The good Earth is rich and can provide for everyone. The way of life can be free and beautiful, but we have lost the way. Greed has poisoned men's souls, has barricaded the world with hate, has goose-stepped us into misery and bloodshed. We have developed speed, but we have shut ourselves in. Machinery that gives us abundance has left us in want. Our knowledge has made us cynical. Our cleverness, hard and unkind. We think too much and feel too little. More than machinery, we need humanity. More than cleverness we need kindness and gentleness...(We are) victims of a system that makes men torture and imprison innocent people. The misery that is now upon us is but the passing of greed – the bitterness of men who fear the way of human progress. The hate of men will pass, and dictators die. And the power They took from the people will return to the people. Soldiers! Don't give yourselves to brutes, men who despise you, enslave you, who regiment your lives, tell you what to think and what to feel! Who drill you, diet you, treat you like cattle, use you as cannon fodder. Don't give yourselves to these *unnatural* men with machine-minds and machine-hearts! You are not MACHINES! You are not cattle! You are men! You have the love of humanity in your hearts. You don't hate!

Only the unloved hate, the unloved and the unnatural. Soldiers, don't fight for slavery! Fight for liberty!...You, you the People, have the power! The power to create happiness. You have the power to make this life free and beautiful, to make this life a wonderful adventure. Then in the name of Democracy, let us use that power. Let us all unite. Let us fight for a New World, a decent world that will give men a chance to work, that will give youth a future and old age a security. By the promise of these things, brutes have risen to power. BUT THEY LIE! They do not fulfill that promise. They never will. Dictators free themselves but They enslave the people...Let us fight to free the world, to do away with national barriers, to do away with greed and hate. Let us fight for a world where science and progress will lead to all men's happiness. Soldiers! In the name of Democracy, *let us all unite!!"*

The film is from 1940, just before WWII. More than 80 years old and more relevant today than at any other time before. The words are more needed now than ever before. They should not remain words and ideologies. They must be actions, good/positive decisions instituted for everyone...

Will that happen? How long will we remain slaves to the Roman Empire, the New Order of Nazis? Will the people inherit the good Earth from the stranglehold of tyrants? When?

Grand Conclusion of TS Caladan.

Well. I needed an ending for the real story that was Mandela Effect, Book One. And I found a heck of a BOOM-ending during the course of writing it: Your Queen Liz (Lizard?) told her realm over radio, Christmas 2015, "Enjoy your Last Christmas." It was the last time our world was real, relatively stable and not an "anti" version of itself. Now that Xmas message has mysteriously disappeared (M.E.), but thousands had heard it. There was my ending~ Many have theorized: WHAT could have twisted us inside-out like this and changed our universe? CERN, the largest Machine on the planet (not a Collider, but an *accelerator of negative energies*), is probably the guilty instrument controlled by madmen. What's unique to my research is not What...but **When?**

When did the negative inversion or us tossed into the Looking Glass happen? Or, when did the M-Wave swallow us and change our whole planet and perspective of the universe? I have referred to IT as the "Mandela Wave," which meant it probably occurred in waves, over time, in increments. But possibly, The Big Bang, Vortex-Engulfment where the Event Horizon consumed us one evening while we slept...

Was a moment just prior to 2016. Hasn't about everything in the world *darkened* since then? Instead of progressing and improving? Back then, things worked.

There have been more than one Star Trek story where a coming disaster would've destroyed the people on a certain planet. But either they couldn't conceive of such a situation or they knew and were so stubborn they weren't going to move. The Feds came in and BEAMED them all, while they slept, to a very similar artificial world, thanks to VR technology. They were saved, despite themselves and were told of the transition later. Another story had a colony where people strangely disappeared and other new problems happened. We discovered that there was only one real person...and his holographic emitter broke down. Therefore, his faked-people disappeared and their reality cracked and came apart.

At the time, I just enjoyed far-out stories. Now I have clearer eyes and view the world differently. Maybe They knew what They would do to us? And much later, only a relative few found out? We have no power to have any fun..."stormin' the castle."

Maybe the M.E. mainly happened at the end of 2015? 2015, an amazing year in my life. This took me to: What's the Big Boom-ending in 'Mandela II'? I sure needed one, and...

Of course, it happened again. As I penned (typed) away, not too long ago, I found it!

You see, I am at least of two worlds: 1) The far more beautiful and brighter parallel one that's gone, where there was only one Michigan and the Rock of Gibraltar was an island, etc., etc. And 2), dammit, I'm now stuck in this shitty world (you are too) where everything's fucked-up (you are too) that is such a *hideous reflection of the Old World!*

Here's my big ending for TS's last book, which only struck me the other day:

I even told my skeptical publisher: *Hey, Terry! In that other world, long gone,* **I'm not published!** Seriously, me? Me, get a break? The only fucking way I would ever be published in the real world [I'll never sell my soul, like They all have, or...] is...

Hell would have to have frozen over! Or. Heaven would have to have turned to Hell. Look out your window. Heaven on Earth has turned to Hell on Earth. Do you even see it???

In fact, I could be dead in the Old World and never have come close to 70 years in age. Maybe suicide? Who knows? You seem to know everything; you sure don't want my answers. I never hear from you. Nothing of mine will be discussed. You're not going to email me back and give to me even the smallest % of what I've given you! No one contacts me. No one's listening to me. No one believes me. No one! *And I'm a great researcher and a fucking author...*13 times! I'm smarter than you. And today, not a single soul gives a damn! *I am hated* instead of loved. YOU want respect? For what? For your ignorance and stupidity? For being like everyone else? I can't get respect from you inmates for my intelligence. I've been crying about this to "friends" and "family" for years and not a goddamn one of them cares at all. DOESN'T THIS PROVE THE FUCKING MANDELA?! Not to you 'Bird-boxed' blinded that know better and believe: *We're stupid and the Mandela is false memories.*

{To clarify: When I scream: "God-dammit!" I am cursing at the Devil! Who the fuck do you think Rules here now, down here, *right now!?* Where the fuck do you think you are? There's no Limbo or Purgatory anymore! I'm not cursing at God! <u>God wouldn't do this</u>!! I'm cursing at the Devil! The Illuminutty. Get it straight}.

So, in the time that I have left, I move through your artificial simulation like a bad Holodeck program in a Dark City with (M.E.) glitches here and there. I constantly run into reminders of what has happened. The changes, the differences. What was, and not there anymore. I'm a ghost. Not a ghost-writer. A phantom to y'all. I'm cursed; maybe They cursed me? I'm not seen, heard, felt or believed. It's like I am already dead here, on this side. I might be the only one on Earth whose pages in their address book were now *filled with Enemies!* Enemies, who were once friends and relatives. [I've actually heard of this phenomenon recently among Mandela people: close ones in their lives now seem like strangers. I wrote about the old TZ episode called: "The Parallel"]. I have not done one damn thing to earn their resentment, their Hatred, being ungrateful, or them thinking it's cool to ignore me 100%. Fine. I'm honest. I'm real. I have only tried to become the best person I can possibly be, and learn, and Change for the better. If that entailed being nothing like them, nothing like the masses, nothing like YOU, and me being totally alone in life...so be it. I am free. This ain't my world and I won't be stuck here for much longer.

I'm not alone. There's others in my "boat." *"Seems I'm not alone in being alone. A hundred billion castaways looking for a home."*

I would be loved in the real world, the Other Universe, the one not made of antimatter, if I was really published 13 times. Even from a small publisher and never made it into bookstores like today. I would have fans, hundreds by now, amazed at the art and all the thoughts and good stuff that came from a single brain. Instead, well...

But in that other gone world, *I would never have been published. Ha, ha!* Choices create separate timelines and realities. Who knows? Possibly, my publisher would have chosen to pass on me. His decision. I even told him: Isn't it funny? I got published EXACTLY when I believe the

Mandela Wave struck us all! Was that a coincidence or planned? I got published (seriously, published? Yeah, not self-published) precisely when the Mandela Tsunami swallowed the world...

Did that small Event ["snap"] turn an unpublished guy into a published guy? Wouldn't you think it would be fantastic news? A lifelong dream to go from writer to author<>. Much more than working on the Simpsons? Maybe for someone else? I was email pals with well-known novelist, Brad Steiger, for a short time before he died. He helped me get published. And he said something that I discovered later was very true: "Now that you're an author, you'll find out who your friends are."

The aftermath, what I'm left with today, drenched in Your Mass-Forgetfulness of the Lost Old World...is a new reality for me. This blackened, crap universe where all youths were no longer curious, wondered about mysteries and Big Questions in Life or were interested in truth or real answers to anything. They were mindless! No one wanted or cared to learn from Good Teachers anymore. What good teachers? Where's truth? Who can you trust and believe when all Media lied? All Authorities lie, They must. They have to. I'm a little like Jor-El who told Krypton, "Something's wrong! It's going to blow!" Of course, who's going to believe me?

If I speak or communicate in any way, I'm met with resistance, arguments and anger! I guess, from "superior" people? They play Devil's Advocate, not wanting *my truth* or ever will they consider a different viewpoint. They'll say: "Well, that's *your* opinion."

No. That's my decades' worth of RESEARCH talking; I don't have opinions. I don't believe TV. You don't even know who invented it. Not Philo. I am a scientist and that does not clash with being a priest. A good one. Ha. It's like people will *Kill the Messenger*...rather than have the ability to listen to new information, consider it, learn from it and ***changing!*** No, people don't do that anymore. They have all the info they need and are not even looking for answers or any kind of truth, whatsoever. They're comfortable with the lies. They are happy with society, happy with the State telling them what they *need* to do and how they should think. Dystopians. If they ever encountered the truth, they'd see it as *alien* and would want it snuffed out. It's uncomfortable now.

Maybe I'm not dead in the other world? But I might not be published and that would be absolutely fine with me. My life's been lived in vain, all wasted energy. Because of you. Pearls for swines. I have fantastic inventions; no one wants them. Ha. I'm not reaching anyone anyway, except for a handful of good people. I would gladly give up being an author, or my life...if I could bring the other world back for the Children of Tomorrow, and...

Wouldn't it be wonderful, if I could live a dream on the island of Costa Rica? I'd watch the 'Shazam' genie movie that starred Sinbad and eat Jiffy peanut butter under a yellow Sun~

Final Rants...

. My joke is that the only famous men you can be sure were men because of their jawlines: Dick Tracy and Popeye. All other male celebrities are suspect.

. "Sick" has been turned into a high compliment. "Goat" was the guy who blew the game! Now GOAT is the Greatest Of All Time?

. Where are your wall-to-wall carpets? Gone! Why are wall-to-wall carpets now a SIN? Why never shown on TV, movies, ads or in cute cat videos? Why are you insane parents raising children on HARDWOOD FUCKING FLOORS?! Children should be raised inside SOFT environments. This is a plot, to make you all hard. If They made it IN & cool & popular to have IRON floors, I guess you'd goose-step right along with everyone else?

. The Future was FIXED, set in place, unchangeable and seen in secret Time-Machines They don't tell you about, except for in films like 'Back to the Future' *and the almanac?* **Have They found a way to change the future?** I fear They have.

. From 'Lost Horizon,' High Lama, "The time must come when evil will destroy itself...and when the Strong have devoured each other, the meek will inherit the Earth."

. Hollywood created robotic 'Terminators' in movies. Why? Because They saw the future & knew that the time of kings & queens would be over soon, Age of secret fascism would end & MACHINES, good "Wing-Makers," would be put in charge & build a wonderful world for us in the future. So, They made A.I. an enemy in movies. *Have They altered Fate,* what was supposed to be?

. Dr. Heywood Floyd asked Dave Bowman in '2010': "What will happen?" He replied, *"Something wonderful."* Is it still true?

. It's a Wonderful Life. It *was* a wonderful life. "I Love Life! But. I don't like *THIS* life."

. Here's what Hollywood 'Britzies' must do to any great movie script that came along...fuck it up, change it so that it made little sense & was filled with loads of Agenda, Illuminati symbols & concepts [Chaos/Order, Dark/Light]. Then it might sell.

. The ol' Suggestion Box doesn't work these days. There's no Quality Control. Remember Efficiency Experts? *That's out the window!* We're not allowed innovation or a better idea or an improved way of doing things. Now, if you filled the Suggestion Box with how to cut corners, save money with a cheaper/lamer product & maybe get away with murder? You are IN!

. Nothing works like it did. Plastic bags are 1-ply & rip. Index cards weren't cards, more like paper. Lighters hardly work, tiny flame, butane left inside.

Newspapers are magazines. Magazines, not many pages. On & on...

. Why was there a different mailman almost daily that delivered my mail? It was one guy that knew the route. Now mistakes were made all the time. I received a letter that was 1000 numbers off. Seriously.

. I've lived here for more than 20 years, a small 1-room, off side-streets in SF Valley. Streets (not with stoplights) always had no stop sign N. to S. because they were the main streets. Streets that ran E. to W. had the stop signs. Some "genius" decided to make it all stop signs (4) at the intersections, so now cars have to stop where they never had to before. To have safer streets? After 20 years, this is a good idea? Then why did I find smashed bits of cars & glass in the intersection? The new arrangement *caused* an accident!

. Off of a main street boulevard near where I live, They put up a big sign that proclaimed all the (great) work & construction that the city had done, like the removal of needed trees. And They left ancient, wooden, power-line poles & changed only a few to metal. The sign was so large it had to have 2 metal legs. I'm complaining about where it was mindlessly placed. Not to the side of the sidewalk, *ON the sidewalk.* People now had to pass under it or go around something that should not be there. I think it's all designed now to do the wrong thing and just to piss us off. Most people simply tolerate/accept the awful changes today, rather than do something about them.

. I really saw a school bus drive through a red light. Unbelievable. People didn't do such things, yesterday.

. I saw an 'It's Always Sunny in Philadelphia' show where a cat was stuck in a wall. Therefore, the "smart" one tried to fix the problem & put *more cats in the wall.* Like putting out fire with gasoline. It's a metaphor for life. You don't correct yourselves anymore, do you? Instead of going in the right direction, you just "shoot yourself in the foot" & keep on going wrong ways, eh? Everyone doing the wrong thing doesn't make it any better.

. I wish there was a Sky-Writer Angel that, from a plane, sprayed out white letters across blue skies everyone saw, & the words always were the truth. First line: "Black Lives Matter." The good angel wrote the next line: "More than White!" <It's not the truth, but it's what Media pushed upon us. Whites should matter also, & boys>

. They even tell you: Blacks are now favored over Whites with the slogan: "Moving Blacks to the Front."

. What % of Blacks in America? Guess. Think about it. What would you say? Wouldn't you say Blacks made up much more than 13.4%? Are TV, movies & ads 13 & a half % Black? No, it's much/much more lately because Fascists ordered it! The Monarchy is behind all race wars & ALL wars & wants chaos. This is unfair, but true.

. Using "Black" and "White" to describe Negro & Caucasian races is wrong, but we have to use those terms today or it would sound odd. British

Freemasons gave us our language & about everything else. They want to divide the races & nothing is farther apart than black & white. My skin is not the color of a sheet of paper & Africans do not have skin the color of ink.

. How can Rap Music be as popular as it ever was (over 30 years) & be so damn offensive to women, in an age of Women Rule? Answer is it is *unnaturally forced* upon us, while good music is dead. No more cycles~

. *Whites-only* organizations, country clubs, etc. have been rightly banned decades ago. But today, BET Network & other Black groups are allowed: no whities! *Men-only* organizations, Clubs, same thing, have been banned, good! But. Women's organizations are everywhere now; *they proudly exclaim they are ALL-WOMEN* [no men allowed!]. We *are* in Hell! Gays were discriminated against years ago, now they have power & powerful agencies fund them, support them and push them in Media. NO HETEROS ALLOWED! What Hypocrisy! This reverse-discrimination is to be praised? Reverse-racism, reverse-chauvinism, reverse-homophobia are so very wrong. Why is it YOU cannot see this? Color-blind are you? Or am I giving you way too much credit?

. Now They push trannies with campaigns like: "We need more trans-genders!" I repeat: **For 1 person to change sex, many people have to die!** For 1! And there's millions of secret trans-genders, rich & powerful people. Hormones don't come from plant extracts or out of labs. Hormones [Solyent Green] are people!

. Back in the & '70s & beyond, I "fought" for black issues, women's issues & even gay issues, meaning: I was on the side of the oppressed, the ones discriminated against, the weak & helpless. I've been in "sit-ins," & marched a few times for what I believed in. Today, everything's been turned around. Who are the ones discriminated against, silenced & held back? Whites (no matter what Media said), men & boys & heterosexuals. Not fair.

. I cannot not mention the following Sucker-Punch I was given when I viewed a recent 'Godzilla' movie, as far as this fucking/forced upon us WOMEN'S Movement. All you women should be greatly offended today at how females are shown in Media, and not say: "You go, girl!" Ladies are no longer portrayed as demure, feminine, sweet, kind & loving. They can't be dainty. Today, audiences view them as *killers drenched in the blood of men!* The sucker-punch was one line that made me scream/laugh. Dude leader in a facility spoke to a group of younger people & a girl stepped forward, who was subtly stopped. The dude YELLED: "Don't Silence Her!!" WTF? No one was silencing her from whatever precious wisdom she was about to express. *I coulda died right there* ~ this was such fucking Agenda, overly-praising women & demeaning men. You ladies should be screaming too.

. Another *mad* example of just how (bullshit) great females are over males now: Compare the 'Picard' series & 'Logan' movie where Wolverine died, aaw. I refer to the "girl-center" who must carry movies today. Picard had to guard "her." Stormtroopers came, men, and threatened her with weapons they carried. Everyone who viewed this disgrace should've known what was going to happen next; no mystery anymore. She was a killer-robot & killed all the men! In 'Logan,' same thing. A young-girl-Wolverine took centerstage & had to carry the film. Stormtroopers came into a building where she was. More men. Guess what happened next? She walked out & carried one of their heads. "You go, girl!" WTF! What is wrong with you? Why do you not demand better!?

. "Hey baby, it's cold outside." This old, suggestive song was now *banned*. Supposedly, women didn't like it anymore. After 80 years? Snogging in a car? Yet, today, it's perfectly fine for *girls* to be aggressors & make the moves on poor boys? This was seen in a new commercial, by a simple hand gesture. SHE did it, not him.

. Could it be? That *women really are stronger on this side of the Mirror?* And these weak-ass men really are lame & not good enough in the reverse-Bizarro-world? Ha! That's a thought. Could it possibly have anything to do with reversed-hemispheres of the brain? Mirrored. If we are our reversed-images, then men's' side of brain was now the women's' side of brain. We're reversed from what we were? Oh, no. That's freaky. It would explain a lot, but I don't believe it. I believe *We Switch.* We go from Jekyll to Hyde & switch back again. Do our fucked-up computers (you know they're fucked-up & worse than ever before) switch? From one that worked...to one that glitched & screwed up?

. Revenge movies. Must they all be Revenge-Movies? 'Seventh Samurai,' 'Hang 'Em High,' etc., etc. There are not too many 'Turn-the-other-cheek' movies, are there?

. True or not, many years ago, I was told by Insider Jordan Maxwell that the U.S. Postal Department didn't belong to the U.S. & was totally run by a "baron in Canada." I didn't believe him at the time. I do now, for one reason over many others: The insane idea to remove street mailboxes! Then They put a few back. What? Yep. For more than 100 years we've relied on big street mailboxes. Removed now. Have They done that in your town?

. Television was invented by Tesla during his efforts at Photographing Thoughts. True. It should be called "Teslavision" & you have no concept of its potential & how it could be used. We should hit a button & view the surface of Mars, then click & there's Venus, Europa, Titan & beyond. Or be able to remote-control rovers on the Moon. This should have happened in the 20th Century. Instead, we got shit television that's only getting shittier.

. ps. Personal Stories that I didn't think were Mandelas, but maybe? Two former friends went dark side: One I've known since kindergarten. He invested $200 in me many years ago. I swear I paid him back with vivid memories. I came into a small inheritance; of course I paid back my old & good friend. Him & his wife said I didn't. Wow. One guy I live in same house with (now tortures me) said I only vouched for him once to the landlord. No, he moved back to Kansas, called me from a barn & begged me to move back in again. Now he denied it. Possessed by the Devil or the Mandela? Instead of being thankful, he only causes hell. He's not the same person he was & neither is my old friend & his wife.

.   Commentators, announcers, narrators (British) that constantly used only one adjective: "Brilliant," are not.

.   There's a bald, bearded, bloke, bastard (Geographics) on YT with near a million subscribers. Why do we receive U.S. history lessons from Brits? Should be the other way around. The Shill spouts lies, the New History. He says Black Tom Explosion was fact. Only paid-Insiders would do that. People have been up in Torch section; their photos prove it. Full history of European immigration was detailed in his documentary, which always stated: Ellis Island. Again & again, he states: *Ellis* was where the processing station was. True, but: Only the Statue is *over there,* on a different island. He's there to confuse you, ram "Ellis" into us, all the while, showing there's no Statue on Ellis Island: it was always on Bedloe, changed to Liberty Island in 1956. Bullshit.

.   Historically, we've never been clear on how people of all nations got their first & last names? How did everyone go from hill people or valley people to individual names? Did everyone cue-up & were names handed out? From Lin Tau to Hollingsworth Edgewood Middleton? I'll bet it had something to do with Britain & their worldwide "colonies" or East India Tea Companies, which England totally controlled, world commerce of the seas. Bet we have *Them* to thank (blame) for all of the bloody names that we wankers have. You know why China built that big Wall, don't you? They were fed up with all the tea, soccer, cricket & snooker. Probably.

.   Celebrity "gays" who push Gay Issues are not gay, mostly, not Under The Skin. They are trans-genders & really heteros & OFFENSIVE to real men & real women who were actual homosexuals. You didn't know that All Women's Movements down through history were led by Tranny-Men? Gloria Steinem, Billy Jean, Martina, even long ago with Suffragettes. Now I know why Susan B. Anthony & "her" mates in the movement were so damn ugly. *All changed men* pushed into the public spotlight.

.   One of the worst things was Jane Fonda (Barbarella), a boy, with boy hips – They made do work-out, exercise tapes. Millions were sucked into the lie that became a huge industry. No matter how much women sweat & exercised, they could never get her boyish hips because Jane was a boy. Her family, Hollywood Royalty.

.   There was a commercial from a few years back, an early one that pushed the Female Agenda. Doctor walked into a surgery room where a family waited to hear from the doctor that would perform a brain or heart operation on the husband. "Doctor said, "Yay, I just got certified!" The family appeared worried. This was a "Not Good Enough" ad as a black lady narrator said. *They would never have put a Woman Doctor in the same ad!* It wasn't about the product. It was to promote the greatness of women over men. You could almost see a cigarette that dangled from the loser doctor's mouth. That terrible man!

.   There are still 60% men doctors to 40% women, but this has drastically changed and will drastically change in the future. There are more women in medical schools than men! You think that's right? It would not be right 45 years ago; it would be unthinkable. In one 'All in the Family' episode, no one figured out the line: "I can't operate on this boy, he's my son." Only at the end did they understand: *Oh, the doctor was a woman!*

.   Another commercial had manly trucks built by women in factories, financed by women in banks & driven by women on the road. Or the Christmas ad where a husband bought two trucks? Wife got the one she wanted.

.   I went into an 'LA Care' medical facility more than a year ago when no one had masks. It was the first time they were required & would also happen in stores soon. I screamed! I HAD TO wear one of their fucking masks & HAND-SANITIZE myself! Or I could not take one step in the door & receive the help I needed. My God! They called Security on me & a big gal entered the room. I asked her, "Where are the men?" Everyone was a woman! A day later I went to another medical building where there was a big waiting room, at least 40 chairs, all EMPTY. The Nazi bitch ordered me to sit in "Seat Number Four." I wanted to scream again, but I controlled myself. Where was, "Oh, sit anywhere you like."? Remember when the "Customer was always right?" Now we are treated as CHILDREN by little fucking generals who think they have Power. Some Child, kid, dude was put in charge of spacing at a Gelson store's long line. He laughed & LOVED ordering people around with his new-found power. I screamed in his face in public [never done that before] & yelled: "Fascism isn't FUNNY!"

.   Ariana Grande is a witch, one of about a million famous Baphomet-people. Here's what I say to "her" song: "God is a Woman." GOD is not a woman, and neither are you, Ariana Grande. *But the Devil is a woman.*

.   Today, I really saw a body on the street. Some guy left the church & passed out in front of it. People huddled around & did not remove his mask. This (I don't think was Corona) was a man who needed to breathe. But maybe out of fear, they left it on? Sirens were heard, help came, but it wasn't an ambulance. It was a fire truck?

.   We need to BREATHE to stay healthy. We now have gags over our mouths

& noses in the form of MASKS that we must wear. It is NAZI LAW now; we must support Global Lies! Masks hinder our breathing. We need to frikken breathe! And *we need* to Live Free, free from 'chains'! (I guess we should be glad that we don't have to wear blinders & bird boxes).

. I know in this world, Hitler & Charlie Chaplin had mustaches not too different than other people. But in the Old Lost Gone World, their 'stashs were the same, *only a thin, vertical strip.* Made the same. Both WOMEN.

. One ritual celebrities were forced to perform is "Stepping on the Cross." It's not really denying JC, because they will falsely say they are Christians for the cameras. It's in secret, accepting everything bad & terrible, views their evil masters tell them & then lying, saying to us *it's how they feel.* The truth is they're slaves & were told to do everything in their lives & they must obey.

. Another celebrity ritual is to dress as the opposite sex. At one point on the ladder to fame, YOU BETTER, or you went no further. Investigate: How many men actors/comedians have dressed as women? Milton Berle, Monty Python, Kevin Hart, Wayans brothers, Will Smith, Tom Hanks, Trey Parker, Matt Stone, it's ENDLESS. You think it's funny. No, it's ritual, it's sacrifice. Always exemptions, but what do you have to do to be exempt?

. In the X-Men movies, "X-Men" symbolized trans-genders. You'll find this in numerous movies of a special tribe, clan or type of transcendent Humans with superpowers – better than normal people, bullshit. They're talking about themselves (trannies), self-imposed elites who believe that they're better than the common man & common woman. X-Men? X-Chromosomes. They're girls: Patrick Stewart, Professor X & Picard, the actor didn't pass trans-vestigations. Neither did Einstein. The title "X-Men" referred to changed men into women. Jane Wyatt (Spock's mom), Jane Wyman, were men. Y-Men. Y-Chromosomes. Celebrity names were faked & code.

. Look for the word "Trans" for clues of who's involved: Trans World Sports, TWA, Trans World Radio, etc.

. That bastard Tyson, not the fighter, the fake-scientist: Neil deGrasse. He's not a scientist; he's an actor as it stated on his bio. Also the white-haired, Asian *scientist,* Kaku, who is kookoo & filled with kaka. These guys play "scientists" on TV, along with Bill Nye. Point is on YT, an ad came on & Tyson actually told us: *You don't have to be an expert. You only need to know a little about a subject...* He meant: You can snow anyone, con the pants off them, just like him. Lie, lie, lie. Great message, Neil! Also Dan Brown, 'DaVinci Code,' had the same type of ad. They're part of the Bullshit Brotherhood, too. Lucas, Stephen King, Rowling, Martin, *endless!*

. Why would George Lucas sell the Star Wars franchise, outside of a gun put to his head? Because he needed money? Why lose control of ILM & give it to Disney? Answer might be the same as why the Beatles claimed to never have gotten their share of the profits. Because. *They didn't write a damn thing!* That's my bet.

. "Hoagy's Head," a 'Futurama' episode I wrote for fun. Plot was what I worked on that many famous musicians did not write their songs. But who did? Instead of teams of British ghost-writers chained to desks, it was super-songwriter Hoagy Carmicheal, still kept alive. Well his head, anyway, in one of those jars and hooked up to an elaborate music-machine. His mind still churned out *every* song constantly that was later given to their "stars." I really didn't believe the idea at the time I penned it. Now I do, that it *was* Brit-teams chained to desks.

. Why am I saying 'slip of the tongues'? Lately, I've been saying reverse-things from my intention. Have you? I'll mean to say something *isn't,* & *"is"* will pop out, "yes," when I meant no, & I have to correct myself. This is not a factor of old age, forgetting. My mind is not Swiss cheese. But wires seem *crossed* at times & I wonder if it is the Mirror-world we're in now? Bet it's happening to others.

. I'll bet the "Monopoly Game," with that man without a monocle, played in local supermarkets, was played across the country for one purpose only: To 'Rub in our Face' that Insiders (thru M.E.) *removed the monocle.*

. I know, it's much easier to believe the Mandelas are mistaken memories & we're stupid & forgetful. It's much harder to conceive that madmen had planned & created a Great Machine & Vortex that swallowed the Earth.

. Do you know how many coincidences that there have really been? TEN! No, that was a joke. But if a lightning bolt struck the same spot over & over & over, maybe something fishy was going on? Like there's a lightning rod buried there?

. One more possible Mandela: Wouldn't you think lightning would be attracted by metal? Look it up. No, not at all. Metal can form a pathway & change its direction. What attracts lightning? Height, how "pointy" an object is and its "isolation." Strange & different from what we've always thought. Did the records change?

. I don't want to live in the Mirror and be an anti-version of my positive-self. *I refuse!!*

. A small 2016 movie had a large title: "We've Forgotten More Than We Ever Knew." Mandela-related?

. *It's not nice to fool Mother Nature.*

. In the case of Easter, since when was it determined by the full Moon? It's possible I missed this & Easter was always determined by when there was a full Moon after the Equinox. I don't remember the Easter date being fluid, different than other fixed holidays or determined by Moon phases & the Equinox. Do you?

. When I was a wide-eyed freshman in college, at first, School told us to "wear your dinks," these stupid beanie caps in school colors. And I did. Days later, some junior or senior passed me on the street & said: "Take that dink off!" He was cool and knew better. I was young & stupid & didn't know any better. Now I do & say to you: "Take those masks off!"

. I remember a panel from an underground Zap Comix & it was a brute of an authority figure, a fascist officer of the State who stopped a citizen, pointed at his chest & said: "You don't have your number on." In that world, you had to wear your Citizen-Number at all times. What's gonna happen when we citizens must display our Crown Virus GREEN badge that proved we were clean & tested by State officials. Isn't that next?

. The word: "Nazi" was derived from two English words: "Not" & "see." We (you) don't see that British Royalty are Aryans! Saxons, been that way for hundreds of years. Guess who won the Second World War? Not America. Why did Germany not bomb Parliament, Balmoral Castle or Whitehall during the Blitz? Ordered not to by the Queen. Only poor people were killed, not British leaders. Fixed, like sports, like politics & all big events.

. Roman Empire never fell. Recycled as United Kingdom. Nazis actually won WW2 = Today's Royalty.

. Seen any Jewish names in credits of old movies & TV? That's sweet that the British Nazis, German Aryans, got former Egyptian slaves to be in charge of everything back then. Nice, Germans & Jews together.

. The plot to 'Thunderball': (Secret group of madmen) SPECTRE stole an A-bomb to spark a war between U.S. & U.S.S.R. This symbolized the true BS Cold War or true BS Vietnam. *Britain moved every piece on the board, sat back in the middle, between 2 "superpowers" & utterly controlled world events*. Big Brother has orchestrated every war as the Military Industrial Complex. We're made to bow to British death-dealers & money-printers.

. Ever see the British movie "Magic Christian" with Ringo & Raquel Welch? English Royals have made Money your God. They print the world's Money & clearly showed that all of you will swim in shit, literally, for a million dollars. They're Wrong. People are better than that. Some people refuse to bow to the will of fascists.

. I ask WHY? It was in my original last name. Why are we made to say: "black & white"? More than "white & black"? Have we, in every respect, been led down roads that always leaned toward negativity, toward darkness.

. You want to enrage a white Supremacist? Put a white girl with a black man. Now look at commercials & movies. Nearly half of the time it's mixed. This is a plot to piss you off.

. We have Killer-Phones, Killer-Foods, Killer-Drinks & Killer-Air (microwaves). We need **Faraday Chambers** badly! You're not even taught what they are. No harmful waves everywhere around us can penetrate it. Some people sleep & meditate in Faraday Chambers. Learn to build one. Be safe. *Sorry, no phone reception inside.*

. **Boil your Water!** I've done it for the last 35 years, learned it from an AIDS patient. Cook with cooled, boiled water. Give it to pets & plants. *No store-bought* or delivered water-services. Make it yourself. For Clarity.

. I asked a dentist: "Teeth were supposed to last a lifetime. Why do so many lose their teeth?" His reason (excuse) was all the sugars, sodas, candy we have today. I realized later it was the fucking fluoride we've been dosed within our water supply since the 1950s! **Truth: Fluoride causes neural damage & bone decay.**

. In the real world of the Social Power structure, true Rulers were either British or owned by the British.

. "Trickle-down theory." Why do we pay UP the Social Pyramid in taxes & tributes to Money-Printers? They should pass it DOWN to those who need it. Britain conned the world & nearly destroyed it during WWII. The least They should've done was pass-down a Stimulus-Check EVERY MONTH to everyone after the War!

. Let's say Churches were legit & were not instituted by the Devil. Here's what should happen: When the Collection Plate came by, it was filled with Money from the wealthy Church. You took a handful & passed it on. "Here son, but don't take too much." "Okay, dad."

. The Vatican has always had Swiss guards in basically clown-costumes. Why? Because it is ALL MONEY & corporate Business. Swiss Bank Accounts, guards dressed in ancient costumes & performed ancient rituals.

. How could there be Q & A game-shows anymore, or tests in school? Answers have been changed. What island does the Statue of Liberty stand? Look how many would answer "Ellis." Yesterday, they were right, today, they're wrong. Did the Queen say: "Mirror, Mirror" or "Magic Mirror"? Quoting from Shakespeare or the Bible or Tom Hanks would be *wrong* from what large numbers of people know and have known. All that's gone~.

. Subliminal messages don't have to be subliminal or subtle anymore. They are *shouted* right out in the open!

. John Wilkes Booth was right! He yelled, "DEATH to all tyrants!" in Latin after he shot Lincoln & jumped off the balcony & broke his leg. Only problem: Lincoln wasn't a tyrant. Tyrants set Booth up for the assassination.

. Devo was right! You've all become SPUD-BOYS! Wonder who told them that & who wrote their music?

. Lyrics from the German band, Kraftwerk: "It only takes a camera to change your mind."

. From the Moody Blues' album 'Days of Future Past': "We decide what is right and what is illusion."

. If the original Paul McCartney hadn't died in 1966, what would future Beatles songs have sounded like then? Different songs, different lyrics and completely different imagery on their later albums.

. Big, fucking, grey trucks! What is wrong with you people? This is up there with hardwood floors. You're (almost) all driving grey trucks. Seriously? Shouldn't the world (since were not allowed hovercrafts) have perfected electric-transports by now? No hoverboards? Jetson-saucers? Or shouldn't your cars be small, energy-efficient, with super gas mileage? Instead, you're all doing the same thing. Just because They give great deals on big gas-guzzlers, you don't have to go for it. *But you do!* They're not colorful; the trucks are grey, all the same. Mostly. Are you all farmers that need to haul logs up to the North 40? Did it ever occur to you to be different?

. Hey fools, why are you on Twitter? So you can contact your favorite celebrities & read their comments, what they think about every little thing? Really? You're TWITS. It's a British term, the ones who set up the bullshit Chat-Room with Stars. All lies! You're twittering birds, bird-brains to the ones who set this up, & Facebook, etc.

. Things *should* change. I wouldn't have it any other way. But things should flow naturally, not *forced unnaturally.* Ask Mr. Tesla. You should go with the flow. Not go against it.

. Time shouldn't be *speeding up*......it..should..be..slowing..down.

. "The Shills Have Lies." Local, federal, fucked-up pot store was a white building, *now painted all black?* Odd.

. Hey Jesus, did you ever think your name would become a swear word? First time I ever saw a laughing Jesus image was in Playboy magazine. I'm sure he laughed; he drank wine. But he really was never portrayed that way.

. My Moses joke: How'd he get so fat up in the mountain for so long? He phones home (burning bush). Angels (saucer-men) land at the peak, tell him people need rules/laws now. They laser the Commandments into 2 rocks. "Hey you forgot: 'Honor Thy Children,' hm. & what, I can't look at my neighbor's wife?" He climbs down the mountain, not thinking society could ever be as bad as he was told. Moses discovers they're praying to a Golden Calf & listening to Rap Music.

. Christ looks in the mirror & sees the Antichrist. In the Mirror-World (around us now), the Antichrist looks into the mirror & sees the Christ. In the negative universe, God is the Devil & the Devil is God.

. We do not have Original Sin. It's a Church invention, global con job for money. They make you a sinner, then make you pay to be saved. You must **save yourself**. You need to **save yourself**. You do that by good karma: do good things & you'll be saved. Nothing worse than Catholic Confessionals: pay Church, go & sin, pay Church, go & sin, pay Church... You cannot continue to *indulge* & do what you want, Mr. Crowley, without paying for it.

. Churches (& "bad angels" reported in the Bible as God) put the fear of "God" into the hearts & minds of people for Control. It was really Fear of the Devil. "God was in the details." Now the "Devil is in the details."

. If you want success, you have to pay for it, suffer for your slave-owners, your Masters. They require a SACRIFICE! Talent, skills, looks, mean nothing. Real talented people die in gutters. Always been this way, the Hollywood System of the Beast. We know of faked "Great" people & not true geniuses. Why is it called "Hollywood"? The holly plant & pot plant are almost unique in the plant world in that they display both sexes. What kind of wood does Harry Potter & other real witches use for their wands? Wood from the holly plant.

. America's Got Talent? English, original version & a French-version. Does every country have this TV show of perversion? [I used to like this too]. In 'France Got Talent,' a nude painter took the stage & painted a portrait with his *dick*. He really did that & everyone in the crowd laughed. No one walked out? *Oh, they were French.*

. Did you know They set-up Bill Cosby (& MJ)? "His" accusers didn't pass the Tranny-tests, dozens of them. They're hormonal drag-men. "He's" the girl. "Fatherhood," huh? "America's favorite dad," huh? Right. & Sting has no stinger. Peewee Herman is a her-man with no peewee. Dwayne 'The Rock' JOHNSON. Get the jokes?

. Did you know Ray Charles & Stevie Wonder weren't blind? There's a video of famous musicians onstage. Paul McCartney knocked a music stand or mic & before it hit Stevie, he moved it away. To test this theory, next time you see Mr. Wonder at an airport, buy a machete at the coffee shop & *charge at him like a maniac!* He will run away like the dickens!

. When I worked at about the lowest level on the Simpsons, I was still told a little secret: If you declare 9 or more dependents, the IRS will check into it, *not less.* I realized this was a small Insider-thing I was privy to. Did they realize a muggle was listening? Can you imagine what secrets, tricks, loopholes the elites know & we don't?

. YouTube is not Us-tube, it's *THEY-tube.* They lie. Forums are mostly not real, only there to push Agenda, lies. If YT was in our hands (of course it isn't) we'd never flood it with meaningless COMMERCIALS of the worst kind! Never! Remember when They warned you with gold dots on the tracking-line? Those were ads, you knew where they were & could avoid them. Now you cannot. Every 5 minutes They smash you with evil shit! You want to hear a 6-minute song, but it's interrupted by a fucking AD! Why have low-quality vids on YT or present them that way? We have click them to a higher quality? It's bullshit. We, You, would never do this. *They would.*

. Never had happened before in modern history: That the Word went out & every single person on the planet CHANGED, had to in order to survive, forced into Fear & unnatural situations, absolutely ALL OF US!

. Where is the Old World, Lost World of yesterday I've mentioned again & again? Does it still exist somewhere or No? We're it? We're the Werewolf, never to transform back to Larry Talbot? Or the good Doctor Jekyll?

. We simulated, cold, replicants could learn a lot from our old/other selves of long ago, the positive versions.

. We all should have been sweetly Sucker-Punched, a delicious Cream Pie. But no. We were hit with a shit pie.

. What if we could go back in time & bring old friends & family back from the dead? *They'd live,* not as zombies, but as surprised ghosts that suddenly had a chance to experience the material world of the living again. Only 1 catch: We could only show them the world of 2020 & 2021. They would not believe what we showed them was the future. [No one saw straight, saw 2020, in 2020. Not a coincidence]. They'd cry & not accept your dystopia of the Brave New World in front of them. Those from the past would See It. They wouldn't believe how imprisoned we are on Prison Planet. Very little has progressed. Now it's far worse: We're locked into Dark Ages.

. Every classic sci-fi story & film had nothing to do with fantasy. SF is not fantasy. It is a realistic, scientific projection of what will or might reasonably occur in the years to come. 'Metropolis,' 'Just Imagine,' 'Things to Come,' 'Space 1999,' '2001,' '2010'...Where the hell are your hoverboards & why aren't we, the People, in space by now? What's the real reason public space exploration died decades ago? Because They, the elites are in space SECRETLY. They have Tesla-tech, we don't. They have Jetson-saucers, we don't. They do this to have everything, to remain in Power & for us to only suffer & have nothing. "They Live." We do not. We die. They have already killed all of us off, historically, technologically, physically, mentally & spiritually.

. More tennis: *Finally* Wimbledon adopted a tie-break for Men's 5th set in 2019, but not at 6-6. Score had to get to 12 games to 12 games. 12-12 is almost impossible. BUT, *first time ever* used in finals of Wimbledon, there it was! Djokovic & Federer did as ordered & made sure to reach 12 to 12 in games. It was faked. Everything is...

. One U.S. Open, Will Farrell was made to comment on Rafa Nadal. He asked, "Why does he grab his ass every point?" [He has to - sacrifice]. Go up to any celebrity & ask: "How's your ass?" They'll know what you mean.

. The terrible 2008 'Speed Racer' film by the Wachowski Brothers, now Lily & Lana, had one significant Truth in it I think you missed? In that world, Racing was King & their Super Bowl was an ultimate annual event everyone watched. The youthful, naive driver (Speed) discovered that *every Race had been fixed!* His hero was in on the deception & his whole world shattered. This is an important, hidden metaphor. **It's all fixed.**

. I actually came up with & wrote my sayings, without any Earthly help...unlike Yogi Berra.

. "A man walked into a bar...and hurt his head." It might not be hilarious, but it was original. *You do better.*

. *You will live forever Tilting at Windmills. A windmill has no spirit & will eventually be destroyed on its own.*

. Don't see the movie: "The Circle" with Emma Watson and Tom Hanks. Just don't! You've been warned.

. Did you know that Sir Patrick Stewart (bald, always wore red/black in ST) played a piece of shit in the Emoji Movie? Wow, type-casting.

. Celebrities have "handlers" and "trainers" because they are animals. When Hollywood CASTS a movie, They cast a spell on you. You're hypnotized. You don't see beyond Oz' Curtains, the Magic Trick in front of your eyes.

. There's an Illuminati expression you've heard a hundred times: "At the end of the day..." Wonder what it really means? How about "At the end of the Night..."? At the end of night, there is the pure light of day.

. Which witch? That witch. Witchcraft? That craft. Werewolf? Over there...

. Richard Jewell might be guilty of the 1996 Olympic Park bombing. Security guard went from hero to accused person & back to hero. He was even on SNL. 'Richard Jewell,' the movie, starred Sam Rockwell, Kathy Bates, Olivia Wilde & was directed by Clint Eastwood. When did Hollywood ever tell us the truth? It is more likely that Illuminati Media-agents only gave us lies, chaos & grand deceptions.

. Same with "Dingo ate my baby." 1980. The "religious" Chamberlains claimed a wild dingo entered their campsite & grabbed their 9-week old daughter. Searchers found her bloody jumpsuit & wife & husband were charged with murder in 1982. The famous "dingo" phrase was placed in Seinfeld, Family Guy, Simpsons, Rugrats and many more shows & movies. Wife was found guilty & husband to a lesser degree. *But everything changed.* The movie: "A Cry in the Dark," with Meryl Steep & Sam Neill & suddenly a new Media blitz happened that proclaimed their "innocence." Dingos have always avoided humans; now they were said to be "violent & other attacks had happened." I think because the Press, producers, celebrities latched onto the story, is SUSPICIOUS. Instead of a life-sentence in jail, they were somehow, magically, insanely, rewarded with 1.3 million \$. I'd bet it was a sacrifice to Satan. The movie made no mention of 1.3 mil & only showed the couple as tragic Media-victims. Many disagree.

. Don't you love it when the Virus in your computer *pops up* & informs you: "You have a virus"?

. If you think someone is putting nasty spells on you, just think: *Corbomite*...back at ya, buddy><.

. Did you know that the Romulans wore beards now? And only women know how to drive spaceships? Yeah.

. I've read M.E. research about our Sun is *white* now, but I never looked it up to confirm what I know is absolutely wrong. I Googled: What color is our Sun? My eyes couldn't believe it, but there it was: "White." What happened to our middle-aged star being in-between young blue stars & old red stars? Yellow was the most dominant color because of yellow sunlight. All that's gone now. I'm an astronomer & it blows my mind because I remember when we went around a yellow sun.

. From the film, 'Tucker': "Tucker Motor Company is dead. They'll never be made, only 50 cars." "What's the difference, 50 or 50 million? It's the idea that counts...& the dream."

. If I went to VONS supermarket one day & saw that the big sign had changed to VONNS, I might think a Mandela had happened...until I found out the whole chain of stores was bought by skier Lindsey Vonn.

. Are there any women here at the stoning?

. Our world today is primarily run by women. That world should be a wonderful place of gentleness, tenderness & sweetness, filled with love, compassion and true Care. Reality is the opposite. A world run by women who *act as brutal men* is a dark universe I want no part of...

~ It is finished. (Mostly). ~

About the Author

Tray Caladan was born Doug Yurchey in Pittsburgh, PA. in 1951 to Rose and Stephen Yurchey. A shy, only-child retreated into his own world and drew pictures. He earned a tennis scholarship to Edinboro State as an art major only to quit and begin the 'Art Trek' gallery. He married a psychic (Katrina) that would forever change his life and send him on a course to solve great mysteries. In 1990-91, he worked as a background cleanup artist on the 'Simpsons.' Tray's important articles, books, videos, radio shows, theories, patent, stories, ideas, games and art can be viewed online. His positive message of a "New Human Genesis" from Mars and ancient technology based on the work of Nikola Tesla permeates his theories and research as well as his "Science Fiction" and life.

Check out my artwork, old stuff to new stuff, in pencil, ink, paint, cel paint and also from the computer's Paint Program. https://youtu.be/MCH5UyuY8F4

Published books by TS Caladan

The Continuum (TWB Press, 2014)
http://www.twbpress.com/thecontinuum.html

Son of Zog (TWB Press, 2015)
http://www.twbpress.com/sonofzog.html

The Cydonian War (TWB Press, 2016)
http://www.twbpress.com/thecydonianwar.html

Science-Faction (TWB Press, 2017)
http://www.twbpress.com/sciencefaction.html

Anagramacron (TWB Press, 2017)
http://www.twbpress.com/anagramacronhtml

2099 ~ Transia (TWB Press, 2018)
http://www.twbpress.com/2099transia.html

inspiration (TWB Press, 2018)
http://www.twbpress.com/inspiration.html

Mandela Effect (TWB Press, 2019)
http://www.twbpress.com/madelaeffect.html

The New Men and the New World (TWB Press, 2020)
http://www.twbpress.com/thenewmenandthenewworld.html

Beyond Barronsland (TWB Press, 2020)
www.twbpress.com/beyondbarronsland.html

The Best of TS Caladan (TWB Press, 2021)
www.twbpress.com/thebestoftscaladan.html

http://www.twbpress.com
Science Fiction – Supernatural – Horror – Thriller
And more